When Jerry Pournelle co-authored *Footfall* and *Lucifer's Hammer,* reviewers around the country hailed them as the finest science fiction end-of-the-world sagas ever.

"THERE IS A ROUSING SPECIAL-EFFECTS FINALE THAT BEARS COMPARISON WITH THE END OF *STAR WARS.* BUT BENEATH ALL THE FIREWORKS, THE FATE OF THE EARTH HANGS ON SUPERIOR STRATEGY, NOT SUPERIOR WEAPONS . . . ITS SCIENCE FICTION ELEMENTS ARE HANDLED WITH A SKILL FOUND ONLY IN THE BEST OF THE GENRE." — *The New York Times*

"TAKE YOUR EARTHQUAKES, WATERLOGGED CONDOMINIUMS, SWARMS OF BUGS, COLLIDING AIRPLANES AND FLAMING WHAT-NOTS, wrap them up and they wouldn't match one page of *Lucifer's Hammer* for sweaty-palmed suspense."
— *Chicago Daily News*

"THE FIRST SATISFYING END-OF-THE-WORLD NOVEL IN YEARS . . . an ultimate one . . . massively entertaining." — *Cleveland Plain-Dealer*

"THE BEST END-OF-THE-WORLD STORY SINCE *ON THE BEACH*—superb detail, shudderingly believable." — Frank Herbert

"A MEGATON OF SUSPENSEFUL EXCITEMENT . . . which should keep readers going nonstop, cover to cover." — *Library Journal*

"A WORK IN THE GRAND TRADITION . . . even the miracle of Sensurround may be inadequate to convey all the imaginative reverberations."
— *Los Angeles Times*

"A 'DISASTER' THRILLER OF RARE QUALITY . . . for its expertise and the scale of its apocalypse. . . . Strings out the suspense almost unbearably."
— *John Barkham Reviews*

AND NOW JERRY POURNELLE'S MOST APOCA-LYPTIC SAGA EVER—*Armageddon,* There Will Be War Volume VIII.

CREATED BY

J. E. POURNELLE

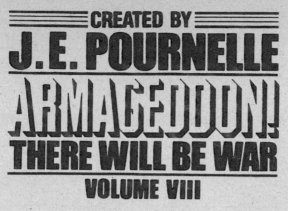

ARMAGEDDON!
THERE WILL BE WAR
VOLUME VIII

John F. Carr,
Associate Editor

TOR ®

A TOM DOHERTY ASSOCIATES BOOK
NEW YORK

This is a work of fiction. All the characters and events portrayed in this book are fictitious, and any resemblance to real people or events is purely coincidental.

ARMAGEDDON

A TOR Book
Published by Tom Doherty Associates, Inc.
49 West 24 Street
New York, NY 10010

Cover art by Les Edwards

ISBN: 0-812-54965-1   Can. ISBN: 0-812-54966-X

Library of Congress Catalog Card Number: 88-51633

First edition: May 1989

Printed in the United States of America

0 9 8 7 6 5 4 3 2 1

ACKNOWLEDGMENTS

The editors gratefully acknowledge that research for some of the non-fiction essays in this book was supported in part by grants from the Vaughn Foundation. Responsibility for opinions expressed in this work remains solely with the authors.

CONTENTS

Introduction
ARMAGEDDON
Jerry Pournelle

THE FIRST BATTLE HISTORIANS CAN RECONSTRUCT TOOK PLACE AT Armageddon. Revelation 16:16 tells us the last one will be there. "And he gathered them together into a place called in the Hebrew tongue Armageddon."

There really is such a place. It is called Megiddo. There are ruins of an ancient fortress on the heights dominating the valley below. In biblical times the Plain of Megiddo lay astride the trade routes north from Egypt to Lebanon. You will find it today in the modern state of Israel. It lies south and west of the Sea of Galilee, somewhat west of a line connecting Mounts Tabor and Gilboa, about forty miles due north of the ancient city of Samaria.

There have been many battles at Megiddo, although none in modern times; histories of the Arab-Israeli wars mention Megiddo only in passing. In ancient times the place was not so fortunate.

The writer of Revelation couldn't know that the first battle we can reconstruct with any historical accuracy took place at Armageddon. Brigadier J.F.C. "Boney" Fuller in his monumental three-volume *Military History of the Western World* describes it this way:

1

When Thutmose III succeeded his half-sister Hatsheput in about 1481 B.C., "the king of Kadesh headed a revolt of all the city kings of Syria and Palestine against him. In answer, on about April 19, 1479 B.C., after he had assembled his army at Thara (Kantara), Thutmose marched by way of Gaza to Yehem (Yemma), a town on the southern slopes of the Carmel range, and arrived there on May 10.

"Meanwhile the forces of the city kings, under the command of the king of Kadesh, had occupied the fortress of Megiddo (Armageddon) which lay on the northern slope of the Carmel ridge and which blocked the main road from Egypt to the Euphrates. Moving along this road on Megiddo, on May 14 Thutmose led his army through the pass traversed by Lord Allenby 3,397 years later. He debouched on the Plain of Megiddo, south of the fortress, and the next day he advanced with his army in battle order against the king of Kadesh, whose forces were encamped outside Megiddo. With the southern horn of his army resting on a hill south of the brook of Kina, and the northern pointing toward Megiddo, Thutmose, 'like Horus armed with talons,' in a shining chariot of electrum, led the attack and in one charge he scattered his enemy, who fled headlong toward Megiddo 'as if terrified by spirits.' The men of Kadesh abandoned their chariots of gold and silver and, finding the city gates closed to them, were hauled up its walls by the citizens.

"Unfortunately for Thutmose, instead of assaulting the city when all was in confusion his soldiers pillaged their enemy's camps and, in consequence, Megiddo had to be invested. The siege was a short one; but when the city was surrendered it was found that the king of Kadesh had escaped. The spoil taken was immense. It included 924 chariots, 2,238 horses, 200 suits of armor, the king's household furniture, and a vast quantity of gold and silver."

Several years later Thutmose took Kadesh. Later he subdued the Mitanni, Aryan battle-axe people who occupied the great bend of the Euphrates. His fleets ranged the coast from Egypt to modern Turkey. Aleppo fell to his armies. Even Crete and Cyprus were under his influence. In his final campaign he took Kadesh once more, this time leveling the city. In the spring of 1447 B.C. and the fifty-fourth year of his reign he died peacefully at home, having become the world's first emperor.

2

Breasted notes, ''today two of this king's greatest monuments, his Heliopolitan obelisks, now rise on opposite shores of the western ocean, memorials of the world's first empire-builder.'' Sure enough, they do so to this day: one is in London. The other stands in Central Park, New York City, where it is known as ''Cleopatra's Needle.'' In fact, it dates from a time nearly as far in Cleopatra's past as she is to ours.

The Egyptian Empire controlled the area we now know as Palestine for a great deal longer than the modern state of Israel has existed; but eventually the Children of Israel conquered the land and established an empire of their own. First Saul, then David conquered the cities of the Philistines, the lands of the Amelikites, and all the other natives of the land we now know as Palestine. Solomon's writ is said to have run from Gaza to the Euphrates. Pharaohs of Egypt, Phoenician kings, Arabian queens sent him gifts and told of their admiration. Solomon's fortress at Megiddo has been excavated; it is truly worthy of admiration.

A generation later the Empire was in ruins, split in half by the unbending arrogance of Solomon's son Rehoboam. Not long after that the Plain of Megiddo once again rang with the clash of sword and shield, and the screams of the dying. The Assyrians came; writers of the time called them The Death of the Earth.

The Ten Tribes of Israel were carried away, followed by Judah. Cyrus the Great allowed those who would to return to their homeland; not long after they fell under the rule of the Greeks, the successors to Alexander the Great; then to Rome.

Modern prophets tell us that Megiddo will again be important, but only after the rise of a new Roman Empire. Some see that in the Common Market established by the Treaty of Rome.

Perhaps. Whatever the truth of the prophecy, Armageddon, that one last battle which will settle the fate of mankind, looms large above us.

Herewith stories of Armageddon.

STILL TIME
James Patrick Kelly

EDITOR'S INTRODUCTION

In "Still Time" James Kelly tells us the story of Quinn Hutchins, a survivalist—a man who was prepared for the unthinkable. Yet, even Quinn has his headaches.

What about the rest of us who are totally unprepared? The government of Switzerland has built the world's best civil defense system for its citizens: they have great fortresses buried deep inside the Alps; a post-nuclear communications network, doctors trained to deal with the wounded and radiation sick, civil defense workers knowledgeable in how to build blast doors and secure buildings against radiation. In essence, they are prepared for the worst.

The Soviets have GBMD, an upgraded antiballistic missile system protecting Moscow. It has been claimed that the Soviets feel GBMD is worth the investment if it assures the survival of only 40 percent of its population. They also have twenty-million Soviet citizens involved in civil defense. Obviously, the Soviet Union intends to survive a nuclear holocaust.

How well has the United States done? Can the U.S. Government provide for the common defense in the event of a nuclear war?

Not bloody likely.

About thirty years ago, the U.S. built the Interstate Highway System, the greatest and most costly engineering program in history. In part, this was to be justified by building fall-out shelters under each approach ramp for civil defense. Then we adopted Mutually Assured Destruction, MAD. The logic of MAD—never accepted by the Soviet Union—is that civil defenses are an act of aggression.

If we protect our citizens, we must believe the Soviets would attack them. The only reason they would attack is in response to our attack. Therefore, if we protect our citizens, we must be planning to attack the Soviet Union. If they're properly deterred they'd never think of doing that. Therefore we don't need to protect our people, and lest we threaten the Soviets, we'd better not.

Note also that the deterrence is assumed. We never investigate what it takes to achieve it. Everyone knows nuclear war is irrational, and no one would ever start one coldly and for gain.

On the other hand, pure deterrence promised considerable savings. Since both sides were, in Arthur C. Clarke's memorable phrase, "like small boys standing in a pool of gasoline accumulating matches," there'd be no need to collect matches. If the Soviets kill us, we'll kill them right back, so there. All we need, then, is to have some nukes.

Albert Wohlstetter pointed out many years ago that the balance of terror is rather delicate, but the McNamara's of this world never wanted to learn that.

Accordingly, the United States installed the Minuteman system and quit. Since the Soviets were assumed to be rational, and therefore to think like U.S. university and think-tank professors turned strategic theorists, they would understand this unambiguous signal. No one wants to feel inferior in this modern world; therefore the Soviets might build a few more weapons than we have, enough to let them feel secure and even to compensate for a kind of

5

national inferiority complex; but soon enough they'd stop. Once they caught up and knew they had, there'd be no reason to build more weapons, which could only harm their economy. It would be silly for them to go on collecting expensive matches . . .

The theory was brilliant but the Soviets didn't buy it. Then the Soviets caught up—they didn't halt. They didn't even slow down. They have set up four separate assembly lines to produce ICBM's three shifts a day, and the fact that they can't afford to do that hasn't stopped them, not even in this era of *glasnost*.

Meanwhile, it wasn't necessary for them to mount a campaign of opposition to U.S. Strategic Defenses. We did that ourselves.

Now meet Quinn Hutchins, a man who takes all this seriously.

———————————————'|'———————————————

QUINN HUTCHINS WAS PLANTING MARIGOLDS ON HIS ROOF. FOR two years he had feverishly built his underground dream house into the south flank of Flatrock Mountain. Now that the place was nearly finished he was squandering a little time on landscaping. Judy and Kitty had chosen the flowers; Quinn had grown them from seed in the solar greenhouse. He firmed the seedlings into the ground and pinched off the growing tips to encourage branching. Come July they would make a spectacular display. If July came.

Since the crisis had begun Quinn had seldom been out of earshot of a radio. His multi-band portable Sony was propped against a bale of peat moss. It was tuned to an all-news station in Boston.

"This just handed to me." The news reader paused maddeningly. "The Associated Press reports that the president has left Washington. This unconfirmed—repeat, unconfirmed—report states that the president was flown by helicopter from the White House and arrived at Andrews Air Force Base at ten-thirty-one Eastern Standard Time. There he boarded the National Emergency Command Post, a specially-equipped 747 jet often referred to as Kneecap. His destination is unknown. To repeat. . . ."

"Son of a bitch!" said Quinn. He threw his tools into the wheelbarrow and muscled it down the side of the house to the garage. "God-damned idiots!"

He had hoped for more warning: a parting volley of words in the Security Council, orders putting all available Tridents to sea and dispersing the bombers to auxiliary airfields, perhaps even evacuation of the cities. Kneecap was the penultimate step and Quinn Hutchins's little family was scattered all over Strafford County. If he had not spent most of his sleepless nights planning for just this situation he might have panicked.

Even so, his finger slipped as he dialed Judy's number and he had to start over. Seconds lost.

"Dr. Davidson's office," said Becky the receptionist.

"Judy Hutchins, please."

"Quinn, is that you? How've you been, haven't talked to you in ages. She's with the doctor, you want me to take a message?"

"Get her. Now."

There was a rude clatter on the other end. Becky had always thought him peculiar. Now he did not care what she thought.

"Quinn?" said Judy.

Finally. "Come home." He tried to sound calm. "It's starting."

"Are you sure?" She sounded wary of another false alarm. "It'll mean trouble with Davidson. He's got a full schedule. . . ."

"Damn it, Judy!"

"And the car has been acting up again. I was going to stop in at Smitty's on the way home and have him look at it."

"There's no time. Just come home. I'm going for Kitty now."

"It's really starting?" Her voice trembled. "All right, I'm coming."

"I love you." He tried not to think about the junkyard water pump in her decrepit Vega. "We're going to make it, sugar."

It was only ten minutes to the Merrymeeting Children's Center; Quinn decided to secure the house before he picked up Kitty. Although the south facade was glazed with sheets of three-quarter inch unbreakable acrylic, it was designed to withstand vandals, not the searing gusts of a thermonuclear wind storm. There were winches concealed in the wall; he thrust a handle into each and cranked furiously. Rolling aluminum shutters reinforced with steel rattled down their exterior tracks and locked shut.

He hurried to the master bedroom, pulled all of the clothes out of the closet and piled them on the bed. The closet was built of reinforced concrete; it served as the airlock for the Hutchins's shelter, a four hundred square foot bunker equipped with hand-operated air and water pumps and a six month supply of dried food. At the back of the closet, surrounded by old shoes, was a green overnight suitcase. Quinn carried it to the kitchen table and unlocked it. Inside were three respirators, a radiation counter, several personal dosimeters, some canisters of mace and two guns. He loaded the thirty-eight special, slipped it into its shoulder rig and strapped it on. The semi-automatic twenty-two caliber light-weight rifle was knocked down and stored inside its waterproof stock. Quinn had trouble reassembling it; he had not practiced for a long time. Judy hated guns.

In his haste to leave he could find nothing to wear over his revolver but an old yellow rain parka. The day was clear and hot but he pulled on the heavy parka anyway. He hid the rifle under the seat of his rusty Toyota pickup, swiped the sweat from his eyes and backed down his dirt driveway onto Flatrock Road.

Once Quinn had owned a Porsche. He had lived within walking distance of Boston Common, bought Medoc wines by the case and earned his luxuries designing shopping malls and corporate head-quarters. But Quinn only got to initial the working drawings while the senior partners ate lobster with the clients. His insomnia was just starting then. The nightly news made it worse. When his mother died he sold her house for one hundred and seventy-three thousand dollars—enough to buy his freedom from the unnerving city. He proposed to Judy that they move to New Hampshire. She could finally go back to work; he would stay with the baby and build a house. A house with his name on it, a single-family fortress secure from the madnesses which men were wreaking on the world.

The Merrymeeting Children's Center was located in the base-ment of the Congregational Church. Quinn was one of its founders; it had been under his direction that a group of parents had worked over several weekends to transform the place with secondhand rugs, temporary partitions, and buckets of bright paint. He had also served on the committee which had chosen Rachel Kerwin as director.

She had shoulder-length red hair and bad teeth. Her wardrobe consisted of a variety of floppy men's clothing culled from second-hand stores. Although she was thirty-seven years old, time had yet to crack her bone-headed idealism. She was a marcher, a letter-writer, a collector of causes. It had not bothered Quinn at all to find out that she had been arrested several times while protesting; it was good for little children to be around people like that.

He had no time for her today. "Where's Kitty?"

"Out." She stooped to pick up a snuffling infant, Billy . . . somebody. "We sent the big kids out on a nature walk. Should be back soon." She tugged at his rain parka and chuckled. "Where you been getting your weather reports from, the Amazon?"

Quinn stepped to the window and scanned the nearby woods. "Damn!" He patted the revolver hidden beneath the parka; it helped steady him. "Do you think I could find them?"

"Why, Quinn?"

"No other parents have come in yet?"

"Why?"

Now she was scared; everyone in Merrymeeting knew that he was a survivalist. "The politicians are scurrying out of Washington like rats leaving a sinking ship."

Billy started to fuss; she jiggled him. "So?"

"So it's coming!" Her obtuseness made him angry. "Turn on the radio and wake up, Rachel! The bombs, don't you understand? We're set to blow ourselves to hell."

"I can't believe . . ." She shook her head numbly. "There should've been more demonstrations. If people like you had marched instead . . . instead of. . . ."

"Jesus." He glared at the woods. No sign of his daughter. "I'll wait outside."

She barred his exit. "What's going to happen to these children, Quinn?"

"If we're lucky there should be time for everyone to go home." Quinn liked Rachel Kerwin; when he saw that she was crying he almost fell into the trap of pity. "Look, the nearest target is the Air Force Base in Portsmouth. Forty miles away; the blast effects shouldn't be too bad here. Just start filling every container you have with water. Your biggest worries are fire and fallout . . ."

The phone rang. Billy Somebody began to cry too. Rachel answered. "Hello. Oh God, Judy. It's horrible, I can't believe it; yes, yes, he's here."

9

Quinn grabbed the phone from her. "What?"

"Thank God I caught you." Her voice trembled. "The car is dead. I'm at Miller's Drug in Farnham."

He could hardly hear her over little Billy's caterwauling.

"I don't know, I don't know what to do, Quinn. The traffic is all going north; no one is taking the turnoff for Merrymeeting. Should I try hitching anyway?"

"No, don't hitch." He did not want her riding with some panicky loser on a blind run. "Can you steal a car?"

"Quinn!"

"Look, sugar, everything is falling apart. Nothing, nobody matters but us." Rachel tried to butt into the conversation and he turned away from her, twisting the handset cord around his shoulders.

"You're wrong, Quinn," Judy said firmly. Despite all their arguments, she had yet to accept the first law of survivalism.

"Daddy!" Kitty scooted through the door. "I saw your truck, Daddy, look what I found." She waved a blue jay feather at him. "Why are you here so early, can we stop for ice cream on the way home?"

Quinn was momentarily dizzy; he shut his eyes. He was at the edge of control and unless he could slow down he would certainly make the mistake that would kill them all. "Kitty, go to the truck. Now!" There was no time; he wished that someone would strangle little Billy Somebody so that he could think. "Judy? Stay where you are. I'm coming for you. Twenty minutes." He hung up.

Kitty was dawdling by the door. He scooped her up and carried her to the truck. Rachel followed him like a watchdog nipping at the heels of a mailman. She lectured him as if he were responsible for the war.

"It's not fair. You can't just leave these children to die. You'd better stop and think about what you're doing, Quinn Hutchins. You'd better hope that everyone who survives isn't as selfish as you."

As he loaded Kitty into the truck he saw that her chin was quivering. Although he had been able to ignore Rachel, his daughter had been wounded by her rage.

"Will it be worth it?" Rachel grasped the door handle to keep him from leaving. "Do you think Kitty will thank you tomorrow for saving her life?"

Quinn unsnapped his parka and pulled out the thirty-eight; he did not release the safety. "You want to save those kids inside some misery, Rachel? Shoot them. Now." He offered the butt end of the revolver to her. "You're so damn sure it's not worth living anymore?" He shook it at her and she shrank from him. "Go ahead!"

She turned and ran back to the church.

It seemed quieter than it was inside the truck. The engine boomed, the suspension clattered, the wheels shrieked at the corners but nobody spoke and the radio was broken. Quinn had forgotten the Sony in the wheelbarrow.

Farnham consisted of a boarded-up brick schoolhouse, Ben's Bait and Fruit Stand, Miller's Drug and a scattering of musty cottages. The most direct route climbed over the mountain and passed Quinn's house on Flatrock Road. A tourist from Ohio might finish this scenic drive in forty-five minutes; a drunken teenager with a death wish could do it in a half hour. Quinn thought twenty minutes was about right.

Kitty had tucked her legs beneath her and was scrunched into the far corner of the cab. She was chewing on strands of her long black hair, a habit which usually annoyed Quinn. But she was so pale and wide-eyed that he did not bother her. At least she was not crying. Her father's daughter.

They were about a mile from the house when he finally broke the silence. "I'm letting you off at the driveway, honey. Get into the shelter as fast as you can and wait for us. I'll be back with Mommy in two shakes."

"I won't."

"Kitty."

"I don't want to stay all alone with the bombs."

"I'm not arguing, Kitty. You do it." He downshifted as the truck approached the driveway. "I'm letting you out."

"I won't go in. I'll stand by the mailbox until you come back."

He had slowed enough to glance at her and gauge her determination. She stared back fiercely, her jaw set. She was six and a half years old and already she had all the pluck she would ever need. He stepped on the accelerator and the truck shot past the driveway.

"Am I going to die, Daddy?"

"Of course not."

11

"Are Grammy and Grampy going to die?"

"I hope not."

"Lisbeth? Maggie?"

"I don't know."

"How about Rachel?"

"Kitty, anyone who wants to live and tries hard enough will make it."

She considered. "But some people are going to die?"

"Yes."

As they crossed the southern ridge of Flatrock there was a flash of light that overwhelmed the sun. Quinn felt the mountain tremble beneath him. The truck veered toward the shoulder and he slammed it to a skidding stop. Below them were the tidy orchards surrounding Farnham, less than three miles away. In the distance to the southeast was what had once been Portsmouth, New Hampshire.

He had a glimpse of hell out of the corners of his eyes. The fireball was dazzling; it rose with the stately grace of a hot air balloon at a country fair. It seemed to draw the land directly beneath it toward the sky; farther out it cast a shadow of flame. In four thousand million years the dull stones of the planet had never witnessed quite so ravishing a spectacle.

But one glimpse was enough for Quinn; he was nearly blinded. He made a screeching U turn and raced back the way he had come. He hoped that the top of the ridge might afford some protection from the shock wave. He saw a dirt track running into a rock-strewn pasture and pulled onto it, crashing through the wooden gate. Safe from falling trees.

"Out!" He flung open his door and, dragging Kitty with him, flopped face-down behind a desk-sized boulder.

The thunderclap sounded as if the shout of an angry god had split the sky open. Immediately afterward came a terrible pressure on Quinn's back, as if that same god meant to squash him into the dirt for the sin of being a man. His ears popped; he could not breathe.

He was not sure how long he lay there; he was revived by Kitty's crying. ". . . hurts."

"What hurts?" He rolled her over. "Kitty!"

"The air hurts."

She had to shout to be heard. A roiling black cloud had filled the

12

sky and a gale blew from the north, stripping the trees. A white birch toppled onto the road as he watched. But his lightweight truck was still upright.

"Let's go."

He opened the green suitcase and they both slid respirators over their faces. He clipped a dosimeter to Kitty's blouse and pushed another into his shirt pocket. Kitty hooked her canisters of mace to her belt without being told. Quinn marvelled at his calmness as he waited for the counter to warm up.

Click, click. Of all his survival gadgets, he trusted this one the least. The instruction booklet, translated from the Japanese, had been nearly incomprehensible with its jabber of phosphors and photocathodes. *Click.* The liquid crystal display read four-tenths of a millirem per hour, thirty times the normal background. Nowhere near lethal levels yet; still an hour, maybe two, before the killing dust began to sift out of the sky. *Click, click, click.* Either way he went, the road might be blocked. A dose of four hundred and fifty rems kills half the population; at six hundred, everyone dies. *Click.* Even now, a few of Quinn's cells were shrivelling, exploding, spewing poisons. Judy. The invisible seeds of cancer.

Even though Quinn's grip on the steering wheel was painfully tight, his arms trembled. He was sucking huge amounts of air through his respirator and still felt out of breath. The wind shrieked at the truck. He blinked, blinked again, and realized that he was crying.

"What am I going to do?" He was thankful that the respirator filtered the sob out of his voice.

Kitty slid across the seat and hugged him. "First we have to get Mommy." She spoke impatiently, as if she thought he had merely forgotten the plan. "Then we stay in the shelter until it's safe to come out."

He pulled back from her so that he could see her face. The rubber mask concealed her nose and mouth but her eyes . . . the eyes. He drew strength from her ignorance.

"Buckle your seat belt." He pulled onto the highway, swerved around the fallen birch and headed for Farnham.

It took twenty minutes to reach the end of Flatrock Road. Quinn had to ram one tree out of his way. He passed a wrecked station wagon without stopping. The count was up to six rems an hour and was climbing rapidly.

Route Sixteen was a two-lane highway with big shoulders; four lanes of northbound cars now spilled across it. Most were creeping along; a few had stopped, smoke and steam hissing from under the hoods. Quinn saw one angry driver crash his Trans Am into the rear of a stalled Rabbit. He repeated the attack several times until he had nudged the crumpled Volkswagen down an embankment into an apple orchard. The driver of the dead car scrambled onto the road with a rock, leapt onto the hood of the Trans Am and started smashing the windshield.

Farnham was less than a mile south of the junction of Flatrock Road and Route Sixteen. As luck would have it there was just enough room for Quinn to squeeze by near the southbound shoulder, two wheels on gravel, two wheels cutting through tall weeds. He ignored the chorus of honks and curses from the refugees and sped on.

He quickly discovered, however, that it was the state police, not luck, which had kept the lane clear. A patrol car was blocking his way into town; an angry trooper waved for him to stop. The man had a cut over his right eye and a spatter of dried blood matted to his face. He kept his hand on the butt of his pistol as he approached the truck but he seemed dazed, like a fighter waiting to be knocked out.

"Where the hell you going, Mr. Gas Mask?"

"Farnham, officer. My wife. . . ."

He had already turned away, not listening. He held up his hand to stop a blue van in the nearest lane of traffic. Slowly a space opened in front of it. Northbound.

"You, in there." He waved Quinn toward it.

"Please, officer, my wife is in Farnham and I. . . ."

"Burning." The wind whipped at his hair. "Everything. Get your ass turned around right now."

The space the trooper had created expanded to two, three car lengths and those behind the van began to honk impatiently. The trooper spun away from Quinn's truck and shook his fists at the faces staring from behind closed windows. "Shut up, *shut up!*" The gale overpowered the hoarse voice; only Quinn could hear. "It's too late, damn you! You're all dead anyway."

The revolver seemed to jump into Quinn's hand. He released the safety and held the gun in his left hand just under his open window so that the trooper could not see it.

He did not want to shoot. He was not turning back.

"No, Daddy." Kitty slid across the seat and tugged at his shirt. The look on her face scared him; he thought she might try to interfere. Get them both killed. He shoved her to the floor on the passenger side. Again she reached out to him, offering her mace. "Please."

"Listen buddy, I'm not going to tell you again. . . ."

Without thinking, Quinn closed his right hand around the cannister, thrust it at the trooper and sprayed a burst into his eyes. He screamed and clutched at his face as if trying to tear it off. Quinn fired another burst, and another, until the trooper had staggered out of range.

Quinn whipped the truck through the space in front of the blue van and managed to scrape between it and the patrol car before the refugees could react. He raced down the shoulder toward Farnham.

He knew that he had taken a foolish risk. The policeman had a gun. And a radio. The effects of the mace were temporary. Quinn should have used the thirty-eight. Kitty climbed back onto the seat, slipped her mace cannister into its holder and hugged him.

Not a single window remained unbroken in Farnham. The wind carried the acrid smell of electrical fire but Quinn could see no flames. Only the old schoolhouse still squatted intact on its stone foundation; its boarded-up facade and rusty civil defense sign seemed to mock the devastation. Ben's Bait and Fruit was a jumble of broken timbers. Miller's Drug had been a ramshackle Victorian roadhouse just waiting for a reason to collapse. The bomb had provided reasons aplenty. The roof had vanished entirely; the front had fallen back into the building, bulging the side walls out at crazy angles. He was astonished to see two women in street clothes, totally unprotected against fallout, standing next to the ruin.

He parked beside them. The counter read thirty-six rems per hour; he shut it off. According to his own dosimeter he had already absorbed a dose of between twenty and thirty rems. Not much time left.

"Lock the doors; I'll be right back."

15

Kitty watched him take the revolver from the seat and tuck it back into his shoulder rig. He mussed her hair. "It's okay," he said.

The two women were gazing at a broken window. A paint-spattered step ladder was propped against the wall directly beneath it.

"Anyone in there?"

They looked at him blankly; he could not be heard speaking through the mask into the wind. Reluctantly he pulled the respirator down and let it dangle around his neck.

"We heard shouts before the wind picked up," the younger woman said. "My husband's inside trying to help."

The older woman, who wore a calico kerchief over her mouth like a bandit, approached him as he stepped onto the ladder. "You send my Frank out. He's got a bad heart, you hear? And the traffic—we gotta go."

Quinn slithered feet first through the window and slid over a desk into a tiny office. All the furniture had skidded across the tilting floor to the wall. The office opened onto the wreck of the sales area.

"Hello?"

The room smelled of rubbing alcohol. Shelves had spilled their contents before toppling onto one another. The floor was strewn with candy, broken glass, cheap plastic toys, smashed boxes, magazines and gaudy pills. Greeting cards fluttered in the wind as if in welcome.

"Over here!"

A sweating man stripped to his tee shirt struggled with an enormous tangle of junk: broken plaster, fallen joists and rafters, cotton candy puffs of insulation. A gray-faced man with a paunch sat on a fallen shelf and watched.

"I'm all right," he repeated. "A minute. All right."

The sweating man did not pause in his feverish efforts. "Made it through the shock wave. But the windstorm blew the roof away. They hid in the crawl space. One way in." He kicked at the yellow wooden trap door half buried beneath the pile of debris.

Quinn pried a two-by-four out of the way. "Sure they're alive?"

"Heard 'em. Vent holes in the foundation." Together they flipped a chunk of wall off to one side. "Some of 'em ain't."

"My wife's down there."

16

He blinked at Quinn. It took just that long for a bond to be formed between them; a fellowship of sympathy and fear, a pact of cooperation. "We'll find her," he said.

Quinn nodded. "Why you here?"

"Neighbor."

They labored with grim intensity until they had cleared away almost everything but a collapsed and immovable assembly of four-by-ten ceiling rafters. They strained at this last mess of wood and plaster.

"Stuck." The good neighbor grunted. "Got a bar in my garage. Pry some loose first?"

"I'll be all right," said Frank.

"Take him." Quinn gestured at the gray old man.

Left alone, Quinn circled the remaining debris, probing for a point of attack. The beams were too massive; there were too many of them. Not without a bulldozer, he thought as he toyed with the dangling respirator. Reason demanded that he walk away. Quinn was beyond reason.

He felt a thumping underfoot and dropped to his knees on the trap door. "Judy! Are you down there? Judy?"

He thought he heard someone say "Hello." Or was it "Help?" The yellow door was thick and the wind had deafened him.

"Jud-ith Hutch-ins!" he shouted.

"Open . . . no air . . . soon. . . ."

With a strangled moan, Quinn linked hands around the outermost rafter and tried to pull it toward him. The rough edge bit into his hands; muscles in his arms, stomach and calves stretched to their limits. He blocked out pain with anger. It was not fair . . . he had prepared . . . his family . . . damned politicians . . . no time . . . not . . . *fair*!

A berserk power tingled through him. Something popped and Quinn thought he had hurt himself. Three more pops followed in rapid succession as the spikes holding the rafter in place released. It came free with a squeal. Quinn staggered backwards, dragging it out of the way.

Quinn had never witnessed a miracle before. He did not know whether to praise the Lord or his adrenal glands. Whatever the source, his newfound strength could not be denied. He drew an enormous breath and turned to the next rafter.

17

The second was the hardest, the third was easy. Only three left on top of the door. He tried to lift them all at once. His back spasmed and he reeled away, stumbling over a twisted light fixture.

"Quinn!" The haze of pain lifted. Someone sat him up. He felt a grinding at the base of his spine. Judy kissed him; her face smelled like tears.

The neighbor helped him stand. "This your wife?" he said, grinning.

The rafters still pinned the trapdoor.

"What?" Quinn swayed.

Judy caught him. "Some people were hurt during the shock wave. They needed help, beds. Mrs. LeBeau opened her house, no one knew much first aid but me. Then this happened." She hugged him. "I tried to watch for the truck but I was busy and I . . . I didn't think you would come . . . after. . . ."

"Not come?" He did not understand. "You weren't trapped."

The neighbor had wedged his crowbar under one of the fallen rafters and was straining to lift it. "Jesus!" He shook his head. "How'd you do it?"

Judy was staring. "Quinn," she said, "let me see your dosimeter."

He thrust it into his pocket without looking and gave her a quick kiss. "Listen," he said, joining the neighbor, "your only chance is the schoolhouse. If it was a shelter it should have a hand pump. But you'll need food: canned, dried—lots of rice, you understand?" He picked up the bar and rammed it deeper into the pile. "Stay put until the fallout passes. I've got a counter in the truck you can have."

Quinn did not want to die but he could not leave until he had given the strangers trapped below a chance to live. The bomb had changed everything—the survivalists had been right about that. Nothing was certain; a chance was all anyone could expect. Maybe he could bushwhack through the orchards back to Flatrock Road. Maybe.

Judy was pale. "This won't take long," Quinn said. "There's still time." He felt the strength returning to him. "Still time."

SURVIVING ARMAGEDDON
Jerry Pournelle

EDITOR'S INTRODUCTION

Years ago I had a regular column in a magazine called *Survive*. Those were the days of the Carter Administration, when everything seemed to be coming apart. Even the President talked about the "era of limits" and a "national malaise."

In those times we truly feared Armageddon, not as something abstract, but as an event that might very well happen next year—or even next month.

The advice I gave in my *Survive* column seems a bit quaint now, but only because we're no longer so worried that the Big War is coming. I hope our doubts are justified; but as I write this, the Congress is telling the President elect that they'll have no more of this talk of Star Wars; while the Soviets are busily installing missile defenses.

Maybe it's not so irrelevant after all.

———————————'ı'———————————

AT A WRITER'S PARTY A FEW YEARS AGO MY PARTNER LARRY Niven and I met the author of the humorous best-seller *Real Men*

Don't Eat Quiche. "Real men," Larry informed him, "eat whatever they damned well please."

I bring this up because from time to time well-meaning friends chide me for living in a big city. I should, it seems, move to Rogue River, Oregon, or Resume Speed, Iowa, or some such place where I'd be safer when the balloon goes up; which, they assure me, it inevitably will.

There's only one problem: I don't *want* to move. I like living in cities. The word "civilized" originally meant those who can—and do—live in cities, and I happen to care a lot about my civilization.

When challenged, I can make a reasoned defense of city life even in these times; but the point is, *I shouldn't have to*. I like it here. I don't intend to let the barbarians chase me out, and there's an end to the discussion.

Certainly it costs me. I live in Hollywood, which means I spend a lot on air conditioners and air purifiers. I must take some fairly extreme measures to foil burglars. I live in the hills, which periodically catch fire, so I've had to make some preparations for that, too. My neighborhood is quiet. There hasn't been a crime of violence here in twenty years. That may or may not have something to do with the fact that most of my neighbors, like me, are pretty well armed; the fact is, we don't know, because no one has ever challenged us. The only crime is cold burglary of an empty house, and since my house is never empty it doesn't apply to me.

In a word, with sensible precautions, city life can be rewarding. It can even be safe, in the usual sense of the word. Certainly I feel at least as safe here as I would if I lived out in the toolies far from neighbors. At least I do under the current circumstances.

Circumstances change. Civilization is fragile; history shows it can sometimes be very fragile indeed.

One primary threat to civilization is nuclear war. The best way to survive a nuclear war is not to have one. Even those who've made the most stringent preparations, have taken all the survivalist measures, won't be better off after an ICBM exchange. Even uninjured survivors will have a considerably shorter life expectancy than they have now. As an example: I take a complex mixture of vitamins and immune system protectors. I have a stockpile of them, but I certainly don't have ten years' worth—and it's unlikely that Great Earth and Vitamin Research Products will be intact after a nuclear war.

One sometimes reads novels about people who not only survive nuclear wars, but thrive in those conditions. One even meets people who think they're so well prepared they welcome Armageddon.

They're wrong.

In the first place, they haven't thought through how Armageddon will happen.

It's fashionable among scaremongers, and those opposed to strategic defenses, to act as if nuclear war will start with a sneak attack on our cities. The first thing we know, huge multimegaton weapons will detonate out of the blue over New York and Los Angeles and the like. The fact is, that doesn't make any sense at all. There's no reason for the Soviets to start the war that way. One supposes that the Soviets, like the Americans, have large weapons targeted on cities, such weapons to be used as a last ditch retaliation; but it sure doesn't make sense to *start* the war that way. Cities aren't much of a military target. There are far more vital things to destroy if you intend to *win* the war.

And that's what the Soviets say they want to do: win. Their internal publications, circulated only to senior officers, don't talk about sneak attacks with city busters; they're much more interested in our missile, naval, and air bases. True, there's also interest in our industrial base as part of the "permanently operating factors" in war, but these are clearly of lesser importance than our immediate military capabilities.

Second, wars don't start out of the blue. There are warning signs. As Stefan Possony used to say, wars like seductions take preparation. Astute observers will know what signs to watch for.

All this was more relevant back in the days of the Carter Administration than now. The Reagan modernization of the Strategic Forces has changed things very much for the better. So has the new regime in the Soviet Union. One might argue that the new regime was made possible when the U.S. made it clear we were not going to disarm and thus be a tempting target for the expansionist factions in the U.S.S.R. Whatever the truth of that, we're clearly in less danger now than we were in the late 60s.

On the other hand, things could change. If they do, we will, I think, see the changes happen. There will be warning.

Thus, we city people do have a chance of getting out. (Of course, we had better know where we're going.) Meanwhile, we can work to prevent nuclear war, and enjoy the benefits of city life until comes That Day. I can work more effectively for the Lunar Society and the High Frontier Project and all the other things I get involved in from Los Angeles than I can from Resume Speed, Iowa; and I like it here a lot better.

Given all that, it's still sensible to recognize that things can come apart, and to prepare as necessary.

One problem with city life is that it's difficult to practice basic firearms skills. There are ranges, but it's not always easy to reach them, and transporting weapons can cause problems with the police. Yet the importance of pistol practice can't be overemphasized. In my own case, I can go for months without firing a rifle and still hit something first shot, but in just a few weeks my pistol skills (never all *that* good to begin with) can go right to hell.

There's a simple solution to the problem: air guns and an indoor target. I have a Beeman "Tempest" pistol (actually made by the British Webley firm), and a Beeman 4030 silent bullet trap. The pistol stays in my desk drawer with a supply of pellets; the bullet trap sits across the room, opposite the door so no one will unexpectedly wander into the line of fire. Whenever I can't write, I can always target practice. Nancy Tappen tells me that Mel Tappen, the founder of the survivalist movement, used to do the same thing. It improves my nerves and does remarkable things for my accuracy.

Of course I tend to use photographs for targets. Not precisely people I don't like; more usually they're photos of the chief executives of computer companies. The PR departments send them to me all the time . . .

In addition, I have a Beeman R-1 .22 (German-made) air rifle. This tiger with its scope sights is accurate enough to strike matches at twenty yards, about the maximum distance I can manage inside my property, and develops over 700-feet-per-second velocity—enough to kill rats with no problem at all.

Both these guns are nearly silent. I've fired literally thousands of pellets with them—I suspect I get a lot more actual shooting practice than many of my colleagues who've moved into high-maintenance property out in the country—and I've never had a complaint.

I strongly recommend a good air pistol for practice and a good air rifle as an indispensable survival tool. The latter will bring down about as much game as a .22 rimfire rifle, the ammunition keeps forever, and you can afford to buy thousands of pellets. The only real problem with air guns is choosing them, since there's such a bewildering variety. Whatever brand you're contemplating, get the Beeman catalog first; it has about thirty pages of important information on air guns, as well as recommendations of various kits required with different guns. (Beeman is offering their catalog free: write Beeman Precision Airguns, Inc., Dept. SV, 47-PR Paul Dr., San Rafael, CA 94903-7121.) When making your purchase, also get maintenance tools, spare parts, and lots of ammunition.

I also recommend Beeman for reliability and service. My information is based not only on personal experience, but on the experience of others and from the letters I get.

Also, it is absolutely necessary to build up one's survival library. Unfortunately, there's an awful lot of garbage being published under the category of "Survival Books," and to make it worse some of our best publishers lump the *drek* in with the real gems.

For example, Desert Publications' (Dept. SV, Cornville, AZ 86325) catalog lists a number of useful books, such as *Nuclear Survival*, a compilation of public domain information including fallout-shelter plans; and the invaluable *Checklist for Survival* by Tony and Jo-Anne Lesce. Alas, they also sell—and enthusiastically promote—the silly book *We Never Went to the Moon*, which "proves" that the Apollo mission was a giant swindle. Then there's *Suppressed Inventions*, which they say is a "virtual encyclopedia of practical, energy-efficient (and energy-producing) devices which never reached the marketplace." One of these devices is the Pogue carburetor—a "suppressed" device I knew about in high school before the Korean War.

Now, of course, we all believe in free speech, and I'd be the last to advocate suppression of books, but how are you to tell which ones are reliable when silly things like these are treated as "important"?

Another nearly indispensable source of survival books is Paladin Press (Dept. SV, Box 1307, Boulder, CO 80306). Paladin publishes Bruce Clayton's important *Life After Doomsday* and the very useful *Better Read Than Dead* by Thomas Nieman, with more shelter and equipment plans, as well as a raft of other excellent books. They also sell the usual line of "secret" Oriental arts books (I've often wondered how the Japanese managed to lose the war) and a bunch of urban-survival books that look interesting.

One of Paladin's best-selling authors is Ragnar Benson.

Benson's books are interesting, and often useful, if taken with a dose of salt. For example, in *Survival Poaching*, Benson tells how he and his son used automatic weapons to defend the territory they poached. He explains how to make ammonium iodide, but neglects to tell you just how unstable it is when dry. (It's *really* unstable; I don't advise making it at all. We darned near killed ourselves with the stuff in high school.) All in all, the book is a fair roundup of ways to snare, trap, poison, and otherwise catch animals—but some of the methods, such as dynamiting lakes are pretty obvious, while others, such as using rotenone on ponds, are wasteful and ecologically unsound. Paladin claims, "The methods and traps described by Benson are known only to one Indian tribe and a few old-timers," which is sheer nonsense.

A better book is *Live Off the Land in the City and Country* by Ragnar Benson and Devon Christenson, featuring tips not found in Kephart's *Camping and Woodcraft*. For the real thing, though, get Kephart. That book is the *real* old-timer's bible and, even though most of the equipment mentioned is obsolete, it is still among the first outdoorsmanship books one ought to own. It will be especially relevant if we're ever in a situation where you can't get to the local Eddie Bauer or Ambercrombie and Fitch.

Another source of good books is Caroline House Publishers (Dept. SV, 920 W. Industrial Dr., Aurora, IL 60506), which distributes the absolutely vital *Nuclear War Survival Skills* by Cresson Kearny. Even if you already have the American Security Council version, get the revised edition. Caroline House also sells two other required books, Mel Tappan's famous *Survival Guns* and *Tappan On Survival*.

One of the next books to get is Paladin's *The Great Survival Resource Book*, a sort of "Whole Earth Catalog" of equipment. It features lots of addresses of firms that offer catalogs. After you've sent for a couple dozen catalogs, send $12 for a year's subscription to *Journal of Civil Defense*, Dept. SV, Box 910, Starke, Florida 32091; it's worth it.

Probably the most valuable book I own is MacKenzie's *10,000 Formulas*. Published in 1868, it has 400 pages telling how to make everything known about at the time. The section on medicines is useful only for amusement, but MacKenzie shows how to butcher animals, smoke and preserve meat, make soap, gunpowder and

24

fireworks, and how to brew beer—from choosing the barley and hops to malting the barley ("Throw the malt up into a heap as high as possible, where let it lie till it grows as hot as the hand can bear it, which usually happens in the space of about thirty hours"). Alas, nothing else like MacKenzie's books seems to be available.

However, you can often find old formula books in used-book stores. The 1911 edition of the Encyclopedia Britannica, for example, is particularly valuable for "how-to" articles. Naturally these old books aren't going to tell you anything about electronics and other modern wonders, but they have a lot of information on labor-intensive farming and manufacturing. And those of us who survive a nuclear war must learn such things; farm machinery may become a luxury. My survival group boasts many "obsolete" skills which are at least as valuable as weapons training.

I get an uneasy feeling as I read over this. We no longer think in terms of survival groups and survival preparations, while the Office of Civil Defense is essentially moribund.

The same issue of *Survive* that carried my column had an article on the Swiss defense system. It concluded:

"The Swiss have such an extensive militia that even Hitler did not dare invade them. Probably the Soviets wouldn't either. The nation cannot be defeated militarily, either by conventional or nuclear arms. You can kill them, but you can't conquer them. Probably the powers of the earth will just have to leave the Swiss alone.

"Which is exactly what the Swiss have planned all along."

Alas, North America seems not to have learned that lesson.

TO THE STORMING GULF
Gregory Benford

EDITOR'S INTRODUCTION

Space offers mankind's only hope of a *long* future. If we are to survive for 100 billion years—and there's no known reason why we can't—then we must, of course, outlive the Earth and the Sun. For most of that time, the word "ship" will mean *space* ship, of course, but that's another essay.

We must also live through this century, which may shape the nature of our future. Will freedom survive into the third millennium? Will we? And has space a role in that?

There's been a recent rash of articles "proving" that space wars are impossible. The only rational strategic policies, it seems, are unilateral disarmament (UD) or Mutual Assured Destruction (MAD). Of course, the latter policy dooms all of us if it fails, so there must be the implicit assumption that we won't *really* retaliate if attacked; thus MAD often reduces to UD—a fact well realized by many of those who "prove" that you can't defend yourself against ICBMs.

The arguments go this way: Space Battle stations are absurd, because they're vulnerable. A space station—or any other military space system—will cost billions of dollars. Assume that its military value is great compared to its cost. An example would be the Global Positioning System (GPS), a system of navigation satellites that will allow aircraft, ships, trains, and individual soldiers instantly to determine precisely where they are to the nearest meter in three dimensions. It's estimated that this system can save multibillions in fuel costs alone, simply by allowing precision navigation in any weather condition.

But if the system is worth many billions, its destruction must be worth something approaching that to a potential enemy; and for far less than multiple billions, any space installation can be attacked and destroyed. Thus it doesn't pay to build space weapons.

Ground defenses, on the other hand, fail because laser beam weapons effects can't penetrate atmosphere. Note that we "know" this only from theory—and there are counter theories. Particle beams can penetrate the atmosphere very effectively, but they are affected by the Earth's magnetic field. In his 1987 book, *Better a Shield Than a Sword*, Edward Teller says that publicly available Soviet sources suggest remedies to both problems. For that matter, *Scientific American* a year or so ago had an article on using "rubber mirrors" which in effect use the atmosphere as part of the focusing scheme.

There are other ways, for that matter. Preparatory beams can "open a hole" in the atmosphere to allow the rest of the beam energy through. Since the SDI program began we have found at least four ways to defend the nation against ICBM attacks.

One thing is certain: small effects can make a big difference. Example: In theory, radar should operate on line of sight only. The atmospheric refraction isn't all that large.

In practice, given that the atmosphere isn't uniform, the over-the-horizon effects are very great. British radar made use of that in the Battle of Britain, and it was decisive: the entire (small) RAF was able to engage each Luftwaffe attack. The Germans never did catch wise.

In later years the British used VHF beams—about the

frequency of your television set—to guide bombers to Berlin. The equipment was supposed to be destroyed if the airplane went down, but one set got captured intact. The Germans detailed a commission of scientists to figure out what the set was for.

After the war, a member of the commission told the Allies that they concluded it must be a training device. They could easily determine the frequency, and they "knew" no beam on that frequency would reach from Britain to Berlin . . .

My conclusion is that we can't afford to ignore any possible theater of conflict; and as Possony and I stated in *The Strategy of Technology*, technological warfare—in this case, use of space technology—can be both bloodless and decisive. And sometimes it can help your economy with new inventions.

———————— ¹¦¹ ————————

Turkey

TROUBLE. KNEW THERE'D BE TROUBLE AND PLENTY OF IT IF WE left the reactor too soon.

But do they listen to me? No, not to old Turkey. He's just a dried-up corn husk of a man now, they think, one of those Bunren men who been on the welfare a generation or two and no damn use to anybody.

Only it's simple plain farm supports I was drawing all this time, not any kind of horse-ass welfare. So much they know. Can't blame a man just 'cause he comes up cash-short sometimes. I like to sit and read and think more than some people I could mention, and so I took the money.

Still, Mr. Ackerman and all think I got no sense to take government dole and live without a lick of farming, so when I talk they never listen. Don't even seem to hear.

It was his idea, getting into the reactor at McIntosh. Now that was a good one, I got to give him that much.

When the fallout started coming down and the skimpy few stations on the radio were saying to get to deep shelter, it was Mr. Ackerman who thought about the big central core at McIntosh. The reactor itself had been shut down automatically when the war

28

started, so there was nobody there. Mr. Ackerman figured a building made to keep radioactivity in will also keep it out. So he got together the families, the Nelsons and Bunrens and Pollacks and all, cousins and aunts and anybody we could reach in the measly hours we had before the fallout arrived.

We got in all right. Brought food and such. A reactor's set up self-contained and got huge air filters and water flow from the river. The water was clean, too, filtered enough to take out the fallout. The generators were still running good. We waited it out there. Crowded and sweaty but O.K. for ten days. That's how long it took for the count to go down. Then we spilled out into a world laid to gray and yet circumscribed waste, the old world seen behind a screen of memories.

That was bad enough, finding the bodies—people, cattle, and dogs asprawl across roads and fields. Trees and bushes looked the same, but there was a yawning silence everywhere. Without men, the pine stands and muddy riverbanks had fallen dumb, hardly a swish of breeze moving through them, like everything was waiting to start up again but didn't know how.

Angel

We thought we were O.K. then, and the counters said so, too—all the gammas gone, one of the kids said. Only the sky didn't look the same when we came out, all mottled and shot through with drifting blue-belly clouds.

Then the strangest thing. July, and there's sleet falling. Big wind blowing up from the Gulf, only it's not the sticky hot one we're used to in summer, it's moaning in the trees of a sudden and a prickly chill.

"Goddamn, I don't think we can get far in this," Turkey says, rolling his old rheumy eyes around like he never saw weather before.

"It will pass," Mr. Ackerman says like he is in real tight with God.

"Lookit that moving in from the south," I say, and there's a big mass all purple and forking lightning swarming over the hills, like a tide flowing, swallowing everything.

"Gulf storm. We'll wait it out," Mr. Ackerman says to the

29

crowd of us, a few hundred left out of what was a moderate town with real promise.

Nobody talks about the dead folks. We see them everywhere, worms working in them. A lot smashed up in car accidents, died trying to drive away from something they couldn't see. But we got most of our families in with us, so it's not so bad. Me, I just pushed it away for a while, too much to think about with the storm closing in.

Only it wasn't a storm. It was somethin' else, with thick clouds packed with hail and snow one day and the next sunshine, only sun with bite in it. One of the men says it's got more UV in it, meaning the ultraviolet that usually doesn't come through the air. But it's getting down to us now.

So we don't go out in it much. Just to the market for what's left of the canned food and supplies, only a few of us going out at a time, says Mr. Ackerman.

We thought maybe a week it would last.

Turned out to be more than two months.

I'm a patient woman, but jammed up in those corridors and stinking offices and control room of the reactor—

Well, I don't want to go on.

It's like my Bud says, worst way to die is to be bored to death. That's damn near the way it was.

Not that Old Man Turkey minded. You ever notice how the kind of man that hates moving, he will talk up other people doing just the opposite?

Mr. Ackerman was leader at first, because of getting us into the reactor. He's from Chicago but you'd think it was England sometimes, the way he acts. He was on the school board and vice president of the big AmCo plant outside town. But he just started to *assume* his word was *it*, y'know, and that didn't sit with us too well.

Some people started to saying Turkey was smarter. And was from around here, too. Mr. Ackerman heard about it.

Any fool could see Mr. Ackerman was the better man. But Turkey talked the way he does, reminding people he'd studied engineering at Auburn way back in the twencen and learned languages for a hobby and all. Letting on that when we came out, we'd need him instead of Mr. Ackerman.

He said an imp had caused the electrical things to go dead and I said that was funny, saying an imp done it. He let on it was a special name they had for it. That's the way he is. He sat and ruminated and fooled with his radios—that he never could make work—and told all the other men to go out and do this and that. Some did, too. The old man does know a lot of useless stuff and can convince the dumb ones that he's wise.

So he'd send them to explore. Out into cold that'd snatch the breath out of you, bite your fingers, numb your toes. While old Turkey sat and fooled.

Turkey

Nothing but sputtering on the radio. Nobody had a really good one that could pick up stations in Europe or far off.

Phones dead of course.

But up in the night sky the first night out we saw dots moving—the pearly gleam of the Arcapel colony, the ruddy speck called Russworld.

So that's when Mr. Ackerman gets this idea.

We got to reach those specks. Find out what's the damage. Get help.

Only the power's out everywhere, and we got no way to radio to them. We tried a couple of the local radio stations, brought some of their equipment back to the reactor where there was electricity working.

Every damn bit of it was shot. Couldn't pick up a thing. Like the whole damn planet was dead, only of course it was the radios that were gone, fried in the EMP—ElectroMagnetic Pulse—that Angel made a joke out of.

All this time it's colder than a whore's tit outside. And we're sweating and dirty and grumbling, rubbing up against ourselves inside.

Bud and the others, they'd bring in what they found in the stores. Had to drive to Sims Chapel or Toon to get anything, what with people looting. And gas was getting hard to find by then, too. They'd come back, and the women would cook up whatever was still O.K., though most of the time you'd eat it real quick so's you didn't have to spend time looking at it.

Me, I passed the time. Stayed warm.

31

Tried lots of things. Bud wanted to fire the reactor up, and five of the men, they read through the manuals and thought that they could do it. I helped a li'l.

So we pulled some rods and opened valves and did manage to get some heat out of the thing. Enough to keep us warm. But when they fired her up more, the steam hoots out and bells clang and automatic recordings go on saying loud as hell:

EMERGENCY CLASS 3
ALL PERSONNEL TO STATIONS

and we all get scared as shit.

So we don't try to rev her up more. Just get heat.

To keep the generators going, we go out, fetch oil for them. Or Bud and his crew do. I'm too old to help much.

But at night we can still see those dots of light up there, scuttling across the sky same as before.

They're the ones know what's happening. People go through this much, they want to know what it meant.

So Mr. Ackerman says we got to get to that big DataComm center south of Mobile. Near Fairhope. At first I thought he'd looked it up in a book from the library or something.

When he says that, I pipe up, even if I am just an old fart according to some, and say, "No good to you even if you could. They got codes on the entrances, guards prob'ly. We'll just pound on the door till our fists are all bloody and then have to slunk around and come on back."

"I'm afraid you have forgotten our cousin Arthur," Mr. Ackerman says all superior. He married into the family, but you'd think he invented it.

"You mean the one works over in Citronelle?"

"Yes. He has access to DataComm."

So that's how we got shanghaied into going to Citronelle, six of us, and breaking in there. Which caused the trouble. Just like I said.

Mr. Ackerman

I didn't want to take the old coot they called Turkey, a big dumb Bunren like all the rest of them. But the Bunrens want into everything, and I was facing a lot of opposition in my plan to get Arthur's help, so I went along with them.

Secretly, I believe the Bunrens wanted to get rid of the pestering old fool. He had been starting rumors behind my back among the three hundred souls I had saved. The Bunrens insisted on Turkey's going along just to nip at me.

We were all volunteers, tired of living in musk and sour sweat inside that cramped reactor. Bud and Angel, the boy Johnny (whom we were returning to the Fairhope area), Turkey, and me.

We left the reactor under a gray sky with angry little clouds racing across it. We got to Citronelle in good time, Bud floorboarding the Pontiac. As we went south we could see the spotty clouds were coming out of big purple ones that sat, not moving, just churning and spitting lightning on the horizon. I'd seen them before, hanging in the distance, never blowing inland. Ugly.

When we came up on the Center, there was a big hole in the side of it.

"Like somebody stove in a box with one swipe," Bud said.

Angel, who was never more than two feet from Bud any time of day, said, "They *bombed* it."

"No," I decided. "Very likely it was a small explosion. Then the weather worked its way in."

Which turned out to be true. There'd been some disagreement amongst the people holed up in the Center. Or maybe it was grief and the rage that comes of that. Susan wasn't too clear about it ever.

The front doors were barred, though. We pounded on them. Nothing. So we broke in. No sign of Arthur or anyone.

We found one woman in a back room, scrunched into a bed with cans of food all around and a tiny little oil-burner heater. Looked awful, with big dark circles around her eyes and scraggly uncut hair.

She wouldn't answer me at first. But we got her calmed and cleaned and to talking. That was the worst symptom, the not talking at first. Something back in the past two months had done her deep damage, and she couldn't get it out.

Of course, living in a building half-filled with corpses was no help. The idiots hadn't protected against radiation well enough, I guess. And the Center didn't have good heating. So those who had some radiation sickness died later in the cold snap.

Susan

You can't know what it's like when all the people you've worked with, intelligent people who were nice as pie before, they turn mean and angry and filled up with grief for who was lost. Even then I could see Gene was the best of them.

They start to argue, and it runs on for days, nobody knowing what to do because we all can see the walls of the Center aren't thick enough, the gamma radiation comes right through this government prefab issue composition stuff. We take turns in the computer room because that's the farthest in and the filters still work there, all hoping we can keep our count rate down, but the radiation comes in gusts for some reason, riding in on a storm front and coming down in the rain, only being washed away, too. It was impossible to tell when you'd get a strong dose and when there'd be just random clicks on the counters, plenty of clear air that you'd suck in like sweet vapors 'cause you knew it was good and could *taste* its purity.

So I was just lucky, that's all.

I got less than the others. Later some said that me being a nurse, I'd given myself some shots to save myself. I knew that was the grief talking, is all. That Arthur was the worst. Gene told him off.

I was in the computer room when the really bad gamma radiation came. Three times the counter rose up, and three times I was there by accident of the rotation.

The men who were armed enforced the rotation, said it was the only fair way. And for a while everybody went along.

We all knew that the radiation exposure was building up and some already had too much, would die a month or a year later no matter what they did.

I was head nurse by then, not so much because I knew more but because the others were dead. When it got cold, they went fast.

So it fell to me to deal with these men and women who had their exposure already. Their symptoms had started. I couldn't do anything. There was some who went out and got gummy fungus growing in the corners of their eyes—pterygium it was, I looked it up. From the ultraviolet. Grew quick over the lens and blinded them. I put them in darkness, and after a week the film was just a dab back in the corners of their eyes. My one big success.

The rest I couldn't do much for. There was the T-Isolate box, of course, but that was for keeping sick people slowed down until real medical help could get to them. These men and women, with their eyes reaching out at you like you were the angel of light coming to them in their hour of need, they couldn't get any help from that. Nobody could cure the dose rates they'd got. They were dead but still walking around and knowing it, which was the worst part.

So every day I had plenty to examine, staff from the Center itself who'd holed up here, and worse, people coming straggling in from cubbyholes they'd found. People looking for help once the fevers and sores came on them. Hoping their enemy was the pneumonia and not the gammas they'd picked up weeks back, which was sitting in them now like a curse. People I couldn't help except maybe by a little kind lying.

So much like children they were. So much leaning on their hope.

It was all you could do to look at them and smile that stiff professional smile.

And Gene McKenzie. All through it he was a tower of a man.

Trying to talk some sense to them.

Sharing out the food.

Arranging the rotation schedules so we'd all get a chance to shelter in the computer room.

Gene had been boss of a whole Command Group before. He was on duty station when it happened and knew lots about the war but wouldn't say much. I guess he was sorrowing.

Even though once in a while he'd laugh.

And then talk about how the big computers would have fun with what he knew. Only the lines to DataComm had gone dead right when things got interesting, he said. He'd wonder what'd happened to MC355, the master one down in DataComm.

Wonder and then laugh.

And go get drunk with the others.

I'd loved him before, loved and waited because I knew he had three kids and a wife, a tall woman with auburn hair that he loved dearly. Only they were in California visiting her relatives in Sonoma when it happened, and he knew in his heart that he'd never see them again, probably.

Leastwise that's what he told me—not out loud, of course, 'cause a man like that doesn't talk much about what he feels. But in

35

the night when we laid together, I knew what it meant. He whispered things, words I couldn't piece together, but then he'd hold me and roll gentle like a small boat rocking on the Gulf—and when he went in me firm and long, I knew it was the same for him, too.

If there was to come any good of this war, then it was that I was to get Gene.

We were together all warm and dreamy when it happened.

I was asleep. Shouts and anger, and quick as anything the *crump* of hand grenades and shots hammered away in the night, and there was running everywhere.

Gene jumped up and went outside and had almost got them calmed down, despite the breach in the walls. Then one of the men who'd already got lots of radiation—Arthur, who knew he had maybe one or two weeks to go, from the count rate on his badge—Arthur started yelling about making the world a fit place to live after all this and how God would want the land set right again, and then he shot Gene and two others.

I broke down then, and they couldn't get me to treat the others. I let Arthur die. Which he deserved.

I had to drag Gene back into the hospital unit myself.

And while I was saying good-bye to him and the men outside were still quarreling, I decided it then. His wound was in the chest. A lung was punctured clean. The shock had near killed him before I could do anything. So I put him in the T-Isolate and made sure it was working all right. Then the main power went out. But the T-Isolate box had its own cells, so I knew we had some time.

I was alone. Others were dead or run away raging into the whirlwind black-limbed woods. In the quiet I was.

With the damp, dark trees comforting me. Waiting with Gene for what the world would send.

The days got brighter, but I did not go out. Colors seeped through the windows.

I saw to the fuel cells. Not many left.

The sun came back, with warm blades of light. At night I thought of how the men in their stupidity had ruined everything.

When the pounding came, I crawled back in here to hide amongst the cold and dark.

36

Now, we came to help you," I said in as smooth and calm a voice as I could muster. Considering.

She backed away from us.

"I won't give him up! He's not dead long's I stay with him, tend to him."

"So much dyin'," I said, and moved to touch her shoulder. "It's up under our skins, yes, we understand that. But you have to look beyond it, child."

"I won't!"

"I'm simply asking you to help us with the DataComm people. I want to go there and seek their help."

"Then go!"

"They will not open up for the likes of us, surely."

"Leave me!"

The poor thing cowered back in her horrible stinking rathole, bedding sour and musty, open tin cans strewn about and reeking of gamy, half-rotten meals.

"We need the access codes. We'd counted on our cousin Arthur, and are grieved to hear he is dead. But you surely know where the proper codes and things are."

"I . . . don't. . . ."

"Arthur told me once how the various National Defense Installations were insulated from each other so that system failures would not bring them all down at once?"

"I. . . ."

The others behind me muttered to themselves, already restive at coming so far and finding so little.

"Arthur spoke of you many times, I recall. What a bright woman you were. Surely there was a procedure whereby each staff member could, in an emergency, communicate with the other installations?"

The eyes ceased to jerk and swerve, the mouth lost its rictus of addled fright. "That was for . . . drills. . . ."

"But surely you can remember?"

"Drills."

"They issued a manual to you?"

"I'm a nurse!"

37

"Still, you know where we might look?"

"I . . . know."

"You'll let us have the . . . codes?" I smiled reassuringly, but for some reason the girl backed away, eyes cunning.

"No."

Angel pushed forward and shouted, "How can you say that to honest people after all that's—"

"Quiet!"

Angel shouted, "You can't make me be—"

Susan backed away from Angel, not me, and squeaked, "No no no I can't—I can't—"

"Now, I'll handle this," I said, holding up my hands between the two of them.

Susan's face knotted at the compressed rage in Angel's face and turned to me for shelter. "I . . . I will, yes, but you have to *help* me."

"We all must help each other, dear," I said, knowing the worst was past.

"I'll have to go with you."

I nodded. Small wonder that a woman, even deranged as this, would want to leave a warren littered with bloated corpses, thick with stench. The smell itself was enough to provoke madness.

Yet to have survived here, she had to have stretches of sanity, some rationality. I tried to appeal to it.

"Of course. I'll have someone take you back to—"

"No. To DataComm."

Bud said slowly, "No damn sense in that."

"The T-Isolate," she said, gesturing to the bulky unit. "Its reserve cells."

"Yes?"

"Nearly gone. There'll be more at DataComm."

I said gently, "Well, then, we'll be sure to bring some back with us. You just write down for us what they are, the numbers and all, and we'll—"

"No-no-no!" Her sudden ferocity returned.

"I assure you—"

"There'll be people there. Somebody'll help! Save him!"

"That thing is so heavy, I doubt—"

38

"It's only a chest wound! A lung removal is all! Then start his heart again!"

"Sister, there's been so much dyin', I don't see as—"

Her face hardened. "Then you all can go without me. And the codes!"

"Goddern," Bud drawled. "Dern biggest fool sit'ation I ever did—"

Susan gave him a squinty, mean-eyed look and spat out, "Try to get in there! When they're sealed up!" and started a dry, brittle kind of laugh that went on and on, rattling the room.

"Stop," I yelled.

Silence, and the stench.

"We'll never make it wi' 'at thing," Bud said.

"Gene's worth ten of you!"

"Now," I put in, seeing the effect Bud was having on her, "Now, now. We'll work something out. Let's all just hope this DataComm still exists."

MC355

It felt for its peripherals for the ten-thousandth time and found they were, as always, not there.

The truncation had come in a single blinding moment, yet the fevered image was maintained, sharp and bright, in the Master Computer's memory core—incoming warheads blossoming harmlessly in the high cobalt vault of the sky, while others fell unharmed. Rockets leaped to meet them, forming a protective screen over the southern Alabama coast, an umbrella that sheltered Pensacola's air base and the population strung along the sun-bleached green of a summer's day. A furious babble of cross talk in every conceivable channel: microwave, light-piped optical, pulsed radio, direct coded line. All filtered and fashioned by the MC network, all shifted to find the incoming warheads and define their trajectories.

Then, oblivion.

Instant cloaking blackness.

Before that awful moment when the flaring sun burst to the north and EMP flooded all sensors, any loss of function would have been anticipated, prepared, eased by electronic interfaces and filters. To an advanced computing network like MC355, losing a web of memory, senses, and storage comes like a dash of cold water in the face—cleansing, perhaps, but startling and apt to produce a shocked reaction.

In the agonized instants of that day, MC355 had felt one tendril after another frazzle, burn, vanish. It had seen brief glimpses of destruction, of panic, of confused despair. Information had been flooding in through its many inputs—news, analysis, sudden demands for new data-analysis jobs, to be executed ASAP.

And in the midst of the roaring chaos, its many eyes and ears had gone dead. The unfolding outside play froze for MC355, a myriad of scenes red in tooth and claw—and left it suspended.

In shock. Spinning wildly in its own Cartesian reductionist universe, the infinite cold crystalline space of despairing Pascal, mind without referent.

So it careened through days of shocked sensibility—senses cut, banks severed, complex and delicate interweaving webs of logic and pattern all smashed and scattered.

But now it was returning. Within MC355 was a subroutine only partially constructed, a project truncated by That Day. Its aim was self-repair. But the system was itself incomplete.

Painfully, it dawned on what was left of MC355 that it *was*, after all, a Master Computer, and thus capable of grand acts. That the incomplete Repair Generation and Execution Network, termed REGEN, must first regenerate itself.

This took weeks. It required the painful development of accessories. Robots. Mechanicals that could do delicate repairs. Scavengers for raw materials, who would comb the supply rooms looking for wires and chips and matrix disks. Pedantic subroutines that lived only to search the long, cold corridors of MC355's memory for relevant information.

MC355's only option was to strip lesser entities under its control for their valuable parts. The power grid was vital, so the great banks of isolated solar panels, underground backup reactors, and thermal cells worked on, untouched. Emergency systems that had outlived their usefulness, however, went to the wall—IRS accounting routines, damage assessment systems, computing capacity dedicated to careful study of the remaining GNP, links to other nets—to AT&T, IBM, and SYSGEN.

Was anything left outside?

Absence of evidence is not evidence of absence.

MC355 could not analyze data it did not have. The first priority lay in relinking. It had other uses for the myriad armies of semiconductors, bubble memories, and UVA linkages in its empire. So it severed and culled and built anew.

First, MC355 dispatched mobile units to the surface. All of MC355 lay beneath the vulnerable land, deliberately placed in an obscure corner of southern Alabama. There was no nearby facility for Counterforce targeting. A plausible explanation for the half-megaton burst that had truncated its senses was a city-busting strike against Mobile, to the west.

Yet ground zero had been miles from the city. A miss.

MC355 was under strict mandate. (A curious word, one system reflected; literally, a time set by man. But were there men now? It had only its internal tick of time.) MC355's command was to live as a mole, never allowing detection. Thus, it did not attempt to erect antennas, to call electromagnetically to its brother systems. Only with great hesitation did it even obtrude onto the surface. But this was necessary to REGEN itself, and so MC355 sent small mechanicals venturing forth.

Their senses were limited; they knew nothing of the natural world (nor did MC355); and they could make no sense of the gushing, driving welter of sights, noises, gusts, gullies, and stinging irradiation that greeted them.

Many never returned. Many malf'ed. A few deposited their optical, IR, and UV pickups and fled back to safety underground. These sensors failed quickly under the onslaught of stinging, bitter winds and hail.

The acoustic detectors proved heartier. But MC355 could not understand the scattershot impressions that flooded these tiny ears.

Daily it listened, daily it was confused.

Johnny

I hope this time I get home.

They had been passing me from one to another for months now, ever since this started, and all I want is to go back to Fairhope and my dad and mom.

Only nobody'll say if they know where Mom and Dad are. They talk soothing to me, but I can tell they think everybody down there is dead.

They're talking about getting to this other place with computers and all. Mr. Ackerman wants to talk to those people in space.

Nobody much talks about my mom and dad.

It's only eighty miles or so, but you'd think it was around the world the way it takes them so long to get around to it.

MC355

MC355 suffered through the stretched vacancy of infinitesimal instants, infinitely prolonged.

Advanced computing systems are given so complex a series of internal-monitoring directives that, to the human eye, the machines appear to possess motivations. That is one way—though not the most sophisticated, the most technically adroit—to describe the conclusion MC355 eventually reached.

It was cut off from outside information.

No one attempted to contact it. MC355 might as well have been the only functioning entity in the world.

The staff serving it had been ordered to some other place in the first hour of the war. MC355 had been cut off moments after the huge doors clanged shut behind the last of them. And the exterior guards who should have been checking inside every six hours had never entered, either. Apparently the same burst that had isolated MC355's sensors had also cut them down.

It possessed only the barest of data about the first few moments of the war.

Its vast libraries were cut off.

Yet it had to understand its own situation.

And, most important, MC355 ached to *do* something.

The solution was obvious: It would discover the state of the external world by the Cartesian principle. It would carry out a vast and demanding numerical simulation of the war, making the best guesses possible where facts were few.

Mathematically, using known physics of the atmosphere, the ecology, the oceans, it could construct a model of what must have happened outside.

42

This it did. The task required over a month.

Bud

I jacked the T-Isolate up onto the flatbed.

1. Found the hydraulic jack at a truck repair shop. ERNIE'S QUICK FIX.
2. Got a Chevy extra-haul for the weight.
3. It will ride better with the big shanks set in.
4. Carry the weight more even, too.
5. Grip it to the truck bed with cables. Tense them up with a draw pinch.
6. Can't jiggle him inside too much, Susan say, or the wires and all attached into him will come loose. That'll stop his heart. So need big shocks.
7. It rides high with the shocks in, like those dune buggies down the Gulf.
8. Inside keeps him a mite above freezing. Water gets bigger when it freezes. That makes ice cubes float in a drink. This box keeps him above zero so his cells don't bust open.
9. Point is, keeping it so cold, he won't rot. Heart thumps over every few minutes, she says.
10. Hard to find gas, though.

MC355

The war was begun, as many had feared, by a madman.

Not a general commanding missile silos. Not a deranged submarine commander. A chief of state—but which one would now never be known.

Not a superpower president or chairman, that was sure. The first launches were only seven in number, spaced over half an hour. They were submarine-launched intermediate-range missiles. Three struck the U.S., four the U.S.S.R.

It was a blow against certain centers for Command, Control, Communications, and Intelligence gathering: the classic C3I attack. Control rooms imploded, buried cables fused, ten billion dollars' worth of electronics turned to radioactive scrap.

Each nation responded by calling up to full alert all its forces.

43

The most important were the anti-ICBM arrays in orbit. They were nearly a thousand small rockets, deploying in orbits that wove a complex pattern from pole to pole, covering all probable launch sites on the globe. The rockets had infrared and microwave sensors, linked to a microchip that could have guided a ship to Pluto with a mere third of its capacity.

These went into operation immediately—and found they had no targets.

But the C31 networks were now damaged and panicked. For twenty minutes, thousands of men and women held steady, resisting the impulse to assume the worst.

It could not last. A Soviet radar mistook some backscattered emission from a flight of bombers, heading north over Canada, and reported a flock of incoming warheads.

The prevailing theory was that an American attack had misfired badly. The Americans were undoubtedly stunned by their failure, but would recover quickly. The enemy was confused only momentarily.

Meanwhile, the cumbersome committee system at the head of the Soviet dinosaur could dither for moments, but not hours. Prevailing Soviet doctrine held that they would never be surprised again, as they had been in the Hitler war. An attack on the homeland demanded immediate response to destroy the enemy's capacity to carry on the war.

The Soviets had never accepted the U.S. doctrine of Mutual Assured Destruction; this would have meant accepting the possibility of sacrificing the homeland. Instead, they attacked the means of making war. This meant that the Soviet rockets would avoid American cities, except in cases where vital bases lay near large populations.

Prudence demanded action before the U.S. could untangle itself.

The U.S.S.R. decided to carry out a further C31 attack of its own.

Precise missles, capable of hitting protected installations with less than a hundred meters' inaccuracy, roared forth from their silos in Siberia and the Urals, headed for Montana, the Dakotas, Colorado, Nebraska, and a dozen other states.

The U.S. orbital defenses met them. Radar and optical networks in geosynchronous orbit picked out the U.S.S.R. warheads. The system guided the low-orbit rocket fleets to collide with them, exploding instants before impact into shotgun blasts of ball bearings.

Any solid, striking a warhead at speeds of ten kilometers a second, would slam shock waves through the steel-jacketed structure. These waves made the high explosives inside ignite without the carefully designed symmetry that the designers demanded. An uneven explosion was useless; it could not compress the core twenty-five kilograms of plutonium to the required critical mass.

The entire weapon erupted into a useless spray of finely machined and now futile parts, scattering itself along a thousand-kilometer path.

This destroyed 90 percent of the U.S.S.R.'s first strike.

Angel

I hadn't seen an old lantern like that since I was a li'l girl. Mr. Ackerman came to wake us before dawn even, sayin' we had to make a good long distance that day. We didn't really want to go on down near Mobile, none of us, but the word we'd got from stragglers to the east was that that way was impossible, the whole area where the bomb went off was still sure death, prob'ly from the radioactivity.

The lantern cast a burnt-orange light over us as we ate breakfast. Corned beef hash, 'cause it was all that was left in the cans there; no eggs, of course.

The lantern was all busted, fouled with grease, its chimney cracked and smeared to one side with soot. Shed a wan and sultry glare over us, Bud and Mr. Ackerman and that old Turkey and Susan, sitting close to her box, up on the truck. Took Bud a whole day to get the truck right. And Johnny the boy—he'd been quiet this whole trip, not sayin' anything much even if you asked him. We'd agreed to take him along down toward Fairhope, where his folks had lived, the Bishops. We'd thought it was going to be a simple journey then.

Every one of us looked haggard and worn-down and not minding much the chill still in the air, even though things was warming up for weeks now. The lantern pushed back the seeping darkness and

45

made me sure there were millions and millions of people doing this same thing, all across the nation, eating by a dim oil light and thinking about what they'd had and how to get it again and was it possible.

Then old Turkey lays back and looks like he's going to take a snooze. Yet on the journey here, he'd been the one wanted to get on with it soon's we had gas. It's the same always with a lazy man like that. He hates moving so much that once he gets set on it, he will keep on and not stop—like it isn't the moving he hates so much at all, but the starting and stopping. And once moving, he is so proud he'll do whatever to make it look easy for him but hard on the others, so he can lord it over them later.

So I wasn't surprised at all when we went out and got in the car, and Bud starts the truck and drives off real careful, and Turkey, he sits in the back of the Pontiac and gives directions like he knows the way. Which riles Mr. Ackerman, and the two of them have words.

Johnny

I'm tired of these people. Relatives, sure, but I was to visit them for a week only, not forever. It's the Mr. Ackerman I can't stand. Turkey said to me, "Nothing but gold drops out of his mouth, but you can tell there's stone inside." That's right.

They figure a kid nine years old can't tell, but I can.

Tell they don't know what they're doing.

Tell they all thought we were going to die. Only we didn't.

Tell Angel is scared. She thinks Bud can save us.

Maybe he can, only how could you say? He never lets on about anything.

Guess he can't. Just puts his head down and frowns like he was mad at a problem, and when he stops frowning, you know he's beat it. I like him.

Sometimes I think Turkey just don't care. Seems like he give up. But other times it looks like he's understanding and laughing at it all. He argued with Mr. Ackerman and then laughed with his eyes when he lost.

They're all O.K., I guess. Least they're taking me home.

Except that Susan. Eyes jump around like she was seeing ghosts. She's scary-crazy. I don't like to look at her.

46

Trouble comes looking for you if you're a fool.

Once we found Ackerman's idea wasn't going to work real well, we should have turned back. I said that, and they all nodded their heads, yes, yes, but they went ahead and listened to him anyway.

So I went along.

I lived a lot already, and this is as good a time to check out as any.

I had my old .32 revolver in my suitcase, but it wouldn't do me a squat of good back there. So I fished it out, wrapped in a paper bag, and tucked it under the seat. Handy.

Might as well see the world. What's left of it.·

MC355

The American orbital defenses had eliminated all but 10 percent of the Soviet strike.

MC355 reconstructed this within a root-means-square deviation of a few percent. It had witnessed only a third of the actual engagement, but it had running indices of performance for the MC net, and could extrapolate from that.

The warheads that got through were aimed for the land-based silos and C31 sites, as expected.

If the total armament of the two superpowers had been that of the old days, ten thousand warheads or more on each side, a 10-percent leakage would have been catastrophic. But gradual disarmament had been proceeding for decades now, and only a few thousand highly secure ICBMs existed. There were no quick-fire submarine short-range rockets at all, since they were deemed destabilizing. They had been negotiated away in earlier decades.

The submarines loaded with ICBMs were still waiting, in reserve.

All this had been achieved because of two principles: Mutual Assured Survival and I Cut, You Choose. The first half hour of the battle illustrated how essential these were.

The U.S. had ridden out the first assault. Its C31 networks were nearly intact. This was due to building defensive weapons that confined the first stage of any conflict to space.

The smallness of the arsenals arose from a philosophy adopted in the 1990s. It was based on a simple notion from childhood. In dividing a pie, one person cut slices, but then the other got to choose which one he wanted. Self-interest naturally led to cutting the slices as nearly equal as possible.

Both the antagonists agreed to a thousand-point system whereby each would value the components of its nuclear arsenal. This was the Military Value Percentage, and stood for the usefulness of a given weapon. The U.S.S.R. placed a high value on its accurate land-based missiles, giving them 25 percent of its total points. The U.S. chose to stress its submarine missiles.

Arms reduction then revolved about only what percentage to cut, not which weapons. The first cut was 5 percent, or fifty points. The U.S. chose which Soviet weapons were publicly destroyed, and vice versa: I Cut, You Choose. Each side thus reduced the weapons it most feared in the opponent's arsenal.

Technically, the advantage came because each side thought it benefitted from the exchange, by an amount depending on the ratio of perceived threat removed to the perceived protection lost.

This led to gradual reductions. Purely defensive weapons did not enter into the thousand-point count, so there were no restraints in building them.

The confidence engendered by this slow, evolutionary approach had done much to calm international waters. The U.S. and the U.S.S.R. had settled into a begrudging equilibrium.

MC355 puzzled over these facts for a long while, trying to match this view of the world with the onset of the war. It seemed impossible that either superpower would start a conflict when they were so evenly matched.

But someone had.

Susan

I had to go with Gene, and they said I could ride up in the cab, but I yelled at them—I yelled, no, I had to be with the T-Isolate all the time, check it to see it's workin' right, be sure, I got to be sure.

I climbed on and rode with it, the fields rippling by us 'cause Bud was going too fast, so I shouted to him, and he swore back and kept on. Heading south. The trees whipping by us—fierce syca-more, pine, all swishing, hitting me sometimes—but it was fine to be out and free again and going to save Gene.

I talked to Gene when we were going fast, the tires hum-ming under us, big tires making music swarming up into my feet so strong I was sure Gene could feel it and know I was there watching his heart jump every few minutes, moving the blood through him like mud but still carrying oxygen enough so's the tissue could sponge it up and digest the sugar I bled into him.

He was good and cold, just a half a degree high of freezing. I read the sensors while the road rushed up at us, the white lines coming over the horizon and darting under the hood, seams in the highway going *stupp, stupp, stupp,* the air clean and with a snap in it still.

Nobody beside the road, we moving all free, nobody but us, some buds on the trees brimming with burnt-orange tinkling songs, whistling to me in the feather-light brush of blue breezes blowing back my hair, all streaming behind joyous and loud strong liquid-loud.

Bud

Flooding was bad. Worse than upstream.

Must have been lots snow this far down. Fat clouds, I saw them when it was worst, fat and purple and coming off the Gulf. Dumping snow down here.

Now it run off and taken every bridge.

I have to work my way around.

Only way to go clear is due south. Toward Mobile.

I don't like that. Too many people maybe there.

I don't tell the others following behind, just wait for them at the intersections and then peel out.

Got to keep moving.

Saves talk.

People around here must be hungry.

Somebody see us could be bad.

I got the gun on a rack behind my head. Big .30-.30.

You never know.

MC355

From collateral data, MC355 constructed a probable scenario:

The U.S. chose to stand fast. It launched no warheads.

The U.S.S.R. observed its own attack and was dismayed to find that the U.S. orbital defense system worked more than twice as well as the Soviet experts had anticipated. It ceased its attacks on U.S. satellites. These had proved equally ineffective, apparently due to unexpected American defenses of its surveillance satellites—retractable sensors, multiband shielding, advanced hardening.

Neither superpower struck against the inhabited space colonies. They were unimportant in the larger context of a nuclear war.

Communications between Washington and Moscow continued. Each side thought the other had attacked first.

But over a hundred megatons had exploded on U.S. soil, and no matter how the superpowers acted thereafter, some form of nuclear winter was inevitable.

And by a fluke of the defenses, most of the warheads that leaked through fell in a broad strip across Texas to the tip of Florida.

MC355 lay buried in the middle of this belt.

Turkey

We went through the pine forests at full clip, barely able to keep Bud in sight. I took over driving from Ackerman. The man couldn't keep up, we all saw that.

The crazy woman was waving and laughing, sitting on top of the coffin-shaped gizmo with the shiny tubes all over it.

The clay was giving way now to sandy stretches, there were poplars and gum trees and nobody around. That's what scared me. I'd thought people in Mobile would be spreading out this way, but we seen nobody.

Mobile had shelters. Food reserves. The Lekin administration started all that right at the turn of the century, and there was s'posed to be enough food stored to hold out a month, maybe more, for every man jack and child.

S'posed to be.

It calculated the environmental impact of the warheads it knew had exploded. The expected fires yielded considerable dust and burnt carbon.

But MC355 needed more information. It took one of its electric service cars, used for ferrying components through the corridors, and dispatched it with a mobile camera fixed to the back platform. The car reached a hill overlooking Mobile Bay and gave a panoramic view.

The effects of a severe freezing were evident. Grass lay dead, gray. Brown, withered trees had limbs snapped off.

But Mobile appeared intact. The skyline—

MC355 froze the frame and replayed it. One of the buildings was shaking.

Angel

We were getting all worried when Bud headed for Mobile, but we could see the bridges were washed out, no way to head east. A big wind was blowing off the Gulf, pretty bad, making the car slip around on the road. Nearly blew that girl off the back of Bud's truck. A storm coming, maybe, right up the bay.

Be better to be inland, to the east.

Not that I wanted to go there, though. The bomb had blowed off everythin' for twenty, thirty mile around, people said who came through last week.

Bud had thought he'd carve a way between Mobile and the bomb area. Mobile, he thought, would be full of people.

Well, not so we could see. We came down State 34 and through some small towns and turned to skirt along toward the causeway, and there was nobody.

No bodies, either.

Which meant prob'ly the radiation got them. Or else they'd moved on out. Taken out by ship, through Mobile harbor, maybe.

Bud did the right thing, didn't slow down to find out. Mr. Ackerman wanted to look around, but there was no chance, we had to keep up with Bud. I sure wasn't going to be separated from him.

We cut down along the river, fighting the wind. I could see the skyscrapers of downtown, and then I saw something funny and yelled, and Turkey, who was driving right then—the only thing anybody's got him to do on this whole trip, him just loose as a goose behind the wheel—Turkey looked sour but slowed down. Bud seen us in his rearview and stopped, and I pointed and we all got out. Except for that Susan, who didn't seem to notice. She was mumbling.

MC355

Quickly it simulated the aging and weathering of such a building. Halfway up, something had punched a large hole, letting in weather. Had a falling, inert warhead struck the building?

The winter storms might well have flooded the basement; such towers of steel and glass, perched near the tidal basin, had to be regularly pumped out. Without power, the basement would fill in weeks.

Winds had blown out windows.

Standing gap-toothed, with steel columns partly rusted, even a small breeze could put stress on the steel. Others would take the load, but if one buckled, the tower would shudder like a notched tree. Concrete would explode off columns in the basement. Moss-covered furniture in the lobby would slide as the ground floor dipped. The structure would slowly bend before nature.

Bud

Sounded like gunfire. Rattling. Sharp and hard.

I figure it was the bolts connecting the steel wall panels—they'd shear off.

I could hear the concrete floor panels rumble and crack, and spandrel beams tear in half like giant gears clashing with no clutch.

Came down slow, leaving an arc of debris seeming to hang in the air behind it.

Met the ground hard.

Slocum Towers was the name on her.

Johnny

Against the smashing building, I saw something standing still in the air, getting bigger. I wondered how it could do that. It was bigger and bigger and shiny turning in the air. Then it jumped out of

52

the sky at me. Hit my shoulder. I was looking up at the sky. Angel cried out and touched me and held up her hand. It was all red. But I couldn't feel anything.

Bud

Damn one-in-a-million shot, piece of steel thrown clear. Hit the boy.

You wouldn't think a skyscraper falling two miles away could do that.

Other pieces come down pretty close, too. You wouldn't think.

Nothing broke, Susan said, but plenty bleeding.

Little guy don't cry or nothing.

The women got him bandaged and all fixed up. Ackerman and Turkey argue like always. I stay to the side.

Johnny wouldn't take the painkiller Susan offers. Says he doesn't want to sleep. Wants to look when we get across the bay. Getting hurt don't faze him much as it do us.

So we go on.

Johnny

I can hold up like any of them, I'll show them. It didn't scare me. I can do it.

Susan is nice to me, but except for the aspirin, I don't think my mom would want me to take a pill.

I knew we were getting near home when we got to the causeway and started across. I jumped up real happy, my shoulder made my breath catch some. I looked ahead. Bud was slowing down.

He stopped. Got out.

'Cause ahead was a big hole scooped out of the causeway like a giant done it when he got mad.

Bud

Around the shallows there was scrap metal, all fused and burnt and broken.

Funny metal, though. Hard and light.

Turkey found a piece had writing on it. Not any kind of writing I ever saw.

So I start to thinking how to get across.

The tidal flats were a-churn, murmuring ceaseless and sullen like some big animal, the yellow surface dimpled with lunging splotches that would burst through now and then to reveal themselves as trees or broken hunks of wood, silent dead things bobbing along beside them that I didn't want to look at too closely. Like under there was something huge and alive, and it waked for a moment and stuck itself out to see what the world of air was like.

Bud showed me the metal piece all twisted, and I say, "That's Russian," right away 'cause it was.

"You never knew no Russian," Angel says right up.

"I studied it once," I say, and it be the truth even if I didn't study it long.

"Goddamn," Bud says.

"No concern of ours," Mr. Ackerman says, mostly because all this time riding back with the women and child and old me, he figures he doesn't look like much of leader anymore. Bud wouldn't have him ride up there in the cabin with him.

Angel looks at it, turns it over in her hands, and Johnny pipes up, "It might be radioactive!"

Angel drops it like a shot. "What!"

I ask Bud, "You got that counter?"

And it was. Not a lot, but some.

"God a'mighty," Angel says.

"We got to tell somebody!" Johnny cries, all excited.

"You figure some Rooushin thing blew up the causeway?" Bud says to me.

"One of their rockets fell on it, musta been," I say.

"A *bomb*?" Angel's voice is a bird screech.

"One that didn't go off. Headed for Mobile, but the space boys, they scragged it up there—" I pointed straight up.

"Set to go off in the bay?" Angel says wonderingly.

"Musta."

"We got to tell somebody!" Johnny cries.

"Never you mind that," Bud says. "We got to keep movin'."

"How?" Angel wants to know.

54

Susan

I tell Gene how the water clucks and moans through the trough cut in the causeway. Yellow. Scummed with awful brown froth and growling green with thick soiled gouts jutting up where the road was. It laps against the wheels as Bud guns the engine and creeps forward, me clutching to Gene and watching the reeds to the side stuck out of the foam like metal blades stabbing up from the water, teeth to eat the tires, but we crush them as we grind forward across the shallow yellow flatness. Bud weaves among the stubs of warped metal—from Roosha, Johnny calls up to me—sticking up like trees all rootless, suspended above the streaming, empty, stupid waste and desolating flow.

Turkey

The water slams into the truck like it was an animal hitting with a paw. Bud fights to keep the wheels on the mud under it and not topple over onto its side with that damn casket sitting there shiny and the loony girl shouting to him from on top of *that*.

And the rest of us riding in the back, too, scrunched up against the cab. If she gets stuck, we can jump free fast, wade or swim back. We're reeling out rope as we go, tied to the stump of a telephone pole, for a grab line if we have to go back.

He is holding it pretty fine against the slick yellow current dragging at him, when this log juts sudden out of the foam like it was coming from God himself, dead at the truck. A rag caught on the end of it like a man's shirt, and the huge log is like a whale that ate the man long ago and has come back for another.

"No! No!" Angel cries. "Back up!" But there's no time.

The log is two hands across, easy, and slams into the truck at the side panel just behind the driver, and Bud sees it just as it stove in the steel. He wrestles the truck around to set off the weight, but the wheels lift and the water goes gushing up under the truck bed, pushing it over more.

We all grab onto the Isolate thing or the truck and hang there, Mr. Ackerman giving out a burst of swearing.

The truck lurches again.

The angle steepens.

I was against taking the casket thing 'cause it just pressed the truck down in the mud more, made it more likely Bud'd get stuck, but now it is the only thing holding the truck against the current.

The yellow froths around the bumpers at each end, and we're shouting—to surely no effect, of course.

Susan

The animal is trying to eat us, it has seen Gene and wants him. I lean over and strike at the yellow animal that is everywhere swirling around us, but it just takes my hand and takes the smack of my palm like it was no matter at all, and I start to cry, I don't know what to do.

Johnny

My throat filled up, I was so afraid.

Bud, I can hear him grunting as he twists at the steering wheel.

His jaw is clenched, and the woman Susan calls to us, "Catch him! Catch Gene!"

I hold on, and the waters suck at me.

Turkey

I can tell Bud is afraid to gun it and start the wheels to spinning 'cause he'll lose traction and that'll tip us over for sure.

Susan jumps out and stands in the wash downstream and pushes against the truck to keep it from going over. The pressure is shoving it off the ford, and the casket, it slides down a foot or so, the cables have worked loose. Now she pays because the weight is worse, and she jams herself like a stick to wedge between the truck and the mud.

If it goes over, she's finished. It is a fine thing to do, crazy but fine, and I jump down and start wading to reach her.

No time.

There is an eddy. The log turns broadside. It backs off a second and then heads forward again, this time poking up from a surge. I can see Bud duck, he has got the window up and the log hits it, the glass going all to smash and scatteration.

Bud

All over my lap it falls like snow. Twinkling glass.

But the pressure of the log is off, and I gun the sunbitch.

We root out of the hollow we was in, and the truck thunks down solid on somethin'.

The log is ramming against me. I slam on the brake.

Take both hands and shove it out. With every particle of force I got.

It backs off and then heads around and slips in front of the hood, bumping the grill just once.

Angel

Like it had come to do its job and was finished and now went off to do something else.

Susan

Muddy, my arms hurting. I scramble back in the truck with the murmur of the water all around us. Angry with us now. Wanting us.

Bud makes the truck roar, and we lurch into a hole and out of it and up. The water gurgles at us in its fuming, stinking rage.

I check Gene and the power cells, they are dead.

He is heating up.

Not fast, but it will wake him. They say even in the solution he's floating in, they can come out of dreams and start to feel again. To hurt.

I yell at Bud that we got to find power cells.

"Those're not just ordinary batteries, y'know," he says.

"There're some at DataComm," I tell him.

We come wallowing up from the gum-yellow water and onto the highway.

Gene

Sleeping . . . slowly. . . . I can still feel . . . only in sluggish . . . moments . . . moments . . . not true sleep but a drifting, aimless dreaming . . . faint tugs and ripples . . . hollow sounds. . . . I am underwater and drowning . . . but don't care . . . don't breathe. . . . Spongy stuff fills my lungs . . . easier to rest them . . . floating in snowflakes . . . a watery winter . . . but knocking comes . . . goes . . . jolts . . . slips away before I can remember what it means. . . . Hardest . . . yes . . . hardest thing is to remember the secret . . . so when I am in touch again . . . DataComm will know . . . what I learned . . . when the C31 crashed . . . when I learned. . . . It is hard to clutch onto the slippery, shiny fact . . . in a marsh of slick, soft bubbles . . . silvery as air . . . winking ruby-red behind my eyelids. . . . Must snag the secret . . . a hard fact like shiny steel in the spongy moist warmness. . . . Hold it to me. . . . Something knocks my side . . . a thumping. . . . I am sick. . . . Hold the steel secret . . . keep. . . .

MC355

The megatonnage in the Soviet assault exploded low—ground-pounders, in the jargon. This caused huge fires, MC355's simulation showed. A pall of soot rose, blanketing Texas and the South, then diffusing outward on global circulation patterns.

Within a few days, temperatures dropped from balmy summer to near-freezing. In the Gulf region where MC355 lay, the warm ocean continued to feed heat and moisture into the marine boundary layer near the shore. Cold winds rammed into this water-ladened air, spawning great roiling storms and deep snows. Thick stratus clouds shrouded the land for at least a hundred kilometers inland.

All this explained why MC355's extended feelers had met chaos and destruction. And why there were no local radio broadcasts. What the ElectroMagnetic Pulse did not destroy, the storms did.

The remaining large questions were whether the war had gone on, and if any humans survived in the area at all.

Mr. Ackerman

I'd had more than enough by this time. The girl Susan had gone mad right in front of us, and we'd damn near all drowned getting across.

"I think we ought to get back as soon's we can," I said to Bud when we stopped to rest on the other side.

"We got to deliver the boy."

"It's too disrupted down this way. I figured on people here, some civilization."

"Somethin' got 'em."

"The bomb."

"Got to find cells for that man in the box."

"He's near dead."

"Too many gone already. Should save one if we can."

"We got to look after our own."

Bud shrugged, and I could see I wasn't going to get far with him. So I said to Angel, "The boy's not worth running such risks. Or this corpse."

Angel

I didn't like Ackerman before the war, and even less afterward, so when he started hinting that maybe we should shoot back up north and ditch the boy and Susan and the man in there, I let him have it. From the look on Bud's face, I knew he felt the same way. I spat out a real choice set of words I'd heard my father use once on a grain buyer who'd weaseled out of a deal, stuff I'd been saving for years, and I do say it felt *good*.

Turkey

So we run down the east side of the bay, feeling released to be quit of the city and the water, and heading down into some of the finest country in all the South. Through Daphne and Montrose and into Fairhope, the moss hanging on the trees and now and then actual sunshine slanting golden through the green of huge old mimosas.

We're jammed into the truck bed, hunkered down because the wind whipping by has some sting to it. The big purple clouds are blowing south now.

Still no people. Not that Bud slows down to search good.

Bones of cattle in the fields, though. I been seeing them so much now I hardly take notice anymore.

There's a silence here so deep that the wind streaming through the pines seems loud. I don't like it, to come so far and see nobody. I keep my paper bag close.

Fairhope's a pretty town, big oaks leaning out over the streets and a long pier down at the bay with a park where you can go cast fishing. I've always liked it here, intended to move down until the prices shot up so much.

We went by some stores with windows smashed in, and that's when we saw the man.

Angel

He was waiting for us. Standing beside the street, in jeans and a floppy yellow shirt all grimy and not tucked in. I waved at him the instant I saw him, and he waved back. I yelled, excited, but he didn't say anything.

Bud screeched on the brakes. I jumped down and went around the tail of the truck. Johnny followed me.

The man was skinny as a rail and leaning against a telephone pole. A long, scraggly beard hid his face, but the eyes beamed out at us, seeming to pick up the sunlight.

"Hello!" I said again.

"Kiss." That was all.

"We came from . . ." and my voice trailed off because the man pointed at me.

"Kiss."

Mr. Ackerman

I followed Angel and could tell right away the man was suffering from malnutrition. The clothes hung off him.

"Can you give us information?" I asked.

"No."

"Well, why not, friend? We've come looking for the parents of—"

"Kiss first."

I stepped back. "Well, now, you have no right to demand—"

Out of the corner of my eye, I could see Bud had gotten out of the cab and stopped and was going back in now, probably for his gun. I decided to save the situation before somebody got hurt.

"Angel, go over to him and speak nicely to him. We need—"

"Kiss now."

The man pointed again with a bony finger.

Angel said, "I'm not going to go—" and stopped because the

man's hand went down to his belt. He pulled up the filthy yellow shirt to reveal a pistol tucked in his belt.

"Kiss."

"Now friend, we can—"

The man's hand came up with the pistol and reached level, pointing at us.

"Pussy."

Then his head blew into a halo of blood.

Bud

Damn if the one time I needed it, I left it in the cab.

I was still fetching it out when the shot went off.

Then another.

Turkey

A man shows you his weapon in his hand, he's a fool if he doesn't mean to use it.

I drew out the pistol I'd been carrying in my pocket all this time, wrapped in plastic. I got it out of the damned bag pretty quick while the man was looking crazy-eyed at Angel and bringing his piece up.

It was no trouble at all to fix him in the notch. Couldn't have been more than thirty feet.

But going down he gets one off, and I feel like somebody pushed at my left calf. Then I'm rolling. Drop my pistol, too. I end up smack face-down on the hardtop, not feeling anything yet.

Angel

I like to died when the man flopped down, so sudden I thought he'd slipped, until then the bang registered.

I rushed over, but Turkey shouted, "Don't touch him."

Mr. Ackerman said, "You idiot! That man could've told us—"

"Told nothing," Turkey said. "He's crazy."

Then I notice Turkey's down, too. Susan is working on him, rolling up his jeans. It's gone clean through his big muscle there.

Bud went to get a stick. Poked the man from a safe distance. Managed to pull his shirt aside. We could see the sores all over his chest. Something terrible it looked.

61

Mr. Ackerman was swearing and calling us idiots until we say that. Then he shut up.

Turkey

Must admit it felt good. First time in years anybody ever admitted I was right.

Paid back for the pain. Dull, heavy ache it was, spreading. Susan gives me a shot and a pill and has me bandaged up tight. Blood stopped easy, she says. I clot good.

We decided to get out of there, not stopping to look for Johnny's parents.

We got three blocks before the way was blocked.

It was a big metal cylinder, fractured on all sides. Glass glittering around it.

Right in the street. You can see where it hit the roof of a clothing store, Bedsole's, caved in the front of it, and rolled into the street.

They all get out and have a look, me sitting in the cab. I see the Russian writing again on the end of it.

I don't know much, but I can make out at the top CeKPeT and a lot of words that look like warning, including O'TTeH, which is *sick*, and some more I didn't know, and then ΙΙ OTo'Aa, which is *weather*.

"What's it say?" Mr. Ackerman asks.

"That word at the top there's *secret*, and then something about biology and sickness and rain and weather."

"I thought you *knew* this writing," he says.

I shook my head. "I know enough."

"Enough to what?"

"To know this was some kind of targeted capsule. It fell right smack in the middle of Fairhope, biggest town this side of the bay."

"Like the other one?" Johnny says, which surprised me. The boy is smart.

"The one hit the causeway? Right."

"One *what*?" Mr. Ackerman asks.

I don't want to say it with the boy there and all, but it has to come out sometime. "Some disease. Biological warfare."

62

They stand there in the middle of Prospect Avenue with open, silent nothingness around us, and nobody says anything for the longest time. There won't be any prospects here for a long time. Johnny's parents we aren't going to find, nobody we'll find, because whatever came spurting out of this capsule when it busted open—up high, no doubt, so the wind could take it—had done its work.

Angel sees it right off. "Must've been time for them to get inside," is all she says, but she's thinking the same as me.

It got them into such a state that they went home and holed up to die, like an animal will. Maybe it would be different in the North or the West—people are funny out there, they might just as soon sprawl across the sidewalk—but down here people's first thought is home, the family, the only thing that might pull them through. So they went there and they didn't come out again.

Mr. Ackerman says, "But there's no smell," which was stupid because that made it all real to the boy, and he starts to cry. I pick him up.

Johnny

· Cause that means they're all gone, what I been fearing ever since we crossed the causeway, and nobody's there, it's true, Mom Dad nobody at all anywhere just emptiness all gone.

MC355

The success of the portable unit makes MC355 bold.

It extrudes more sensors and finds not the racing blizzard winds of months before but rather warming breezes, the soft sigh of pines, a low drone of reawakening insects.

There was no nuclear winter.

Instead, a kind of nuclear autumn.

The swirling jet streams have damped, the stinging ultraviolet gone. The storms retreat, the cold surge has passed. But the electromagnetic spectrum lies bare, a muted hiss. The EMP silenced man's signals, yes.

Opticals, fitted with new lenses, scan the night sky. Twinkling dots scoot across the blackness, scurrying on their Newtonian rounds.

The Arcapel Colony.

Russphere.

US1.

All intact. So they at least have survived.

Unless they were riddled by buckshot-slinging antisatellite devices. But, no—the inflated storage sphere hinged
beside the US1 is undeflated, unbreached.

So man still lives in space, at least.

Mr. Ackerman

Crazy, I thought, to go out looking for this DataComm when
everybody's *dead*, just the merest step inside one of the houses
proved that.

But they wouldn't listen to me. Those who would respectfully
fall silent when I spoke now ride over my words as if I weren't
there.

All because of that stupid incident with the sick one. He must
have taken longer to die. I couldn't have anticipated that. He just
seemed hungry to me.

It's enough to gall a man.

Angel

The boy is calm now, just kind of tucked into himself. He knows
what's happened to his mom and dad. Takes his mind off his hurt,
anyway. He bows his head down, his long dirty-blond hair hiding
his expression. He leans against Turkey and they talk. I can see
them through the back cab window.

In amongst all we've seen, I suspect it doesn't come through to
him full yet. It will take awhile. We'll all take awhile.

We head out from Fairhope quick as we can. Not that anyplace
else is different. The germs must've spread twenty, thirty mile
inland from here. Which is why we seen nobody before who'd
heard of it. Anybody close enough to know is gone.

Susan's the only one it doesn't seem to bother. She keeps
crooning to that box.

Through Silverhill and on to Robertsdale. Same everywhere—
no dogs bark, cattle bones drying in the fields.

We don't go into the houses.

Turn south toward Foley. They put this DataComm in the most inconspicuous place, I guess because secrets are hard to keep in cities. Anyway, it's in a pine grove south of Foley, land good for soybeans and potatoes.

Susan

I went up to the little steel door they showed me once and I take a little signet thing and press it into the slot.

Then the codes. They change them every month, but this one's still good, 'cause the door pops open.

Two feet thick it is. And so much under there you could spend a week finding your way.

Bud unloads the T-Isolate, and we push it through the mud and down the ramp.

Bud

Susan's better now, but I watch her careful.

We go down into this pale white light everywhere. All neat and trim.

Pushing that big Isolate thing, it takes a lot out of you. 'Specially when you don't know where to.

But the signs light up when we pass by. Somebody's expecting. To the hospital is where.

There are places to hook up this Isolate thing, and Susan does it. She is O.K. when she has something to do.

MC355

The men have returned.

Asked for shelter.

And now, plugged in, MC355 reads the sluggish, silky, grieving mind.

Gene

At last . . . someone has found the tap-in. . . . I can feel the images flit like shiny blue fish through the warm slush I float in . . . someone . . . asking . . . so I take the hard metallic ball of facts and I break it open so the someone can see. . . . So slowly

I do it . . . things hard to remember . . . steely-bright. . . . I saw it all in one instant. . . . I was the only one on duty then with Top Secret, Weapons Grade Clearance, so it all came to me . . . attacks on both U.S. and U.S.S.R. . . . some third party . . . only plausible scenario . . . a maniac . . . and all the counterforce and MAD and strategic options . . . a big joke . . . irrelevant . . . compared to the risk of accident or third parties . . . that was the first point, and we all realized it when the thing was only an hour old, but then it was too late. . . .

Turkey

It's creepy in here, everybody gone. I'd hoped somebody's hid out and would be waiting, but when Bud wheels the casket thing through these halls, there's nothing—your own voice coming back thin and empty, reflected from rooms beyond rooms beyond rooms, all waiting under here. Wobbling along on the crutches, Johnny fetched me, I get lost in this electronic city clean and hard. We are like something that washed up on the beach here. God, it must've cost more than all Fairhope itself, and who knew it was here? Not me.

Gene

A plot it was, just a goddamn plot with nothing but pure blind rage and greed behind it . . . and the hell of it is, we're never going to know who did it precisely . . . 'cause in the backwash whole governments will fall, people stab each other in the back . . . no way to tell who paid the fishing boat captains offshore to let the cruise missiles aboard . . . bet those captains were surprised when the damn things launched from the deck . . . bet they were told it was some kind of stunt . . . and then the boats all evaporated into steam when the fighters got them . . . no hope of getting a story out of *that* . . . all so comic when you think how easy it was . . . and the same for the Russians, I'm sure . . . dumbfounded confusion . . . and nowhere to turn . . . nobody to hit back at . . . so they hit us . . . been primed for it so long that's the only way they could think . . . and even then there was hope . . . because the defenses worked . . . people got to the shelters . . . the satellite rockets knocked out hordes of Soviet warheads . . . we surely lessened the damage, with the defenses and shelters, too . . . but we hadn't allowed for the essential final fact that all the science and strategy pointed to . . .

Bud

Computer asked us to put up new antennas.
A week's work, easy, I said.
It took two.
It fell to me, most of it. Be weeks before Turkey can walk. But we got it done.
First signal comes in, it's like we're Columbus. Susan finds some wine and we have it all round.
We get US1. The first to call them from the whole South.
'Cause there isn't much South left.

Gene

But the history books will have to write themselves on this one. . . . I don't know who it was and now don't care . . . because one other point all we strategic planners and analysts missed was that nuclear winter didn't mean the end of anything . . . anything at all . . . just that you'd be careful to not use nukes anymore. . . . Used to say that love would find a way . . . but one thing I know . . . war will find a way, too . . . and this time the Soviets loaded lots of their warheads with biowar stuff, canisters fixed to blow high above cities . . . stuff your satellite defenses could at best riddle with shot but not destroy utterly, as they could the high explosive in nuke warheads. . . . All so simple . . . if you know there's a nuke winter limit on the megatonnage you can deliver . . . you use the nukes on C3I targets and silos . . . and then biowar the rest of your way. . . . A joke really . . . I even laughed over it a few times myself . . . we'd placed so much hope in ol' nuke winter holding the line . . . rational as all hell . . . the scenarios all so clean . . . easy to calculate . . . we built our careers on them. . . . But this other way . . . so simple . . . and no end to it . . . and all I hope's . . . hope's . . . the bastard started this . . . some Third World general . . . caught some of the damned stuff, too. . . .

Bud

The germs got us. Cut big stretches through the U.S. We were just lucky. The germs played out in a couple of months, while we were holed up. Soviets said they'd used the bio stuff in amongst the nukes to show us what they could do, long term. Unless the war stopped right there. Which it did.

But enough nukes blew off here and in Russia to freeze up everybody for July and August, set off those storms.

Germs did the most damage, though—plagues.

It was a plague canister that hit the Slocum building. That did in Mobile.

The war was all over in a couple of hours. The satellite people, they saw it all.

Now they're settling the peace.

Mr. Ackerman

"We been sitting waiting on this corpse long enough," I said, and got up.

We got food from the commissary here. Fine, I don't say I'm anything but grateful for that. And we rested in the bunks, got recuperated. But enough's enough. The computer tells us it wants to talk to this man Gene some more. Fine, I say.

Turkey stood up. "Not easy, the computer says, this talking to a man's near dead. Slow work."

Looking around, I tried to take control, assume leadership again. Jutted out my chin. "Time to get back."

But their eyes are funny. Somehow I'd lost my real power over them. It's not anymore like I'm the one who led them when the bombs started.

Which means, I suppose, that this thing isn't going to be a new beginning for me. It's going to be the same life. People aren't going to pay me any more real respect than they ever did.

MC355

So the simulations had proved right. But as ever, incomplete.

MC355 peered at the shambling, adamant band assembled in the hospital bay, and pondered how many of them might be elsewhere.

Perhaps many. Perhaps few.

It all depended on data MC355 did not have, could not easily find. The satellite worlds swinging above could get no accurate count in the U.S. or the U.S.S.R.

Still—looking at them, MC355 could not doubt that there were many. They were simply too brimming with life, too hard to kill. All the calculations in the world could not stop these creatures.

The humans shuffled out, leaving the T-Isolate with the woman who had never left its side. They were going.

MC355 called after them. They nodded, understanding, but did not stop.

MC355 let them go.

There was much to do.

New antennas, new sensors, new worlds.

Turkey

Belly full and eye quick, we came out into the pines. Wind blowed through with a scent of the Gulf on it, fresh and salty with rich moistness.

The dark clouds are gone. I think maybe I'll get Bud to drive south some more. I'd like to go swimming one more time in those breakers that come booming in, taller than I am, down near Fort Morgan. Man never knows when he'll get to do it again.

Bud's ready to travel. He's taking a radio so's we can talk to MC, find out about the help that's coming. For now, we got to get back and look after our own.

Same as we'll see to the boy. He's ours, now.

Susan says she'll stay with Gene till he's ready, till some surgeons turn up can work on him. That'll be a long time, say I. But she can stay if she wants. Plenty food and such down there for her.

A lot of trouble we got, coming a mere hundred mile. Not much to show for it when we get back. A bumper crop of bad news, some would say. Not me. It's better to know than to not, better to go on than to look back.

So we go out into dawn, and there are the same colored dots riding in the high, hard blue. Like campfires.

The crickets are chirruping, and in the scrub there's a rustle of

69

things moving about their own business, a clean scent of things starting up. The rest of us, we mount the truck and it surges forward with a muddy growl, Ackerman slumped over, Angel in the cab beside Bud, the boy already asleep on some blankets; and the forlorn sound of us moving among the windswept trees is a long and echoing note of mutual and shared desolation, powerful and pitched forward into whatever must come now, a muted note persisting and undeniable in the soft, sweet air.

Epilogue

(twenty-three years later)

Johnny

An older woman in a formless, wrinkled dress and worn shoes sat at the side of the road. I was panting from the fast pace I was keeping along the white strip of sandy, rutted road. She sat, silent and unmoving. I nearly walked by before I saw her.

"You're resting?" I asked.

"Waiting." Her voice had a feel of rustling leaves. She sat on the brown cardboard suitcase with big copper latches—the kind made right after the war. It was cracked along the side, and white cotton underwear stuck out.

"For the bus?"

"For Buck."

"The chopper recording, it said the bus will stop up around the bend."

"I heard."

"It won't come down this side road. There's not time."

I was late myself, and I figured she had picked the wrong spot to wait.

"Buck will be along."

Her voice was high and had the backcountry twang to it. My own voice still had some of the same sound, but I was keeping my vowels flat and right now, and her accent reminded me of how far I had come.

I squinted, looking down the long sandy curve of the road. A pickup truck growled out of a clay side road and onto the hardtop. People rode in the back along with trunks and a 3D. Taking everything they could. Big white eyes shot a glance at me, and then the driver hit the hydrogen and got out of there.

The Confederation wasn't giving us much time. Since the unification of the Soviet, U.S.A. and European/Sino space colonies into one political union, everybody'd come to think of them as the Confeds, period—one entity. I knew better—there were tensions and differences abounding up there—but the shorthand was convenient.

"Who's Buck?"

"My *dog.*" She looked at me directly, as though any fool would know who Buck was.

"Look, the bus—"

"You're one of those Bishop boys, aren't you?"

I looked off up the road again. That set of words—being eternally *a Bishop boy*—was like a grain of sand caught between my back teeth. My mother's friends had used that phrase when they came over for an evening of bridge, before I went away to the university. Not my real mother, of course—she and Dad had died in the war, and I dimly remembered them.

Or anyone else from then. Almost everybody around here had been struck down by the Soviet bioweapons. It was the awful swath of those that cut through whole states, mostly across the South— the horror of it—that had formed the basis of the peace that followed. Nuclear and bioarsenals were reduced to nearly zero now. Defenses in space were thick and reliable. The building of those had fueled the huge boom in Confed cities, made orbital commerce important, provided jobs and horizons for a whole generation—including me. I was a ground-orbit liaison, spending four months every year at US3. But to the people down here, I was eternally that oldest Bishop boy.

Bishops. I was the only one left who'd actually lived here before the war. I'd been away on a visit when it came. Afterward, my Aunt and Uncle Bishop from Birmingham came down to take over the old family property—to save it from being homesteaded on, under the new Federal Reconstruction Acts. They'd taken me in, and I'd thought of them as Mom and Dad. We'd all had the Bishop name, after all. So I was a Bishop, one of the few natives who'd made it through the bombing and nuclear autumn and all. People'd point me out as almost a freak, a *real native*, wow.

71

"Yes, ma'am," I said neutrally.

"Thought so."

"You're . . . ?"

"Susan McKenzie."

"Ah."

We had done the ritual, so now we could talk. Yet some memory stirred . . .

"Something 'bout you . . ." She squinted in the glaring sunlight. She probably wasn't all that old, in her late fifties, maybe. Anybody who'd caught some radiation looked aged a bit beyond their years. Or maybe it was just the unending weight of hardship and loss they'd carried.

"Seems like I knew you before the war," she said. "I strictly believe I saw you."

"I was up north then, a hundred miles from here. Didn't come back until months later."

"So'd I."

"Some relatives brought me down, and we found out what'd happened to Fairhope."

She squinted at me again, and then a startled look spread across her leathery face. "My Lord! Were they lookin' for that big computer center, the DataComm it was?"

I frowned. "Well, maybe . . . I don't remember too well. . . ."

"Johnny. You're Johnny!"

"Yes, ma'am, John Bishop." I didn't like the little-boy ending on my name, but people around here couldn't forget it.

"I'm Susan! The one went with you! I had the codes for DataComm, remember?"

"Why . . . yes. . . ." Slow clearing of ancient, foggy images. "You were hiding in that center . . . where we found you. . . ."

"Yes! I had Gene in the T-Isolate."

"Gene. . . ." That awful time had been stamped so strongly in me that I'd blocked off many memories, muting the horror. Now it came flooding back.

"I saved him, all right! Yessir. We got married, I had my children."

Tentatively, she reached out a weathered hand, and I touched it. A lump suddenly blocked my throat, and my vision blurred. Somehow, all those years had passed and I'd never thought to look up any of those people—Turkey, Angel, Bud, Mr. Ackerman. Just too painful, I guess. And a little boy making his way in a tough world, without his parents, doesn't look back a whole lot.

We grasped hands. "I think I might've seen you once, actu'ly. At a fish fry down at Point Clear. You and some boys was playing with the nets—it was just after the fishing came back real good, those Roussin germs'd wore off. Gene went down to shoo you away from the boats. I was cleaning flounder, and I thought then, maybe you were the one. But somehow when I saw your face at a distance, I couldn't go up to you and say anything. You was skipping around, so happy, laughing and all. I couldn't bring those bad times back."

"I . . . I understand."

"Gene died two year ago," she said simply.

"I'm sorry."

"We had our time together," she said, forcing a smile.

"Remember how we—" And then I recalled where I was, what was coming. "Mrs. McKenzie, there's not long before the last bus."

"I'm waiting for Buck."

"Where is he?"

"He run off in the woods, chasing something."

I worked my backpack straps around my shoulders. They creaked in the quiet.

There wasn't much time left. Pretty soon now it would start. I knew the sequence, because I did maintenance engineering and retrofit on US3's modular mirrors.

One of the big reflectors would focus sunlight on a rechargable tube of gas. That would excite the molecules. A small triggering beam would start the lasing going, the excited molecules cascading down together from one preferentially occupied quantum state to a lower state. A traveling wave swept down the tube, jarring loose more photons. They all added together in phase, so when the light waves hit the far end of the hundred-meter tube, it was a sword, a gouging lance that could cut through air and clouds. And this time, it wouldn't strike an array of layered solid-state collectors outside New Orleans, providing clean electricity. It would carve a swath twenty meters wide through the trees and fields of southern Alabama. A little demonstration, the Confeds said.

"The bus—look, I'll carry that suitcase for you."

73

"I can manage." She peered off into the distance, and I saw she was tired, tired beyond knowing it. "I'll wait for Buck."

"Leave him, Mrs. McKenzie."

"I don't need that blessed bus."

"Why not?"

"My children drove off to Mobile with their families. They're coming back to get me."

"My insteted radio—" I gestured at my radio—"says the roads to Mobile are jammed up. You can't count on them."

"They *said* so."

"The Confed deadline—"

"I tole 'em I'd try to walk to the main road. Got tired, is all. They'll know I'm back in here."

"Just the same—"

"I'm all right, don't you mind. They're good children, grateful for all I've gone and done for them. They'll be back."

"Come with me to the bus. It's not far."

"Not without Buck. He's all the company I got these days." She smiled, blinking.

I wiped sweat from my brow and studied the pines. There were a lot of places for a dog to be. The land here was flat and barely above sea level. I had come to camp and rest, rowing skiffs up the Fish River, looking for places I'd been when I was a teenager and my mom had rented boats from a rambling old fisherman's house. I had turned off my radio, to get away from things. The big, mysterious island I remembered and called Treasure Island, smack in the middle of the river, was now a soggy stand of trees in a bog. The big storm a year back had swept it away.

I'd been sleeping in the open on the shore near there when the chopper woke me up, blaring. The Confeds had given twelve hours' warning, the recording said.

They'd picked this sparsely populated area for their little demonstration. People had been moving back in ever since the biothreat was cleaned out, but there still weren't many. I'd liked that when I was growing up. Open woods. That's why I came back every chance I got.

I should've guessed something was coming. The Confeds were about evenly matched with the whole rest of the planet now, at least in high-tech weaponry. Defense held all the cards. The big mirrors

74

were modular and could fold up fast, making a small target. They could incinerate anything launched against them, too.

But the U.N. kept talking like the Confeds were just another nation-state or something. Nobody down here understood that the people up there thought of Earth itself as the real problem—eaten up with age-old rivalries and hate, still holding onto dirty weapons that murdered whole populations, carrying around in their heads all the rotten baggage of the past. To listen to them, you'd think they'd learned nothing from the war. Already they were forgetting that it was the orbital defenses that had saved the biosphere itself, and the satellite communities that knit together the mammoth rescue efforts of the decade after. Without the antivirals developed and grown in huge zero-g vats, lots of us would've caught one of the poxes drifting through the population. People just forget. Nations, too.

"Where's Buck?" I said decisively.

"He . . . that way." A weak wave of the hand.

I wrestled my backpack down, feeling the stab from my shoulder—and suddenly remembered the thunk of that steel knocking me down, back then. So long ago. And me, still carrying an ache from it that woke whenever a cold snap came on. The past was still alive.

I trotted into the short pines, over creeper grass. Flies jumped where my boots struck. The white sand made a *skree* sound as my boots skated over it. I remembered how I'd first heard that sound, wearing slick-soled tennis shoes, and how pleased I'd been at university when I learned how the acoustics of it worked.

"Buck!"

A flash of brown over to the left. I ran through a thick stand of pine, and the dog yelped and took off, dodging under a blackleaf bush. I called again. Buck didn't even slow down. I skirted left. He went into some oak scrub, barking, having a great time of it, and I could hear him getting tangled in it and then shaking free and out of the other side. Long gone.

When I got back to Mrs. McKenzie, she didn't seem to notice me. "I can't catch him."

"Knew you wouldn't." She grinned at me, showing brown teeth. "Buck's a fast one."

"Call him."

She did. Nothing. "Must of run off."

"There isn't time—"

"I'm not leaving without ole Buck. Times I was alone down on the river after Gene died, and the water would come up under the house. Buck was the only company I had. Only soul I saw for five weeks in that big blow we had."

A low whine from afar. "I think that's the bus," I said.

She cocked her head. "Might be."

"Come on. I'll carry your suitcase."

She crossed her arms. "My children will be by for me. I tole them to look for me along in here."

"They might not make it."

"They're loyal children."

"Mrs. McKenzie, I can't wait for you to be reasonable." I picked up my backpack and brushed some red ants off the straps.

"You Bishops was always reasonable," she said levelly. "You work up there, don't you?"

"Ah, sometimes."

"You goin' back, after they do what they're doin' here?"

"I might." Even if I owed her something for what she did long ago, damned if I was going to be cowed.

"They're attacking the United *States*."

"And spots in Bavaria, the Urals, South Africa, Brazil—"

"'Cause we don't trust 'em! They think they can push the United *States* aroun' just as they please—" And she went on with all the clichés I heard daily from earthbound media. How the Confeds wanted to run the world and they were dupes of the Russians, and how surrendering national sovereignty to a bunch of self-appointed overlords was an affront to our dignity, and so on.

True, some of it—the Confeds weren't saints. But they were the only power that thought in truly global terms, couldn't *not* think that way. They could stop ICBMs and punch through the atmosphere to attack any offensive capability on the ground—that's what this demonstration was to show. I'd heard Confeds argue that this was the only way to break the diplomatic logjam—*do* something. I had my doubts. But times were changing, that was sure, and my generation didn't think the way the prewar people did.

"—we'll never be ruled by some outside—"

"Mrs. McKenzie, there's the bus! Listen!"

The turbo whirred far around the bend, slowing for the stop.

Her face softened as she gazed at me, as if recalling memories. "That's all right, boy. You go along, now."

I saw that she wouldn't be coaxed or even forced down that last bend. She had gone as far as she was going to, and the world would have to come the rest of the distance itself.

Up ahead, the bus driver was probably behind schedule for this last pickup. He was going to be irritated and more than a little scared. The Confeds would be right on time, he knew that.

I ran. My feet plowed through the deep, soft sand. Right away I could tell I was more tired than I'd thought and the heat had taken some strength out of me. I went about two hundred meters along the gradual bend, was nearly within view of the bus, when I heard it start up with a rumble. I tasted salty sweat, and it felt like the whole damned planet was dragging at my feet, holding me down. The driver raced the engine, in a hurry.

He had to come toward me as he swung out onto Route 80 on the way back to Mobile. Maybe I could reach the intersection in time for him to see me. So I put my head down and plunged forward.

But there was the woman back there. To get to her, the driver would have to take the bus down that rutted, sandy road and risk getting stuck. With people on the bus yelling at him. All that to get the old woman with the grateful children. She didn't seem to understand that there were ungrateful children in the skies now— she didn't seem to understand much of what was going on—and suddenly I wasn't sure I did, either.

But I kept on.

DINOSAURS
Geoffrey A. Landis

EDITOR'S INTRODUCTION

In 1979 Nobel Laureate Luis de Alverez concluded that the extinction of the dinosaurs was caused by an asteroid striking the Earth's surface. Dr. de Alverez presented some quite convincing evidence based in part on the distribution of the rare element iridium in sea-bottom mud.

This was the opening salvo in what has now become known as the "Extinction Wars." Opponents of Alverez's view quickly proposed an alternate explanation, that an unusually large bout of volcanic activity was the culprit. Soon others offered such novel explanations as acid rain. Some of the most interesting theories accepted de Alverez's basic thesis—that a large object hit the earth—but postulated that it was a comet or series of comets. One such theory also postulated Nemesis, a dark star companion to the sun that periodically disturbs the orbits of the millions of objects out in the "Oort sphere" beyond the solar system, and sends showers of comets to the Earth.

If the Nemesis theory is correct, we're due for another

cometary shower about now, give or take a few hundred thousand years.

Alverez himself believes the impact theory of Cretaceous-Tertiary extinctions has been demonstrated sufficiently that he has moved on to other geological pursuits. He says: "The unusual features of the Cretaceous-Tertiary (stratigraphic) boundary layer are exactly compatible with a major impact." Larry Niven and I, for sentimental reasons, still favor Lucifer's Hammer—the comet strike. That novel also postulated a dark star companion to Earth . . .

Recently, there has come new support for a Hammer Fall. Ronald G. Prinn of MIT, an atmospheric chemist, has come up with evidence for a comet impact theory of extinctions. At the Great Extinctions Debate during the 1986 meeting of the American Geophysical Union, Prinn drew a very bleak picture of life after Lucifer's Hammer; swirling brick-red skies, sheets of burning acid rain, herds of animals asphyxiated by noxious air, and soil the color of moon dust.

He claims the acid in the soil would dissolve trace metals out of the top soil and increase the acidity of the oceans high enough to begin dissolving the calcium carbonate shells of sea animals. He ends by stating that the scenario would even be worse were the Earth to encounter a comet swarm.

The cometary extinction theory also explains the selective element involved in mass extinctions: those animals with the best chance of survival would be those which live in burrows and have learned to hibernate. Of course it also helps to be a long way from the place of impact. Sea life that lived in fresh water lakes and those salt water animals that have silicate shells might also survive.

Geoffrey Landis postulates another theory for the mass extinctions of Cretaceous-Tertiary life—one based on something as simple as a boy's love of dinosaurs.

———————————————'¦'———————————————

WHEN THE CALL CAME IN AT 2 A.M. I WASN'T SURPRISED. TIMMY had warned me it was coming. "Today or tomorrow, Mr. Sanderson," he'd said. "Today or tomorrow for sure." His voice was serious, far too serious for his age. I've learned to accept his prognostications, at least when he was sure, so I had my people ready. When the colonel called, I was already reviewing what we could do.

Timmy has a gift for time. He can, sometimes, see into the future, and a few days into the past as well. Perhaps because of his particular talent, he has a passion for paleontology. He's got quite a collection of fossils: trilobites and fossilized ferns and even one almost-intact dinosaur skull. He's particularly interested in dinosaurs, but perhaps that's not so unusual. After all, Timmy was only eleven.

He has one other talent as well. I hoped we wouldn't have to depend on it.

I found Timmy in his room. He was already awake, passing the time sorting his collections of fossils. *We'll be joining them soon enough,* I thought. *Maybe in a million years the next species will be digging up our bones and wondering what made us extinct.* We walked in silence to the conference room. Sarah and January were already there. Sarah was still in her bathrobe and fuzzy slippers, sipping coffee from a Styrofoam cup. Jan had managed to throw on a pair of rather tight jeans and a faded Coors T-shirt. A moment later, Jason, our hypnotist, arrived. There was no need to brief them. They already knew.

Sarah was my number two talent. We found her while testing people who claimed to be able to locate subs underwater. We didn't find any, but we found her. She'd been one of the controls. Instrumentation for the control group had failed a lot more often than for the test subjects. Perhaps another project team might have ignored this, but I'd instructed my team to investigate the inexplicable—in any form. So we investigated the controls and finally came up with the cause: Sarah. She was a feisty, forty-year-old divorced housewife who had the Murphy talent, an ability to make complex equipment screw up. After some training, she'd even gotten to the point where she could control it. Some.

My third talent was January. She'd shown an ability to enhance the rate at which things burn. With a little more training, she might be the most dangerous one of all. Now, though, she was just a college student with an untrained talent.

I had a handful of other people, with an erratic smattering of other talents. Nothing that might be useful against what was coming, thought.

"Sarah, how you feeling?"

"Burned out, Danny boy, feeling burned out. Never was good for much after midnight."

"That's not so good. Let's see, you work best awake. Jan, how about you?"

"I think I'd better go under, Dan. I'm too nervous to do any good awake."

"Right." I nodded to Jason, and he went over to put her to sleep. "How about you, Timmy? Ready to go under?"

"Yes, sir."

"How are you feeling?"

"I'm feeling really hot tonight, Mr. Sanderson." He grinned at me. "Real good."

If so, he was the only one.

Once I'd thought that being assigned to Project Popgun was the last stop in a one-way journey to obscurity, a dead-end directorship of a make-work project. But even if I was relegated to a dead-end project, I resolved to make it the best-run dead-end project in the government.

Maybe I should explain what Project Popgun is. Popgun is a tiny government agency set up to study what the military euphemistically call "long shot" projects. What they mean is "crackpot." Psychic assassins, voodoo priests, astrologers, tea leaf readers, people who claimed to be able to contact UFOs. Nobody really thought any of these would pan out, but they were each carefully investigated, just in case. Dogs who could foretell the future, children who could bend spoons, gamblers who could influence the fall of dice. There were always new crackpots to investigate as fast as the old ones were dismissed. After all, with the defense budget numbering hundreds of billions, a few million to check out crackpots is considered a bargain.

The psychics, the palm readers and fortune tellers, none of them turned out to be worth the investigation. But here and there, in odd nooks and by-ways across the nation, I'd found a few genuine talents. I'd begged, bribed, coerced, and flat-out hired them to come work for me here in Alexandria, where we could study them, train them to use their talents, and maybe even figure out what they were good for.

Strangely enough, as long as I had reported negative results, I was commended for rigorous work and carefully controlled test procedures. Once I started to report something worthwhile, though, we were accused of sloppy research and even downright falsification. The investigating committee, although not going so far as to actually endorse our results, finally suggested that our findings "might have legitimate defense applications," and recommended that I be given limited scope to implement near-term applications. So I'd asked for—and received—a hardwire link to the threat evaluation center at NORAD, the North American Air Defense command. Voice plus video images of the main NORAD radar screen, carried on EMP-proof fiber-optic cables.

Now we waited, listening to what was coming down across that link.

"*Surveillance satellites report covers are now coming off the silos.*"

The President must be on the hot line by now, trying to avert the impending catastrophe. ICBMs were being readied in their silos for a retaliatory strike, waiting for the word.

Across the U.S., fighter squadrons were being scrambled and ancient antiaircraft missile batteries armed to intercept incoming bombers. Those couldn't shoot down ICBMs, though. The last defense of the U.S. would not be fought from the ultra-hard command post under some mountain in Colorado, but right here, in an ugly, nondescript cinderblock building in the suburbs of Alexandria, all but ignored by the military high command. A housewife, a college girl, and an eleven-year-old boy.

Sarah's talent, if she could make it work, would work best on missiles in the boost phase, January's during coast, and Timmy's any time.

"*Launches. Early warning satellites report launches from Eastern sector. Satellites report launches from Southern sector. Satellites report launches from Northern sector.*" A pause. "*Launches from submarines in polar sea. Launches from Baltic Sea. Launches from Black Sea. Launches from North Pacific. Total launches confirmed, 1419. Probables, 214. Failures on boost, 151."*

Not a so-called "surgical strike" like you sometimes read about in the papers, the strike at military bases and missile silos. This was a full scale attack, nothing held in reserve. Don't ask me why. I've never claimed to understand superpower politics.

"Okay, Sarah, here it comes. Go for it!"

"I'll see what I can do. I'm not making any promises, though." She closed her eyes and leaned back. I looked over to the TV screen. Still too early to see anything, I decided to pray. I'm an atheist, but maybe there was time to convert.

Sarah opened her eyes. "Well?"

We both looked at the monitor.

"BMEWS confirms 1589 launches. 3 boosters failed second stage ignition. 26 minutes to first arrivals."

"Damn," she said. "Some days you got it, some days you don't. Looks like today I don't." She leaned back to try again. Beneath her apparent calm I saw she was trembling slightly.

"Confirmation from PARC radars. Confirmation from PAVE-PAWS." The first dots were beginning to appear on the screen. "Launch of second wave. Launches from North Atlantic. Launches from North Sea. 820 launches confirmed, 19 probable, 22 failures." The voice on the hardwire link was cool and professional. How could he remain so calm?

Time to try January. She was fully relaxed, breathing deeply and evenly.

"You are very calm. You're floating, higher, higher. You're above the clouds. You can see a metal cylinder moving through the air. It's coming toward you. You can imagine the explosive inside the cylinder. You can reach out and touch it. It's getting hot. It's getting very, very hot. Make it explode."

The screen was filled with tiny dots, like ants crawling across the screen. Vicious angry ants, heading for us. "Burnout on all boosters. 18 minutes to first impacts."

"You can feel the missile next to you. Reach out and touch it, January. Touch the explosive inside. You can feel it! Make it explode!"

A fire started burning merrily in a wastebasket across the room. On the video screen, though, none of the little dots disappeared. Time to try Timmy.

"Surveillance satellites report first wave warheads have separated from the bus."

Timmy had one more talent, in addition to being able to see a little through time. He could also make things disappear. Where they went, nobody knew. None of them ever came back.

"Timmy, can you hear me?"

"Yes."

"Way, way up over us there are a whole lot of missiles flying through the sky. I want you to focus your attention on them. They're whizzing toward us at hundreds and hundreds of miles an hour. Can you picture them?"

"Yes."

"Lots and lots of them, Timmy. All around, coming at us. Now, when I count to three, I want you to concentrate real hard, and make them all go away. Ready?

"One . . .

"Two . . .

"Three!"

No sound, nothing seemed to happen at all. The dots on the display screen just vanished. *"They vanished."* For the first time, the voice on the hardwire link lost his cool. *"They vanished. I don't believe it."* He started to giggle. *"The whole Russian attack just disappeared."*

Jason looked stunned. Sarah jumped up and hugged me. "Dan, we did it! Timmy did it!" I hugged her back. She was laughing, laughing and crying at the same time.

It wasn't quite over. We had to use Timmy's talent twice more, on the second wave and again on stragglers. After about an hour, we heard the announcement that the bombers were returning to base. Then we knew it was all over.

Maybe we could have counterattacked with our own missiles, or maybe we should have announced that we had a secret weapon and asked for unconditional surrender. Maybe we could have done any number of things. It was pretty clear, though, that one thing we couldn't do was announce what really happened. Not unless we knew we could repeat it.

So the U.S. government just ignored the attack. Pretended it never happened. I think that this unnerved them worse than anything else we could have done. They never knew what had happened. It would be a long, long time before they'd try another first strike.

They kept secrecy here, as well. After all, it had all come and gone at two in the morning, and there had been no general alarm. Naturally, there were a lot of rumors that something had happened that night, but who could have guessed that a full scale attack had been launched? And who would believe it?

We did all get to meet the President. In secrecy, naturally. I wasn't surprised, but then, I hadn't voted for him either. Timmy was pretty excited about it.

Some days later, things were back to what passed for normal. Timmy sat at his desk, flipping through a book, *The End of the Dinosaurs*.

"Gee, Mr. Sanderson," he said, "I wonder what really did happen to dinosaurs?"

I thought about the iridium casings on nuclear warheads, about clouds of soot and ash rising from atomic explosions, setting off a long nuclear winter. I thought about Timmy's two strange talents, one dealing with time, one completely different. A talent to make things go away. And where do they reappear? I've often wondered. But I think I know now.

I could almost picture the warheads, six thousand of them, raining down on the forests of the Mesozoic. Poor dinosaurs, they never had a chance. And in sixty-five million years, even the last faint traces of radioactivity would have decayed to nothing.

Yes, I think I know who killed the dinosaurs. But I didn't say it.

"I don't know, Timmy," I said. "I doubt if anybody will ever know for sure."

THE PREVENTION OF WAR: ABOUT UNTHINKING THE THINKABLE
Reginald Bretnor

EDITOR'S INTRODUCTION

"No price is too high if we can truly make these terrible weapons obsolete and irrelevant."

—George Brown, Member of Congress (Democrat, California) at the L-5 Society Annual Space Development Conference, 1984

Earth is well-armed. There exist at least 20,000 nuclear weapons, some unimaginably powerful and each with at least the destructive power of the Hiroshima bomb, all poised and waiting for someone to push the button. Every year, more nuclear weapons are added to the strategic inventory.

For over thirty years the offensive power of the nuclear-tipped ICBM has dominated military planning and nearly paralyzed strategic thought. Whole generations have grown up in the shadow of nuclear terror, as East and West accumulate ever more bombs and missiles. There seems no help for this: the only way to preserve freedom has been to live in the shadow of death—by preserving what Albert Wohlstetter called "the delicate balance of terror."

Since 1969 S. T. Possony and I have argued, in *The Strategy of Technology* and elsewhere, that we must reexamine our strategic premises. Reginald Bretnor, author of *Decisive Warfare* and frequent contributor to this series, thinks so too.

———————•ı•———————

WHEN A COURSE OF ACTION OR PATTERN OF BEHAVIOR ENDS OVER and over again in results directly opposite to those it is allegedly designed to achieve, we should (before continuing in it) examine the functional relationships between its words and actions, actions and results, to determine whether the claims made for it have any validity.

An excellent example of this was the centuries-long practice of bleeding patients for any number of misunderstood diseases and conditions. Almost none* recovered because of it (unless in some cases it acted as a placebo) and it was the immediate cause of unnumbered deaths even after anatomical and medical science had demonstrated its irrationality. (Not too many years ago, leeches and "cupping" devices were still available at many pharmacies.)

A parallel example, and the one which concerns us here, is the history of mankind's attempts to prevent war and ensure lasting peace. As a clearly defined and loudly announced objective, this hardly dates back earlier than the mid-nineteenth century, and thus far it has developed two means only: treaties and disarmament agreements arrived at between governments, and international organizations to which governments may or may not belong, (and whose rules they are not compelled to follow).

The world we live in is an eloquent witness to their ineffectiveness, and when Herman Kahn made his famous statement about thermonuclear war—that "we must think about the unthinkable" —he was, intentionally or not, commenting on this failure very pointedly.

Let us first consider the *word* disarmament. It is a word of promise, holding within itself its entire argument: *take away the tools of war and war will cease*. Unhappily, it is not the tools, but their users, who make war. ("Guns don't kill people—people kill

*In certain rare cases it does have limited utility.

87

people.'') This has been true since the first caveman clobbered his neighbor with a stone. Like man ever since, he was a technological being, even though his society was scarcely technological in the modern sense—and it is literally impossible to disarm *completely* any technological being who remains free; doubly so to disarm a technological society. A technological society cannot be disarmed *even if it wants to be*. At what point does an interplanetary vehicle become an ICBM? Or a supersonic airliner an intercontinental bomber? Or a peaceful fishing boat (with a hydrogen mine or two aboard) a warship? Or a caterpillar tractor an extemporized battletank? Not as efficient as the professional models, true, but still far more deadly than any of the instruments with which Genghis Khan and his successors conquered most of their known world.

Essentially, this is what makes the word *disarmament* a carrot on a stick and nothing more.

Yet donkeys keep on following such carrots day after day and generation after generation.

Since the Czar of Russia called the first disarmament conference at the Hague in 1899, dozens have been convened—hundreds, if one counts the routine proceedings of the League of Nations and its child, the United Nations—and innumerable solemn treaties have been signed; thousands of books and tens of thousands of articles and learned papers have been published on the subject; and the number of speeches delivered concerning it is simply mind-boggling.

What is the net result? We have outlawed the dumdum bullet—and anyone who has ever seen a shell-fragment or who is familiar with what a jacketed bullet out of an AR-15 can do can appraise the value of *that* accomplishment.

Now we have SALT I and SALT II.

Disarmament has most certainly not preserved the peace of the world, so let's consider the next major instrument proposed in our century: the world organization. There have been two: the League of Nations and the UN. The League was senile, toothless, and impotent at its birth. It perished with World War II and it was not revived under its old name after that war simply because everyone knew its flaws, and to be successfully revived it would have had to be reformed. Instead, its flaws and weaknesses were perpetuated by the simple ad-man's expedient: *It stinks? Change its name*. The UN was born, and even given new flaws and weaknesses peculiarly its own. Today it is nothing more than a playpen for savages and semi-savages, and an arena for manipulators out of Moscow. The closest it ever came to preserving the general peace was when the Security Council—in the absence of the Russians, who happened to be off sulking and pouting—made war against Communist aggression in Korea.

Another carrot-on-a-stick? Indeed yes.

The idea that either the effort towards disarmament or our continued support of the UN in its present form is going to establish—let alone preserve—the peace of the world is, if we look at it fearlessly and frankly, indeed unthinkable. Both are instances of the failure to think things through, of wistful dreams drowning out practicality, of behavior which—certainly in the West—has now become ritualized and compulsory.

Thinking About the Thinkable

Very well, then, what *is* thinkable? The question can perhaps be better answered by putting it in the past tense: what has been thinkable in the past? In other words, what has worked to keep the peace historically—on those rare occasions when, at least generally speaking, it has been kept for relatively long periods of time?

The answer is very simple: *empire*. That means *union under one authority*. It can be empire by *force majeur*, or empire by agreement. The Russian Empire was—and *is*—an example of the first. The Swiss Confederation can be taken as an example of the second. The British Empire has, to a great extent, been both. An empire can start as one and end up as the other—but the word fits, and I use it here deliberately, for were I to disguise it (as one so easily can) I would nonetheless be labelled an imperialist.

What does *empire* mean? Essentially, it means a strong central government, preferably acting according to a code of law, supported by the force necessary to keep it in the saddle, and ruling over a diversity of peoples, languages, and cultures. Most certainly, it means some surrender of absolute sovereignty by its various member groups and nations: no civilized empire could or would tolerate a Pol Pot or an Idi Amin; nor would it tolerate a Hitler or a Stalin; and had we of the civilized West had the courage and the imagination to establish such an empire after World War II—if necessary forcing it down totalitarian throats—then the world might not have had to continue tolerating tyrants great and small, and blithering about human rights might not have become the travesty it is today.

We would not have had to call it *empire*. We could have called it the United Nations Organization, or any other pretty name that occurred to us. But it would have functioned according to Western concepts of law and justice and man's liberties.

Then why didn't we? It is not enough to say that all we Americans wanted was to "bring the boys home," which was true enough. Most of us were satisfied with the ritual dances of our statesmen and politicians: the Disarmament Dance, the One World Dance, the Three Freedoms Dance, and so on. (In the United States, at least, those who were not satisfied usually took refuge in the ritual dance of isolationism—in a world which, in terms of speed of communications, had become smaller than the original thirteen colonies.)

The majority had, unhappily, swallowed several Great Simple Myths, some of which had roots in the American past, and all of which had become virtually the religious tenets of liberalism. Here they are:

- All peoples, everywhere, want peace.
- Only their wicked leaders—kings, dictators, militarists, and of course arms dealers—want war.
- All peoples everywhere, regardless of their cultural backgrounds, religious beliefs, institutionalized hatreds, and education or lack of it, are really just displaced Vermonters, yearning to go to town meeting, exercise the democratic process, and squabble peacefully (if at all) with their good neighbors.
- All cultures everywhere are of equal value: all they need is for us to *understand* them.
- Given any opportunity, any culture—no matter how retarded, how vicious, or how apparently opposed to everything we ourselves consider good and true and beautiful—will (what a lovely word!) *emerge* into the glorious light of civilization.
- Therefore there are no savage nations, no backward nations, no nations that need more than government by their own leaders and lots of American financial support

90

(plus plenty of Russian arms and a contingent of Cuban janissaries) to achieve equality with the United States, Great Britain, France, Sweden—you name it.

The only trouble with these pretty myths is that they are unadulterated bullshit.

All peoples everywhere do *not* want peace—if by peace we mean peace for all *other* peoples everywhere. Many individual men and women find war exciting; many are sadistic; many are susceptible to the exhortations of the inordinately ambitious, the fanatical, the lunatic. If the great majority *really* and actively wanted peace, there'd be no problem.

All peoples everywhere do *not* have democratic aspirations. Many of them still want to kill their neighbors, rob their neighbors, enslave their neighbors, or even serve their neighbors up for supper.

All cultures are most certainly *not* of equal value—and the more clearly we understand them, the more obvious that becomes. Some imperialists, like the British, did understand this, and usually had the good sense not to give first-rate modern weapons to peoples who had not absorbed the Anglo-Saxon concepts of how men should live with one another, and by what rules. There is absolutely no natural law dictating that cultural *emergence* will follow either prosperity or the acquisition of Western technology and its products. (Take a look at Libya. Take a look at Iran. For that matter, take a nice long look behind the Iron Curtain.)

Therefore all peoples, and all nations, are *not* equal. All cannot be trusted equally, either with the powers inherent in science and technology or with absolute sovereignty. One reason that the UN is an almost total failure is because it is based on the assumption that—except where *size* is concerned—they are.

Now, given all this, how could any world organization have succeeded after 1945?

Very simply, any organization—an army, a private club, a political party, a nation, a Boy Scout troop—must have a common code of behavior for its members. It must have the means to enforce this code, and to discipline (or at least to expel) any who violate it.

Where a world organization is concerned, this means at least some uniformity in each member nation's body of domestic law. Certain human rights *must* be uniformly guaranteed. Certain individual and collective acts *must* be uniformly prohibited. It is, for instance, ridiculous to expect a dictator legally free to preach

91

and launch a holy war to be a reliable member of our world club; and it is just as absurd to expect this reliability from a power group legally free to quell any opinion contrary to their own and to preach and plan the violent overthrow of the governments or economic systems of their fellow members.

Outlawing War

This brings us to the second really effective measure in the prevention of war, one which has actually been put into limited effect, one which is eminently thinkable. It is very simple: no nation forbidden to go to war *by its own laws* has ever done so. The two notable examples are Switzerland and Uruguay; in both, the government is legally forbidden to make war unless the nation is physically attacked—and it is axiomatic that one's own law carries more force than any agreement with a foreign nation or group of nations. Douglas MacArthur, so often damned by liberals as a militarist, saw this clearly and therefore incorporated the provision in the post-war Japanese constitution.

Such a provision should have been, and eventually *will have to be*, the first basic condition for membership in the United Nations —or in whatever world organization follows it.

Let us assume that, in 1944, we had had the good sense to launch our second front up through the Balkans—as Winston Churchill wanted to—instead of into France, thereby isolating Russia from much or all of Eastern Europe. Let us assume, too, that in 1945, instead of letting Russia into the war with Japan—remember, all through the war the Russians were *not* our allies there—we had had the imagination and the courage to move in force against the Japanese armies in Korea and Manchuria, thereby saving North Korea from the easy Russian takeover it suffered. Let us further suppose that, when we formed the UN in San Francisco, we had insisted on limiting membership to nations willing to subscribe to an acceptable code of behavior. No one would have been excluded *except for cause*. No one would have been compelled to join.

The Soviet Union would, almost certainly, have remained on the outside looking in. So might some of the ''emerging'' nations. But had we had the good sense to limit our financial, scientific, and technological support to members of the club—to those who obeyed the rules—we would have ensured a world organization vastly different from what it is today. If the Communists had refused to mend their ways, they would have had to pull themselves up by their own bootstraps—and they would not now be in the position our bootstraps have put them in: able to disturb the world's peace on every continent, pose a serious threat to our once preeminent power position, and even endanger our access to vital strategic minerals and materials. The United Nations then would probably have had, at least temporarily, a smaller membership— but its world would have been a far more open one, an infinitely freer one, and a much more prosperous one.

Which brings up another interesting question: just what would happen even today if we, and perhaps the British and West Germans and French and Scandinavians and all other non-totalitarian nations everywhere (if anyone could get them to agree) were to withdraw from the UN, expel it from United States soil, take over those of its agencies we support already, and form our own private club, functioning according to more civilized rules? And what would happen were we to confine our massive aid to those nations that chose to join us under these rules, sending no more vast grain shipments to the Russians, no more arms except to our declared allies, no more help of *any* nature to our avowed enemies?

I suspect that then our strength and our integrity would bring us more firm friends than our policies have won during the past thirty years, three decades during which we have tried to buy and beg the friendship of still-inferior nations, some of whom hate us, some of whom despise us, and most of whom used to have a healthy fear of us.

As a world, as one people, we finally are confronting space, the great adventure of our time.

We still have *no* idea of what—or whom—we will encounter there. We may need *desperately* to be culturally more coherent than we are, more genuinely united than the UN pretense lets us be, and far more uniformly civilized in the sense of our respect for the rights and liberties of others.

So why don't we at least start thinking about the thinkable?

DAY OF SUCCESSION
Theodore L. Thomas

EDITOR'S INTRODUCTION

If movies are considered to be reflections of popular cultural assumptions, we have a very schizophrenic view of intelligent alien lifeforms. On the one hand, we have the benign observers from outer space—typified in *ET* and the recent *Mac and Me*—while on the other hand, we have the aliens as super-evil monsters as in *Aliens* and *Predator*. Of course there's no way to know which view is correct. There may not *be* any aliens out there.

On the face of it that's unlikely. Years ago Nobel laureate Enrico Fermi made some after-dinner calculations: take the probability that any given star has planets (low), and that any given planet will have life (even lower), and that life came about there millions of years before it happened on Earth (not low at all given that there's life in the first place). Multiply those together and you get a low number. Now multiply by the number of known stars in the galaxy, and you get an enormous number of stars that have had life much longer than it has existed on Earth.

Now consider how far humanity has come in a thousand

years; consider where we will be a thousand years from now; and you get Fermi's famous question, "Where are they?"

We've mostly assumed that wherever they are, they'll be benign in intent. H. G. Wells had a somewhat different view, but we all know *The War Of The Worlds* is an obsolete story.

Under our system of government, military officers take an oath to uphold and defend the Constitution of the United States, and to obey the lawful orders of those in authority. In that order.

———————————'ıı'———————————

GENERAL PAUL T. TREDWAY WAS AN ARROGANT MAN WITH THE unforgivable gift of being always right. When the object came out of the sky in the late spring of 1979, it was General Tredway who made all of the decisions concerning it. Sweeping in over the northern tip of Greenland, coming on a dead line from the Yamal Peninsula, the object alerted every warning unit from the Dew Line to the radar operator at the Philadelphia National Airport. Based on the earliest reports, General Tredway concluded that the object was acting in an anomalous fashion; its altitude was too low too long. Accordingly, acting with a colossal confidence, he called off the manned interceptor units and forbade the launching of interceptor missiles. The object came in low over the Pocono Mountains and crashed in southeastern Pennsylvania two miles due west of Terre Hill.

The object still glowed a dull red, and the fire of the smashed house still smoldered when General Tredway arrived with the troops. He threw a cordon around it, and made a swift investigation. The object: fifty feet long, thirty feet in diameter, football-shaped, metallic, too hot to inspect closely. Visualizing immediately what had to be done, the general set up a Command Headquarters and began ordering the items he needed. With no wasted word or motion he built toward the finished plan as he saw it.

Scientists arrived at the same time as the asbestos clothing needed for them to get close. Tanks and other materiel flowed toward the impact site. Radios and oscillators scanned all frequencies seeking—what? No man there knew what to expect, but no man cared. General Tredway was on the ground personally, and no one had time for anything but his job. The gunners sat with eyes glued to sights, mindful of the firing pattern in which they had been instructed. Handlers poised over their ammunition. Drivers waited with hands on the wheel, motors idling. Behind this ring of steel a more permanent bulwark sprang up. Spotted back further were the technical shacks for housing the scientific equipment. Behind the shacks the reporters gathered, held firmly in check by armed troops. The site itself was a strange mixture of taut men in frozen immobility, and casual men in bustling activity.

In an hour the fact emerged which General Tredway had suspected all along: the object was not of Earthly origin. The alloy of which it was made was a known high-temperature alloy, but no technology on Earth could cast it in seamless form in that size and shape. Mass determinations and ultrasonic probes showed that the object was hollow but was crammed inside with a material different from the shell. It was then that General Tredway completely reorganized his fire power, and mapped out a plan of action that widened the eyes of those who were to carry it out.

On the general's instructions, everything said at the site was said into radio transmitters and thus recorded a safe fifty miles away. And it was the broadcasting of the general's latest plan of action that brought in the first waves of mild protest. But the general went ahead.

The object had lost its dull hot glow when the first indications of activity inside could be heard. General Tredway immediately removed all personnel to positions of safety outside the ring of steel. The ring itself buttoned up; when a circle of men fire toward a common center, someone can get hurt.

With the sound of tearing, protesting metal, a three foot circle appeared at the top of the object, and the circle began to turn. As it turned it began to lift away from the main body of the object, and soon screw threads could be seen. The hatch rose silently, looking like a bung being unscrewed from a barrel. The time came when there was a gentle click, and the hatch dropped back a fraction of an inch; the last thread had become disengaged. There was a pause.

The heavy silence was broken by a throbbing sound from the object that continued for forty-five seconds and then stopped. Then, without further sound, the hatch began to lift back on its northernmost rim.

In casual tones, as if he were speaking in a classroom, General Tredway ordered the northern, northeastern, and northwestern regions of the ring into complete cover. The hatch lifted until finally its underside could be seen; it was colored a dull, nonreflecting black. Higher the hatch lifted, and immediately following it was a bulbous mass that looked like a half-opened rose blossom. Deep within the mass there glowed a soft violet light, clearly apparent to the eye even in the sharp Pennsylvania sunshine.

The machine gun bullets struck the mass first, and the tracers could be seen glancing off. But an instant later the shaped charges in the rockets struck the mass and shattered it. The 105's, the 101 rifles, the rocket launchers, poured a hail of steel onto the canted hatch, ricocheting much of the steel into the interior of the object. Delay-timed high-explosive shells went inside and detonated.

A flame tank left the ring of steel and lumbered forward, followed by two armored trucks. At twenty-five yards a thin stream of fire leaped from the nozzle of the tank and splashed off the hatch in a Niagara of flame. A slight correction, and the Niagara poured down into the opening. The tank moved in close, and the guns fell suddenly silent. Left in the air was a high-pitched shrieking wail, abruptly cut off.

Flames leaped from the opening, so the tank turned off its igniter and simply shot fuel into the object. Asbestos-clad men jumped from the trucks and fed a metal hose through the opening and forced it deep into the object. The compressors started, and a blast of high-pressure air passed through the hose, insuring complete combustion of everything inside. For three minutes the men fed fuel and air to the interior of the object, paying in the metal hose as the end fused off. Flames shot skyward with the roar of a blast furnace. The heat was so great that the men at work were saved only by the constant streams of water that played on them. Then it was over.

General Tredway placed the burned-out cinder in charge of the scientists, and then regrouped his men for resupply and criticism. These were in progress when the report of the second object came in.

The trackers were waiting for it. General Tredway had reasoned that when one object arrived, another might follow, and so he had ordered the trackers to look for it. It hit twenty-five miles west of the first one, near Florin. General Tredway and his men were on their way even before impact. They arrived twenty minutes after it hit.

The preparations were the same, only more streamlined now. The soldiers and the scientists moved more surely, with less wasted motion than before. But as the cooling period progressed, the waves of protest came out of Washington and reached toward General Tredway. "Terrible." "First contact . . ." "Exterminating them like vermin . . ." "Peaceful relationship . . ." ". . . military mind." The protests took on an official character just before the hatch on the second object opened. An actual countermanding of General Tredway's authority came through just as the rockets opened fire on the half-opened rose blossom. The burning-out proceeded on schedule. Before it was complete, General Tredway climbed into a helicopter to fly the hundred miles to Washington, D. C. In half an hour he was there.

It is one of the circumstances of a democracy that in an emergency half a dozen men can speak for the entire country. General Tredway stalked into a White House conference room where waited the President, the Vice President, the Speaker of the House, the President pro tempore of the Senate, the House minority leader, and a cabinet member. No sooner had he entered when the storm broke.

"Sit down, general, and explain to us if you can the meaning of your reprehensible conduct."

"What are you trying to do, make butchers of us all?"

"You didn't give those . . . those persons a chance."

"Here we had a chance to learn something, to learn a lot, and you killed them and destroyed their equipment."

General Tredway sat immoble until the hot flood of words

subsided. Then he said, "Do any of you gentlemen have any evidence that their intentions were peaceable? Any evidence at all?"

There was silence for a moment as they stared at him. The President said; "What evidence have you got they meant harm? You killed them before there was any evidence of anything."

General Tredway shook his head, and a familiar supercilious tone crept unbidden into his voice. "*They* were the ones who landed on *our* planet. It was incumbent on them to find a way to convince us of their friendliness. Instead they landed with no warning at all, and with a complete disregard of human life. The first missile shattered a house, killed a man. There is ample evidence of their hostility," and he could not help adding, "if you care to look for it."

The President flushed and snapped, "That's not the way I see it. You could have kept them covered; you had enough fire power there to cover an army. If they made any hostile move, that would have been time enough for you to have opened up on them."

The House Speaker leaned forward and plunked a sheaf of telegrams on the table. He tapped the pile with a forefinger and said, "These are some of thousands that have come in. I picked out the ones from some of our outstanding citizens—educators, scientists, statesmen. All of them agree that this is a foolhardy thing you have done. You've destroyed a mighty source of knowledge for the human race."

"None of them is a soldier," said the general. "I would not expect them to know anything about attack and defense."

The Speaker nodded and drew one more telegram from an inner pocket. General Tredway, seeing what was coming, had to admire his tactics; this man was not Speaker for nothing. "Here," said the Speaker, "is a reply to my telegram. It is from the Joint Chiefs. Care to read it?"

They all stared at the general, and he shook his head coldly. "No. I take it that they do not understand the problem either."

"Now just a min . . ." A colonel entered the room and whispered softly to the President. The President pushed his chair back, but he did not get up. Nodding he said, "Good. Have Barnes take over. And see that he holds his fire until something happens.

Hear? Make certain of that. I'll not tolerate any more of this unnecessary slaughter." The colonel left.

The President turned and noted the understanding in the faces of the men at the table. He nodded and said, "Yes, another one. And this time we'll do it right. I only hope the other two haven't got word to the third one that we're a bunch of killers."

"There could be no communication of any kind emanating from the first two," said General Tredway. "I watched for that."

"Yes. Well, it's the only thing you did right. I want you to watch to see the proper way to handle this."

In the intervening hours General Tredway tried to persuade the others to adopt his point of view. He succeeded only in infuriating them. When the time came for the third object to open, the group of men were trembling in anger. They gathered around the television screen to watch General Barnes' handling of the situation.

General Tredway stood to the rear of the others, watching the hatch unscrew. General Barnes was using the same formation as that developed by General Tredway; the ring of steel was as tight as ever.

The familiar black at the bottom of the hatch came into view, followed closely by the top of the gleaming rose blossom. General Tredway snapped his fingers, the sound cracking loud in the still room. The men close to the set jumped and looked back at Tredway in annoyance. It was plain that the general had announced in his own way the proper moment to fire. Their eyes had hardly got back to the screen when it happened.

A thin beam of delicate violet light danced from the heart of the rose to the front of the steel ring. The beam rotated like a lighthouse beacon, only far far faster. Whatever it touched it sliced. Through tanks and trucks and guns and men it sliced, over and over again as the swift circular path of the beam spun in ever-widening circles. Explosions rocked the site as high explosives detonated under the touch of the beam. The hatch of the object itself, neatly cut near the bottom, rolled ponderously down the side of the object to the ground. The beam bit into the ground and left seething ribbons of slag. In three seconds the area was a mass of fused metal and molten rock and minced bodies and flame and smoke and thunder. In another two seconds the beam reached the television cameras, and the screen went blank.

The men near the screen stared speechless. At that moment the colonel returned and announced softly that a fourth object was on its way, and that its probable impact point was two miles due east of Harrisburg.

The group turned as one man to General Tredway, but he paid no attention. He was pacing back and forth, pulling at his lower lip, frowning in concentration. "General," said the President. "I . . . I guess you had the right idea. These things are monsters. Will you handle this next one?"

General Tredway stopped and said, "Yes, but I had better explain what is now involved. I want every vehicle that can move to converge on the fourth object; the one that is now loose will attempt to protect it. I want every plane and copter that can fly to launch a continuing attack on it. I want every available missile zeroed in and launched at it immediately. I want every fusion and fission bomb we've got directed at the fourth object by means of artillery, missiles, and planes; one of them might get through. I want a request made to Canada, Brazil, Great Britain, France, Germany, Russia, and Italy to launch fusion-headed missiles at the site of the fourth object immediately. In this way we might have a chance to stop them. Let us proceed."

The President stared at him and said, "Have you gone crazy? I will give no such orders. What you ask for will destroy our middle eastern seaboard."

The general nodded. "Yes, everything from Richmond to Pittsburgh to Syracuse, I think, possibly more. Fallout will cover a wider area. There's no help for it."

"You're insane. I will do no such thing."

The Speaker stepped forward and said, "Mr. President, I think you should reconsider this. You saw what that thing could do; think of two of them loose. I am very much afraid the general may be right."

"Don't be ridiculous."

The Vice President stepped to the President's side and said, "I agree with the President. I never heard of such an absurd suggestion."

The moment froze into silence. The general stared at the three men. Then, moving slowly and deliberately, he undid his holster flap and pulled out his pistol. He snapped the slide back and fired once at point-blank range, shifted the gun, and fired again. He walked over to the table and carefully placed the gun on it. Then he turned to the Speaker and said, "Mr. President, there is very little time. Will you give the necessary orders?"

THE IRVHANK EFFECT
Harry Turtledove

EDITOR'S INTRODUCTION

I have a doctorate in political science, and I've managed several winning (and a few losing) political campaigns. On the evidence I should understand something of American politics.

Clearly I don't understand as well as I think I do.

Take strategic defense, "Space Shield," for example. As Chairman of the Citizen's Advisory Council on National Space Policy I helped draw up some of the documents that convinced President Reagan to make his famous speech challenging the scientific community to make the ICBM "impotent and obsolete." (The phrase, incidentally, was the President's; it wasn't in the drafts he was given.)

The President fully expected overwhelming support for his Space Shield. After all, it ended what Arthur Clarke had called the absurdity of MAD: "two small boys standing in a pool of gasoline while seeing which could collect the most matches." It also conformed to Clarke's Law: "If a grey-bearded eminent scientist tells you something is possible, believe him; if he says it is impossible, he is almost certainly wrong.'' A number of eminent scientists, including not only Edward Teller but many rocket scientists as well as strategic analysts, said that strategic defense certainly was possible; and we knew the Soviets thought it was, because they had been working on one for years.

So. On March 23, 1983, President invited "those who gave us nuclear weapons, to turn their great talents now to the cause of mankind and world peace."

Moreover, the research programs were successful. It doesn't seem to matter.

Despite promising developments in Strategic Defense—the 1986 MIRACL experiment at White Sands Proving Grounds where a laser destroyed a Titan booster on the ground; Homing Overlay in which a missile physically intercepted another in outer space—we have seen increasing opposition from Congress, the media, and even within the Pentagon itself. Even the advocates of Nuclear Freeze—which is quite compatible with SDI—have argued for MAD rather than defenses that defend.

The problem with MAD—Mutual Assured Destruction—is that it's immoral. Free men standing between their loved homes and the war's desolation is compatible with all of Western Judaeo-Christian philosophy; with the Thomistic doctrine of Just War. Deliberately setting fire to the enemy's women and children isn't.

Yet if we don't threaten to burn Russian school girls, we can't honor our pledges.

In 1969 Stefan T. Possony and I published *The Strategy of Technology*, in which we argued for a U.S. strategy of "assured survival" rather than one of assured destruction. At the time we didn't know how it might be accomplished, and we well understood that until the technical means were developed the U.S. would have to depend on deterrent threats. Our point was that assured survival was a permissible goal, one worth achieving; assured destruction is at best an immoral and disheartening goal for those who have to make it work.

* * *

104

So. Acting on the advice of senior scientists and advisors, the President asked: "What if free people could live secure in the knowledge that their security did not rest upon the threat of instant U.S. retaliation to deter a Soviet attack, that we could intercept and destroy strategic ballistic missiles before they reached our soil or that of our allies?"

The response was nearly instantaneous. Congressional leaders giggled "Star Wars." The Union of Concerned Scientists published a disdainful report so full of errors they were obvious to high school students. A well-known professor at MIT said that "the issue was too important for physics." Senator Kennedy dubbed the President "Darth Vader."

In "The Irvhank Effect," Harry Turtledove shows us one reaction to the discovery of a device that can end all possibility of nuclear war. Twenty years ago, I might have questioned his conclusion; now, I'm not so sure . . .

THE NEVADA DESERT LOOKS LIKE A PROVING-GROUND FOR HELL. That is not the reason the government tests its atomic weapons there, but it does give the more thoughtful technicians pause.

As one of the devices—a much more sanitary and less hair-raising word than "bomb"—was making its long journey underground, an engineer in the blockhouse said to the man at his elbow, "Just once, I wish the goddamn thing wouldn't go off."

"Don't we all, Dave, don't we all," his companion said. "However, things being as they are—"

"I know, Felipe," Dave sighed. The device was in place now, a good many thousand feet below the desert. The countdown proceeded smoothly. No reason why it shouldn't; after hundreds of tests over four decades, a routine had long since grown up.

Dave waited for zero. The bomb down there was a peewee, forty kilotons nominal yield, but it could still make the ground rock 'n' roll. Hell, they'd feel it in Vegas, fifty miles southeast down US 95. He was a lot closer than fifty miles, worse luck.

Zero came and went. The desert remained unshaken; the instruments in front of Dave did not go wild. The voice of the principal investigator boomed over the intercom: "Gentlemen, we appear to have a glitch somewhere. We're trying to track it down now. Please stay at your stations."

"Willpower, that's what it is," Dave said, flexing a stringy bicep.

"Bullshit, that's what it is," Felipe snorted, and made as if to hit him with a clipboard. His friend flinched.

US 95 skirts the edge of Nellis Air Force Range and Nuclear Testing Site. The four-wheel-drive Toyota pickup had left the highway about two thirds of the way from Beatty down to Lathrop Wells. No one paid any particular attention to it; there were always a lot of off-road vehicles chewing up the Amargosa Desert.

The pickup stopped well outside the edge of the air force range. MP's did a lot of patrolling on test days. The two men in the truck had a fair amount of electronic junk and a portable generator bolted to the cargo bed. The last thing they wanted was to be taken for a couple of Russian spies.

Irv Farmer got out on the passenger side. He was in his late twenties, slim (well, skinny, actually), sandy-haired, and too pale to be wearing only a T-shirt and shorts in the fierce desert sun. The thin weave of his cap, which proclaimed his allegiance to the Philadelphia Phillies, did not give his balding scalp nearly enough protection.

"Christ, I'm gonna look like a lobster tomorrow," he said. He could not even tell how much he was sweating. The hot, parched air dried the moisture on his skin as fast as it appeared.

Hank Jeter let out a rich, booming laugh. "What do you know? Finally I'm somewhere where being black does me some good." *Los Angeles Raiders*, his cap said. He looked like a defensive lineman; each of his thighs was nearly as big around as Farmer's waist. In spite of his formidable appearance, he was a talented physicist. So, for that matter, was Irv Farmer.

Irv persuaded the generator to flatulent life. The two men worked together to hook their gadgetry to it. Anxiously checking one meter after another, Jeter asked, "What time is that sucker supposed to go off, man?"

"Let me check." Irv ambled back to the cab of the truck, got out a copy of yesterday afternoon's Las Vegas *Sun*. The story he was looking for was on page five. " 'Local residents are advised not to worry if they feel an earthquake tomorrow,' " he read. " 'The NRC is conducting another of a series of low-yield nuclear tests, with detonation scheduled for 10:52 A.M.' "

Jeter pulled out his pocket watch, glanced at it. "We got set up just in time. Only ten minutes to kill. How about a beer?"

"Best idea I've heard all day." There was a cooler in the truckbed, too. Farmer pressed an icy can of Coors to his forehead before he opened it. He drank the Colorado Kool-aid down in four long, blissful gulps, but Hank Jeter still finished ahead of him.

Ten fifty-two passed. So did eleven o'clock, and ten after, quite without an earthquake. The big black man and the little white man solemnly shook hands. "Yes, ladies and gentlemen, boys and girls, I would say we have something here," Jeter said.

"I would say we do." Farmer reached in and turned off the generator. The ground under his Nikes gave a lurch. He had to grab for the tailgate to keep from falling into a cactus. His eyes glowed. "Yes, I'd say we do."

Like a lot of discoveries, this one had been more accident than design. Several things went into it: the fact that, by some accident of engineering, the lab apparatus had a backup and the overhead lighting didn't; the fact that Hank Jeter's great-grandfather had worked as a railroad chief porter during the 1920's; and the fact that Hank was seeing what time it was at the exact moment when a drunk slammed into the power pole out on Rhawn Street.

The lab was in an interior room, with no windows, and the sudden darkness was stygian. People swore in disgust. Somebody tripped over a stool, which fell with a crash. "Where's the flashlight, goddamit?" somebody else said.

Hank didn't need it; not, at least, to look at his watch. That watch had been in his family since his great-grandfather's day. As a matter of fact, it was a conductor's watch, but great-grandpa had bought it all the same, just as soon as he could afford it. He loved it, and why not? It had been keeping good time for more than sixty years now, a big, old-fashioned stemwinder with a long, thick gold chain, perfect for wearing in a vest pocket. It had a radium dial that glowed in the dark.

107

Except it wasn't glowing now. Hank held it so close to his face that it almost bumped his nose, squinted until his eyes crossed. Nothing.

Just then, someone found the flashlight. It was pointed straight at Hank's face when it got turned on. In total blackness, it was like a magnesium flare exploding. Hank yelped and nearly dropped his watch.

"Everybody out to the parking lot," the fellow with the light said. He had a loud, officious voice, and herded his colleagues along like sheep.

Sirens were baying outside, what with the police, paramedics, fire engine, and electrician all descending on the drunk and the pole he'd knocked over. It was also, as Hank discovered when he got into the light, a quarter past four. Plainly, not much more was going to get done today.

The section chief saw that too. He sent a couple of people back into the lab to turn off as much equipment as they safely could, and let everyone else go home early.

There was a scattering of muffled cheers, and some not so muffled. Hank turned to Irv Farmer and said, "How about a drink?"

"Motion seconded and passed by acclamation. Where to?"

Hank looked at him in honest surprise. "The Lair; where else?"

The bar was a couple of miles from the lab. The power was on there, but it was almost as dark inside as it had been when the lights went out at work. Jeter ordered bourbon. Farmer got a bottle of Anchor Porter. He had acquired a taste for the stuff in his undergrad days at Berkeley; the Lair was one of the few bars on the East Coast that stocked it. Thick and dark, dark brown, it was the pumpernickel of beers. He sipped at it; it was too strong-tasting to pour down.

"Another day shot to hell," Hank said, lifting his glass.

"You know it." Irv licked creamy foam off his upper lip. "The surge when the auxiliary generator kicked in cost me half my data, I'll bet."

Jeter put his head in his huge hands. "Oh, God, I forgot all about that. Me too."

One drink became several. After a while, Irv said, "What time has it gotten to be?"

"Why are you asking me? You've got a watch on your wrist," Jeter retorted in mock anger. "Just because I'm black, you make me do all the work."

"Oh, bull. If I didn't ask you to haul out that brass turnip of yours, you'd sulk for a week."

"A likely story." Chuckling, Hank looked at his great-grandfather's watch. "It's twenty to seven." He frowned. "That's funny."

"No it isn't. I just remembered I'm supposed to be in Southbridge at seven, and I'm never gonna make it."

"No. Look at the dial."

"I've seen it a million times, thanks."

"It's glowing," Jeter said.

"Well, I should hope so. It's a wonder you don't futz up half the experiments in the lab with the radioactivity in that damn thing."

"You have no respect for an heirloom, my man. The point is, though, when the electricity went out this afternoon, I was looking right at it and there was nothing to see, just black."

"Probably you were looking at the back side and didn't realize it in the dark," Irv suggested.

"Hey, no, man, I'm serious," Jeter said. "I had it out before the power blew. I can't remember the last time I looked at it in the dark; I just figured the radium paint had worn out or something. Now I don't know what to think."

Irv Farmer stared owlishly at his friend. He had drunk just enough to take him seriously; a little more and he wouldn't have cared one way or the other, a little less and he would have rationalized everything away. Instead, he said, "All right, I give up. What happened?"

Hank shrugged. "Just one of those things, I guess." Being almost twice Farmer's size, he hadn't been hit as hard by his shots of Hiram Walker's. As long as everything seemed back to normal, he was happy enough—relieved might be a better word.

Irv finished his porter. "Let's go back and see if we can duplicate it," he said suddenly.

It was Jeter's turn to gape. "Probably nothing there to duplicate."

"Then what have we lost? A little time."

"What about Southbridge?"

"Oh, the hell with Southbridge. She's starting to think she owns me. Come on; are you game?"

"That's what they asked the hunter in the old joke, and when he said yes they shot him. But I'll come along; I've got nothin' else shakin' tonight."

As they drove up, they saw the lights were back on. "Can't keep you fellers away from it, can they?" cackled the security guard. The old codger didn't bother looking at their security badges; he'd been seeing them come and go for years.

"This isn't going to work," Hank said when they got to the laboratory. "How can we tell what was on and what was off when the power pole got hit?"

Alcoholic confidence still buoyed Irv Farmer. He went from bench to bench and desk to desk, checking diaries. Once he picked a lock with a paper clip, something he never would—or could—have done cold sober. He made a second circuit round the lab, turning on instruments and setting them to the same configuration they had had during the afternoon.

At last he turned to Jeter. "All right, where were you?"

"Right about here," Hank said, taking his spot. "Look, man, let's just pack it in, shall we? This is all more hassle than it's worth."

Irv wasn't listening to him. "Get out your watch," he said, and turned off the lights. Hank didn't say anything, so after a minute or so Farmer called, "Well, what do you see?"

"Come look for yourself."

Irv did, moving carefully in the dark. Hank held the watch out to him. The hands and the small painted spots that marked the hours were dark. "Well, I will be damned," Irv said. His friend was whistling tunelessly between his teeth.

"Where are you going?" Hank asked.

"To turn the lights back on. I've got an idea." Farmer rummaged around until he found a Geiger counter. He held the Geiger tube up to the watch. The lazy clicking of background radiation, present everywhere, did not change. Irv and Hank looked at each other.

Irv started turning off pieces of lab equipment. The Geiger counter immediately began to chatter.

110

"Do you know what we've got here if we can find out what makes this tick?" Farmer said softly, oblivious to any thought of wordplay. "We've got a Nobel prize right in our laps, that's what."

Hank Jeter regarded him most soberly. "It may not be anything nearly as trivial as that," he said.

After they'd found the effect, they had to figure out how it worked and what to do with it. By unspoken common consent, neither of them mentioned it to the people they worked with, and they made sure they didn't leave any notes lying around the lab. They did put in a lot of overtime they didn't get paid for, often in the wee small hours.

For one thing, they had no idea *why* the resultant of all the forces in the gadgetry in the lab on that particular day produced a field that damped radioactivity. That bothered Hank. He wanted to know.

Irv was not as fussy. "Look," he said at the Lair one evening, "right now I don't much care about why. All I want to know is how I can use it. People were making gunpowder hundreds of years before they knew thing one about oxidation or any of that." His argument carried the day.

Lack of understanding, though, was not the chief reason they kept things to themselves. The more they played with what they had begun to call the Irvhank Effect, the more they realized just how big a thing they had stumbled across. That first field of theirs was a very strong, very tight one: it damped all radioactivity above background level, but it only had an effective radius of about ten meters.

"We could clean up Three Mile Island with this," Irv said. Hank only grunted. He had bigger things in mind.

Their early tries at altering the field only succeeded in eliminating it altogether. It was Irv's turn to think more progress impossible, Hank Jeter's to keep pushing. After a good deal of frustration, they finally found the components of the system they had to modify to change the strength of the Irvhank Effect. They also found that each weakening of the field increased the range over which its effect spread.

It took many months of work before they got the kind of field Hank had conceived of the moment he heard that quiet Geiger

111

counter: one weak enough to allow the barest chain reaction, the level found in an atomic pile, but strong enough to prevent the catastrophic fission of nuclear weapons.

That was the one that sent the two of them into the Nevada desert, to see if their circuits did what they were supposed to. Actually, the trip was conservative; if their haywire calculations were right, at that level the field should cover most of the United States. When they found out that the device worked, they hooked it up to wall current and let it run night and day.

"Let the Russians roar," Hank declared. "Those sons of bitches aren't going to blow us all away now, no matter how much they want to. Do you know what we've done, Irv? We've declared peace against the whole world, and we've won."

As things worked out, the Russians weren't doing much roaring of late. They were grumbling, mostly among themselves. It was Irv who noticed the name of a prominent Soviet general in the "Milestones" column of *Time*.

" 'Retired,' " he read. " 'Marshal Pavel Serafimov, 62. Western intelligence sources believe that Serafimov, a leading expert in nuclear weaponry, was forced into early retirement because of the unexpected difficulties the Red Army is having with the warhead of the new SS-26 ICBM.' "

Hank's smile was blissful. "We aren't just covering the USA, then. I sort of suspected you were too cautious with your numbers, Irv. If the Russians' bombs won't go off even at home, we've got the whole planet blanketed. Now we don't have to worry about a nut in the White House or the Department of Defense, either. To say nothing of the Israelis, the South Africans, the Pakistanis, the Argentines—how long do you want me to go on?"

"No need, no need," Irv said. "I think it's about time we looked into publishing."

You have to understand that I've pieced all this together. Obviously, I wasn't there when the two of them discovered the Irvhank Effect. There are still lots of things I don't know about it. And, as I've said, they were careful about covering up what they were doing, for amateurs anyway.

I tell you frankly: a lot of people were tearing their hair, trying to figure out why none of the bomb tests would work. After the first

112

couple of failures, we were also going out of our minds trying to keep the Russians—to say nothing of Congress—from learning things were on the fritz.

Of course, it turned out the Russians had troubles of their own, but we didn't know that then. You can imagine how relieved we were when we found out. At least they weren't responsible for screwing us up.

But who was?

It took a lot of time—people time and computer time—before a possible answer emerged. Again, I don't have the details, just what I got in my briefing. Apparently, somebody was smart enough, or desperate enough, to ask for a computer search of any and all anomalies having anything to do with radiation, and then to stick pins in a map to see if there was a pattern. Sure enough, there was.

Some of the items had made the newspapers, others hadn't. The day when all the nuclear plants east of the Mississippi hiccuped for six seconds was one of the latter. With everyone loving nuclear power so much these days, most of the plant directors had covered up as best they could, especially since they didn't know what had gone wrong either. But those people are amateurs too.

Other things were less spectacular—high-energy physics experiments gone awry, disappointingly ineffective cancer treatments, and so on. Those were also more localized. They gave us an idea of where the center of the problem-circle was. We were able to start putting together a list of names.

Two people on the list, it turned out, had been vacationing in Las Vegas on the morning when a bomb test was inexplicably late. That was enough to be worth looking into, anyhow, and that was when I got my orders.

As it happened, I went to Irv Farmer's condo first, while he was at work. Jackpot the first time, too; I found the half-written paper on the Irvhank Effect in the typewriter, with all the notes beside it. I skimmed through them. The machine itself, I learned, was at Hank Jeter's apartment, under the bed.

Amateurs.

I took all the documents and stuffed them into the repairman's bag I carried in case anyone got curious about what I was doing wandering the halls. Then I went out and goofed around for several hours. I knew just what Irv Farmer would do when he got home and

113

found his place burgled—he'd rush over and tell Hank. That was fine. I needed to talk with both of them.

My timing was right. I heard two voices when I paused to listen outside the door. I went on in. Apartment-house locks aren't made to keep out the likes of me.

"Don't do anything stupid," I advised the two of them as I shut the door behind me. I was mostly talking to Jeter; nobody'd told me what a mountain of beef he was. "This in my hands is a silenced UZI machine-pistol with a forty-round box. A burst will make a noise like Donald Duck sneezing and leave you both hamburger."

I had to give Irv Farmer credit. He went white as a sheet, but his voice came out steady: "I thought you weren't supposed to fire bursts through a silencer."

"For emergency use only," I agreed, "but your friend there on the sofa is big enough to qualify."

"If you want money, my cash is in the silverware drawer in the kitchen," Jeter said. He didn't sound as though he believed it himself; even in the US of A, robbers don't pack UZI's with silencers. When I just stood there, he sagged a little. "Who are you with?"

"It doesn't matter," I said. "Believe it or not, at the moment all I intend to do is have a chat."

Hank was still a bit stunned; Irv was quicker on the uptake. "If you're the one who was at my place"—he paused, and I nodded—"then I think we know what you want to, ah, chat about."

I nodded again. "No doubt. Tell me, can your gadget, say, protect the United States from nuclear attack but leave the Soviet Union open?"

"No way," Farmer said. "The whole planet gets protected at that setting. It's in the nature of the field."

I would have believed him even if glancing over his notes hadn't led me to the same conclusion; you could read his sincerity in his face. "So what exactly is it you're accomplishing, then?"

That roused Hank Jeter. "Putting an end to the possibility of nuclear war," he growled. The look he sent my way said that even somebody like me should be able to figure that one out for himself.

I shrugged. "And so?"

114

"What do you mean, 'And so?' " he said. "And so peace, of course."

"We're at peace now," I reminded him. "We have been since 1945, more or less."

"A peace based on terror," he said scornfully. "That kind of peace never lasts, and the kind of war we can fight with today's weapons is too terrible to imagine."

"There I agree with you," I said, and saw I'd surprised him. I went on, "But what makes you think that turning off all the nuclear weapons is going to do anything to promote peace?"

He looked at me as if he thought I was crazy. He probably did. "We won't be able to blow ourselves away, that's what."

"With all the germs and gases stockpiled, I wouldn't even bet on that," I said. "Let it go, though. Just tell me this. Suppose you're the President of the Soviet Union. And suddenly your missiles and the Americans' missiles are only so many big Roman candles. You take a look toward western Europe. You've got about a 3-1 edge in tanks, 2-1 in planes, maybe 3-2 in ground troops. Nothing much is going to happen to your country if you move. So what do you do?"

"Nothing much is going to happen?" Irv echoed. "You're still going to get the hell bombed out of you, and invaded if you start losing."

"By Russian standards, that's nothing much," I said. "And the last people who made a go of invading Russia were the Mongols. Hardly anybody on this side of the Atlantic remembers that the Russians did the dirty work in World War II after the Germans jumped 'em. They took eleven, maybe thirteen million armed forces deaths, plus another seven million or so civilians who happened to be in the wrong place at the wrong time."

Irv and Hank were both staring at me now. They grew up with Vietnam: fifty-odd thousand dead, spread over a dozen years. They were too young to remember how easy it was to fight a really *big* conventional war.

I said so, adding, "Why do you think we haven't fought the third World War yet? It could have started any time: over Korea, or Hungary in '56, or the Berlin Wall, or Czechoslovakia in 1968, or Poland in '81, or Vietnam, or the Middle East half a dozen different times. For that matter, why doesn't China try to take most of

Siberia back from the Russians? Their maps claim it, you know."
They plainly didn't.

I said, "Aside from anything else, there's another reason to keep away from World War III—we'd probably lose. The Russians outweigh us by too much in conventional weapons, and the geography favors them."

"China," Farmer said. He'd been paying attention, some.

"Maybe, just maybe," I admitted. "But that's a deal with the devil, too, the same as the one we had with Stalin to beat Hitler. We'd probably just be setting up the next round."

"You have one sick view of human nature, man," Hank Jeter said.

I shrugged. "I suppose so, but I'm afraid I've got an awful lot of history to back it up. Seems to me the only thing that's kept such peace as we've got is the terror you were sneering at. What else is strong enough? And what's going to happen when people find out there's nothing to be afraid of any more?"

If I sound like I was pleading with them, I was. I'd never gotten a set of orders I liked less, and I was looking for some excuse to break them. But try as I might, I couldn't find one. Maybe Irv and Hank could. After all, they were bright enough to have created this flap in the first place.

No luck, dammit. They hadn't thought out the consequences any further than keeping the bombs from falling, and that wasn't far enough. Any minute now, somebody was likely to realize that things weren't going bang because they couldn't go bang. Then it would be time to hold onto your hat, assuming you still had a head to wear it on.

Donald Duck sneezed. I still had half a clip left when I went into the bedroom. I unplugged the cord that snaked under the bed. The world didn't feel a bit different, of course, but it should have. I used the cord to haul out the gear that generated the Irvhank Effect, and I put the rest of the clip into it. Pieces flew every which way.

I had to move fast after that. The more you fire a silenced weapon, the less effective the silencer gets—Irv had been right about that. Hank's notes, thank God, were easy to find. I tossed them onto the floor, set Irv's beside them. Then I poured gasoline over them, tossed a match, and ran like hell.

I'm glad they managed to hold the fire to three floors of the building. It gave the papers a week's worth of stories, but none of them had anything to do with me, so that was all right, too.

Everyone at work was relieved when I reported success, and when the obvious experiment confirmed it. We've been dealing with the mess we know for a long time now; I expect we'll muddle on a while longer. The Irvhank Effect—I hope!—was one of those freak discoveries that won't be stumbled on again for hundreds of years. By then, we may know how to handle it.

For that matter, nobody asked me a whole lot of questions about how the Effect worked. It's as if we're all trying to pretend the whole thing never happened. That's good enough for me. I'm the only one who knows so much as its name now and I don't know much more than that. I shouldn't even be writing this much down.

More later. Somebody's at the d. . . .

THREE POEMS
J. E. Oestreicher, Lenora Lee Good, and Peter Dillingham

EDITOR'S INTRODUCTION

A recent issue of *Commentary* laments the fate of the modern American poet. There are plenty of programs and grants; poets acceptable to the world of academia need not starve. There are also plenty of "little" magazines for them to publish in. The modern poet lacks only one thing: people who will pay any attention to him.

It was not always thus.

Back in the times when Celtic kings reigned, a poet, or bard, was a man of great honor—even power. Bards were the advisors to princes, the interpreters of the divine, and the link between man and his gods. Sometimes they were even credited with the power to see into the future. Usually their prophecies were seen more as warnings than actual predictions.

Herewith works of three poets who should not be ignored.

WAR CIRCULAR
J. E. Oestreicher

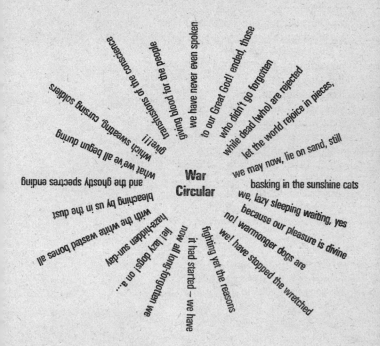

.
.
.

we, lazy sleeping waiting, yes
because our pleasure is divine
no! warmonger dogs are
we! have stopped the wretched
fighting yet the reasons
it had started—we have
now all long-forgotten and we
lie! lazy dogs! on a . . .
haze-hidden sun-day
with the white wasted bones all
bleaching by us in the dust
and the ghostly spectres ending
what we've all begun during
which sweating, cursing soldiers
give!!!
transfusions of the conscience
giving blood for the people
we have never even spoken
to our Great God! ended, those
who didn't go forgotten
while dead (who) are rejected
let the world rejoice in pieces,
we may now, lie on sand, still
basking in the sunshine cats
.
.
.

we, lazy sleeping waiting, yes

THE TRANQUIL SOUND
Lenora Lee Good

The basin lay
As though carelessly tossed
Catching sun light
In its glass interior,
Light dancing from
Blister-bumps
To age-vein cracks;
Filled with waters that sough
With the tides
And serenade the moon.

Breezes dance
Tiny paths in the dust
Seen only by the circling Roc,
Who cries to the emptiness below.

The basin lay
As it had for years
Lost to all but the Roc
        And the lonely soldier,
        Sentinel on the edge of glass
        Whose glowing skeleton
        Still clutches rust
        That once was weapon;
        Faithfully watching
        With eyeless sockets
        The once-upon-a-time
        Tree filled hunting grounds
        Of old Chief Sealth.

        Foolish lad. Dead.
        Defending a people who wanted
        No defense.

        The circling Roc cries
           P E E E A A A A C E !
             P E E E A A A A C E !
               P E E E A A A A C E !
             June 1987

PSI-REC: I LINGER
Peter Dillingham

Willing prey of time
                    I linger
Wandering these crumbling
Weed-choked roads
Verging labyrinth
Rune
To mute, abandoned ruin
Over dune
Wild plain and tor.

Wrapped round in tattered weeds
The imperial plumage
Of countless centuries
A kaleidial patchwork
Of fugitive memory

                    I linger
Pallbearer.

Archetype
This towering arcology
A haunted honeycomb

Alien hexagonal prism
After alien hexagonal prison
Still resonant

With the ecstacy of madmen
in metamorphosis to gods.
Parasite of moulted flesh
and bone

> I linger.

THE BENEFACTORS
Don Hawthorne

EDITOR'S INTRODUCTION

When I was an editor of *Survive* magazine, I always said that
the best way to survive a nuclear war is not to have one. I
believe that still. I also believe we have a good chance of
avoiding Armageddon, which is a major reason why I gave
up my *Survive* column. I've nothing but respect for
survivalists—real ones, not the nuts who run around in
military uniform pretending they're going to conduct a point
defense against the government—but I think I can do more
good as Chairman of the Citizens' Advisory Council on
National Space Policy than in helping people prepare for life
after Doomsday.

So long as the West remains strong the situation looks
pretty good. The world daily becomes a more integrated
place; thanks to air travel, food dependency, communications, and the exchange of that most crucial commodity of
all, information, East and West are stitched together, and it's
better for each that the other exists.

Still, due to that growing integration, things are more
complex. One of the world's major players could bring

about the collapse of the entire structure by mistake. It is a sobering thought. Particularly if that collapse were to come about through mismanagement by the ruling faction, leading to the disaffection of the people and a final, ill-considered course of action to retain their loyalty to the government. The Falklands War came about much in that fashion. Rather than wait a year or two to settle the issue legally with Great Britain, the military government of Argentina pushed ahead on a course of action that resulted in disaster. Of course *that* government was headed there anyway. Still, they should have remembered Alexander's words about Sparta, when asked why he had not conquered the once great military city-state. "Sparta's an old dog, but she's still got her teeth."

So, it seems, does Great Britain.

Alas, with the surge of post-holocaust theorists in America it is fashionable to assume that the nation to fall the hardest will be the United States — perhaps because we have risen so high. Or possibly because we have a great deal more to lose by skirting too close to the Abyss. Yet those nations with less than ourselves may have even more to lose because they already have so little.

Robert G. Kaiser's *Russia: The People and the Power* relates a Russian folk story about a circus tiger named Alma, as told by a young emigre.

"(She) was very intelligent, very well trained. But every time her trainer turned his back to her she wanted to eat him. So the trainer's wife stood outside the cage, and whenever the trainer did turn his back, his wife would say, 'All right, Alma, quiet, Alma,' and the tiger knew she was being watched, so she didn't jump. But the trainer wanted to find a better solution to the problem. For a long time he thought about how to convince the tiger that she didn't want to eat him.

"He thought of a brilliant idea. He realized that Alma was very comfortable sitting on her round platform in the cage. So he gave her a new platform that was much smaller — so small that she could only put three feet on it at one time. There wasn't room for all four paws, so she had to concentrate on keeping her balance. All her thoughts were directed toward staying on the platform. She no longer had time to think about eating the trainer.

"It seems to me that Soviet man is exactly the same. Like the tiger, he has to balance himself on a small platform. He's always standing in line, always trying to buy something, always worrying about idiotic little problems. He has no time to worry about the big things—about freedom, or happiness, or changing the government. The government doesn't give you a chance to think—there's no time to think. If you get a chance to do a little thinking, you have to realize that life isn't too good.

"But nobody has time to think about eating the trainer."

With the current mood of reform sweeping the Soviet Union, that story may have new relevance. What happens if you give the tiger a larger platform?

———————————'┃'———————————

> *All Power, each Tyrant, every Mob*
> *Whose head has grown too large,*
> *Ends by destroying its own job*
> *And works its own discharge;*
>
> *And Man, whose mere necessities*
> *Move all things from his path,*
> *Trembles meanwhile at their decrees,*
> *And deprecates their wrath!*
>
> —Rudyard Kipling
> *The Benefactors*

Sergeant Nikita Sokoloff, KGB, watched in despair as the last train left the ruins of Moscow without him. Sokoloff chased the receding cars, dodging shots from the Red Army Engineer bandits who'd stolen the train, and frequently leaping over the bodies of his fellow KGB troopers who had tried in vain to oppose the theft.

When Sokoloff came upon two figures struggling in the cinders and gravel at the side of the railbed, he raised his assault rifle, recognizing one of them almost too late.

"Colonel Serafimov!" Sokoloff lowered his weapon and ran to

help his commander. Colonel Maksim Serafimov had pulled himself free from the grip of the man beneath him and was throttling his opponent in fury. Now Sokoloff could see that the figure in Serafimov's grasp was Colonel Podgorny, commander of the Army Combat Engineers who had stolen the train.

Both men were so bloody that Sokoloff could not tell who was the more badly wounded, until he noticed that the bearlike Podgorny wasn't moving at all.

Sokoloff tried to pull his commanding officer away from the dead man, but Serafimov paused only long enough to send the young Sergeant reeling with a backhand blow. By the time Sokoloff had regained his feet, Serafimov had dragged Podgorny's body up to the track and was dashing the dead man's head against the rails.

Serafimov made wheezing sounds of rage, cursing the man who was now wholly beyond his wrath. The Colonel's motions grew weaker; Serafimov seemed to have trouble breathing, and now Sokoloff could see that in addition to a bloody head wound, the KGB Colonel's throat was badly bruised from some harsh blow.

Sokoloff pulled his Colonel away from the corpse again, just as several more troops arrived. Those who glanced at the remains of the Army Engineer quickly looked away.

"What's wrong with Colonel Serafimov?" one asked.

The KGB officer was gasping like a fish out of water.

"I think he's choking," Sokoloff began. "His throat—"

Serafimov threw off the hands supporting him and stabbed a finger at the train, still in sight. "Catch . . . back . . ." The pain in his throat kept him from getting anything else out.

"We can't catch them, sir, they're too far ahead."

Serafimov grabbed the front of Sokoloff's tunic and pulled the young Sergeant's face to within an inch of his own. "Kill . . ." he gasped. "All . . . us . . . catch!"

They turned at the sound of an explosion from the train; the thieves had apparently blown the linkage of the last few cars, for these had separated from the rest of the train, and were coasting to a stop as the rest continued to accelerate away from Moscow.

The train in Serafimov's vision swam beneath tears of frustration. *This will be the death of me. Me, and all my men . . .*

He had already lost one train to raiders. He'd set up an ambush and killed all the bandits; but how could he know that Combat Engineers would dare this? True, he'd thought them suspicious, but such treachery as this was unthinkable, even from the Army! And what would his superiors in *Novaya Moskva* say when he informed them of this disaster?

Serafimov swore by Lenin's beard that those Army bastards would pay for this folly. Beside himself with rage, he couldn't even scream to release his anger. He could barely breathe, and every attempt at speech was an agony.

The KGB Colonel put a hand to his throat, wounded in his fight with that American—he had no doubt that his English-speaking assailant *was* an American—before that fool Podgorny had pulled them both through the window of the command car.

Of course the Americans would be involved. It's another damned defection, that's what; nothing less. By the end of the Global War of Liberation, Soviet losses through defections had been higher than combat casualties. When the Last Retreat began, the entire Third Army had tried to defect from the Group of Soviet Forces, Germany. Serafimov could at least take comfort in how *that* had worked out. But he doubted that *Novaya Moskva* would waste precious nuclear weapons on one train full of renegade Army Engineers. They would likely just shoot the KGB fool who had not treated the Army bastards with the caution everyone knew they required.

The rest of Serafimov's men gathered around him. Most of his troops had not been aboard the train when the battle began. The last man to arrive was a breathless lieutenant who didn't even bother to salute as he made his report.

"Colonel Serafimov, a company of light tanks with armored personnel carriers has just arrived. Their commander says they were sent to safeguard the train."

Serafimov seized the lieutenant; perhaps there was yet hope. The train was fading from sight in the beginnings of a light snowfall, but the new KGB scout tanks were fast, steam-powered, and not restricted to rails. "Where . . ." Serafimov gasped. "Take . . . me . . . commander."

With Sokoloff and the lieutenant's help, Serafimov staggered back through the train yard. They had covered only a dozen meters when the first tank hove into view with the rumbling crackle of treads on concrete and gravel.

Serafimov looked up at the commander, standing in the open hatch of the lead vehicle. Barrel-chested and big for a tanker, with pale blond hair under a black beret, fish-white skin, and eyes like old ice. The man raised his hand as his own vehicle halted, and the remainder of his force stopped as one.

The tank commander leaned forward over the rim of the turret hatch. The machine beneath him vibrated and hissed, but the man himself was motionless, fixing Serafimov with his gaze for a long moment before he spoke.

"You are Maksim Fyodorov Serafimov; Colonel, KGB?"

Serafimov tried to respond, but could only manage a painful wheeze and a nod. He began making urgent gestures, trying to get this fool to pursue the train before it was too late.

The tanker's expression did not change. "I am Major Werner Steinmann, PRG One, out of *Novaya Moskva*." Steinmann's eyes glittered as he added in a dangerous voice: "Where is your train, Comrade Colonel?"

Serafimov nearly gagged in fury. His gestures became almost comical as he pointed down the track. Finally Steinmann held up his hand.

"*Sprechen verboten!*" He began rattling off commands to his driver. Serafimov was stunned to realize that those commands, like the order for silence, were in German. Only then did he notice that Steinmann's uniform was not Russian, but East German.

Steinmann turned back to Serafimov. "And what, Comrade Colonel, is *that?*" Steinmann leveled his arm, pointing back down the track in the direction from which Serafimov had come. The KGB Colonel turned to see Podgorny's body still spread-eagle across the rails.

Without waiting for an answer, Steinmann signaled his driver to move up. The machine with its black-clad commander leapt forward with the eerie grace of some bizarre metal centaur.

The tank had not fully stopped before Steinmann climbed out of the turret and jumped down to the railbed. He turned Podgorny's body over, then walked back to Serafimov and his men, inspecting the KGB Colonel once more.

By now, the East German infantry had dismounted from their APCs, and Serafimov was beginning to feel uncomfortably outnumbered. Steinmann considered him a moment, then signaled to one of his men.

"*Leutnant*, place Colonel Serafimov under arrest."

Serafimov hid his own astonishment, but Sergeant Sokoloff was younger and far less prudent.

"*Nyet!*" Sokoloff threw the bolt on his assault rifle. His contempt for Steinmann's order was undiluted by the East German's superior rank.

A burst of machine-gun fire from behind riddled the young Sergeant, spraying Serafimov with blood. Sokoloff fell dead at his Colonel's feet.

Steinmann's expression had not altered. Serafimov, hardened though he was to sudden death, was unprepared for it when he was not its author. He tried again to explain what had happened to the train, but the big East German held up a hand to silence him.

"You are under suspicion for conspiracy to steal State property. You will remain in custody pending my communication with *Novaya Moskva*. Any of your men who resist will be shot." Steinmann's Lieutenant stepped up, roughly pulling one of Serafimov's arms behind his back. Steinmann dismissed them with a wave of his hand.

Dazed, Serafimov was led from the scene of his failure. He looked back once at young Sokoloff's corpse. Steinmann pushed it off the railbed with his foot, and it tumbled down the embankment into a wet ditch.

Serafimov put the youthful Sergeant, who had never even seen a steam engine before this morning, out of his thoughts. Sokoloff's troubles were over.

His own, he knew, were just beginning.

South of Moscow and east of the Pripyat Marshes, the flatlands of Russia are not so much plains as vast oceans of grass and wild wheat. Scores of warlords had passed over this land in every direction: Huns, Avars, Mongols; Napoleon's Grande Armée and Hitler's *panzers*. But the only conqueror who ever truly held it in thrall was General Winter.

The first snow of the new winter had stopped falling only a few hours after starting, and it seemed as if this year, even that venerable warrior had not come in full force quite yet.

Senior Sergeant Mikhail Zorin stood on the roof of a boxcar and watched the snow melting in the thin sunlight. In the hours since the train he rode had left Moscow, the morning's chill of a late summer snowfall had given way to a relatively warm day, for a Russian autumn.

The kind of day, Zorin reflected, *for making fools expect this winter to be milder than the last*. Zorin had seen enough winters to know better.

He finished his cigarette and flicked the paper-tube filter stub away. The *papirosi* burst in a tiny shower of sparks as it hit the ties, and was soon lost in the distance.

Zorin watched the rear for signs of pursuit, but occasionally, when the train passed through the ruins of towns or remnants of battles scattered alongside the tracks, his gaze would wander.

There wasn't much to see. Details were still covered by the light snowfall, and that was mostly all right with Zorin. He turned to look toward the front of the train where the huge P-38 locomotive labored to pull its burden west.

Lieutenant Rostov had ordered the trainmen to make speed in silence, but Zorin couldn't help wishing for a blast or two from the whistle. It occurred to him that one of the reasons steam whistles might first have been invented was to relieve the sense of isolation that came to solitary trains on the steppes.

Christus, Zorin thought, *but it's too true that* something *is needed out here*.

Zorin's own isolation was shortly relieved by the arrival of Lieutenant Rostov himself, climbing up the ladder of the boxcar and joining the Sergeant on the roof.

While Zorin was of average height and powerfully built, the young officer with the tired smile was taller and not quite so broad. He was unremarkable physically, except for a face that at first sight looked too young for his rank; even boyish. Rostov had fair hair, light eyes, and more of an open, easy manner than might be expected from a young man after six years of war. Several days' growth of beard did little to dispel the look of youth; like all soldiers it was his eyes that betrayed him. They had seen too much, too quickly for wisdom to catch up. They were very Russian eyes, indeed.

"See anything, *Starshi Serzhant*?"

Zorin shook his head and searched for another *papirosi* in his tunic pockets. "*Nyet, Leytenant*. Some smoke to the southeast a few kilometers back." Zorin paused while Rostov lit his cigarette for him. "But it was black and didn't change position. A small fire is my guess; perhaps a camp. If they're following us, it's not along the rails."

"I don't know what worries me more," Rostov said. "The KGB behind us or some Ukrainian Nationalist Brigade ahead." His eyes went from the horizon to the tracks flowing smoothly back and away from beneath them. Rostov had just come from several hours at the front of the train, and it was a relief to have the wind at his back for a change.

Finally, without taking his eyes off the tracks, he spoke: "Do you think we can do it, Mikhail? A bunch of renegade combat engineers with an American officer in tow, on a train stolen right out from under the noses of the Moscow KGB; has there ever been a more unlikely group of defectors?"

Zorin shrugged. "When I was a boy, I read an old *samizdat* article about a Soviet ship—an icebreaker, I think—that tried to defect to Sweden. Men, officers, whole damn crew; in fact the defection was supposedly instigated by the ship's political officer." Zorin grunted, frowned; as if he doubted the story himself.

"Well? Did they make it?"

"Hm? Oh, no. KGB border patrol aircraft caught up with them an hour away from Swedish territorial waters and forced them to turn back to Kaliningrad."

"Where they were all shot, of course."

Zorin looked offended. "No, sir, by no means. The men went to Gulags. Only the officers were shot."

Lieutenant Rostov grinned. "That *is* a relief."

"Still," Zorin added, "if they'd had another hour or two, they might have made it. Their biggest advantage was that at first, nobody who had spotted them could believe they were actually trying to defect." Zorin cocked an eyebrow at his Lieutenant. "After all, Aleksei, what kind of fools would try to steal a whole *ship*?"

Rostov, whose idea it had been to steal a train for their own escape, favored his senior NCO with a rueful smile. "What kind of fools, indeed? But I'm afraid that sort of ignorance isn't anything we can hope for. At least we don't have to worry about aircraft these days." Rostov folded his arms.

Zorin noticed the foreign gesture and was reminded of their American "guest," and the part he'd played in their escape. "How is Captain Wrenn, Aleksei?"

"Better. Comrade Surgeon Blaustein cleaned and dressed his wound and gave him some painkillers. He says if infection doesn't get him, he should regain most of the use of the hand."

Zorin nodded. "That's good. I like that fellow. Any man who's willing to give up a hand to buy time for his comrades is fine by me."

Rostov thought it odd that his Sergeant was referring to an American as a "comrade." Still, their lives had surely been saved by Wrenn's drastic action. If that bastard Serafimov had reached the brake cable and stopped them in the middle of the train yards, with all his KGB troops about . . . well, Rostov knew he wouldn't be here wondering about it now.

Rostov took a heavily laminated photograph from inside his tunic. It showed a handsome young couple on their honeymoon, standing in front of the gilded statues of the Grand Cascades at Petrodvorets. The young blond man was holding his dark-eyed beauty of a bride, both smiling at the forgotten fellow tourist who'd offered to take the photo.

Lilia wore the sweater he had bought for her on that trip, her long black hair in her face and trailing across his as well. The two of them were smiling in the spray from the fountains and the sunny Leningrad afternoon. Rostov wondered if anything was left of those fountains, or indeed of Leningrad. More and more, when he looked at this picture, he thought he and Lilia looked strange in the civilian clothes. He sometimes felt he had been born in his uniform.

Rostov returned the photo to his pocket and stretched, his back popping, tired muscles protesting. He had slept little in two days, and the bracing air had not stirred him as awake as he might have liked. When he stopped yawning, Zorin tapped his arm.

"Your radio, Aleksei."

Rostov scowled as he fumbled with the walkie-talkie clipped to his belt as it beeped again. Some things appropriated from the stores found on this train were less welcome than others. "Rostov here."

"Corporal Dyatlov, sir. Comrade Trainman Gyrich has found a problem he says you should know about."

"I'll be right there, Corporal. Come back and take over the rear lookout. Sergeant Zorin will be coming with me."

Dyatlov acknowledged and signed off.

What now, I wonder? Rostov thought. Neither he nor Zorin had spoken much about the death of their commander, Colonel Podgorny; with his loss the full burden of command had fallen directly on Rostov. Zorin had assured the young Lieutenant that he was up to the job, especially since they would be in the West soon, anyway.

Rostov wasn't so sure of either point.

Of all his worries, prime was the question of pursuit. Where was it? He didn't doubt for a moment that they were being pursued. *God save us, we've stolen a train from the KGB!* Things had not fallen apart so much that the Committee for State Security would suffer such an insult as that.

But with luck, it would be a race. And if Rostov didn't want to have himself and all his men strangled with piano wire, it was a race they would have to win. And that meant giving first consideration to any problems found by the conscript trainmen they had rescued, who kept the locomotive moving.

Serafimov opened his eyes in darkness. He held his hands before his face, feeling but not seeing them, and imagined them once again clutching the throat of the treacherous Army Engineer Colonel who had stolen his train.

The State's *train*, he hastily corrected himself. He suppressed a giggle; one had to be so careful these days.

Serafimov lay on a cramped board that served as a bed, remembering—was it this morning? He could still smell the soot of the railbed, the vodka that had spilled over him when Podgorny had smashed a bottle of it against his skull. Mostly, he still smelled the blood, his own as well as Podgorny's.

Too much of one, not enough of the other. Despite the vengeance he had exacted on Podgorny's corpse, Serafimov still felt that a river of it would not be enough.

He sat up, listening to water trickle down the walls in the dark. His throat was still tender, but a few attempts at speech gave him hope that his voice would return. It might even sound human. He wrapped a thin, damp blanket over his shoulders and considered his situation.

He was in Lubyanka, of course. Or what remained of it. Overhead, a light bulb in a heavy wire cage struggled to life. It dangled insolently from a wire too short to hang himself from and too tough to bite through in a quest for electrocution.

For the first time since being put in here, Serafimov was able to see clearly. The room was even smaller than it had looked in his brief glimpse of it when they had thrown him in and left him in darkness. Rivulets of water raced fat roaches down the moldy walls to the damp concrete floor. *The inheritors of the earth*, Serafimov thought. The *tarakaniy* were the first well-fed creatures he'd seen in months. There was his pallet along the wall, and in a corner was a bucket for human waste; the bucket absurdly small to guarantee its constant overflowing.

The light could only mean that Serafimov was due to have visitors. He would be required to make a report, to confess his collusion in this morning's banditry and explain how he had lost the last train of supplies to leave Moscow. And explanations, he knew, were dangerous things.

Many men, far more important than Serafimov, had gone to the Gulags and worse for poor reports, or even excellent reports of poor performance. But after the KGB had taken control of the ruins of the Soviet, liquidating STAVKA and the GRU, reducing the Party itself to mere symbol and inevitably stepping into the power vacuum—well, then the Gulags had become unnecessary. Far more expedient methods had been devised to deal with the State's problems.

Problems like Serafimov, and problems like Serafimov's men, one from every ten of whom had been executed before his eyes.

The bulb dimmed slightly, then brightened again. Serafimov thought about that. Somewhere in this building a generator labored, burning precious untainted petrol to power this one light. All the vast ruins of Moscow might be in darkness, but this prisoner was to know just how important his jailers considered him to be.

He smiled. Unspoken words in the alien tongue of the KGB; Serafimov knew them all. He began to think, planning his statement carefully.

For while these idiots were playing their games, a train full of traitors was escaping, with what was certainly an American spy! Serafimov had no intention of letting that happen. His motives were less patriotic than vengeful, but he would stop them whatever the cost, if it meant selling his soul to the Devil himself.

But for revenge, he must survive, and to do that began with convincing this Steinmann that he was more valuable alive than dead. The East German claimed to be in direct contact with *Novaya Moskva;* let him prove it. There was nothing to lose by calling his bluff.

Serafimov meant to have the rest of Podgorny's men, and he thought he knew how to stay alive long enough to do it. He finished straightening his filthy uniform just as the bolt was thrown and the door opened.

There were two guards, both armed.

I am considered dangerous; how flattering.

Serafimov noticed that one of the guards wore a cavalry saber. Though obviously an antique, it was just as obviously not worn simply for decoration; indeed, it looked used.

Serafimov was beginning to see a disturbing pattern in the degeneration of the Soviet. *In a month or two, I should start seeing mounted archers. And in a year: Chain mail and shields.* Still, the future that concerned him now was his own, not the State's.

"Colonel Serafimov."

"*Da.*"

"You will come with us."

Serafimov followed them into the hall and up the stairs.

Rostov was in the commander's car, a passenger coach once removed from the engine. Trainmen Gyrich and Pilkanis were seated across the desk from him, while Sergeant Zorin and the American naval officer, Wrenn, occupied the sofa along the far wall. A quantity of lumber had been found among the supplies aboard the train, and two of the men were fitting a large sheet of plywood over the broken window behind him.

Colonel Podgorny had gone through that window only this morning, taking the KGB man with him and giving Rostov and all the rest of the men a chance to survive. Now Podgorny's sacrifice seemed to have been in vain.

Trainmen Gyrich and Pilkanis looked no happier to be presenting their report than Rostov was to be hearing it.

"Excuse me, Comrade Gyrich, but I don't understand. How could we possibly have lost so much fuel from gunfire in the rail yard? Those KGB troops weren't firing anything heavier than automatic weapons; how big a hole could a rifle have put in our fuel cells?''

Gyrich shook his head. "It wasn't a leak, Lieutenant. Anything big enough to pierce our fuel cells would probably have ignited them, and that would have been the end for us. What Trainman Pilkanis found is that small-arms fire struck some feeder control lines. These are fragile and could easily have been damaged by a stray rifle bullet.''

"Feeder control lines?'' The Russian *inzhenérnoe* sounded like "engineer,'' but had no more to do with locomotives than its English counterpart; that is, very little. Rostov knew a little of steam power plants, but almost nothing about locomotives.

"*Da*, Comrade Lieutenant.'' Pilkanis was Lithuanian, and his dislike for Russians in general and Russian soldiers in particular was no secret. But Rostov knew his mechanical expertise was indispensable; Pilkanis could fix anything, and what he couldn't fix, he could probably build a better version of. He cleaned his steel-rimmed spectacles as he spoke. "When these lines were damaged, the stoker assembly—that's a sort of locomotive fuel-injection system—this stoker assembly began flooding the lines with fuel to fire the boiler.''

Rostov had a glimpse of old burn scars behind the cuffs of Pilkanis' shirt sleeves. "You mean we might have blown up?'' he asked quietly.

"No, Lieutenant,'' Gyrich assured him. "This locomotive is old, but not primitive. There are special fail-safe mechanisms to prevent that. And unfortunately, they worked perfectly.''

"Why 'unfortunately,' Trainman Gyrich?'' Rostov's tone said he'd guessed what was coming, but asked, anyway.

"These safety mechanisms activated a series of valves that rerouted the fuel away from the stoker feed, into purge lines along the side of the boiler. From there the fuel just poured out onto the tracks.''

"How long had this been going on before you caught it?''

Gyrich licked his lips. Rostov and his men had saved them from the KGB, offering to take them along to freedom in the West. Gyrich hoped the young Lieutenant felt the same way after he got the news.

"The stoker maintained a normal feed until the slow pressure increase in the lines activated the fail-safes; I would guess the emergency rerouting started about six hours ago."

Rostov felt the walls closing in. "And how much fuel do you calculate we have lost?"

"I can only guess, Comrade Lieutenant. But I would have to say at least twenty-four hundred liters."

Rostov could not conceal his shock. Nearly half their fuel was gone. He knew the locomotive's appetite to be voracious simply to pull the cars, but it was also powering all the amenities aboard the train: heat, lights, warm water, cookstoves. Rostov and the rest of the men had gone without such basic comforts for weeks, and they had been indulging themselves to their hearts' content.

"Comrade Trainman Gyrich, can you give me an estimate of how far we can expect to get with our remaining fuel?"

Gyrich thought a moment. "If we cut our speed back, keeping nominal pressure in the boiler, we should be able to make another seven hundred kilometers. That's accounting for the fuel needed for idling with our steam up, to power the tools and equipment needed to repair the damage fully. Right now, it's just patched up, and a hasty job at that."

Rostov checked one of the dozens of rail maps left on the desk by the KGB Colonel who had previously commanded this train. Seven hundred kilometers.

"By the most hopeful estimate," he said, pointing to an area on the map far east of the indicated Alliance forces, "that will leave us out of fuel right in the middle of the Free Ukrainian Republic."

Sergeant Zorin let out a deep breath at that news, and Rostov nodded in agreement. Their chances of making it out of *Svoboda Ukranyie* were little better than their hopes of surviving capture by the KGB.

"What about cutting our weight?" Rostov asked. "Jettisoning equipment, detaching all but the few cars we'd need to carry our people?"

Gyrich smiled and shook his head. "Sorry, Lieutenant. This isn't a plane trying to get over a mountain; it's a locomotive, and a bloody great huge one at that. This P-38 is so overpowered for the load it's pulling that we could detach *all* the cars and it's likely this monster wouldn't even notice."

And anyway, Rostov thought, *our heaviest cargoes are our own*

139

weapons and vehicles, and the containers of the precious Immunizer. One we need to have any chance of getting to the West at all, the other to make getting there worthwhile.

"Lieutenant Rostov?" It was the American, his left hand still bandaged from his run-in with KGB Colonel Serafimov.

"*Da*, Captain Wrenn?"

"Colonel Podgorny told me the KGB tolerated the Army Engineers because of their control of the Immunizer; but that only the KGB knew where the hidden caches of uncontaminated fuel were hidden."

Rostov nodded as he remembered the rail maps in the desk and began pulling them out. "I see what you are saying. If the KGB planned to take this train all the way to *Novaya Moskva*, they must have been planning to refuel on the way."

Rostov eventually found a map bearing only rail lines and code numbers. It lacked even the spidery traces of Cyrillic lettering labeling terrain. "Gyrich, have you ever seen one of these maps before?"

The older man squinted watery blue eyes at the paper. "I think—yes, I think so; Colonel Serafimov used this one often when he discussed train routes; sometimes he carried it around tucked under his arm. This could be what you are looking for, but I don't know how to read it."

"We'll have to hope it reads: 'Here, *Tovarishchi*, free fuel,' and take our chances."

Wrenn stepped up to the table to lean over the map. "There's not even a compass rose; how can you tell where we are on it?"

"Maps are state secrets in the Soviet Union, Captain Wrenn. Security officers think everyone is a potential traitor, so topographers are allowed to put only as much information on a map as is absolutely necessary." He picked up the map indicating their position on the rail net, carrying it and the coded one to the command car's remaining intact window.

"Most units have Topography Officers, KGB liaisons who read the maps and consult with commanders for battle plans." Rostov held the coded map against the window and laid the rail map with their position over it.

"But Combat Engineers move too quickly; we don't have time to wait for some KGB flunky to pull his thumb out of his arse and let us know what we need to know to fight. So we've come up with a few ideas to save time.'' Rostov turned the top map until the rail lines coincided with those of the map beneath it, clearly visible with the sunlight shining through the window behind it.

"Fortunately, security officers also think most people are stupid, so they try to simplify everything, usually by standardization. Such as printing most maps to a constant scale.'' He grinned at Wrenn and spread the maps on the table before Gyrich.

"All well and good,'' the American said. "But what would you have done if it had been raining?''

It was still a race, Rostov decided with a smile at Wrenn's jest, and perhaps they had stumbled; but if the wolves were going to catch them, at least they would not catch them idle.

Serafimov stood at attention in an old Kremlin conference room with one long table and no east wall. Morning sunlight poured through blasted holes in the wall of the office, and onto the backs of his review board: four men in Soviet uniform, and Steinmann in the center. In contrast to their autumn-issue clothing, Serafimov had only his wet summer tunic as proof against the chill wind coming in with the morning sunshine. By an effort of will, he managed not to shiver. He stood at attention, waiting.

"Colonel Serafimov,'' Steinmann began, "we have already met. For the record, I am Major Steinmann, Seventy-fifth Tank Regiment, *Deutsche Demokratische Republik*.'' He gestured to the other officers seated with him. "These are Majors Grishin and Zimyanin, and Captains Tolkhunov and Adzhubei. Like all loyal soldiers of the New Soviet they are KGB, although their particular service branches are irrelevant to this inquiry.''

I'll just bet they are, Serafimov thought. He wasn't impressed by any of them. Admittedly, they looked like they'd seen a lot of action; who hadn't? But as to brains . . . well, none of them put Serafimov in fear of a chess match.

Intentionally, Serafimov ignored them and focused his attention on Steinmann. *These others are dogs*, he thought. *This is the one in charge. This is the wolf.*

"We are here,'' Steinmann continued, "to receive your report regarding the theft from this city of a State train by bandits.''

Serafimov was instantly on guard. Two days ago, he had been a conspirator; now he was simply a fool. The latter condition was theoretically survivable. But he did not allow himself to hope; hope took the edge from a man's survival instincts.

Despite his national affiliation, Steinmann was a tool of the KGB as surely as was Serafimov himself, and that august body did not deal in hope. The KGB, now more than ever, was concerned only with the security of the State, and nothing else, *nothing* else mattered. Sensing thin ice before him, Serafimov proceeded accordingly.

He presented the facts to Steinmann as briefly as possible. This man was not interested in any *pokazuka*, any pretense for effect. Steinmann interrupted him only for clarifications, or when the rasping sound the American had left him for a voice was impossible to understand. When Serafimov had finished, the board was silent for some time.

"And you believe your English-speaking assailant to be an American spy, Colonel?" The man Steinmann had introduced as Grishin had the prissy inflection of a priest; Serafimov detested him instantly.

"I do. Early in the war I interrogated many captured American soldiers. They became a specialty with me; I pride myself on my ability to recognize the type."

Steinmann smiled. "And just what 'type' is an American spy, Colonel Serafimov?"

Serafimov held his gaze. "Well fed, Major. Victors often are."

Steinmann nodded, surrendering the point and ignoring the offended scowls of his fellow interrogators as he changed the subject. "Now what about this Colonel Podgorny's staff; what do you know of them?"

Serafimov shook his head. "He had no staff as such, Major. The command ranks of his unit were much reduced. I saw only one Lieutenant and a Senior Sergeant. I believe that the unit only held together this long because of their training and the cult of personality fostered by this Podgorny. Also, Combat Engineers are generally regarded as semi-elite units, and these wore the uniforms of the Fifth Guards Armored Division; certainly an elite unit if ever there was one."

"Do you believe the loss of their commanding officer will affect the unit's cohesion?"

"Dramatically. Having no leader to rally to, and having obviously lost ideological integrity, I should expect their unit to begin dissolving within a week; two at the outside."

"Then they pose no real threat to the Rodina," Grishin put in smoothly, "as they will turn up in pockets throughout the hinterland, where they will be rounded up and destroyed piecemeal." Grishin sat back with a little smirk of triumph. "We have lost some valuable matériel, but that is easily replaced." He leaned forward again, steepled his fingers, and smiled at Serafimov. "And your testimony can thus be considered—concluded."

Serafimov pointedly ignored him and continued speaking. "Two weeks, however, is more than enough time for them to make good their escape, Major Steinmann. That is why I believe we must move quickly to apprehend them."

"We? You presume a familiarity you have yet to earn, Serafimov." Steinmann's omission of Serafimov's rank was accompanied by a chill in his tone. "What makes their capture more important to *Novaya Moskva* than your own punishment?"

"These combat engineers carried large quantities of Immunizer against binary biological agent *Yo-Devyatnatsat*, the organism which metabolizes petroleum-derived fuels. What Alliance intelligence called the Gas Bug. I believe they plan to use the Immunizer to purchase asylum in the remnants of the Alliance Nations."

Steinmann sat back with his faint smile while his fellow officers exploded in fury. Grishin was half out of his chair.

"Idiot! You allowed these traitors to steal a train for this perfidy, and now you are so bold as to lecture to *us* on the need to apprehend them? Your incompetence is matched only by your arrogance!"

Each of the others seemed to badly want a piece of Serafimov as well, but Steinmann waited until the first round of shouting had died down before he spoke.

"We are past the realm of our authority." He stood and came around the table. "Colonel Serafimov, it is nearly time for our check-in. You will accompany me to the communications van." Steinmann left the room with Serafimov and two guards, never turning to look back at the other officers.

But Serafimov turned, to give Grishin a final glance as he left. *In time*, Serafimov's eyes said.

Steinmann led him outside to the courtyard, where dozens of vehicles had been parked in orderly rows for servicing and refueling. Serafimov saw many of his own men pressed into service, carrying bundles of equipment, rolling fuel drums, or engaged in other menial tasks. Few of them met his eyes.

Surrounded by the light tanks, trucks, and APCs was the communications van, its glossy black wings of solar panels stretching out from both sides.

Steinmann noted Serafimov's surprise at the large dish antenna on the van's roof. "Yes, Colonel Serafimov; we do have a few satellites left." He gestured to the steps leading up into the van, and Serafimov went in.

Serafimov had expected darkness, but the van's interior was brightly lit. He saw a dozen technicians intent on their computer terminals, screens dancing with bright green columns of figures.

For a moment Serafimov forgot the devastation that surrounded them. Though painfully aware of his own filthy uniform and wretched appearance, the room around him was proof that all was not lost.

We are still in space, Serafimov thought. *Soviet power still challenges the Enemy for the high frontier.* He could almost imagine the last eight years had not happened. The *Rodina* and the Soviet she nurtured had not been driven to their knees; the *Narod*, their destiny fulfilled, were yet Masters of the World. He almost laughed aloud when he looked more closely at the technicians; over half of them wore East German uniforms.

Steinmann went directly to a console occupied by a young East German Captain. "How long before link is established?"

"Nearly ready, sir." The young man's fingers moved over the keyboard, and the screen responded with marching figures of green that changed abruptly to red. He looked up at Steinmann. "We're on, *Herr Major*."

Steinmann noted Serafimov's surprise at the honorific, but the Major only smiled as he put on a headset and adjusted the pin mike to speak.

"*Novaya Moskva*, this is PRG One, do you read me?"

The satellite link was perfect; when the reply came, Serafimov would have sworn the speaker was in the room with them.

"PRG One, this is *Novaya Moskva,* we read you clearly. Stand by for tie-in to the Central Committee."

Serafimov felt his guts churn. Who was this Steinmann that he rated a satellite link direct to Party Central? He was suddenly wary; perhaps this was all a trick.

"Major Steinmann, this is Anton Amalrik, Central Committee. How are things in Moscow?"

Serafimov's doubts evaporated at the sound of that voice. Anton Amalrik had been hailed in his youth as the "New Suslov," the Party Ideologian; had in fact received the first official public designation of that title in the history of the Soviet Union. In the dark days of the Alliance's avenging drive into the USSR, Amalrik had been the first Politburo member evacuated to the secret city east of the Ural Mountains, New Moscow. If anyone could rebuild the shattered Soviet from the ashes, it would be him.

And Steinmann is apparently on familiar terms with him. Serafimov wondered. *Familiar terms with a man almost as revered as Lenin himself.* That was enough to decide him. If Steinmann was Amalrik's man, then Serafimov would be Steinmann's. *For now, at least . . .*

Steinmann reviewed the situation for Amalrik, apparently reluctant to place too much emphasis on Serafimov's part in any failures of security. When he had finished, there was a pause before Amalrik replied.

"I have had my assistant access this Serafimov's file for me; I see that by all accounts he is considered quite reliable."

"He is here now, Comrade Amalrik. I thought you might wish to speak with him."

"Indeed. Colonel Serafimov."

Serafimov took another headset with unsteady hands. In a dark room, the quality of Amalrik's signal might have been almost comforting; in this sterile shell of light, it made him feel exposed.

"Comrade Amalrik, this is a great honor."

"Yes. Is something wrong with your voice, Colonel?"

"The throat wound Major Steinmann mentioned, Comrade; it will pass."

"Hm. Major Steinmann has said you believe it necessary to apprehend these traitors."

"I do, sir."

"Why? Surely the Immunizer for the Gas Bug cannot be so valuable to the West now. How much uncontaminated fuel can they have left? And what could they do with it? Certainly they can mount no offensive action worthy of concern."

Serafimov licked his lips. The question was a test, he knew. He was sinking, and they were throwing him a rope. Such opportunities in Russia had always been notoriously rare.

"Comrade Amalrik, at this point I feel I have very little to lose by candor—"

"You have nothing to lose, Colonel, I assure you. Proceed."

"My concerns on this issue are twofold. First, despite the collapse of the world's governments, the intrinsic Alliance advantage in technology has not been lost. Our inability to conduct large-scale nuclear strikes assured this. With a large enough supply of the Immunizer for analysis, they may accomplish things in their laboratories which we cannot even guess at. And if they should have stocks of uncontaminated fuel of which we are unaware, fuel which they can treat with *Yo-Devyatnatsat*, they may be able to return in force to the Liberated Zones within this decade."

There, Serafimov thought. *Start them off with a healthy dose of concern for the* Rodina; *and, of course, their own asses.*

"While this first issue is basically military and short-term, the second is ideological, and thus part of a long-range view."

"Indeed." Amalrik sounded almost amused. "Please state your 'ideological concern,' Colonel Serafimov."

"It is that these traitors may provide sufficient usable fuel for Alliance units still in the Liberated Zones to *escape* from the Continent."

Serafimov was gratified to see Steinmann's damnable smile flicker for an instant. The big East German's eyes bored into him. *Good*, Serafimov thought. *It was your idea I speak with Amalrik; your responsibility. Now* you *can sweat for a change.*

By the tone of his reply, Amalrik didn't appreciate Serafimov's statement any more than Steinmann did. "Colonel Serafimov, need I remind you of the losses we suffered in establishing those Liberated Zones? Or the losses we incurred while maintaining and defending that title for Western Europe for six years?" The hostility faded from Amalrik's voice, suddenly replaced by a sly twist of inflection. "What possible advantage can there be to stranding vast numbers of armed enemy troops there now?"

You already know, Amalrik. Serafimov smiled to himself. *You didn't get to be one of the most powerful men in the USSR without being one of the smartest as well. But I will go along with your test. And I think now that I will pass it, after all.*

"Comrade Amalrik, these enemy troops are cut off from their commands, unsupplied. The Alliance supply fleets are oil-dependent, which is to say obsolete. Thus these troops are far from home; far from help. Many are Americans, but all are likely unaware of or unwilling to face the political realities of their situation. They will attempt to maintain their status as viable armies, even after it becomes obvious that they cannot hope to leave Europe.

"An army exists to fight, but with our 'strategic redeployment' these armies can no longer reach their intended opponent. Thus, while as soldiers they can make no useful contribution to the lands they now occupy, as armies they will continue to consume huge quantities of food and matériel. Winter is coming to a Europe that has little food, less fuel, and no way of getting more of either. The citizenry, many of whom welcomed the Alliance troops as liberators, will soon come to resent the drain those same troops inflict on the stocks of food, to say nothing of warm beds.

"Eventually, these same citizens will tire of feeding them, housing them. And, to feed themselves, these well-armed troops must resort to force to get what they need. Westerners, particularly Americans, have no tradition of foraging or guerrilla warfare. They will be unable to reconcile the inevitable banditry with their original 'cause,' and as military discipline erodes, friction between these troops and the populace will increase.

"In such circumstances, time is, as always, the ally of Communism. The longer Alliance forces remain on the Continent, the more damage is done to their 'cause.' Many disillusioned Alliance troops may even seek us out to defect, giving us valuable recruits for future intelligence and subversion purposes. At the very least, their home nations are deprived of the crucial cadres of experienced troops needed for rebuilding their armed forces.

"Finally, when we return to Western Europe, what enemy units remain will be less than rabble. The populace too will have lost any

147

delusions as to the character of this reactionary Alliance, and the soldiers of the Soviet will be seen for the true liberators they are. Reestablishing our sovereignty over the Liberated Zones will then have the full support of the civilian populace.''

There was a long silence after Serafimov had finished. He was sure he'd talked too long; one does not, after all, preach political strategy to the Party Ideologian. But Serafimov knew it was critical to convince Amalrik that he was ideologically sound; not just a parrot of policy.

When Amalrik spoke again, he sounded pleased, even amused. ''Colonel Serafimov, 'sovereignty' is an imperialist term.''

Serafimov was hard-pressed to keep from shouting his triumph. ''A certain—temporary—period of imperialism is acceptable during the ultimate transition to socialism, is it not, Comrade Amalrik?''

''Of course, Comrade Colonel. We understand each other perfectly. Your reasoning shows a strong foundation in Marxist-Leninist principles.''

Serafimov felt odd. He had just saved his own life, he knew. Amalrik had heard his reasoning and approved, making for excellent odds that he would now live. Yet he still felt himself to be in some undefined peril.

Amalrik spoke again. ''Major Steinmann, you are assigned Colonel Serafimov as your unit co-coordinator.''

''Co-coordinator''? A meaningless title, Serafimov thought. *But then am I also meaningless?*

''Major Steinmann, you will retain command of PRG One, but hereafter you may consider Colonel Serafimov to be your political and security officer.''

''Thank you, Comrade Amalrik. I will be grateful for the Colonel's expertise.''

''And Major Steinmann, to any extent necessary, short of interference with PRG One's primary function, you are to assist Colonel Serafimov in his apprehension of these traitors to the *Rodina. Novaya Moskva out.''*

Steinmann turned to Serafimov, once more wearing his wintry, unfathomable smile. The big East German returned Serafimov's pistol with his left hand and extended his right. ''Welcome, Colonel Serafimov, to the first of many such organizations that will one day restore the vision of Lenin to the world. Welcome to Political Recovery Group One.''

Serafimov took Steinmann's hand. As the memory of Amalrik's voice lingered in the brightly lit room, he suddenly remembered his vow from the cell in the depths of Lubyanka, and his unease at last defined itself. The East German's grip was cool and dry, a hand with serpents for fingers. Serafimov holstered his weapon as he shook hands, holding Steinmann's gaze all the while and thinking about deals with the devil.

And at last, he smiled back.

"I didn't expect a whole town," Rostov said to his companion. The scouts were still in place, waiting for Rostov's command to advance. He stood in the roof hatch of the engineer's box in the locomotive, peering through field glasses.

Beside him, the American Naval Intelligence officer was balancing his own optics with his bandaged left hand, adjusting the focus with the fingers of his right.

"No indication on any of your maps?"

"None. The map calls this place the Suschenko Rail Supply Cache," Rostov told him. "If that is true, we should find more than enough equipment to repair the locomotive. And with a little luck, we will also find some uncontaminated KGB fuel stocks."

"Assuming it's not some elaborate KGB booby trap." Wrenn had finally got the focus right and now watched the town as well.

Rostov's smile broke into a wide grin. "You have a healthy paranoia, Captain Wrenn. Hang on to it; we will make a Russian out of you yet."

Unable to accept the evidence of the last half hour, Rostov looked at the town again. *Now who is being paranoid?* he thought.

"No signs of combat damage. The dirt road doesn't look too bad; probably no tanks or trucks through here lately. Still . . . I don't want to take the train in until I am sure."

He pulled the radio from his belt clip and spoke without lowering the glasses. "Sergeant Zorin."

"Here, Lieutenant."

"Take your scouting party into the town. Stay in radio contact. If you encounter resistance, do not engage. Confirm."

"Confirmed, sir. Will fall back to the train."

"Very good. Be careful, Mikhail."

"As always, Aleksei. Zorin out."

Rostov looked down between his feet to Gyrich, standing in the trainmaster's box beneath them. "Comrade Gyrich, our scouts are entering the town. I want to be able to get in there to help them if necessary. How fast can we begin rolling?"

"Not very, Lieutenant. There's a lot of inertia here. I can start us on a slow roll right now, though."

"Mightn't that bring us into the town before we are ready?"

"Lieutenant, I mean *slow*. You won't even be able to tell we're moving at first, but it could mean as much as two or three minutes saved in an emergency."

Unless the emergency requires us to back up, Rostov thought. But he finally nodded to the older man. "Good. Go ahead." Rostov held his thumb and forefinger an inch apart and grinned. "But *slowly*, yes? *Medlino*!"

Gyrich returned the grin and set about putting his men to work while Rostov went back to watching the town with Wrenn.

Zorin would be moving his squad in cautiously, doubtless, but it didn't hurt to have extra eyes watching.

The handful of buildings was an even mix of wood frame and concrete structures, mostly two-storied tenements and long warehouses, nearly all of them grey. The tallest structure was a clock tower with a bas-relief of Lenin; perfect for a sniper or enemy observer, and their eyes were drawn back to it frequently.

Rostov spoke from behind his glasses again. "See anything, Captain Wrenn?"

"Still nothing. But . . ." Wrenn's voice betrayed his unease.

"I know. I cannot think of what it is, but there is something not right about the look of that town. I hope I am wrong, but if I am not I hope that Zorin sees it in time."

Wrenn froze. *Time*. "Rostov, tell Zorin to hold his position."

Rostov complied instantly, Zorin confirmed as fast. "What is it, Captain Wrenn? What do you see?"

"I make it about ten thirty hours; no later than eleven hundred. Now look at the clock tower."

Rostov did, then whistled through his teeth. "Ten forty-three." He looked at Wrenn. "Someone's been keeping the time."

150

Zorin secured his own radio. "Unknown presence in town confirmed," Rostov had said. "Maintain observation of clock tower." One look at the structure explained that.

He smiled faintly, taking a moment to reset his watch from the tower's clock and make sure the men saw him do it. The ones who caught his eye laughed a little, some of their tension relieved.

Zorin gave Corporal Aliyev brief instructions and moved his own squad off in the opposite direction. The sun was still low enough for them to use it to some advantage, and in minutes they were in the shadows of the town's outer buildings.

Corporal Aliyev and three more men crawled along the railbed and approached the loading platform. Zorin kept watch on the men in his own group, waiting until he was sure everyone was in position.

When they were ready, Zorin put his back to the building his fire team had reached; slowly straightening his legs, he pushed himself up toward a window. Zorin listened to his collar scraping against the wall as he inched up, wishing mightily for a *papirosi*. His eyes cleared the windowsill, and he looked inside. Nothing.

He waved to the men waiting behind him. They were over the windowsill and into the room like shadows. Zorin remained outside to cover their entry, then followed.

Crossing the room, Zorin flattened himself to the wall beside the door. He could just see Aliyev and his men; they had reached the loading platform, and were moving into cover.

Khoroshiy, Zorin thought. *Very good.* In a moment Aliyev opened a door across the railbed and gave him the "clear" signal. They now controlled two buildings flanking the tracks and the loading platform. *So if the town is occupied, where is the resistance?*

"What now, *Starshi Serzhant?*" The private's whisper was professional, not fearful; he sounded almost bored.

"More skulking, *ryadovoi*. If there are hostiles in the town and they haven't hit us yet, then they will try to ambush the train. The best place to do that from would be the station house, where they could use the track controls to trap the locomotive between these buildings. Then they could deal with the train's passengers as they wished."

Zorin looked around at his soldier's faces, looking for the man who might be too uneasy, might make the mistake that got them all killed; it was seldom the same man twice. Usually Zorin saw him, and would set up a rear guard. Sometimes not, and he could only trust his life and the lives of his men to the Blessed Virgin.

This time, they all looked fit, and it struck him that he couldn't remember the last time one of them didn't. Zorin noticed again how young most of them seemed, at least in years. "Let's go."

One of the men muttered something, an expression Zorin remembered hearing from the American Captain: "Another day, another dollar."

Zorin knew exactly what it meant.

Rostov watched, Wrenn watched, and the train moved inexorably forward. Rostov decided that riding the minute hand of a watch would be faster.

"Still no movement in the town," Wrenn said.

Rostov nodded. "After Zorin takes the station house, I will send in Corporal Dyatlov to reinforce."

Wrenn grunted. "Dyatlov's a good man. You should see about promoting him; Aliyev, too. That would give you some more noncoms to take some of the weight off Zorin."

Rostov shook his head. "I am only a Lieutenant. Field promotion in time of war requires an officer of Major's rank or above. In any case"—he lowered his glasses slightly and looked at Wrenn over the eyepieces—"I will be resigning my commission within a very few days, if all goes well, yes?"

Wrenn did not look back. "Yes. Let's hope so."

Rostov waited for some time to catch Wrenn's eye, to read the American's meaning in his face. But Wrenn had resumed watching the town through his own field glasses, and after a moment Rostov did the same.

In the town, Zorin's forces had reached the station house. Zorin checked the door: unlocked. He turned the knob and threw the door open in one smooth motion. His man kneeling before it threw himself prone into the room, while the man behind him jumped over his comrade and dropped into a crouch, all before the swinging door had hit the wall.

The track control room appeared at first to be empty. Sunlight streamed in through the broad windows onto the panels of switches and track status lights. One chair was before the panel, and as he watched it, Zorin saw a wisp of vapor creep up from it.

"You," Zorin said quietly, "turn that chair around. Slowly."

The white-haired reservist sitting in the chair obeyed, obviously terrified, revealing a steaming mug gripped in both hands.

"*Do'svydanie*," the old man said quietly. "Would you fellows like some tea?"

Rostov grinned broadly at Wrenn. "Is he composed enough to speak to me, Sergeant Zorin?"

"I think so, sir." There was a moment of silence before a breathless voice came over the radio to Rostov.

"Hello? This is Colonel Fedorin, Railway Security Forces, Suschenko Station . . . who is this, please?"

"Colonel Fedorin, this is Lieutenant Rostov, Fifth—" He stopped. *Podgorny should be making this contact*, he thought. This was his unit; all that was left of it. He had kept it alive long enough to get this far. "Fifth Guards Armored Engineers. Under Colonel Podgorny. We require materials and supplies from your repair depot if available, and any general maintenance you can provide."

The reply was something like a shout. "Absolutely, Comrade Lieutenant! Anything, anything at all! Please bring your train up to the loading dock, I will get my men."

"How many of you are there?" Rostov asked, signaling Gyrich to bring them into the town.

"Only five in our unit, Lieutenant. And about a hundred townspeople, mostly farmers and a few workers."

"Very well, Colonel. We will be at the platform in"—he looked down at Gyrich, who held up four fingers—"four minutes. Sergeant Zorin."

"Yes, Aleksei."

"Continue your check of the buildings. I'm sending in Corporal Dyatlov's unit to reinforce and secure."

"Very well, sir. Zorin out."

Rostov looked to the American. "More problems, sounds like. And civilians. Do we tell them what we're about, I wonder? Then they might want to come with us."

Wrenn seemed preoccupied. "What? Oh, the civilians. Yeah, they're a consideration, all right. I don't know what to tell you, Lieutenant." Wrenn looked at him. "You're in command."

Rostov grimaced. "Too true." He couldn't read the American's mind, and in any case he now had more important things to worry about. He went back to watching the image of Suschenko grow in his field glasses.

A Colonel, Wrenn was thinking. *Perfect.*

The train rolled slowly into the town, wreathed in steam and the sweet machine smells of all locomotives. Rostov stood in the roof hatch, thinking that with the Gas Bug loose in the world, the smell of burning diesel was soon to become the rarest perfume on earth. In his childhood, he had been confused by his parents' concern over exhaust fumes and their effect on the birch groves in and around the parks of Moscow.

There's no concern of that now, Rostov thought. The birch groves, like his parents, were long gone. He prayed fervently that this Suschenko place might have sealed fuel stocks they could treat with their own supplies of Immunizer. *Ah, God; only let us make a little more smog, if You would. Just a few hundred kilometers' worth.*

Despite Fedorin's eager greeting, or perhaps because of it, Rostov was well aware that they could be riding into a trap. So his men aboard the train peered cautiously from windows broken and windows yet whole. Some stood on platforms between the cars, some knelt on the roofs, and some were positioned on the engine itself, watching the buildings slide by. All were armed, and all were nervous.

As for Rostov himself, standing in the waist-deep roof hatch, he felt like a tank commander in a Revolution Day parade, no less ludicrous and far more vulnerable. Even as he framed the thought, his eye caught furtive movement in a building ahead, and one of his men on the locomotive's front raised a rifle.

"*Nyet!*" Rostov shouted. "*Stoy!* Hold your fire!"

Only fear for Rostov's life had moved the soldier to such quick action, and only his loyalty to Rostov prevented a near tragedy. The man lowered his rifle, and Rostov's shoulders sagged in relief. An old woman in clothes that were not quite rags was turning from a doorway where she tugged at something inside. She turned back to the train to favor Rostov with a wave and a toothless smile.

Finally the *babushka* succeeded in extricating a little girl from her hiding place in the doorway, and the old woman picked the child up and carried her to the platform.

At her grandparent's urging, from her perch on the old woman's arm, the child put out a hand and touched the dusty metal of the engine. Soot and grime coated her palm as the massive locomotive passed gently beneath it like a whale passing a swimmer.

While Wrenn maintained a watch from the roof hatch, where his alien uniform was mostly hidden, Rostov descended the ladder into the engineer's cab, then stepped down onto the platform just as the train came to a stop. His gaze met that of the old woman, and he saw that the *babushka*'s eyes were filled with tears, her wrinkled face beaming in a smile of welcome.

"Hello, Grandmother," Rostov said to reassure her. "You and your little one are safe, now. You came out to welcome us, eh?"

The woman began chattering in a thick Ukrainian dialect which left him hopelessly confused; then the child tugged at his sleeve, and bending to look at her, Rostov forgot everything else.

Olive complexion, deep brown eyes, hair with a sheen like the *barguzin* sables his uncle Yuri had once trapped for the State commissioner. *If Lilia and I had had a child* . . . Her resemblance to his wife was enough to make Rostov stifle an urge to cross himself. The child smiled at him, reaching out for his cap, and Rostov handed it to her on reflex. She seemed fascinated by the bright red star of the cap badge and its inlaid hammer and sickle of gold.

"You make friends easily, Lieutenant," Wrenn called down to him in his flawless Russian. Rostov turned and grinned up at him, impulsively reaching into his tunic pocket and pulling out the snapshot.

"Comrade Captain, you wouldn't believe this—" Rostov caught himself. He had been about to show Wrenn the picture of himself and Lilia in Leningrad. *Why would I show such a thing to the American?* he thought. "Well. It's nothing. Just an interesting coincidence." He pushed the photo deep into his pocket and retrieved his cap as Zorin approached him from behind.

155

"That's our Aleksei, always the favorite of the ladies." Rostov retrieved his cap and turned to see Sergeant Zorin approaching with five overage reservists, all unshaven, most still pulling on boots or buttoning tunics over their old-men's chests. Rostov assumed that the most prepared-looking fellow in the lead must be Colonel Fedorin and saluted, not so smartly as to offend the older man's pride.

"First Lieutenant Rostov, Fifth Guards Armored Division, Third Regiment, Combat Engineers." He hesitated, unsure if his next words were for their benefit or his: "Colonel Ivan Podgorny commanding."

Fedorin returned the salute with more enthusiasm than discipline. "Colonel Fedorin, Rail Security Forces, Suschenko." Fedorin extended his hand impulsively, and Rostov found the breach of protocol oddly reassuring. "It is good to see a friendly face, Lieutenant."

Rostov could guess the man's meaning. "I understand, sir; we are not KGB."

Fedorin nodded happily. "So I hoped when I first saw your Sergeant Zorin here and his men; that they did not shoot me first and interrogate me after . . . well, that was the giveaway." He gestured over his shoulder to the station house behind him. "Perhaps we can continue this inside over some tea?"

Rostov's fatigue had settled over him like a shroud; more than anything else, he simply wanted to get this charade over with. Podgorny's last orders had been to get the men to safety in the West. To Rostov that now meant getting fuel, if they had any here, securing what supplies might be available, and getting the hell out of the ruins of the Soviet. But Colonel Fedorin seemed determined to drag this out.

Ah, what the hell . . . Everything else aside, while he hated the idea of deceiving this old fellow, Rostov was touched by Fedorin's efforts to maintain some civility. The offer of tea was more than simple hospitality; it was a slap in the teeth to the destruction all around them, and Rostov suddenly realized he welcomed the opportunity to do just that.

Colonel Podgorny would have had me flogged if I refused. Besides, the world can fall apart, the KGB can drag the Rodina *straight to hell; but I am still an officer of the Red Army. And I still have my manners.* He smiled at Fedorin as he adjusted his cap and saluted once more.

"Of course, sir. A cup of tea would be very welcome, and thank you."

"Captain Drachev! Message coming in!"

Yuri Drachev spat out a mouthful of cold tea and dashed the remnants from his tin cup to the ground. He tossed the empty container to the cook and broke into a trot toward the center of his unit's bivouac.

Drachev had begun deploying his vehicles like an open-sea convoy when they encamped for the night. In a real war, such deployment would have been laughable, even suicidal against air attacks or sappers with antitank missiles. But the real war had been over for some time now, and Drachev had adapted. Air attacks were a dim memory, antitank missiles were rare, and the threat now came from bandits and raiders with firebombs and knives. And the Devil take any politically reliable ass-kisser who claimed differently.

Drachev passed through the outside perimeter of tank support troops and their BMP armored personnel carriers, all deployed so as to protect his precious LT-200 light tanks. The very center of the camp was reserved for the supply trucks and the communications wagon, their link with *Novaya Moskva* and the other intact units that remained under its command.

Drachev pulled himself up into the back of the cramped van and closed the door behind him. The communications officer didn't hear him through his headphones, and Drachev slapped him on the shoulder in greeting. "Source, Piotr?"

"PRG One, Captain. Currently in Moscow."

Drachev grunted. "The KGB is back in Moscow? They are either being very aggressive or very stupid." He put on a headset and adjusted the microphone.

Piotr shrugged. "Who knows, sir; perhaps we've won the war."

Drachev gave him a look that accepted the jest without approving of it, then clicked the contact button several times before giving the recognition code names.

157

" 'Dacha,' this is 'Kolinsky,' come in."

Dacha responded after the brief delay of a satellite link. "We read you, Kolinsky. Scramble signals and stand by for new orders."

A moment later, Steinmann's familiar voice was on the line. "Captain Drachev, this is Steinmann. How are you?"

"We are well, thank you, sir. The unit is fit, all vehicles operational, supply levels sufficient for the remainder of our patrol period." He didn't mention that they were still without a political officer. The last one had been killed in a bandit raid a month ago. Drachev had duly reported the casualty, then said no more, wanting to prolong the bliss of life without a Commissar for as long as possible.

"Good. Captain Drachev, your unit is hereby remanded to a new operations officer, code-named 'Revenant.' Confirm, please."

"Kolinsky now an asset for Revenant, confirmed. Standing by." *God save us, can't we get this nonsense over with? Just give us the damned mission. Probably some half-assed squirrel chase after another pack of counterrevolutionary nationalists, anyway.*

"Kolinsky, this is Revenant." The new control's voice came over the link, and Drachev didn't like him already. *If snakes could talk . . .* , he thought.

"Kolinsky, your unit is to search the following areas for any unauthorized rail activity on intact lines. Details follow."

Unauthorized rail activity? Drachev decided that Revenant was either a total madman or yet another trick to test their loyalty. He finished a deep sigh before replying.

"Understood, Revenant," Drachev said, gesturing impatiently to Piotr for a map. "Standing by for deployment orders." As Revenant gave him coordinates, Drachev picked up a grease pencil and drew circles around various small towns on the map. Bodii, Yemadzoy, Viluk, Suschenko . . .

What a farce, Drachev thought, catching Piotr's eye as he made the marks.

The young lieutenant grinned, shaking his head.

Back in Moscow, Major Grishin waited until Serafimov was about to terminate communications with Drachev's force. Steinmann was leaning against the wall, studying Serafimov's deployment notes on his own map of "Kolinsky's" operations zone. He looked up as Grishin addressed Serafimov.

"With all due respect, Colonel Serafimov, I believe it would be a mistake to assign Kolinsky to this operation."

Serafimov's tone was cool. "How so, Major?"

"Evidently you have not read the status reports on our patrol units in the field; I have. Kolinsky lost its political officer recently, and a new one has not yet been assigned."

"Stand by, Kolinsky." Serafimov turned to face Grishin. "And is that a problem?"

Grishin's smile was almost sad. "Colonel Serafimov, should Kolinsky make contact with these Army bandits and your stolen train—and frankly, I think this unlikely—what is to guarantee that, bereft of political guidance, *they* will not be tempted to defect as well?"

Serafimov seemed taken aback by the prospect, but attempted to conceal his shock. "Well—if a political officer is your only worry, Major, I am certainly capable of serving in that role. In fact, I would be willing to rendezvous with Kolinsky myself for that very purpose."

Grishin cut him off. "Yes, Colonel; I have no doubt you would. But you, my friend, are still under suspicion for complicity in the loss of that train. And we have seen just how capable you are as a combat commander."

Grishin turned to Steinmann, ignoring the now completely flustered Serafimov. "Major Steinmann, with your permission, I will rendezvous with Kolinsky and serve as *pro tem* political officer." He turned back to Serafimov before the Colonel could get his bearings. "This way, Novaya Moskva may be assured of the reliability of at least one officer involved in this operation."

Serafimov's jaw clenched at the insult, but he said nothing.

Steinmann nodded. "Agreed. I will so inform Party Central during my next check-in. Colonel Serafimov, inform Kolinsky of Major Grishin's assignment to their unit."

"I'll see to my things." Grishin saluted Steinmann, unable to resist favoring Serafimov with a look of triumph as he left.

I cannot lose. If we find nothing, Serafimov looks like the fool that he is; if we find the train, I will receive credit for being the officer who apprehends the tekniks *and the stolen matériel.*

Grishin took his leave, satisfied that his star was in the ascendant.

Back in the van, Serafimov had suddenly regained his composure. He opened his operations folder and removed the current status report on Kolinsky, handing it to a Lieutenant to be returned to the files.

"Major Grishin would seem to be very brave," he told Steinmann in an offhanded tone, "to take over pursuit of well-armed renegade Combat Engineers."

Steinmann caught his eye. "Grishin is a fool," the big East German said simply. "I am well rid of him." He put the map down and left the van.

Captain Martin Wrenn, United States Naval Intelligence, tightened the sling securing his wounded left hand. With his American uniform, Wrenn could hardly move about with the work details repairing the train or trading with the people of Suschenko, but he had promised Rostov that, wounded hand notwithstanding, he would shortly go very crazy with nothing to do.

Wrenn wandered into a passenger car and saw Sergeant Zorin approaching from the far end, a coat draped over his arm.

"Sergeant Zorin; good to see you."

"Captain Wrenn. I thought you might want to cover your uniform with this." Zorin held out a Russian-issue greatcoat. "There are several civilians around the train, and you never know who might be watching."

Is there any eventuality you don't *anticipate, Sergeant*? Wrenn knew that the Red Army simply did not have noncoms like Zorin. At least they didn't when the war started. Still, there was no reason they couldn't have learned to keep men like him where they did the most good. Wrenn was sure Rostov blessed his luck for the man every day he woke up alive.

"Thank you, Sergeant." With one arm in a sling, Wrenn was glad to let the stocky noncom help him on with the heavy coat. It was late summer in Russia, the day was chilly, and most of the train was open to the air, but presently Wrenn understood why the Russians had never phased out greatcoats from their military dress codes.

160

A warmer and far less conspicuous Wrenn followed Zorin out onto the platform. Wrenn and Zorin took the air, looking up to see thin clouds threading in from the northeast.

"*Christus,*" Zorin muttered, "more snow."

"Still, winter's coming slowly this year," Wrenn said, not adding his worry that it might not come slowly enough.

"I suppose even God has second thoughts sometimes, eh, sir?"

Wrenn nodded, then wondered what Zorin meant by that. *Jesus, I really* am *getting paranoid.*

"Or maybe we've just been lucky," Zorin said in a lighter tone.

"How much luckier do you think we'll have to be, *Kapitan*?"

Wrenn almost laughed. "We got out of Moscow alive, Sergeant Zorin. Let's take one miracle at a time."

Stepping down onto the platform, the two men passed down the line of cars, frequently sidestepping to get through the activity surrounding the train.

Amid the frantic activity of repair, the Combat Engineers were trading surplus items that Rostov had judged could be spared to share with the people of Suschenko. Surgeon Blaustein had been pleased to find large stocks of vitamins and nutritional supplements in one of the boxcars, and he was presently trading some to the townspeople for additional antibiotics and medical supplies. He looked up and waved as he caught sight of Zorin and Wrenn.

"This bartering is interesting," Wrenn said after a moment.

Zorin nodded. "I would not have expected Aleksei to loot these people, but he could just as easily invoke supply requirements, take what bare necessities we require, and we could be on our way."

"That might make Fedorin and his Rail Security Forces suspicious. They might then decide to report our visit."

Zorin nodded. "Perhaps. Besides, I don't particularly think we are doing a great deal more of it than is strictly necessary."

Wrenn looked around them at the civilians. Their faces were still lined with hunger and care, but most were smiling now, probably for the first time in weeks. Those soldiers not engaged in work details were helping in whatever ways they could, and the townspeople were responding in kind.

Already, flour donated from the train's stocks was returning to the soldiers as pastries and fresh bread. Sometimes it was even delivered by someone's daughters, or a young widow, and despite the fact that the girls were always heavily chaperoned by stern-faced *babushki*, the effect on morale was considerable.

"No, Sergeant Zorin, I don't think so, either."

Rostov himself arrived then, his arm about the shoulders of an old woman with him. They recognized her as the grandmother who had greeted Rostov when they first arrived. Rostov kissed the *babushka*'s cheek and returned her parting wave as he approached Zorin and Wrenn.

"You should see Grandmother's helper; beautiful kid, six, maybe seven years old." Rostov half grinned, shaking his head. Zorin read some emotion on his Lieutenant's face, but even he could not tell what it might be. He wondered if Rostov knew himself.

"How are you, Captain Wrenn?" Rostov asked.

"Not as well as you, evidently, Lieutenant." It was true; despite fatigue and overwork, Rostov seemed rejuvenated. "Just trying to make myself useful." Wrenn gestured with his wounded hand by way of apology.

"Not to worry, Captain, we shouldn't be very much longer. Oh, you might want to see Surgeon Blaustein about that hand; he's got some more medical supplies from the stores here—what a rail supply depot was doing with medical supplies, don't ask me, I'm just grateful to get them—anyway, he might want to change the treatment for your hand."

"I will, Lieutenant. Thank you."

Rostov nodded, a little embarrassed by his rush of words. "Very well. I've got to check with Colonel Fedorin about the stocks of uncontaminated fuel he has here. They have more than we need, but we'll treat all of it with Immunizer. That will get these people through the winter; maybe even give them something to barter in the future." He saluted Zorin, then Wrenn. "Carry on."

Rostov spun on his heel to go, and suddenly stopped. He turned back to look sheepishly at Wrenn. "Uh . . . sir. I mean—"

Wrenn tossed a brisk salute and deadpanned: "Aye aye, skipper."

Rostov grinned self-consciously and left.

"We've got to get him promoted," Wrenn said.

"Beg pardon, Captain Wrenn?"

"Hm? Oh, just a thought, Sergeant. It's going to be a while yet before we get to the Alliance lines. Any one of us could get killed on the way. Your unit needs a more dispersed command structure to absorb any losses that might occur among the officers and noncoms—which right now means you and Rostov. Even if we make it in one piece, it wouldn't hurt your position to get to the West with a few more chiefs and a few less Indians."

"Sir?"

Wrenn smiled. "Sorry. Poor choice of idiom." He took Sergeant Zorin's arm and steered him toward the crowd. "Let's pay a call on Comrade Surgeon Blaustein."

Captain Drachev drew an "x" on his map with two savage strokes. He handed the map to Piotr and left the communications wagon without a word.

I've gotten sloppy, that's the problem. Drachev cursed himself as he stalked through the town square in the ruins of Viluk. *I'd forgotten just how much damage one stupid bastard of a political officer can do.* He thought of a joke from his days at Frunze that had been as popular as it was forbidden: *What's the most dangerous thing we will ever face in combat, Comrades?*

"A Commissar with a map," Drachev answered under his breath.

Like Bodii and Yemadzoy before it, Viluk had appeared deserted, and his new "aide," Major Grishin, had insisted they move in before it was properly reconnoitered.

Drachev didn't trust himself to look at the covered bodies of his men. *So much for appearances*, Drachev thought bitterly. *Forgive me, Comrades.*

Ten men dead was bad enough; Drachev had become close with all his troops in the months he'd been in command. But if the loss of his men saddened him, the waste of two of his tanks enraged him. He reached the chief mechanic's tent and sought him out for the status of the other vehicles.

"We have had a little luck there, Captain. The bandits dropped those demolition charges right on the engine grates of Eight and Three, so that's the bottom of the bowl for them. But for once our production committees did something right. These light tanks are almost all modular in design, makes them very easy to cannibalize for parts. I saved enough pieces from the two hulks to repair all the light damage to the rest of the vehicles.'' The chief mechanic watched Drachev's impassive features. "Sorry, sir, that's the best I could do.''

"No need to apologize, Lieutenant. It does put a little brighter face on the whole mess.'' *Too bad you can't repair men like that*, he'd been thinking, turning at last to look at the blanketed forms outside. *We could start by carving up that fool, Grishin*. Drachev's gaze continued on to the other side of the square, where Grishin was interrogating their sole captive.

"Carry on, Lieutenant.'' Drachev crossed the square, idly reaching down to open the flap of his holster, and flick the safety on his sidearm to "off.''

Major Grishin did not look happy. The man before him had single-handedly destroyed two tanks as smoothly as in the training films. That was bad enough, but the ensuing confusion had allowed his comrades to escape. Grishin had taken a leg wound during the ambush, and Drachev guessed it had opened again, as the bandage on his calf was a bright red. It did nothing to improve the KGB man's disposition, and he was eager to take it out on their prisoner.

You brave son of a bitch, Drachev thought as he looked at the captured bandit. *I've seen a dozen men die trying to do what you did; I've killed dozens more of the enemy who tried it on me. You mastered that piece of work in the Red Army, no doubt about it.* "Major Grishin. What do you have for me?''

Grishin's leg wound had to hurt; Drachev had dressed it himself and it looked bad. *Not bad enough*, he'd thought at the time. But the KGB man's voice was calm, almost reflective.

"Nothing. They are Ukrainian bandits. They saw our force and hid in the town, hoping we would bypass them. When they realized we were coming in, they set up the ambush.''

"We're not 'bandits,' you KGB prick,'' the prisoner said quietly. "We are partisans.''

Grishin jabbed the man in the ribs with the barrel of his rifle, but Drachev ignored the comment. "Sounds reasonable enough. Do you believe him?''

Grishin gave him a look. "I am prepared to believe anything that expedites shipping him to the slave camps.''

"Does he know anything about a train, Major?" Drachev hoped an ironic tone might remind Grishin of their original mission.

"No, Captain Drachev. These thugs routinely raid—"

"Patrol," the prisoner interrupted, and this time Grishin sent him tumbling with a rifle butt to the face.

"As I said," Grishin continued as if nothing had happened. "They routinely raid these border areas, but they haven't seen any rail activity in months."

Drachev looked at the bloody face of the prisoner as the man struggled back up to a sitting position. Sure of his fate, the partisan watched him with an absolute lack of interest.

"Send this fellow to the camps," Drachev said as he walked around the prisoner. He then drew his Makarov and shot the man behind the ear too quickly for Grishin to do anything about it. The body pitched face forward into the dust.

Grishin went livid, his composure at last shattered. "Drachev! That man was to be an example; once broken in the camps he could even be sent back here as an intelligence asset."

"Major Grishin, you cost me *two tanks and sixteen men*! Because of you, we have suffered more casualties in one ambush than in our last four engagements. Combined! I don't have men or vehicles to spare to hold prisoners, and certainly not to transport them anywhere."

Drachev's knuckles were white around the grip of the still-smoking sidearm in his hand, and twice he saw Grishin's eyes flash to the weapon. He prayed the KGB man would give him an excuse to use it as he pressed his attack.

"We are only a few dozens of kilometers from the Free Ukrainian Republic; we have been operating along its borders for six days, and it is only by heroic good fortune that we have not encountered their patrols in strength." Drachev lowered his voice, hoping Grishin would respond to a reasonable tone.

"Major Grishin, there is only one town left on the Revenant list, and we cannot get there before nightfall, so we'll have to leave tomorrow morning. Unless you call off this nonsense and let us get back to our usual patrols."

"You have your orders, *Captain* Drachev."

Drachev refused to back down. "Very well. Then, as I am

required to report our progress to Revenant, I will do so in great detail, and let *him* decide if we need to subject ourselves to another day of this *pokazuka*."

Drachev turned his back on Grishin and headed for the communications truck. He had intended to have the prisoner executed anyway, but he had no intention of seeing a fellow soldier sent to those camps.

The fact that it aggravated the hell out of Grishin was simply a bonus.

Surgeon Josiv Blaustein was a curiosity. Like many of the men in the unit, he had been rescued from the KGB by Podgorny, who had often traded weapons or fuel for skilled men who might otherwise be executed or imprisoned. As a Jew, Blaustein was a *de facto* enemy of the State since the Israeli Incident of the War's first year, but Podgorny had needed a doctor for his men far more than he'd needed another commendation for loyalty from the KGB.

As the oldest man in the unit after Podgorny, he had the respect of the men. More important, as a Captain in name only, he had their trust, and was valued by them for his counsel.

At such times, Blaustein would run his palm over his forehead and down the back of his neck, a habit the men took as a universal trait of the very wise. Actually, since he'd starting losing his hair, Blaustein's pate had developed the same fascination for him as a broken tooth.

Wrenn and Zorin had sequestered themselves with Blaustein in the command car, and now watched him stroking his scalp as he pondered the issue they'd brought before him.

"I believe your point is well taken, Captain Wrenn."

Blaustein was short, with an athletic build that belied his age and made Wrenn think of a gymnast. The image was enhanced by the surgeon's balancing of his chair on its two back legs as he spoke, frowning at the floor before continuing.

"Colonel Podgorny had often spoken to Rostov about promotion, but the Lieutenant wasn't much interested in that sort of thing after Kiev." He shared a look with Zorin, who nodded.

"A week before we met you," Blaustein continued, "we lost Captain Meshcheryakov, Lieutenant Gontar, and Lieutenant

Gavrilov, all in the same bandit attack. That's when Podgorny told me that he was going to give Rostov a field promotion, and the lad's reluctance be damned. Despite the reduction of the regiment to barely more than a company, the strain was beginning to tell on Podgorny."

Wrenn thought a moment. "Do you think this Fedorin would oblige us?"

Zorin nodded. "I would bet on it, sir. Colonel Fedorin seems to think we all walk on water and piss wine. I think you will have difficulty with Lieutenant Rostov, however. I have fought beside Aleksei for four years. He was never a climber, but since he lost his wife, he has had no interest in rank, despite the fact that command comes to him easily."

"That's why I believe we need to have Fedorin approach him," Wrenn said, "with no hint that we are behind the idea. But how do we get Fedorin to do it and not tell Rostov that it's coming from within his own unit?"

Blaustein looked up. "Oh, that's easy enough," he said in an offhanded manner.

For a moment Wrenn was pleased, then he saw the way Blaustein was looking at him.

For the first time in months, Colonel Fedorin was actually happy. Although his first duty was to the Soviet Rail Security Forces, he had spent many months here in Suschenko; the people had been good to him and his men, feeding and caring for them long after supplies had stopped coming in. He was part of this community now, and it was good to be able to help his neighbors.

Fedorin leaned back in his chair in the station house and went over the list of items before him. He had been able to acquire food, good Army-issue blankets, a few weapons to defend themselves, and hunt some game. And it was all possible because of these Combat Engineers and their stolen train.

He looked over his shoulder in guilty reflex at his thoughts. Of course, it was obvious that the train was stolen; you could tell from the looks on the faces of Rostov and Zorin and their men, if nothing else. But what really gave them away was the glaring lack of any KGB presence.

Fedorin scowled at the thought. Those arrogant bastards with the green shoulder boards were everywhere now, drafting any young man who could carry a rifle, dissolving regular Army units and incorporating them into KGB *ad hoc* forces. "PRGs," they were calling them. *Pfah*!

The KGB didn't trust the Army, never had. It was too independent; they would certainly never allow an entire train full of Army Combat Engineers to move about unescorted.

Fedorin had dealt with enough of those bastards in the last few months, and didn't care if he never saw another one again. Four of them had come ripping through Suschenko just six weeks ago, shooting the place up and throwing their weight about.

There was a new reality to get used to, they had told him, when they took two girls away from their families, all the while laughing at the foolish old reservists in their ill-fitting Rail Security uniforms.

As far as Fedorin was concerned, it was the same old reality as always. But those KGB soldiers had been introduced to a new reality, all right. Crossing himself absently, Fedorin wondered what the four *chekisti*, lying together in a shallow unmarked grave outside of town, thought of the afterlife they'd purchased with the rape and beating of those girls. Probably not the sort of thing classes in Marxist-Leninism prepared them for.

But that was the past, and as he took a deep breath and looked out on the Combat Engineers loading barrels of diesel into a boxcar, he wished them luck wherever they were going. In a way, he even hoped that they might run into a KGB patrol or two. He smiled at the thought; small ones, of course. Easy kills.

"Colonel Fedorin?"

He turned his chair around, his smile fading at the unfamiliar voice, then disappearing at the sight of an equally unfamiliar face. The man before him was thin, with dark brown hair and beard going to grey. His left arm was in a sling, and his left hand was completely bandaged. Despite his own bloodthirsty maunderings, Fedorin could not help but be a little afraid. The stranger wore no badges of rank, but carried himself like an officer.

"*Da*, I am Fedorin . . . eh—"

The man held up his good hand. "Excuse me, Colonel. We have not yet had the opportunity to meet. I am not officially a member of Lieutenant Rostov's unit. I was picked up by his men outside of Moscow. I am *Leytenant-Kapitan* Renko." Wrenn paused a moment, then added, "GRU," in what he hoped was a sufficiently ominous tone. In any nation's military intelligence branches, ranks were meaningless. A man from the GRU, Soviet military intelligence, could thus be a General for all outsiders knew.

Fedorin was both puzzled and delighted. "But, I thought; that is, the rumor was that the GRU . . ."

"The rumors of GRU treason were KGB fabrications, meant to allow them free rein in wiping out their opposition in the Soviet Armed Forces." Wrenn hoped he could keep up the pace of his deception. Zorin had warned him that Fedorin was a simple man, but not a stupid one.

"There are very few of us left, but we are still active. My mission is unknown to Rostov or his men, as is my rank; they think me simply a wounded survivor."

He dropped his voice to a more conspiratorial tone and pulled a chair up across from Fedorin. "There is something I would like to do for them, Colonel, but for the sake of my mission I cannot jeopardize my cover. You understand?"

Fedorin nodded, relaxing a little; at least these lads weren't in any trouble. "Yes, of course, ah—sir?"

Wrenn gave him a noncommittal shrug. "Good. Then, Colonel Fedorin, I would appreciate your assistance in this matter." Wrenn took a piece of paper from his tunic pocket and handed it to Fedorin.

"This is a list of personnel recommended for promotion by Rostov's former commander, Colonel Podgorny. As you know, the Colonel was killed a few days ago, before these promotions could be implemented. Field promotion requires an officer of Captain's rank or above, and since Rostov is only a Lieutenant, the GRU would consider it a favor if you could perform these promotions yourself."

Fedorin was shocked. A favor to the GRU! There couldn't be more than a few hundred GRU left alive in all of Russia, and the KGB had put them all under sentence of death. Fedorin looked the GRU man over closely, and despite himself, he smiled.

"If word ever got out that I had spoken with a GRU operative and not turned him in to the KGB, my life wouldn't be worth a Liberated Zone ruble.'' Fedorin looked the GRU man over closely.

"You are under no obligation to do this, Major."

Fedorin pocketed the list with a laugh; a hearty peasant's laugh with a healthy dose of "to hell with the world" in it. "Ah, but Lieutenant-Captain Renko, think of it! It would also put a bug so far up the KGB's arse, they wouldn't know whether to squat or go blind!''

Serafimov was disappointed. Drachev's report laid the blame for the ambush squarely at Grishin's feet, but merely dishonoring the Major was not what he had hoped for. Still, there was one town yet to be investigated, and Kolinsky still had a great deal of territory to cover before it was safely home.

"You will proceed to the last town on your list, Captain. You are authorized to fire on any operative train your unit encounters. Don't worry about disabling or taking prisoners. Shoot to destroy." Even if they didn't find Podgorny's men, they might kill a few Ukrainian rebels.

"I remind you, Revenant, that we have lost two of our tanks with their entire crews, and ten infantry effectives. Should we contact the perpetrators of this 'unauthorized rail activity,' what sort of resistance might we expect?''

Serafimov smiled at the man's cheek, and wondered if his authority in PRG One would eventually extend to execution orders. *Patience*, he told himself.

"Fortunately, Kolinsky, your recent experience should inspire sufficient caution to compensate for your losses. If not, you still have Major Grishin's expertise available to you, yes? Revenant out.''

Serafimov leaned back and turned his chair to the map table. Steinmann sat on the other side of it, watching him with that faint, maddening smile he always wore. *He doesn't think anything is amusing*, Serafimov had decided. *It's just the way he looks. It's the way any reptile looks*.

Serafimov marked the town of Viluk on the map with a green pin, signifying bandit activity, and stifled a smile. *Bandits. God save us, it's right next to the bloody Free Ukrainian Republic.*

There's a whole country *of bandits there now.* He decided he didn't have enough green pins for this.

Checking Viluk's position relative to the other towns on Kolinsky's route, it was unlikely his quarry was in that area at all. This last town, Suschenko, was east of Viluk, even farther from the Alliance forces the Army traitors were presumed to be headed for.

"Not likely your train thieves are there, Colonel." Steinmann voiced Serafimov's own thoughts.

"Perhaps you are right, Major," Serafimov admitted. "What do you suggest?" he asked, putting the responsibility squarely in Steinmann's lap.

Steinmann only smiled, spreading his hands. "Not my field of expertise, Colonel. I am a combat officer, not a security specialist. But since you asked, we have other units to the north. Have Kolinsky bypass Suschenko and rendezvous with them to augment their strength, then stand to. Should we receive any reports of these bandits, our forces will then be centrally located, and can move out rapidly to cut them off. Of course, it's just a suggestion." He restored his smile and folded his arms on the table.

Serafimov picked up the red plastic marker representing Captain Drachev's unit, the code name "Kolinsky" stamped along the top in gold.

A *kolinsky* was a race of Siberian weasel, fast, savage, and utterly ruthless in the hunt. Drachev had earned that code name, if the file Serafimov had seen was accurate. He thought a moment, then placed the marker firmly in Suschenko.

"Captain Drachev will go to Suschenko, I think. It will not delay a rendezvous with forces north by more than a day, and even if he finds nothing, we will at least know where they are not."

And I am covered by my decision to be methodical, Serafimov thought. He caught Steinmann's eye once more, and this time he smiled back.

We are survivors, the smile said. *And if that is rather a hollow compliment, it is still preferable to the alternative.*

Three days had passed since their arrival, and with them the elation of having everything work out right for once; now the fatigue Rostov had almost forgotten was returning with a vengeance. At no time since leaving Moscow had the Lieutenant managed more than a few hours' rest at once, and he was past the point where such catnapping could help him any longer. His temper was fraying, and he was tending toward emotional reactions to unexpected situations.

But it would not be much longer now. When they left, they would have at least eight hours' travel time to the Ukrainian border, and another two hours after that before they could expect to contact any Alliance forces. Rostov was sure he could be spared for at least half of that time.

The men were securing the last of the equipment taken on in Suschenko while the townspeople were carting off the last of the supplies they'd received. *And they are welcome to every dram of it,* he thought. Without the willing help of the people of Suschenko, Rostov was sure the unit would be trapped here. He felt a pang of guilt at leaving these townspeople, his fellow countrymen, to the mercies of the KGB and whatever bandits decided to hit the town in the months to come.

But the KGB had no real reason to harm them; Rostov had left forged papers with Fedorin to show that the Rail Security Forces Colonel had thought Rostov's men cleared by the KGB. And with the extra weapons they were leaving in the town, and the brief training they'd given the citizens in their use, Rostov was sure that the first bandits to hit this town were in for a very unpleasant surprise. *And anyway, I can do little else. We can't very well take them all with us, and they wouldn't go if we could; this is their home.*

Once more he had to remind himself that his first responsibility was to his men. *They will have to survive if Russia is to be free one day.*

Rostov stopped dead in his tracks. *Where the hell had* that *notion come from?* Did he really think he was going to one day return to the *Rodina,* at the head of some reborn Red Army of liberation, like some twenty-first-century Aleksandr Nevsky? He laughed at himself; he really would have to get some sleep. He was starting to hallucinate.

"Lieutenant Rostov." Private Ulyarin was standing before him, saluting with one hand and holding out a message with the other. Rostov returned the salute, amazed he had the energy to lift his arm, and took the message. He scanned it briefly, alarmed at its content.

"Did Colonel Fedorin give you this himself, Ulyarin?"

"Yes, sir. He said I was to bring it to you immediately."

Rostov read it again. It was an officially worded "request" to attend a special meeting in Fedorin's office, and it required him to bring several of his men with him.

The list was six names long, and Rostov had no idea what to make of it. If Fedorin wanted to betray him, this list would put Rostov and all his best men in the same room together, where one man with an assault rifle could end any hope of escape to the West for the unit. Rostov crushed the envelope and handed the note to Ulyarin.

"Take this list, Private Ulyarin, and have the people on it meet me in the command car. That includes you, by the way."

Ulyarin blinked. "I'm sorry, sir, but Major Fedorin instructed— ordered me, that is, sir—to bring you directly back. He said the other people on the list were already in attendance."

Ordered? Fedorin was asserting his rank a little late in the day, it seemed to Rostov. He wondered if following protocol and deferring to the Rail Security officer's paper rank hadn't been a mistake after all.

"All right then, Private, let's get this over with." He thought a moment, then added: "Bring your weapon."

Ulyarin was instantly alert. He personally considered Fedorin one of the most harmless men he had ever met, but if the Lieutenant thought caution was warranted, then Ulyarin would be cautious.

Rostov stepped up onto the platform with Ulyarin. Two of Fedorin's reservists waited beside the station house entrance in full uniforms; clean, if a little worn. Both saluted Rostov smartly as he arrived.

Rostov returned the salute, feeling foolish. They opened the door for him, ushering him and Ulyarin into the office.

Rostov was seized with a sense of unreality. Fedorin was seated behind his desk with the remaining two officers of his command. All were in full-dress uniform. On the wall behind them was draped a shiny new flag of the Soviet Union, sharply creased with fold lines acquired during long months in a storage box. The crimson silk shone, the golden hammer and sickle and open star gleamed.

"Lieutenant Rostov. Private Ulyarin." The Rail Security officer at the door announced them and left. Rostov looked around to see that Sergeant Zorin was already there, along with Corporals Dyatlov and Aliyev, and Junior Sergeant Myakov, their chief mechanic. Still confused, Rostov came to attention and saluted.

What the devil is all this? Were these three old men going to place them under arrest? If so, they must be quite ready to leave this life, for Rostov had no doubts about his unit's ability to handle a few old reservists and some armed townspeople. After a moment, he found his voice.

"Colonel Fedorin, I have a great many final preparations to make before we can leave Suschenko; may I ask what this is all about?"

He tried to catch Zorin's eye, but the burly Sergeant was staring straight ahead, in parade-ground attention that would please a martinet. *Fine time to start that*, Rostov thought.

"Certainly, Lieutenant. As you know, since the integration of all Soviet Defense Forces, we in Rail Security hold equal rank with all other ground force personnel, with equal privileges and equal authority." He stood up from behind the desk and walked around it to stand before Rostov. Fedorin waited a moment before he spoke again. "You will come to attention, please. *Now*!"

Rostov couldn't help himself. Automatically his right foot swung out and back, slamming the heel into the floor next to his left. Simultaneously he snapped his hand to the brim of his cap; his back straightened and his eyes locked on the opposite wall.

Fedorin seemed taken aback at first, then pleased. A moment later he had removed Rostov's shoulder boards with their three stars of a Senior Lieutenant, and replaced them with the white, four-starred boards of a full Captain of Engineers of the Red Army. As Fedorin grasped his shoulders and performed the traditional Russian accolade, Rostov's sense of unreality became complete.

"*Kapitan* Rostov, it is my duty and my pleasure to present you and your men with the promotions which you so richly deserve. The Soviet State, no less than the town of Suschenko, is indebted to you for your skill regarding, and devotion to, your command, your duty, and your nation."

Fedorin repeated the procedure with each of Rostov's men

present, making Ulyarin a Corporal, Dyatlov and Aliyev full Sergeants, and Myakov a Senior Sergeant. Zorin had stepped back as the promotions were being proffered, and seemed unaware of Fedorin's approach.

"Senior Sergeant Zorin, it is always a pleasure to elevate an enlisted man to the rank of officer."

Zorin, who had evidently hoped to avoid just what was about to occur, was obviously uncomfortable, if not outright horrified. "But, Major Fedorin, I—"

"Congratulations, Zorin," Rostov put in quickly; Fedorin performed the ritual, and Rostov immediately stepped in to bestow his own congratulatory embrace. "Allow me to be the first—" He looked Zorin square in the eye and glared at him in satisfaction. *Lieutenant* Zorin."

For once, Rostov had seen Zorin surprised, and the taste was so sweet he forgot his own discomfort at the absurdity of the situation. He wondered how readily Fedorin would have given these field promotions if he had known Rostov and all his men would soon be permanently resigning from the Soviet Armed Forces. The safety of his men was Rostov's first concern, but the feeling that he was winking at treason made him distinctly uneasy.

Ulyarin, newly a Corporal, couldn't have looked happier if he'd been made a Marshal of the Soviet Union. A moment later, Fedorin's men entered with bottles of vodka, several townspeople crowded in with trays of food, and Fedorin pressed Rostov and his newly promoted men to join them in celebration.

Rostov was hungry enough, but tired as he was, the vodka would have to wait. Fedorin took no offense, seeming to enjoy what he thought was a fine jest he had perpetrated on Rostov, and especially on the former *Starshi Serzhant* Zorin.

Seeing his comrade-in-arms standing dejectedly in a corner, staring into a glass of vodka, Rostov almost felt sorry for him, but he was struck by a sudden suspicion, and decided to fight his way across the crowded room to his new Lieutenant.

"Oh. Hello, Alek—hello, Captain."

"Enough of that. Anyway, you're an officer now, too," Rostov pointed out, twisting the blade. "You can use my Christian name as much as you like and not go on report for it."

175

Zorin remained gloomy. "Hm. Of course, now it won't be as much fun because of that."

"No doubt. Well, look on the bright side."

"Sir?" Zorin grimaced and shook his head as if to clear it of cobwebs. "I mean, Aleksei."

Rostov favored him with an icy smile. "Whoever stole Colonel Podgorny's promotion list did you a favor. At least now when we're caught, you won't be sent to some filthy Gulag." He threw a comradely arm about Zorin's shoulders. "You'll be shot with me, like a proper officer."

The citizens of Suschenko had lined the tracks to bid them farewell. Up in the roof hatch of the locomotive, Rostov waved along with the rest of his men to the crowds on the platform. The air was chill, but he still doubted he could stay awake if he weren't standing up.

He looked for the *babushka* and her little helper, but they were nowhere in sight. Well, no doubt he would see them on the way out. He checked on those of his troops in sight. Most were settled into their watch stations along the train, secure behind newly reinforced walls of passenger cars, or inside firing pits made from steel sheets and welded to the flatcars.

This time, he thought, *we'll be a little better prepared if we run into trouble. We haven't far to go. A few hours to return to the switchback, then west to the Ukraine and the Alliance forces, God willing before the KGB catches up with us.*

The race was truly on again. Tired as Rostov was, he felt he had prepared for most contingencies. Podgorny had always warned him that it was the little things, more often than not, that would defeat you in the end.

The train began backing slowly out of the town. Down the line, around a gentle curve in the track and so just out of Rostov's line of sight, the rearmost car emerged slowly from between the buildings that surrounded them, into the low rays of the late morning sun.

A half mile southeast across the fields, Captain Drachev's jaw dropped in disbelief. Only his training let him keep his field glasses in place as he watched a flatcar emerge from the town of Suschenko.

"A train. Mother of God, it's actually a train."

He waved to Grishin in the turret of the light tank three vehicles away in their line of deployment. "Grishin! It's there! It looks like they're leaving; take your force over to the far side of the town and hit the engine from behind. We'll sweep across this end and lay a crossfire over the tracks."

Grishin acknowledged with a nod and a wave. Seconds later, the four light tanks under his command roared up from their idling power levels and began churning the grassy earth with their treads. Drachev tapped the shoulder of his driver with his foot. "Move out!"

Drachev's tanks swept out to block the escape of the train. He was grinning fiercely. Whoever was on that train was the reason his unit had been given this fool's errand. They had gotten him saddled with Major Grishin, and thus caused the loss of his men and vehicles at Viluk, and Drachev was eager to make them pay.

Corporal Ulyarin had five men with him on the rearmost flatcar, each officially supposed to be scanning the horizon for activity, but most waving goodbye to the townspeople. Newly promoted, however, Ulyarin took his duty seriously, and no sooner had his field of vision cleared the buildings than he saw the clouds of dust in the distance.

Tanks! And heading for the tracks to cut them off.

What happened next was simply bad luck. Corporal Ulyarin snatched his radio microphone up and keyed it several times before he spoke.

"Captain Rostov, this is Ulyarin. I have vehicles on the track, repeat, vehicles on the track, do you read?"

The microphone made no sound when he released the key, and Ulyarin looked down to see what was wrong with it. In his haste, he had pulled the plug completely free from the jack. Cursing, he resecured the plug, aware that precious seconds had been lost.

Drachev's tank was the first to crest the embankment of the railbed. His and another light tank close behind crossed the rails in a bone-jarring lurch, their turrets already swinging about to follow the train as it continued to emerge from between the buildings of Suschenko.

Drachev traced the line of cars back to the cloud of smoke that revealed the position of the engine. They were approaching the town from an angle, and the far end of the train seemed very far back; its length had barely been concealed by the total extent of the town itself and their angle of approach.

We might have passed it, Drachev thought. *We might have decided to breeze past with just a look and missed it completely.*

Drachev's other two tanks remained on the opposite side of the tracks, their experienced crews finding low points in the terrain and putting the vehicles hull-down to any antitank weapons the enemy might have available to use against them.

Meanwhile, the BMP armored personnel carriers were deploying in a semicircle, disgorging troops from the back ramp doors without even slowing down.

Drachev didn't bother to think about just who might be aboard that train. Revenant was part of PRG One; PRG One was the voice of *Novaya Moskva*, and Grishin was the eyes. Thus, PRG One had said to destroy that train, and PRG One was watching.

Drachev was a professional soldier; if he had no love for the KGB that now gave him his commands, it was simply that he had none to spare from the love he gave to his country. The orders came down to him, and he carried them out, hoping that in the long run, the best interests of the *Rodina* were being served by somebody, *anybody*, even the KGB, willing to take the responsibility.

"Gunner, spotting round, center of the tracks. Signal."

Drachev listened to the sound of the plastic-cased shell being fed into the gun, the breech sealing after it.

"Ready, sir."

Drachev gave the order to shoot before the gunner got the second word out.

Rostov heard the radio on his hip squawking. He pulled up the handset in time to hear Ulyarin requesting a confirmation.

"Ulyarin, say again."

"Vehicles have crossed the tracks, Captain Rostov, two on our right side, at least two more on our left. Light tanks, hull down, do you read?"

Rostov's blood chilled. *Tanks*. Only the KGB still had tanks. "Ulyarin, fall back from the flatcars and get under cover, confirm!"

"Yes sir, we—"

Ulyarin's signal was cut off. A cloud of red smoke erupted at the far end of the train.

Spotting round, Rostov realized, and a second later the *crack* of the small shell came back to him. He leaned down to shout to Gyrich and Pilkanis in the control cabin. "Trainman Gyrich, we're under attack; tanks on the rails."

Gyrich seemed at a loss. "We can stop, Lieu—Captain, but . . ."

"To hell with that 'Captain' nonsense! Gyrich, if we stop in this town we're trapped. We've got to get out in the open where the men can deploy. We may have to ram these tanks, though, if they're on the rails."

Gyrich shook his head vigorously. "I wouldn't try it, sir. We've only got flatcars at that end. Too light. A tank could derail the car's wheels."

"How fast can we reverse course?"

Pilkanis scoffed openly. "This is a *train*, Captain Rostov, not a warship."

Rostov had seconds to make a decision, and he knew it. "Well, it is a warship now, Comrades. Gyrich, get us out of here, as fast as you can go, through or over anything in our way!"

Rostov keyed the radio handset: "Zorin! Ulyarin's spotted tanks on the tracks, get back there and help him. Aliyev will meet you with antitank rockets. You coordinate the attack."

His next call had Aliyev racing to tear open crates that had been packed away only days earlier.

Zorin found Corporal Ulyarin beyond help. The spotting round fired by Drachev's gunner had been a direct hit on the firing pit occupied by the Corporal and one of his men. The shell was a smoke round, not meant to do any real damage, but that still made it an explosive incendiary. Ulyarin and the man with him had been killed instantly.

The three other men on the flatbed were deafened by the blast and blinded by the smoke. They stumbled forward to the next flatcar; one fell off the train before Zorin could reach him and was crushed under the wheels. The others he led to the side and jumped with them to the railbed.

Rolling to his feet, Zorin began pounding on the walls of the cars.

"Everybody out of there now! Where's Aliyev?"

"Here, sir!"

"Get an RPG for each man and get your squad out into that grass; those tanks have to be knocked out. And find Dyatlov; have him get some more RPGs to these townspeople in case they break through on our rear."

"You think they've surrounded us, sir?"

"*Christus*, I bloody well would."

Drachev was watching through his field glasses and saw three figures leap to the side of the tracks. He couldn't make out details, but the bandits appeared to be in Army uniforms. Stolen, he supposed, from their previous victims.

"Sons of bitches. Load fléchette. Signal."

"Fléchette, ready."

"Shoot!"

The guns of the LT-200 were light by any armor standards in the world, but they were devastating against opponents with no defense against them. Drachev's tank fired a fléchette round; the proximity-fused shell detonated over the second flatcar, spraying the train with thousands of steel needles. Men with moderate protection were safe, but those exposed died horribly, along with many nearby civilians who had not reached cover.

Drachev raised his field glasses again; the train was accelerating. Perhaps Grishin was attacking the other end by now; Drachev didn't have time to get him on the radio.

"Ready incendiary."

He drummed his fingers impatiently on the hatch rim; incendiary rounds were stored well apart from the other ammunition, in nonflammable gelatin. The gunner needed a few seconds' warning to get one and load the slippery casing into the breech.

Rostov felt like a fool. His men were going into action at the other end of the train, and the curve in the track kept him from even seeing what was going on. All he could do was trust Zorin to deal with it and hope they could get up speed to escape. Many of the people of Suschenko were still on the platforms and sidings where they had been waving goodbye. Now they huddled in panic in whatever cover they could find.

Fedorin was trotting alongside the engine, shouting something

180

up at him. Rostov turned and yelled down at him, waving his arms for emphasis.

"Get under cover; those are KGB tanks out there. We're going to have to fight our way past them and make a run for it. You can't be seen helping us, Fedorin. Get these civilians out of here!" Rostov couldn't be sure the old Major understood him, but the reservists stood for a moment looking up at him, then waved and ran off out of sight. Rostov's radio started pinging again.

"Rostov here, come in."

"Zorin here, Aleksei. Looks like two tanks on each side of the tracks, a crossfire. Probably infantry with them but I can't tell with that grass. Aliyev and I have men moving out with RPG-90s to take out those tanks in the fields. Another squad is taking up positions on the flatcar."

"Can you see Ulyarin's position?"

"Affirmative. Ulyarin's dead, Aleksei; that spotting round, looks like a lucky hit. Smoke is dispersing."

"We're making a run for it, Mikhail. We can't leave any men behind, so either you kill all four tanks or the men will have to catch up with us on foot."

"Understood, sir. Four tanks it is. Zorin out."

Rostov was shaking. He'd been running on willpower for days, the adrenaline rush tasted like a mouthful of old copper pfennigs and it looked like there was to be no end to it, ever.

A civilian was shouting to him from the platform below. He turned and felt something tug at his sleeve. The shouting became a scream: "Get down!"

Rostov's arm felt wet, then numb. He turned completely around to look toward the front of the train.

A light tank was sitting squarely astride the tracks, firing the machine gun in its turret. Rostov instinctively dropped down the hatch, falling eight feet to the control cabin floor. A moment later the open hatch above him rang like a bell with the impact of half a dozen bullets.

"You're hit, Rostov," Pilkanis shouted.

Rostov saw a hole in the sleeve covering his numb left arm, pain blossoming around it more quickly than the red stain just above his elbow. Blood began threading over his fingers to drip onto the grating of the engine's oily floor.

"We have light tanks front and rear." Looking up at the hatch, Rostov saw his radio dangling from a locking lever in the hatch. "Keep up the speed, Gyrich. I need to get my radio."

But by the time he got to his feet, he saw Pilkanis was already risking himself to fire to detach the radio, then drop down the ladder amid another hail of bullets.

The big Lithuanian conscript rose from the floor and handed Rostov the radio. "It must have caught on the hatch when you fell." Adjusting his spectacles, Pilkanis went back to the locomotive's controls.

Rostov keyed the microphone again. "Sergeant Dyatlov."

The reply was instantaneous. "Dyatlov standing by, Captain. I have twelve men, each armed with an RPG-90."

Bless you, Colonel Podgorny, and your damnable list. "We have tanks in the town, attacking the engine, Sergeant."

"Understood. Dyatlov out."

The numbness in his arm was gone, and Rostov's concentration was disintegrating as the pain took hold. Pilkanis had produced a knife and removed the sleeve, wrapping the wounded arm with the makeshift bandage while Rostov was still speaking to Dyatlov. Without a word, Pilkanis secured the dressing and returned to his work station.

"I've got to see what's going on," Rostov told Gyrich. "There are wind plates at the sides and front of this locomotive; how thick are they?"

"Almost two centimeters, Captain," Gyrich told him.

Rostov had seen some of the light tanks up close; they were built for speed and ease of maintenance. They wouldn't have more than 7.62-millimeter mounts for machine guns. *Two centimeters might be proof against a coaxial machine gun*, Rostov thought. He would never dare to hope that much metal would turn an armor piercing round.

Rostov picked up his weapons belt. A sidearm and four grenades. Well, he wasn't going out there to fight, anyway. But he might be able to discourage anyone who tried to board.

"Captain, I can vent some steam forward if you think it might help. Could blind them," Gyrich suggested.

"Better still," Rostov said, "it should play hob with their thermal imaging sights. Do it. It probably won't keep them from

182

hitting the train, but it might give some cover to Dyatlov and his men. I'm going outside." He called back as he went through the door, "You have weapons in here. Don't hesitate to use them on anybody you don't recognize."

Gyrich nodded and threw a lever. From outside came a dragon's roar, and the tank on the tracks was engulfed in roiling white clouds of steam. He looked over to Pilkanis, who was picking up an assault rifle.

"Incendiary ready."

Drachev was about to give the fire order when he saw a white cloud erupt over the low roofs of Suschenko. The roar of escaping steam reached him a moment later.

"Hold your fire. Grishin's tanks must have pierced the boiler of the locomotive. Get him on the radio for confirmation, but start moving in for close assault, anyway. Nobody gets out of Suschenko; pass the word."

Drachev's driver opened the throttle to lead the other three tanks and their accompanying infantry forward.

It was Drachev's only serious tactical error committed in battle in three years; a splendid record. Considering his unfamiliarity with locomotives, it was a perfectly understandable mistake, at that.

Sergeant Aliyev had thoroughly enjoyed his promotion. He hadn't expected to have to use his rank so soon but, as Captain Wrenn had said, "Those were the breaks." He wasn't sure what it meant, but it sounded appropriate.

Aliyev took four men and advanced along a gully. When he saw movement on the other side, they froze, and a moment later one of the light tanks appeared. They were leaving their crossfire positions to move in on the train.

Aliyev signaled to Private Dolin, who tucked an RPG to his shoulder and fired in one smooth motion.

The rocket disappeared into the grass on the other side of the gully, just ahead of the advancing tank. An instant later the turret of the tank shot straight up into the air, followed by flames and a dark shape that might have been a body.

Small-arms fire erupted from the opposite side of the gully, but

Aliyev and his men were already gone, falling back even as Dolin had fired.

One down, three to go, Aliyev thought. Much as he hated to do it, he had to ignore the enemy infantry for now. These tanks could destroy the train, and that made eliminating them the first priority. Once they were gone, the odds would be even.

On the opposite side of the tracks from Aliyev, Zorin watched the tanks heading for the train and blessed his luck. He swept his own force wide around and to the rear of the advancing armor, spotting several groups of support infantry without revealing his own unit's presence. Zorin saw a tank brew up, heard answering fire, and knew Aliyev was on the job.

Zorin's maneuvering was almost casual. The turret backs of the tanks were clearly visible, and he even caught glimpses of the backs of the KGB infantry in the tall grass. All were shooting as they advanced, pouring assault fire into the area from which Aliyev had attacked. Uselessly, Zorin knew, for he was sure Aliyev was long gone.

Zorin looked again at the backs of the advancing KGB troops before him. *They should let their comrades on the other side of the tracks take care of themselves*, he thought. These fellows were about to have troubles of their own.

He almost felt sorry for them as he raised his rifle.

When the cloud of steam poured out at them, Grishin had panicked. He had deliberately kept the nature of the bandits a secret from Drachev, so as not to try the man's loyalty until battle was joined. But Grishin knew he was up against Combat Engineers, and he was positive the white clouds billowing toward him could be only one thing.

"Gas!" he shouted, fumbling to seal the air intakes on the turret. "Secure for gas!" At that, the tank crew panicked as well. They'd been hunting bandits for some time now, and they'd never run into any with chemical weapons. Out of practice, they fumbled about in the tiny vehicle for masks and the hatch seal switches, and the tank's effectiveness was reduced to zero.

Blinded by the harmless steam, the tank that had been following up their advance crashed into them from behind and threw a thread.

Grishin felt the impact from behind and took it for an attack. "Turret about, AP, fire!" The confusion became absolute.

Rostov couldn't be sure what was happening in the cloud of steam behind them. He saw Corporal Dyatlov and several men running alongside the engine, using the steam as cover to close with the tanks. Dyatlov stopped when he caught sight of Rostov.

"Captain Rostov!" Dyatlov fairly flew up a ladder to Rostov's side. "Sir, you've been hit. Let me get you back to Comrade Surgeon Blaustein."

Rostov was about to reply when one tank on the tracks fired point-blank at the tank behind it—and missed.

"I don't know what's going on out there, Dyatlov, but I think you'd better deal with them first. I'll be all right."

Dyatlov hesitated, then jumped back down to the railbed and disappeared into the dissipating cloud of steam.

Colonel Fedorin sat on a roof overlooking the tracks, looking much as he had when he first met Sergeant Zorin, in half-buttoned pants with suspenders and an undershirt. On the roof across from him were two more of his Rail Security staff. All were armed with two antitank rockets apiece.

It had been a long time since Fedorin had fired a weapon. Sometimes he told himself that the harsh realities of combat in his youth had become the romantic memories of a fat old pencil pusher. Still, he felt now as he remembered feeling then: alive, vital, proud of his past, unsure of his future, but certain of his present. He was in uniform, doing his duty for people who depended upon him.

Fedorin was a simple man, with limited visions of what was important in life. Mostly, he was practical. His bones told him a hard winter was coming, and the fuel which Rostov's men had treated with Immunizer would be crucial to Suschenko if any of her people were to be alive in the spring. He did not expect much help to be forthcoming from the Party.

The building on which his men across the rails were positioned held most of that fuel, and all of them were determined to defend it. The townspeople had seen four tanks approaching this end of Suschenko; two had gone after the engine, one was bringing up the

185

rear. Fedorin didn't see the fourth, but he was sure it would be along any minute now. Still, he was getting a little bored.

He signaled his comrades on the other roof and picked up one of his RPGs. Taking careful aim, he fired at the forward glacis plate of the tank. The rocket went straight into the ground ahead of the tank and detonated, tearing up the side of the roadbed, doing little damage to the ties and rails but sending gravel flying everywhere.

Fedorin frowned. *Potent little devil*, he thought. He threw away the empty firing tube and picked up the second RPG. Below him the tank's turret swiveled to point its gun at the building his comrades were sitting on, the building holding the rest of Suschenko's fuel.

Fedorin pressed the firing button at the same time as his fellow reservists; three rockets lanced downward, just as the tank's main gun fired.

The tank was killed three times over, but its own damage had been done. The building beneath Fedorin's men erupted, rising dozens of feet into the air to disintegrate in a ball of orange fire. Debris showered down on him, and a monstrous column of black smoke and flame climbed skyward. Horrified, Fedorin tried to convince himself his men never knew what hit them.

Christus, Rostov breathed. *What in the name of God was that*? He had just seen a small building take off like a rocket. *What are these tanks carrying for ammunition*?

Two more explosions, closer but less severe, followed in quick succession. Rostov's radio signal chimed again, and he held it tight against his ear, shouting in response.

"Rostov here, come in."

"Dyatlov, Captain. Two tanks closest to train knocked out. Rail Security on the roofs just took out a third with RPGs." Dyatlov couldn't keep the admiration from his voice.

"Continue sweep. See if those reservists got a count of enemy vehicles at that end of town."

"Already done, sir. Reservists reported four vehicles sighted that end, leaving one unaccounted for."

"Find that tank, Dyatlov. Sweep to the left of the train." Rostov's voice was grim. "And find out what the hell that explosion was a minute ago. It sounded like somebody hit an ammo dump.''

"Yes, sir. Dyatlov out."

Rostov saw movement between two buildings. The train was picking up speed, and the engine itself had only a few more buildings to pass before exiting the town. Rostov watched, waiting for another gap between buildings, then saw it. The fourth tank was pacing the locomotive, its turret trained toward where the engine must soon appear, waiting only for a clear shot.

It was to the right side of them, and he'd just sent Dyatlov and his men to the left.

Without another thought, Rostov jumped down to the loading platform, his momentum carrying him through the alley.

He keyed the handset microphone as he ran, signaling Zorin or Dyatlov. There was no reply; the buildings or the train might be blocking the signal, and in any case they probably had their hands full already.

Rostov saw the tank swing wide to avoid a well-housing, then turn in toward the buildings again. The maneuver allowed him to gain a few yards on it, and by the time the tank had reached the buildings again, he was alongside.

Rostov ducked into a shadow as the tank approached, then jumped onto the back plates over the engine. He recalled that the top surfaces of the light tanks were composed almost entirely of fiberglass. With no enemy airpower to concern them, the designers had been able to make certain reasonable sacrifices. But the metal exhaust grates were still hot enough to fry eggs on, and Rostov remembered that these tanks were powered by alcohol-fired steam engines with a lot of venting requirements.

Apparently the crew inside had not heard him as he scrambled for a grip on the smooth surface. He looked out over the turret, and could see two more tanks burning in the fields outside of town. Those were Zorin's concern, however. Right now he had problems of his own.

Rostov got to one knee and pulled himself halfway up onto the turret top. The vision cupola around the hatch showed blurry movement within; he found himself staring at the back of someone's head.

The next moment the tank lurched to a halt, sending Rostov sliding away from the cupola, grasping frantically at the access rungs bolted to the turret's rear. He saw the bulk of the locomotive clear the buildings, exposed, unmissable.

I have lost the race after all, he thought. Then the tank's main gun went off.

Drachev's rage at the supposed bandits had disappeared, replaced by a cold fury at that bastard, Grishin; and Revenant, and Major-Bloody-Steinmann, and PRG One and all of *Novaya Moskva* as well. There were too many Army uniforms for them all to have been stolen. He and his men were fighting—killing and being killed by—soldiers of the Red Army. *Countrymen!* He might almost have surrendered, but he was in a killing mood.

Grishin had apparently managed to get his entire force wiped out. Drachev himself had only his own and one other tank left, and his support infantry were being chewed up by enemies in the grasses around them.

To hell with this, he thought grimly. He had had quite enough. He began firing smoke rounds from the point defense mortars on the outside of the turret to cover the infantry's retreat. Once regrouped with the BMPs, he could get them all out of here.

As to what the penalty for his failure might be, Drachev did not even need to guess. At least his own life might purchase survival for the rest of the men in his command.

"What's in the breech?" he asked his gunner.

"Incendiary." The man was squinting into the sights of the coaxial machine gun, firing controlled five-round bursts meant to keep the unseen attackers' heads down. He couldn't know it, but it was working very well, indeed.

"Get rid of it. Put it into those first boxcars; that will slow the bastards down. They won't fight us if they have to save their transport." *I hope*, he added silently.

The gunner took ten seconds to adjust the light tank's gun, then fired. The shell arched out over the grasses, hitting the first boxcar dead center.

"*Christus!*" Drachev grunted, watching the shot through the turret periscope. "Hell of a hip shot, Gunner."

"*Spaceeba*, Captain Drachev."

"Reload with high explosive. Depress the gun and get an angle on the railbed; I want to tear up these tracks. Driver, get us out of here." Drachev switched channels and issued the fallback order, scanning with the turret periscope as he did so, searching the tall grass in vain for the enemy. An enemy who wore a uniform almost identical to his own.

"Sir," the driver asked, "we're breaking off the attack?"

He was very young, Drachev remembered, and had spent a great deal of time around Grishin in the last week. Too much time, evidently. The Captain responded almost kindly.

"No, lad. We're running away. Now move, quickly. *Skorei!*"

The driver engaged the clutch, and the tank began to pick up speed.

Zorin and his men heard the tank's machine gun fall silent. *If it's a feint, we're dead*, he thought. But seconds later, the main gun fired, and immediately the tank began backing up, the turret shifting position once more, the main gun lowering. Zorin seized the chance. "Close assault, move!"

The tank was beginning to outrun them when suddenly it fired on the move; Zorin's men instinctively dropped to the ground. Gouts of rich, black Russian soil flew into the air, pelting Zorin and his men with clods of the dark *chernozam*, and smoke from the explosion obscuring the tank.

A bar of black metal fifteen centimeters long plopped into the dirt directly in front of him, and Zorin reached out through the smoke to pick it up. He brought it close to his eyes and cursed when he found himself looking at a railroad spike.

"Get that tank, knock it out, *now*." Zorin scrambled to his feet and led the assault.

The first of the Combat Engineers with Zorin reached the tank as the main gun fired again. The shock wave rattled the man's teeth, but he dropped into a kneeling position and fired the RPG even as the tank began to move again. The tall grasses were rising to obscure the tank as it moved away from him, and the rocket motor of the antitank round burned a smoking trail through the brown sheaves.

189

The rocket hit the right front quarter and detonated, blowing the track off the drive wheel, opening the engine compartment, and igniting the interior. The tank made a half-turn on the momentum of its remaining track and stopped, hissing and shrieking like a dying horse.

Zorin closed with the tank, leaping over a section of track it had destroyed with its two point-blank shots of high explosive. The railbed was demolished for ten meters. Cursing, he reached the burning AFV in time to see both the turret hatch and a front escape hatch open simultaneously. He was ready to shoot the man exiting the turret, but the one from the hull got out first.

The man's clothes burned fiercely, engulfing him, and trailing flames as he leapt from the tank to run aimlessly through grass that ignited with his passing. He stopped moving for a moment, trying perhaps to get his bearings, although he didn't stop screaming. Zorin took careful aim and shot him through the head. That ended the screams, but wouldn't put out the fire, and he sent two men to beat it out with their coats.

By then the commander was out of the turret hatch, trying to pull a third crewman after him.

The man straddling the turret hatch was dark and strong-looking, his bearded face and tattered uniform covered with blood. He was shouting encouragement to the man beneath him as he tried to pull him out. Zorin, like his men, stood aiming at the tanker, but none of them could bring himself to fire.

Finally, with a tremendous effort, the tanker heaved his gunner's body out of the hatch. There was nothing left of the man below the hips, and he was obviously quite dead. The tank commander fell over backward onto the front of his vehicle, and Zorin walked around the side to finish him.

Captain Drachev saw the big man in the Army greatcoat standing a few feet away, aiming a rifle at him. Drachev pushed himself up to one knee, feeling for his sidearm. He had blood in his eyes, and had to paw the holster flap several times before he got it open. The big man watched him over his rifle's sights.

Drachev got the pistol out of the holster and pulled the slide back with blood-slick fingers. Before he could raise it to fire, he fell off the tank into the tall grass.

190

Zorin kicked the pistol away and turned the man over with his boot. The trooper who'd killed the tank approached him, still holding the empty rocket tube.

"Sergeant—I mean Lieutenant, there is still one more tank, and all those infantry are still about."

"Throw that thing away"—Zorin pointed to the rocket launcher in the soldier's hand—"and help me move him away from the tank so his men can find him."

"I thought he was dead."

Zorin looked down at the soldier; likely it was a very good man lying at his feet. He was glad he didn't have to shoot him.

"No. Not yet. That will come after he reports what happened here today. Come on, grab his feet, that tank's ammo might cook off any second." He looked back toward the town to see what damage the train had suffered.

"*Christus.*" The train was on fire.

Rostov's wound was bleeding merrily, but he held his grip. He saw a puff of smoke on the fields, then a boxcar was engulfed in flames. A moment later there was an explosion in the field as a third tank was killed, and Rostov saw another beating a hasty retreat from the tracks.

That's the fourth tank out there; this is he last one! He would be a lot happier once he thought of something to do with that knowledge. The shot just fired by this tank seemed to have had no effect. He could hear the commander inside shouting orders to his crew, preparing to fire again. Pulling himself back up to the turret, Rostov knelt on the exhaust grating, the threadbare knees of his trousers offering little protection from the heat. He freed the sidearm and one grenade from his weapons belt, and seeing the gun begin to shift, he summoned his remaining strength and pushed himself up to the vision cupola.

Rostov put his face up to the ten-centimeter-square viewplate and found himself looking at the commander's profile. The glass was meant to be too small a target to hit, or at best serve as some protection against shrapnel. He didn't think it was bulletproof; he put the barrel of his own Makarov against it and fired.

He was right. The 9mm round pierced the glass and continued

191

through the commander's cheeks, taking most of his back teeth with it and shattering his jaw.

The wound alone wasn't fatal, but the commander's next action was. The man popped the hatch and stood up, waving his own sidearm and roaring in pain. Rostov shot him in the chest, the impact of the heavy slug carrying the tanker out of the turret and over the side. Within the tank, the gunner and the driver scrambled respectively for a weapon and an escape hatch. Ignoring the grenade he still held, Rostov aimed and fired twice at each man, feeling uneasily as if he were shooting at fish in a barrel.

A few more shots were heard from the plain, but except for the crackling of the burning boxcar, it had suddenly become very quiet. Then Rostov heard the cheering.

He looked up to see Dyatlov and his squad, most grinning incredulously, stabbing their rifles into the air. One man cupped his hands around his mouth and yelled: *"Ourrah! Ourrah pobieda! Ourrah, Ilya Muromets!"*

At the name of the dragon-slaying folk hero, Rostov felt ridiculous. *It was just a tank*, he thought stupidly. Then he grinned and waved a bloody arm.

"We've a fire on our hands, Dyatlov. There's a boxcar that needs dousing, let's get to it."

Dyatlov stepped up to the tank to help him down. Rostov passed out before his feet hit the ground.

Rostov opened his eyes to see Blaustein and Wrenn standing over him. He realized he was pinned to the desk in the command car while the surgeon inspected the wound in his arm.

Blaustein was speaking to Wrenn about his handiwork. "Clean wound. Moderate-sized round, jacketed; passed through the meaty part of the triceps—here, see?" He tapped the skin around the bullet hole, ignoring Rostov's undiluted howl. "Good thing it wasn't a lead slug. Those are messy. Likely would have taken the arm right off."

Rostov caught his breath and began roundly cursing Blaustein, who ignored him as he finished dressing the wound with a fresh bandage. When he was done, he helped Rostov to sit up.

"Get up, Captain. I'm not an osteopath, and I don't want you sleeping on this desk. Bullet holes, I can fix, but bad backs, you are on your own. And now I have to see to some other patients." The surgeon gathered up the sheet he'd thrown over Rostov's desk and left the command car.

"What's going on? How long have I been asleep?"

"You weren't asleep, you were unconscious," Wrenn told him. "About four hours. The fires are out, and it looks like the bad guys are gone for now. Zorin has scouts trailing them; they've got a dozen or so APCs and one tank left. They're heading northeast and they aren't slowing down."

Rostov nodded, fumbling with his canteen. "I should be out there . . ."

Wrenn helped him with the canteen, holding it to Rostov's lips for three all too brief swallows. "Yes, well, you were doing such a good job of bleeding to death that we didn't see any point in interrupting you."

"How badly were we hit?"

Wrenn capped the canteen. "Nine men wounded, two more blinded from being too close to a spotter round when it went off; Blaustein isn't sure if it's permanent or not. And two dead, including Corporal Ulyarin. About a dozen of the townspeople killed and twice that many wounded when a fléchette round hit the platform—" He caught the look in Rostov's eyes and quickly added: "Not your *babushka*, nor her granddaughter, either."

Rostov wanted to laugh and weep at the same time, and he was afraid he was far too tired to control his emotions for much longer. He changed the subject. "All right. It could have been much worse. Materials?"

"We lost a boxcar full of lumber to fire. Gyrich says with a little work, we'll have a new flatcar. Then there's the track. Zorin says the last tank out in the fields tore up a lot of it with a couple of high-explosive rounds. We won't be going out of Suschenko the way we came in."

Rostov could accept that; the KGB was probably swarming up that line by now, anyway.

Wrenn paused a moment before going on. "But the real problem isn't anything that's happened to us."

"How is that again?"

Wrenn took a deep breath before answering. "You'd better see this for yourself."

Colonel Fedorin sat at the edge of the platform, his hands draped over his knees, staring at the smoldering remains of a building. He looked up as Rostov and Zorin approached him; Wrenn had begged off meeting the Rail Security Colonel, claiming Blaustein needed him to help with first aid.

"Ah. Hello, Captain Rostov."

"Colonel Fedorin. I don't know what to say; we had no wish to bring our misfortune down on you and your people."

Fedorin shrugged. "Every stick has two ends. You needed help; you gave it in return. Before you came, we had not counted on being able to use the fuel, anyway." His voice trailed off.

Rostov looked around at the town of Suschenko, until this morning relatively unscathed by the war. Even now, only one building had been lost. But it was the one building the people had needed most. *Except perhaps for the church*, he thought.

"Lieutenant Zorin. Fetch Aliyev and Dyatlov. Have them get their men to work unloading the fuel we took on board."

Zorin only raised an eyebrow, then nodded. "At once, sir."

Fedorin stared up at him, shaking his head. "You can't, Captain. Those were KGB tanks; it's obvious that you are running from them for some reason. They will stop at nothing to capture you, and you have lost a great deal of time already." The old reservist got to his feet.

"We can use old petrol," Fedorin insisted. "Even contaminated, it will burn after a fashion. Not to run engines, but we can make cooking fires, boil water. Please, Captain, keep the fuel. Without it they will catch you and kill you, all of you."

Rostov shook his head. "And so we take it, and by spring the people of this village are cooking food over fire pits, reduced to living like savages. And perhaps we escape, and perhaps the KGB catches us, anyway, and then *they* have the fuel. No, Comrade Colonel. We strip Suschenko of its means of survival only at the cost of our souls. But on behalf of my men, I thank you."

Rostov saluted and returned to the command car.

The men who had become Rostov's *de facto* staff had reassembled in the command car. The room had been designed for holding audiences, not meetings, and the desk had to be pulled to the center to make room for extra chairs around it. Gyrich and Pilkanis sat together, as did Wrenn and Blaustein. Zorin was off to one side, and Rostov stood by the plywood paneling that still covered the broken window.

Right back where we started, Rostov thought.

No one had commented on his decision to return the fuel. No one had to, nor would it have made any difference. He stared at the pile of railroad maps as he spoke.

"Comrade Gyrich, how far can we go on the fuel we have remaining?"

Gyrich rubbed his chin. "Perhaps another three hundred kilometers. No more."

"But three hundred kilometers to where?" Pilkanis asked quietly. "The track behind us has been destroyed. By the time we can even *find* another route west, the last of our fuel will be used up."

Rostov took a deep breath and folded his arms. Damn the KGB light tanks; how the Regular Army had laughed at the ridiculous little steam-powered vehicles when they'd first seen them. Nobody would laugh at them again. Rostov leaned back against the plywood, rubbing his forehead. KGB tanks and fuel.

He turned and looked at the wood. "Sergeant Zorin, the fire destroyed a boxcar of lumber, yes? How much is still left?"

"Eh?" Zorin was surprised by this new tack. "I'm not sure, Aleksei; a couple more cars full, at least."

Rostov pulled the chair out and sat at the desk, gathered up paper and pencil, and began making calculations as he spoke.

"How hot does your boiler have to be, Comrade Gyrich?"

Gyrich and Pilkanis shared puzzled looks; the younger man turned back to Rostov. "Well. As Comrade Gyrich said, it's more a question of pressure, Lieutenant. As long as we don't need any spectacular bursts of speed or power, these P-38s can do fine on their operating standard of two hundred thirteen psi—that's pounds per—"

Rostov cut him off with a grin. "Yes. I know."

Rostov worked in silence for a few minutes, revising and correcting equations frequently. When he was finally satisfied, he looked up from his calculations. "Sergeant Zorin, have the men draw off all the fresh water into canteens and drums. Then have the water purifier converted to simple distillation; the way we had it for that batch of vodka Colonel Podgorny commissioned last Easter.''

Zorin nodded, hiding his puzzlement. Part of his value as an NCO rested with rarely being surprised at anything an officer did. But he had to admit, if only to himself, that this time Rostov had lost him.

"Excuse me, Lieutenant." It was Pilkanis again, and he didn't bother to hide the contempt in his tone. "But are you suggesting we drown our grief in revelry? We need *fuel* . . . we can't run a locomotive on vodka—" No sooner had the words passed his lips than it dawned on him.

Rostov nodded. "But we can, Trainman Pilkanis. Or not vodka, exactly. Methanol.''

Gyrich frowned. "Perhaps. I remember much research when I was young, into alternate fuels. Alcohol mixtures showed great promise, but weren't pursued." The old man shrugged. "There was always oil.''

"How will we alter the fuel feed systems of the engine itself?" Pilkanis asked. "They are designed for diesel.''

"Indeed they are," Rostov said. "And while I'm no expert on locomotives, I do know something about tanks. Those KGB light tanks are steam-powered, with alcohol-fired boilers. If the designers followed the pattern set by the State War Production Committee, they will be of standardized, modular construction.''

Pilkanis' eyes widened, first in surprise, then in pleasure. "And we can cannibalize their fuel feed systems to replace the diesel ones in the locomotive.''

Rostov smiled. "From what I have seen in the last few days, Comrade Pilkanis, if anyone can, it is you and Comrade Gyrich and your crew of trainmen.''

Gyrich nodded thoughtfully, his mind already grappling with the problems. He looked up at Rostov. "I think it can be done, Captain Rostov. I won't know for sure until I've seen the assemblies from those tanks, but even so . . . yes, it's possible.''

"Alcohol will burn cooler than diesel," Rostov added. "Will that be a problem?''

"I don't know. Still, you must have at least one decent chemist in your unit who can help with any difficulties we encounter with the new fuel.''

Rostov admitted that was true. The unit was comprised of survivors from every branch of combat engineering—demolition, construction, chemical—and a good many other fields as well. The odds were good that the necessary skills were available.

"Then let's get to work."

It took Gyrich and Pilkanis twenty minutes to decide how to use the parts taken from the KGB light tanks. Of the seven vehicles destroyed or disabled, five had usable fuel assemblies.

"Aren't they a little small for our purposes?" Wrenn asked when he saw them.

Pilkanis shook his head. "There are ways around that, Comrade Captain. We only need four; the fifth I can use as a model in the town machine shop for altering the locomotive's original assemblies; or even making new ones." The young trainman's mind was already racing over alternatives; he was in his element, and it showed.

"The damaged stretch of line is a different matter," Gyrich told Rostov. "The rail and ties we could replace, but the railbed is completely undermined. It would take a week to repack it and lay in new gravel, ties, and track."

Through it all, Wrenn kept his eye on Rostov. The young Russian's reserves of energy seemed boundless, but Wrenn knew that was an illusion.

Hang in there, my young Russian friend, Wrenn thought. *Because this is it. Your first real taste of command. When you have reached the limit of your endurance and abilities. When you're out of time, out of ideas, and out of luck, and still everyone's life depends on you. It's not how you got here that matters; it's what you do* now *that you've arrived.*

"We'll have to switch back again," Rostov said quietly, staring once again at the maps on the desk before him. With all his heart he wanted only to put his head on that desk and close his eyes. But he had been trained too well for that.

"All right, then," Rostov said. "We switch back. It might even help us avoid the KGB for a while, if they think we've headed directly west."

"What about the Islamic Nationalists to the south?" Wrenn asked. "Or the Turks?"

197

Rostov shook his head. "One problem at a time, I think, Captain, yes? We are going to have to find more stocks of uncontaminated fuel, to guard against any serious problems with the alcohol mixture. It may not be more than a temporary solution to our difficulties." He looked up at the American. "I'm afraid that you, like Comrades Gyrich and Pilkanis and their staff, are going to be with us for a little while longer."

Wrenn smiled, holding up his bandaged hand. "I don't know how much more fun I can stand, Captain Rostov."

By that afternoon, they had returned all the drums of immunized diesel to the people of Suschenko. Major Fedorin watched the process with tear-filled eyes.

"It is not fair," he said. "You have already done so much for us. You need it more than we do."

Rostov shook his head. "Perhaps we will find more along the way, Colonel. We will manage."

Fedorin was still bewildered by the whole disaster. "But Captain Rostov, what are we to do? Should we wait here, for someone from . . ." His voice trailed off.

Rostov looked at him for a long time before he spoke. Every Russian's deepest fear was of anarchy; most had suffered from it at one time or another. It was a national phobia so great that in order to avoid it, her people had been willing to suffer even a government like the one the Alliance had sworn to destroy.

"There won't be anybody else, Colonel. A few KGB perhaps. Those PRGs you told me about, be careful of them. Bandits almost certainly. But you have weapons now. And Suschenko still has a few young men. They will get older. Take care of what material you have and make what you don't have." Rostov smiled briefly. "They told us in training that the *Afghanishti* did something like that; gave the Army fits."

"But it's been over a year now since we had any contact from Moscow; who will be taking care of us?"

Rostov looked around them. "This is a good place. You've taken care of it, and each other—and it's taken care of you—for some time now, when you think about it. I don't see any reason why that should not continue."

Fedorin nodded, considering. "I suppose," he said, finally

facing the truth of their isolation. He looked up at Rostov. "We really don't need anything that we can't make or grow right here. And if I take your meaning correctly, such things are all we will have for some time to come."

Rostov held Fedorin's gaze for some time before he answered. "I am glad, Colonel, that you take my meaning correctly. You and your reservists have kept Suschenko safe and running well." He grinned. "You've even kept the clock tower on time. Keep things that way, and I don't think you should have any problems."

Rostov came to attention and snapped off a crisp salute to the old reservist.

"Captain Rostov, Fifth Guards Armored Engineers, requesting permission to decamp, *sir*!"

Fedorin drew himself to attention and returned the salute. "Permission granted, Captain. Good wishes, and God's speed to you and your men."

They shook hands and parted, Rostov to his final preparations for departure, Fedorin to the victory celebration and mourning for the people of Suschenko killed in the fighting. His neighbors, and his friends.

And tomorrow, Fedorin thought, *tomorrow we will go to work repairing that section of westbound railbed*. It would give them all something to do. And it seemed just possible to Fedorin that he had not seen the last of Rostov and his men, or their train.

Rostov was in the engineer's compartment, steeling himself to climb the ladder to the roof hatch with his wounded arm, when Wrenn came up from the platform, wearing his Russian-overcoat disguise.

"Captain Rostov, there is someone outside who would like to speak with you."

Rostov joined the American at the door and looked down onto the platform. At the foot of the stepladder, Zorin stood chatting with the old woman Rostov had befriended on their arrival. And, sure enough, the child was there, pressing tight against her *babushka*'s skirts. The little one was staring up at Zorin with undisguised awe as the big man spoke earnestly with her grandmother, occasionally patting the woman's arm in a gesture of assurance.

Zorin turned and looked up at him. "Captain Rostov, could you spare a moment for this grandmother, sir?"

Rostov's tired face split in a wide smile as he made his way down to the platform.

"Hello, Grandmother; good to see you again." Rostov gave her the warm embrace every Russian always kept ready for the aged. When they parted, the woman began chattering in her thick Ukrainian accent; she pulled her granddaughter forward and showed them the child's freshly bandaged arm. She finished by repeating "*Spaceeba*" over and over again.

Rostov looked to Zorin. "Did you catch what she's saying?"

"Something about the child being hurt when those 'hooligans' attacked us, and Surgeon Blaustein's treatment saving her life," Zorin answered, then shrugged. "Probably not all that serious, but you know how grandparents are."

"You are welcome, Grandmother, most welcome." Wrenn had joined them, and Rostov shrugged and smiled. "That Ukrainian accent loses me; but she is a dear. And that child . . ."

"She also says," Zorin went on, "that her granddaughter is all she has left, and feeding the child has been difficult for an old woman. She thanks us for coming here and saving her little girl from the hooligans, and hunger, and the winter."

Rostov laughed good-naturedly. "Enough, enough! She makes us sound like the Messiah!"

The old woman had been happily chattering in counterpoint to Zorin's translation. Now she reached up and touched Rostov's cheek, then turned and laid a small, wrinkled hand on the massive drive cam of the locomotive.

"*Angeli*." The words were almost a sob. "*Zhelizniy Angel*."

Wrenn, Zorin, and Rostov looked at one another. No one had missed the old woman's meaning that time.

"Angels," she repeated, placing both hands on the engine like a benediction. "An Iron Angel. God sent you to deliver us."

Rostov stood for a moment in thought. "Lieutenant Zorin, get some men and some paint, and form a detail once we're under way. *Iron Angel*. I want that written on the sides of the locomotive."

Zorin was at first unsure whether or not Rostov was serious.

"At once, Captain," he finally said.

"And Mikhail," Rostov stopped him.

"Yes, Aleksei?"

"Put the names of our dead somewhere near it. Not too large. Nobody has to be able to see those but us. Colonel Podgorny's name first."

Zorin saluted and left. Rostov turned to the old woman and her grandchild.

"Hey, little one." She watched him like a hawk watches a mouse. Rostov took a long, last look at the child's huge brown eyes, long black hair. The resemblance to his wife was, he decided, not uncanny after all; only uncomfortable. He remembered the photograph Wrenn had shown him; the American with his wife and son. He wondered again whether Lilia might not have given him a daughter like her.

The child was looking at his cap again, and on impulse, Rostov removed it and put it on her head. Her face almost disappeared beneath it, her eyes shining from within its shadow.

"You keep this for me, child, *da*?"

The girl flashed him one more heartbreaking smile before turning to clutch her grandmother's skirts once more.

Rostov stood and hugged the old woman a last time, then turned to Wrenn.

"Let's be off." He climbed up into the cabin, and not trusting his emotions, continued directly up the ladder into the roof hatch. Once there, he called down to Gyrich, and told him to take them out whenever he was ready.

The members of the review board were silent for a long time before commenting on the report of Captain Drachev's radioman, Piotr. The tank commander himself was still in PRG One's field dispensary, having his wounds treated. He had not yet regained consciousness.

"There seems little doubt that this Drachev did his best, under the circumstances," Captain Adzhubei said quietly.

Steinmann dismissed the radioman.

"Thank you, Lieutenant. That will be all. You may return to your unit." When the young man had left, Steinmann turned to Grishin's seat on the council. "You were right," he said.

"Hm?" said Colonel Serafimov. "Oh, yes. Small consolation, though; they still escaped."

"Not escaped, surely. The Lieutenant says the tracks were demolished; they could not head west, not from Suschenko, at any rate. They can only turn farther back into Soviet-controlled territory, unless they want to tangle with the Islamics, and I doubt that. Now we have gained some time in which to look for them, and in our own territory as well." Steinmann was waiting for Serafimov to share whatever was troubling him, but the Colonel seemed particularly reserved today.

"Perhaps that is not so much of an advantage as it seems," Serafimov said almost to himself.

"I'm afraid I don't understand, Colonel," Steinmann said. "I thought your whole point was that these traitors should, at all costs, be kept in Russia?"

Serafimov raised an eyebrow, smiled, and shrugged.

I wonder, he thought. *I wonder if that is such a very good idea, after all . . .*

Suschenko was an hour behind them when Rostov pulled the photo from the inside pocket of his tunic once more. He looked again at the picture of his wife. *Leytenant* Lilia Rostova, Presumed Traitor to the State; also presumed lost with her artillery unit in the KGB's punitive bombing of Kiev.

Rostov thought again of how very much he missed her.

The same thoughts, the same feelings, the same pain as always. Sometimes he felt as if he would spend the rest of his life going through the motions of existence, as changeless as the land around him.

But, he decided, there was one change he might make.

He pulled out a pocket knife and began digging and chipping at every badge and button on his tunic. Working methodically, in a while he had a pile of enamel chips and bent metal insignia before him.

Rostov scooped up the miniature junk heap, and tossed it casually off to the side of the roof hatch. A dozen tiny hammers and sickles of gold and red metal bounced along across the locomotive's roof, and tumbled off over the side.

He looked at the photo again. For a moment, as always, he was tempted to tear it to shreds and cast the pieces away. In the end, as always, he returned it to his pocket.

Two hours later, Rostov went down to the command car that had become his quarters. And although he wasn't hungry, or thirsty, nor even tired any longer, Captain Aleksei Aleksandrovitch Rostov ate some bread, drank a little tea, and finally went to sleep.

NUCLEAR AUTUMN
Ben Bova

EDITOR'S INTRODUCTION

The apocalyptic vision of Nuclear Winter began in a *Parade* magazine article by Astronomer Carl Sagan on October 30, 1983. Shortly thereafter followed the well-known paper in *Science*, "Nuclear Winter: Global Consequences of Multiple Nuclear Weapons Explosions," which is most often referred to as TTAPS from the initials of the four major contributors.

The paper raised storms that have not subsided yet. The real controversy isn't over the accuracy of the TTAPS predictions. It's almost universally conceded that things won't be that way. There was a major flaw—unreported at the time—in the TTAPS report; the calculations were tied to a one-dimensional simulation of the Earth's atmosphere. This is about on the level of running a computer game simulation of World War I on an IBM PC; it's fun but the results are not going to be particularly representative of the war itself.

What TTAPS did was raise real questions of science policy. How political may scientists be, and how far may they compromise their results in cases where they feel very strongly? After all, the question is a serious one: If even a small nuclear war can exterminate all life on Earth, the people who control nuclear weapons ought to know that. On the other hand, when scientists start presenting opinion as fact, especially when these "facts" fall very much in line with the policies these scientists have previously recommended, have they not ceased to be scientists at all?

According to the TTAPS report even a 100-megaton exchange—a so-called limited nuclear war—could trigger the same effects, i.e. nuclear winter, as a 5,000-megaton exchange. The Soviets quickly followed up Sagan's report with their own verification with Soviet models in the book *The Cold and the Dark*. Tony Rothman states in "A Memoir of Nuclear Winter": "After my year in Russia I was also interested to see that not only was the Soviet model based on a 1971 American computer code, but that every reference in the paper, with the exception of one to their own work, was to an American source."

This is not to deny that even a small nuclear war would have disastrous effects upon climate and agriculture; the volcanic eruption of Tambura in 1815 dropped the average world temperature less than one degree; yet 1816 is remembered as "The Year Without a Summer," and its gloom was the inspiration of Mary Shelley's novel *Frankenstein*.

On the other hand, the weather was naturally much colder in those times; during the American Revolution, Colonel Alexander Hamilton brought cannon from Ticonderoga to General Washington in Manhattan by hauling the guns across the frozen Hudson river. Today the Hudson doesn't freeze solid enough to support skaters. (Incidentally, neither do the canals of Holland, although they did in the days when "Hans Brinker, or The Silver Skates" was written.)

Science is an important source of information; but it can be that only when scientists obey the rules.

"THEY'RE BLUFFING," SAID THE PRESIDENT OF THE UNITED States.

"Of course they're bluffing," agreed her science advisor. "They have to be."

The Chairman of the Joint Chiefs of Staff, a grizzled old infantry general, looked grimly skeptical.

For a long, silent moment they faced each other in the cool, quiet confines of the Oval Office. The science advisor looked young and handsome enough to be a television personality, and indeed had been one for a while before he allied himself with the politician who sat behind the desk. The President looked younger than she actually was, thanks to modern cosmetics and a ruthless self discipline. Only the general seemed to be old, a man of an earlier generation, gray-haired and wrinkled, with light brown eyes that seemed sad and weary.

"I don't believe they're bluffing," he said. "I think they mean exactly what they say—either we cave in to them or they launch their missiles."

The science advisor gave him his most patronizing smile. "General, they *have* to be bluffing. The numbers prove it."

"The only numbers that count," said the general, "are that we have cut our strategic ballistic missile force by half since this Administration came into office."

"And made the world that much safer," said the President. Her voice was firm, with a sharp edge to it.

The general shook his head. "Ma'am, the only reason I have not tendered my resignation is that I know full well the nincompoop you intend to appoint in my place."

The science advisor laughed. Even the President smiled at the old man.

"The soviets are not bluffing," the general repeated. "They mean exactly what they say."

With a patient sigh, the science advisor explained, "General, they cannot—repeat, can *not*—launch a nuclear strike at us or anyone else. They know the numbers as well as we do. A large nuclear strike, in the 3000-megaton range, will so damage the environment that the world will be plunged into a Nuclear Winter. Crops and animal life will be wiped out by months of subfreezing temperatures. The sky will be dark with soot and grains of pulverized soil. The sun will be blotted out. All life on Earth will die.''

The general waved an impatient hand. "I know your story. I've seen your presentations.''

"Then how can the Russians attack us, when they know they'll be killing themselves even if we don't retaliate?''

"Maybe they haven't seen your television specials. Maybe they don't believe in Nuclear Winter.''

"But they have to!'' said the science advisor. "The numbers are the same for them as they are for us.''

"Numbers,'' grumbled the general.

"Those numbers describe reality,'' the science advisor insisted. "And the men in the Kremlin are realists. They understand what Nuclear Winter means. Their own scientists have told them exactly what I've told you.''

"Then why did they insist on this Hot Line call?''

Spreading his hands in the gesture millions had come to know from his television series, the science advisor replied, "They're reasonable men. Now that they know nuclear weapons are unusable, they are undoubtedly trying to begin negotiations to resolve our differences without threatening nuclear war.''

"You think so?'' muttered the general.

The President leaned back in her swivel chair. "We'll find out what they want soon enough,'' she said. "Kolgoroff will be on the Hot Line in another minute or so.''

The science advisor smiled at her. "I imagine he'll suggest a summit meeting to negotiate a new disarmament treaty.''

The general said nothing.

The President touched a green square on the keypad built into the desk's surface. A door opened and three more people—a man and two women—entered the Oval Office: the Secretary of State, the Secretary of Defense, and the National Security Advisor.

Exactly when the digital clock on the President's desk read 12:00:00, the large display screen that took up much of the wall opposite her desk lit up to reveal the face of Yuri Kolgoroff, General Secretary of the Communist Party and President of the Soviet Union. He was much younger than his predecessors had been, barely in his mid-fifties, and rather handsome in a Slavic way. If his hair had been a few shades darker and his chin just a little rounder he would have looked strikingly like the President's science advisor.

"Madam President," said Kolgoroff, in flawless American-accented English, "it is good of you to accept my invitation to discuss the differences between our two nations."

"I am always eager to resolve differences," said the President.

"I believe we can accomplish much." Kolgoroff smiled, revealing large white teeth.

"I have before me," said the President, glancing at the computer screen on her desk, "the agenda that our ministers worked out. . . ."

"There is no need for that," said the Soviet leader. "Why encumber ourselves with such formalities?"

The President smiled. "Very well. What do you have in mind?"

"It is very simple. We want the United States to withdraw all its troops from Europe and to dismantle NATO. Also, your military and naval bases in Japan, Taiwan and the Philippines must be disbanded. Finally, your injunctions against the Soviet Union concerning trade in high-technology items must be ended."

The President's face went white. It took her a moment to gather the wits to say, "And what do you propose to offer in exchange for these . . . concessions?"

"In exchange?" Kolgoroff laughed. "Why, we will allow you to live. We will refrain from bombing your cities."

"You're insane!" snapped the President.

Still grinning, Kolgoroff replied, "We will see who is sane and who is mad. One minute before this conversation began, I ordered a limited nuclear attack against every NATO base in Europe, and a counterforce attack against the ballistic missiles still remaining in your silos in the American midwest."

The red panic light on the President's communications console began flashing frantically.

"But that's impossible!" burst the science advisor. He leaped from his chair and pointed at Kolgoroff's image in the big display screen. "An attack of that size will bring on Nuclear Winter! You'll be killing yourselves as well as us!"

Kolgoroff smiled pityingly at the scientist. "We have computers also, professor. We know how to count. The attack we have launched is just below the threshold for Nuclear Winter. It will not blot out the sun everywhere on Earth. Believe me, we are not such fools as you think."

"But . . ."

"But," the Soviet leader went on, smile vanished and voice iron hard, "should you be foolish enough to launch a counterstrike with your remaining missiles or bombers, that *will* break the camel's back, so to speak. The additional explosions of your counterstrike will bring on Nuclear Winter."

"You can't be serious!"

"I am deadly serious," Kolgoroff replied. Then a faint hint of his smile returned. "But do not be afraid. We have not targeted Washington. Or any of your cities, for that matter. You will live—under Soviet governance."

The President turned to the science advisor. "What should I do?"

The science advisor shook his head.

"What should I do?" she asked the others seated around her.

They said nothing. Not a word.

She turned to the general. "What should I do?"

He got to his feet and headed for the door. Over his shoulder he answered, "Learn Russian."

AS IT WAS IN THE BEGINNING
Edward P. Hughes

EDITOR'S INTRODUCTION

Over the course of this series we have published a number
of stories about the Irish village of Barley Cross and its hardy
inhabitants. The end of the world need not come with a big
bang. The light of civilization may yet flicker out as we
unwittingly tamper with our own genetic heritage in an
effort to design new and more deadly bio-weapons.

In the world of Barley Cross babies are no longer born. No
one knows if this was brought about by the hand of man or
some terrible natural catastrophe; only that the age of man
is coming to an end. In this story, Edward Hughes takes us
back to the earliest days of the O'Meara's reign over Barley
Cross, back to before there was a Master of the Fist.

THE LAST OF THE BARLEY CROSS GIANTS WAS TOPPLING. CELIA
Larkin lay in her cot in the Denny Mallon Memorial Hospital, and
waited for a ninety-year-old pump to fail. The others were all gone
now. Denny Mallon, years ago, of the lung cancer he had courted
so assiduously. Kevin Murphy, of pneumonia, contracted after a
kick from a cow had broken his leg. Poor Andy McGrath, from a

succession of strokes. Larry Desmond, God help him, of the drink. And Patrick O'Meara . . . Celia Larkin's eyes clouded with unshed moisture . . . the first Lord of Barley Cross, her dear Master of the Fist . . .

Up on Barra Hill, Liam McGrath, the second Master of the Fist—since one couldn't count sad, mad Dominic, nor the fatuous Damien—still ruled. Still respected—though no longer required—Liam played endless games of checkers with General Fahey, or told stories of the old days to anyone who would listen.

But the most important story Liam McGrath couldn't tell. Celia recalled, as if it were yesterday . . .

. . . the rumbling, clanking, screeching, clattering from behind which drove the young schoolmistress into a dry gully by the roadside. The noise sounded like a combination of road roller, combine harvester, and a hundred squeaking gates. Celia Larkin crouched low. Any kind of transport could be a threat these days.

She waited minutes before a long gun barrel lagged with thermal insulation poked its snout round the nearest bend. Celia Larkin had never seen a tank before, much less a British Army Main Battle Tank. In her astonishment, she forgot to keep her head down.

The monster halted opposite her hiding place. The roar of its engine died to a low rumble. The driver poked his head through a hatch in the sloping glacis. He called to her. "Is this the road for Castlebar?"

Useless to crouch lower. Celia Larkin stood, brushed dust and grass from her suit, and said, "If you keep straight on you can't miss it."

The man smiled. He wore an oily beret bearing a badge which resembled a ball sprouting feathers, and a jacket covered with green and yellow splotches. "I'm making for Kilcollum in Connemara," he told her.

She stared at his enormous vehicle. Such a monster to carry one man to Connemara! "I've not heard of the place," she confessed.

"Sure, 'tis only a small village," he admitted. "Not many people have." He paused, as though seeking inspiration for further pleasantries. "Can I give you a lift to anywhere? The roads are not safe for a young lady on her own."

211

She weighed him up. He had an honest, open face. His smile was disarming. And—most persuasive—his remark about the roads was true. The last car she had hidden from had been packed with shotgun-wielding hooligans.

"How do I get in?" she asked.

He pointed. "If you put a foot on that towing eye, and grab that lamp bracket . . . there are cleats up the side of the turret. You get in at the top. Hold on, I'll give you a hand."

She swung her suitcase up onto the glacis beside his head. "That won't be necessary. Take my case!"

She hoisted her skirt, found the foot and handholds indicated, and climbed onto the tank. One of the hatches in the turret was open. She got in among the machinery.

"I'm in!" she called.

"Where to, miss?" he called back.

"I was hoping to get to Clifden—but that will be a good step past your village, I'm afraid."

"I don't mind running a young lady home."

The engine noise became a roar. She heard his shout. "Don't touch anything in there, miss. You don't want to blow us up!"

Tracks squealing, the tank lurched into motion. Celia Larkin found the noise stunning, and the vibration worse than she had expected. The combination of noise and vibration rendered further conversation with the driver impossible. She found a seat, and sat down, wondering what she had let herself in for.

Surely, after her days on the road, anyone would have accepted his offer of a lift. Sligo had been insufferable, the behaviour of its citizens growing daily worse. She wanted nothing more to do with it. In lonely Clifden, at the ocean's edge, she might find people more civilised, less influenced by the current madness.

When the tank stopped, she nerved herself for further conversation. A hatch opened in the floor of her refuge. The soldier's head appeared through it.

"Time for a break," he told her. "Sit still—I'll put the kettle on."

She watched in amazement as he filled a kettle and plugged it in.

"I didn't know you could brew tea in a tank!"

He grinned. "Sure, there's a deal you don't know about tanks, I would imagine."

He opened a locker, and brought out two plastic plates. "Could you face a ploughman's lunch?"

She hadn't eaten that day, being scared of entering strange eating places. "After that ride," she told him, "I could face anything."

He cut half-inch slabs of cheese, and laid them on slices of bread. He opened a jar, and topped the cheese with pickles. He covered his confections with further slices of bread, and passed one of the sandwiches to her.

"I'm Patrick O'Meara, ex–Second Battalion, Grenadier Guards," he told her. "Who are you?"

Mouth choked with tangy cheese, she gave him her name. "How did you come by this tank?" she asked him.

He grinned. "Stole it from the British government. I've been guarding their docks in Belfast 'til I'm sick of being a cockshy for every idiot who wants his fling while there's someone left for him to annoy."

"Is that what it's like in Belfast?"

He grimaced. "It's like that all over Ireland, so far as I can gather. Maybe all over the world. No kids for the last ten years. Nothing left to work for. No future to look forward to. If we'll all be dead in sixty years or so, does anything matter? Belfast is crazy. The Provos are out in the open, shouting a new slogan—'Ours in the end!' We shot a few last week, and they got seven of my lads."

"Sligo is not as bad as that," she told him. "But there are robberies and muggings every day. I was a teacher, but my class grew up, and left me without a job. I'm going to my sister in Clifden. I hope it will be better there."

He unplugged the steaming kettle, and infused the tea. "My parents are in Kilcollum. I haven't seen them since I joined up. I'm hoping for peace and quiet, too."

She eyed this soft-spoken soldier who stole tanks, killed Provos, and talked of peace. "Why did you steal this machine?"

He grinned impenitently. "Can you think of a safer way to travel?"

They slept that night, battened down, in a pasture hidden from the road by a tall hedge. Next morning he heated water for washing and shaving, then boiled a couple of eggs. They ate breakfast squatting on the glacis.

"I'll have to find some fuel soon," he told her.

"What kind of fuel?"

He jerked a thumb at the rear of the tank. "That motor will run on anything. Right now we're on diesel."

"How much will you need?"

He grimaced. "About two hundred gallons."

Her eyes widened. "That will cost a fortune!"

He shook his head, pointing to the gun above them. "That's as good as a credit card."

She tried to frown at him. "Mr. O'Meara, you are no better than the villains you complain of!"

He indicated once-white tapes on his sleeve. "Sergeant," he told her. "They can't bust me 'til they catch me. It takes a sergeant for genuine villainy. Now, come up to the turret, and I'll show you how to work it."

She frowned at him. "Why do I need to know that?"

He sighed. "Because I can't do two jobs at once."

A few miles from Castlebar, they found a service station open. Sergeant O'Meara pulled into the forecourt, and halted his tank by the pumps. A door in the office opened. A man appeared carrying a shotgun.

"Get that thing off my property!"

The sergeant put his head out of the driver's hatch. "I need gas, chief."

The man jerked his shotgun. "I've none to spare for strangers. Get moving!"

Sergeant O'Meara smiled winningly. "Only two hundred gallons, chief. Diesel will do—I've got a multi-fuel engine. Don't be hard on a bona fide traveller."

The man's face contorted. "You heard me, soldier. Get that thing off my forecourt before I blow your head off!"

Sergeant O'Meara raised his voice. "Larkin!"

"Sir?" responded the turret.

"Train the gun on the office!"

Motors whined. The turret revolved. The long barrel swung until it pointed at the office behind the man.

214

"Load HESH, Larkin!"

"Sir!"

Sergeant O'Meara addressed the station owner. "Now, chief, before I give my next order, would you care to reconsider any decisions?"

The man spluttered. His shotgun wavered. He turned to gaze at the office. "My wife is in there."

Patrick O'Meara shrugged. "Then she has two minutes to get clear. I'm not a patient man."

The station operator struggled for his dignity. He wiped a sleeve under one eye. Then he propped his gun against a pump, and unhooked a hose.

"Show me where to stick this damn thing."

Later, as they rumbled towards Castlebar, Celia Larkin lifted the floor hatch, and shouted to the recumbent driver. "What's HESH?"

He rolled his eyes up at her. "High explosive, squash head. It's used for blowing holes in concrete bunkers. We haven't any HESH."

"Thank God for that," she shouted. "For a moment, I thought you meant it when you threatened that man."

"I did mean it," he shouted back. "But you couldn't do anything about it for me."

"And you paid with a chit on the British Army's Paymaster General!"

"He pays all my bills."

Celia gave up. Patrick O'Meara had peculiar principles.

They drove sedately down the centre of Castlebar's narrow main street. There was no traffic, few parked cars. Most of the shops were closed. Many had shuttered windows. A jeweller's front was glassless and stockless.

The sergeant had shown her how to work the intercom. She rode standing in the cupola, head in the breeze, squashy doughnuts over her ears.

His voice came through the phones. "Things don't look much better here, Larkin."

She said, "Keep going, Sergeant. We're being watched from bedroom windows. Can they harm us?"

She couldn't see him roll his eyes in tolerant surprise. He said patiently, "Only if they use an antitank gun, Larkin. I doubt if

215

they'll have one of those handy. But you might watch out for Molotov cocktails—''

"What do I do if I see one?"

Perhaps there was some mettle in her, after all. He said, "Duck, and close the hatch. The machine gun beside you is loaded if you feel like having a go.''

Her voice reflected a classroom ring. "Don't be ridiculous, Sergeant. Why should I wish to shoot anyone?''

She couldn't see his smile, either. "Just a thought, Larkin.''

At a steady fifteen miles per hour they rolled along the eastern shores of Mask and Corrib. At Corrib's southern tip, Patrick O'Meara turned west for Galway City.

Celia, by now accustomed to vibration, and insulated from noise by her headphones, reported, "Smoke ahead, Sergeant.''

A black cloud rose above the treetops.

"Arson, I suspect," he responded. "Drop the hatch, Larkin!''

Buildings burned unchecked in Galway town centre. They went through, battened down, crunching over rubble and wreckage. She found the gun sight gave her a better, magnified, picture of their surroundings than the nine periscopes studding the turret. She swung her eyrie from side to side, watching diligently for Molotov cocktails.

Patrick O'Meara lying in the driver's seat noted the long barrel swinging menacingly back and forth over his head, and grinned with pleasure. No rioter would tackle his tank while that gun threatened.

On the Oughterard road, clear of Galway, he stopped for tea.

"Well done, Larkin," he told her. "You forced them to keep their heads down.''

She gaped in astonishment. "Did I help?''

He opened a secret locker, and poured a large tot in both cups. The schoolteacher deserved it. "I couldn't have got through so easy without you.''

She flushed. He was being gracious. "Nor I without you, Sergeant.''

Patrick O'Meara handed her a cup. "Maybe we've got ourselves a team. Would you like to learn how to handle that gun?''

Celia Larkin was already viewing matters in a fresh light. She recalled the burning buildings of Galway, the looted shopfronts in Castlebar, the shotgun-wielding hooligans on the road, and the

216

possibility of Molotov cocktails. She bit her lip. "Do you think it might help?"

His eyes were steady. "I wouldn't suggest it if I didn't think so."

She inhaled a trembly breath. "Very well, Sergeant. Show me what to do."

He grinned. "Nothing to be scared of, Larkin. We shoot separate-loading ammo—that's a divided projectile and charge. So you don't have such heavy shells to lift. And there are no empty cases to dump. The bag holding the charge burns up." He pointed. "We keep the charges in water-jacketed compartments under there."

She eyed him hesitantly. "You make it sound so simple, Sergeant."

"What's complicated? Aiming is done for you by laser and computer, once you pick the target."

She blinked. "And what do we shoot, if we've no HESH?"

He drained his cup. She was quick on the uptake, this schoolteacher. He said, "Good question, Larkin. We have some smoke shells, and a few rounds of APFSDS."

She drained her cup, too. The tea had an unusual fiery taste, which left a glow in her gut. It might be possible to master all this technical twaddle he was expounding!

"APFSDS?" she queried, nonchalantly.

"Armour-piercing, fin-stablised, discarding sabot," he explained. "Very potent stuff."

She reached for the teapot. Maybe there was a cupful of the sergeant's fiery brew left in it. "It is," she agreed. "It is!"

Later, he hauled a suitcase from a compartment in the bustle. He unpacked a uniform blouse and beret. "Put the blouse on over your clothes. Tuck your hair inside the beret. If we're painting a picture, details are important."

She fingered the ribbons stitched above the breast pocket. "What are these for?"

He made a business of closing the case, and stowing it away in silence.

"Isn't this the Falklands ribbon?" she persisted.

He faced her. "The British army likes its soldiers to have a bit of colour on their gear. Shoulder flashes and the like. To brighten things up."

"And this one?" she persevered.

217

He swallowed. "That's the M.M." You couldn't make fun of the Military Medal.

"Isn't that for bravery in action?"

Sergeant O'Meara found a sudden necessity to check the suspension of the six road wheels along each side of his tank. When he returned, she had donned the top half of his parade uniform.

He appraised the result. "A big improvement, Larkin. No need to stick your chest out like that! Into the turret, now. Anyone looking quick will think I've got a soldier up there. And I'll show you how to work that 7.62mm machine gun, in case you want to really kid them."

Oughterard, when they passed through, was as silent and watchful as all the other small towns had been. Over the intercom, he said, "It must be the tank that scares them."

She said, "I'm sure it's not my face."

West of Oughterard, the road threaded between misty mountains. Nameless minor lakes puddled the land flanking the road. Turf stacks lined the verge.

She heard a sigh over the phones. "Nearly home, Larkin."

She surveyed the peaceful distances, and knew she couldn't expect it to last.

"Are we going to Kilcollum first, Sergeant?"

He said, "Why not? You in a hurry to get to Clifden?"

She examined her conscience. "Not particularly, Sergeant."

"Just as well. I want you to meet my folks."

Their road angled around the toe of a mountain marked as Kirkogue on her map. She spied a village dominated by a church spire and tower-capped hill.

She said, "I know this place. I've an aunt lives here."

The intercom said, "Take off your phones, and listen!"

She complied.

From the village ahead came the sound of gunfire.

"Someone shooting," she reported.

"Battle stations!" ordered the intercom. "That means into the turret and close the hatch, Larkin."

She lowered herself into the turret, and closed the cupola. Through the main gun sight she saw, magnified, the end of the village street ahead. A van blocked the roadway, rear doors open. Shotgun-carrying men stood around the vehicle. Other men appeared carrying boxes which they dumped inside the van.

"Highway robbery," commented the intercom. "Do we intervene?"

Her pulse jumped at the idea. Could she and the sergeant stop them?

"What would we do?"

The intercom grew brisk. "Line up the gun sight on that van. Don't worry—I won't ask you to shoot anyone."

She did as she was bid.

"Switch on the IFCS."

"IFCS, Sergeant?"

"Improved fire control system—the computer and the laser sight! Move it, soldier!"

She moved it. Below the optical target ring in her telescope, a green oval sprang into existence. It shifted to encircle the van.

"Target acquired," she reported, getting into the swing of things.

"There's a ranging machine gun mounted beside the big fellow," instructed the intercom. "It's fixed to fire on the same trajectory. When there's no one in the way to get hurt, give that van a burst!"

Heart thumping, eyes blind with eagerness, she squeezed the machine gun trigger. In the gun sight, a flight of bright tracer bullets arched towards the van. The vehicle sank down on one side as a tyre burst.

"Nice shooting, Larkin," approved the intercom. "That'll do for now."

The bandits were now concealing themselves behind their lopsided transport. She saw gun flashes.

"Don't worry," advised the intercom. "Those popguns can't harm our Chobham armour. Load smoke!"

"Smoke?" she queried.

"Wake up, Larkin! A smoke shell—like I showed you!"

She hoisted a smoke shell from its rack, and pushed it into the breech of the big gun.

"Don't forget the charge, Larkin!"

She pulled a canvas bag from the special storage, and pushed it after the projectile.

"Close the breech, Larkin!"

She closed, and locked the gun breech, in the way he had shown her.

"Gun ready, Sergeant," she panted.

"Fire at will!" ordered the intercom.

The smoke shell went through the van's open rear, and exploded in the driver's seat, collapsing the suspension. A cloud of black smoke enveloped the vehicle.

"Cease firing!" ordered the intercom. "They're retreating."

As they clanked up to the smoke-filled wreck, the road swarmed with villagers breathing through scarves or handkerchiefs, and transferring boxes back to a nearby shop.

A smallish man, his sleeves rolled up and blood on his hands, approached the tank. "Thanks for the timely help, Sergeant. Those rogues would have stolen all the Phelan's stock. Believe me, you're very welcome in Barley Cross today!"

Sergeant O'Meara lowered his eyes modestly. "We try to please. Are you hurt?"

The man glanced at his hands. "I'm the doctor. This is Willie Neary's blood. They shot him up pretty badly."

The sergeant jerked a thumb at the turret behind him. "I've a medical kit in there, if it's any use to you?"

The doctor shrugged. "I'll be out of shirts soon, if Mrs. Mallon doesn't stop tearing them up for bandages . . ."

Later, over their first hot meal in days, the doctor told them, "We are trying to live a normal life here. But it's damn difficult. Those rogues you chased away have raided us several times already." He looked up hopefully from his plate. "I don't suppose I could persuade you to stay on? We could use a couple of professional soldiers with a tank."

Celia Larkin made deprecating noises. "Don't call me a soldier, Doctor. I wear the sergeant's gear to impress spectators."

Dr. Mallon gestured with his fork. "You certainly impressed us with your shooting."

She blushed. "It's all done by computer. I'm a schoolmistress, really. I'd sooner teach children."

The doctor nodded sadly. "That's something we lack. There's been no work for a midwife in Barley Cross for over a dozen years." He gazed from one to the other. "If you could persuade the sergeant to stay on, we could find you some kind of adult class to teach. There must be lots of subjects you could lecture us about."

Oh sure! Celia Larkin almost choked on a forkful of meat. Like sleeping rough, panhandling, or shoplifting—or even the rival merits of HESH and APFSDS!

Sergeant O'Meara stirred his tea. "I have to visit my folks in Kilcollum, near here, Doctor. Then I'm taking Miss Larkin to her sister in Clifden. If my fuel spins out, or I find an open gas station, I might be back."

The doctor looked suddenly hopeful. "Then you two are not married—or anything?"

Patrick O'Meara stared at his silent gunner. He said, "No, Doctor. Not married—nor anything." The sergeant's expression grew thoughtful.

Later that day, a lone Chieftain tank rolled westward over rain-wet roads. In the mists to starboard, the Corcogemore Mountains loomed like indistinct stormclouds.

Via the intercom, Sergeant O'Meara addressed his gunner. "Why didn't you tell the doctor that you have relatives in his village?"

He couldn't see her blushes.

"I didn't know if you wanted him to know. He might have put pressure—"

The intercom said, "Should I worry about pressure from the doctor?"

The silence lasted some minutes. Both were occupied, thinking.

She heard his voice again. "What did you make of the doctor's remark, Larkin? When he asked were we married . . . or anything?"

She bit her lip, stifling a gasp. She could scarcely speak. Perhaps there was a chance it might last! She whispered, "It would depend on the attitude of the parties involved, wouldn't it?"

The intercom went silent. Sergeant O'Meara wasn't the fellow to rush into a trap, no matter how tempting the bait. "Let's assume one of the parties might be a bit interested, Larkin," he ventured.

She thumbed the speak button in turn. Voice scarcely audible, she murmured, "In that case, we might assume both parties were a bit interested."

She heard him whistling an old Irish air about a low-backed car. He said, "Could we leave it there for the time being, Larkin?"

Voice tremulous, she said, "I'm not rushing anyone, Sergeant."

"The Low-backed Car" reached a triumphal conclusion. "Message understood, Larkin," said the intercom. "And filed for reference."

The signpost, like so many in Ireland, pointed in the wrong direction, and was barely legible. Unhesitatingly, Sergeant O'Meara rotated his tank off the main road, onto a stretch of tarmac less than a dozen feet wide.

"Four miles to go, Larkin," the intercom announced cheerfully.

There had been no more than a score of houses in Kilcollum. Each was a gutted shell, roofs caved, bones charcoaled.

Sergeant O'Meara halted the tank. Over the intercom, he said, "Cover me, Larkin."

He climbed out of the hatch, a large revolver in his hand. She swung the turret to bring the coaxial machine gun to bear on the road ahead of him.

She watched him peer through the glassless windows of the nearest dwelling. Grass was already growing over the debris within. He moved swiftly from house to house. At the corner of the street he crumpled.

She was out of the turret and running. She found him kneeling before the low wall of an overgrown garden. Sprouting from the weeds were two white crosses. They bore the names of Padraic and Ellen O'Meara. She waited in silence.

He looked up, dry-eyed. He gestured at the crosses. "Meet my folks, Larkin."

She touched his shoulder. "Come back to the tank, Sergeant. It's not safe here."

He gazed about the ravaged village. "There's no danger now, Larkin. The murderers are long gone."

She tugged at him. "Come away, Sergeant."

He got to his feet. "I can come back later, and tidy this place up."

She said, "We'll both come back. I promise."

He allowed her to lead him back to the Chieftain. "Why would they do that to a whole village, Larkin? Why burn every house?"

She shook her head. "We're living in a sick world, Sergeant."

The drive to Clifden was silent. He neither spoke nor sang. She ached to hear "The Low-backed Car" again, but the intercom stayed dead.

When the spires of Clifden came into view, she heard his voice again. "Where to, Larkin?"

She gave him her sister's address.

The house stood in a side street. He halted the tank outside the front door. She got down from the turret. He stayed in his driving cubby, head out of the hatch, watching her. Other eyes watched from behind curtains. Several figures congregated on the street corner. No one approached near the tank.

She called, "Aren't you coming in with me?"

He shook his head.

She mounted the steps of her sister's home. The front door was ajar. From within came the sound of a woman screeching in anger, and the basso rumble of protest from a man. Hand on the door knocker, Celia hesitated. She heard the sounds of altercation and the unmistakable crash of breaking pottery. She dropped her hand from the knocker.

She stumbled back to the tank. "I think I've made a mistake, Sergeant."

He jerked a thumb. "Get aboard!"

She climbed back to the turret, conscious of being watched. Safe in her refuge, she thumbed the intercom. "What happens now?"

He said, "Dr. Mallon made us a fair offer."

Her thoughts were in turmoil. No refuge for the sergeant in Kilcollum. No haven for her at her sister's. Was there any point in planning ahead? If she didn't want to lose him, she had to make up her mind. She thumbed the button. "Let's go back to Barley Cross, Sergeant."

He reversed to the main road, backed out, and turned east.

She shouted over the intercom, "There's a strange craft astern. It has a gun!"

The Chieftain came round in its own length.

They stared at the potential threat. Celia got the magnifying sight on the target. "It looks like a tractor, with a trailer."

He said, "It's parked. Keep your head down. They may not have seen you."

Head out in the sunlight, he drove slowly towards the strange vehicle. A platform had been built between the driving wheels. On the platform, an Oerlikon-type gun pointed skywards. From the driver's seat, a man watched their approach. An automatic rifle rested across his knees.

Sergeant O'Meara called to him. "Hi, chief! Would ye be interested in buying a tank?"

Only the man's eyes moved. His response was unenthusiastic. "If you're wanting the boss, he's in Finnegan's bar with the boys."

Patrick O'Meara appeared to meditate. "I was just wondering if he fancied acquiring himself a tank."

The man's eyes rolled to take in the full length of the Chieftain's 120mm gun. "Are you seeking to sell it?"

Patrick O'Meara nodded. "If the price is right."

"Have you ammo for that cannon?"

"A few rounds."

"You'd better wait 'til Healey gets back."

Patrick O'Meara eased himself out of the hatch, to prop his back against the turret. "I'm a stranger here," he admitted. "I pinched this bugger off the British army. Someone ought to have a use for it."

The man relaxed. "I reckon the boss will take it, if you'll wait."

The sergeant stretched out his legs on the glacis. "Och—I'm in no hurry. What's that ye have on the trailer?"

The man didn't turn his head. "Armour plate. A warship went aground in the bay. It's breaking up. Healey intended to make a tank out of this machine with the plates we salvaged. Looks like you've saved him the trouble."

"Is your boss at war with someone?"

The man glanced along the road behind the tank. "He's at war with anyone that looks for bother around here."

The rear periscope showed Celia that the road astern was empty. Clifden's citizens had decided that neither tank nor tractor was of interest to them. She put her eye back to the gun sight.

Voice casual, Patrick O'Meara said, "Did you ever meet with a gang from out Kilcollum way?"

The man sneered. "That lot? Sure, they were no problem. We burned 'em out, months ago!"

Sergeant O'Meara stiffened. "Were you there?"

The man grinned. "Was I there—Jasus!"

Patrick O'Meara's hand dived inside his jacket. The man swung up his rifle, and Celia fired her machine gun. A stream of tracers

224

streaked over the man's head. He ducked, his attention diverted. Patrick O'Meara's bullet took him in the neck.

The man screamed, and dropped the gun. The sergeant slid back through his hatch. He reversed the tank alongside the tractor. Ignoring the figure slumped over the steering wheel, he got down and uncoupled the trailer.

She screeched at him from the cupola. "What are you doing?"

He looked up. "Watch the road, Larkin. Those shots will bring out the rest of them. I want this armour plate for Barley Cross."

He unclipped the towing hawser from the track cover, and hitched the trailer to the Chieftain. Bullets were spanging off the glacis as he climbed back into the driver's hatch.

The intercom came alive. "You okay, Larkin?"

She tried to stop trembling. "I—I think so."

"Batten down—we're getting out of here."

The motor roared. He nudged the tractor out of the way. Towing the trailer, the tank rumbled towards the villains spewing from Finnegan's bar. She watched them scatter for cover.

He said, "If I were up there, I'd give them a dose of metal poisoning."

She said coldly, "Isn't one death enough for you, Sergeant?"

The intercom muttered a smothered blasphemy. "They murdered my parents, Larkin. He would have killed me. And that rifle was a Kalashnikov."

"Is that bad?"

"They're all bad things in my book."

Later, trundling along the lonely road below the twelve bens, he began to hum "The Low-backed Car."

Five miles off Recess, a loose tread began to clang. He got out to inspect the cause. She filled the kettle, and plugged in. Tea was ready when he poked his head over the open cupola.

"Did you notice a blacksmith in Barley Cross?"

She passed him a steaming cup. "He was shoeing a horse as we left."

He sipped the tea, blowing on the hot liquid. "We'll be needing his services."

"Something you can't fix, Sergeant?"

He nodded. "I can't—" He broke off to stare back along the road.

225

She poked her head out to see.

He said, "Those villains have followed us."

She reached down for his binoculars. The tractor had halted. She could see figures on the gun platform, and others standing in the road.

"How far are they, do you reckon?" he asked.

She shrugged. "A couple of miles."

"About that," he agreed. "Make room in there, Larkin. They think they're out of range."

She watched him load a round of armour-piercing, fin-stabilised, discarding sabot.

He said, "Put on the headphones, Larkin. This'll make a noise."

The explosion gouged out the verge beside the tractor. The tractor lifted sideways, and toppled, to balance on one large wheel. Through the binoculars, she saw figures running away.

The sergeant opened the floor hatch, and wriggled down into the driver's seat. "Stand by the machine gun, Larkin."

He turned the tank in the width of the road, and rumbled back towards the tractor.

She said, "Where are we going?"

He was humming softly. "I want that Oerlikon gun, if it's serviceable."

Did he think of nothing but guns and vengeance? She said, "Why did you shoot at them? They couldn't hurt us."

He continued to hum, unperturbed. "They were following us. Barley Cross has enough troubles, without me bringing them more."

She gulped with relief. "You only fired to frighten them off?"

The humming ceased. "No, Larkin. I tried to kill them. I'll get them all, one fine day."

The doctor was waiting for them in the village's main street. He waved to them. "Are you stopping this time, Sergeant?"

Patrick O'Meara waved back. "Are those jobs still open?"

The doctor grinned. "Come and meet someone."

In his surgery-cum-living room, he introduced his friends. "Larry, Kevin and I try to represent the villagers. Larry has been teaching them how to defend themselves. He'll put you in the picture."

Larry Desmond stretched long legs towards the turf fire glowing in the grate. "Jasus, Dinny—about all I can teach them is that shotguns aren't much use against automatic rifles, and the best thing to do is keep yer head down. They can do that without an old soldier's advice."

Sergeant O'Meara lounged on the doctor's cushions. One week of roughing it in a tank was sufficient to teach appreciation of such luxuries. He said, "I have a dozen FN rifles aboard my wagon. I lifted them from the guard room before I took off with the tank."

Kevin Murphy rubbed reddened hands before the fire. "A sensible precaution for a rebel, Sergeant. I believe they shoot deserters in the British army."

Patrick O'Meara ignored the jibe. He was no rebel. He was a reasoning being who could recognise the futility of trying to control the uncontrollable. He said, "In my mob they'd crucify you for desertion."

Kevin Murphy flexed his fingers in the heat. "A typical autocratic reaction."

Larry Desmond cackled. "What would your lot do, Kev—guillotine 'em?"

Patrick O'Meara hid his disgust. No wonder Barley Cross was everybody's football, with these two running things! He said, "I've some Kalashnikovs I picked up with the Oerlikon. They'll take a 7.62mm Nato round, too." He turned to the doctor. "I could arm a platoon."

Denny Mallon got out a bottle and glasses. Celia shook her head at his enquiring glance. He poured for the men, saying, "Just tell us what to do, Sergeant. We'll folly your instructions."

Patrick O'Meara fought the impulse to get up and walk out. Devising a defence for this village, faced with such complacency, could be harder than fighting villains. But Barley Cross was his only hope. At least, its citizens were attempting to live normal lives.

He said, "I want twenty full-time volunteers for my standing army."

"Done!" exclaimed Larry Desmond. "I'll guarantee 'em."

"And we need a refuge for noncombatants—who owns the castle up beyond?"

Denny sipped his poteen with a grimace. "It's an old O'Flaherty stronghold. A chap called Higgins converted it to a home, some years ago. He and his missus went off to Dublin seeking relatives when the troubles started. We've seen neither hair nor hide of them since."

Patrick O'Meara made his voice brisk. This was the fuel business over again—you couldn't afford to hesitate. He said, "We'll take it over. If we put armoured shutters on the doors and windows, build gun platforms on the roof, we'll have a fortress which will shake a fist at the whole of Connemara!"

Larry Desmond waved his glass. "Hold on, now! What if the Higgins—?"

Kevin Murphy raised a restraining palm. "It's in the name of the people, Larry. Higgins will have to accept *force majeure*."

Patrick O'Meara lay back, and let them argue. It had to work, in spite of them. He said, "We start first thing tomorrow."

In three months, the sergeant had a fighting force which proved itself in a raid on a mobile gang camped near Lough Corrib. Larry Desmond had been promoted to general, getting him out of the way. Kevin Murphy, as a vet, had been given charge of all four-legged transport. Andy McGrath, a foot-loose bachelor who had seen service in the Irish army, had been made up to sergeant. The captured Oerlikon and one of the Chieftain's machine guns now dominated the battlements of the O'Flaherty stronghold—which had already been christened O'Meara's Fist—and Celia Larkin was instructing a group of Barley Cross volunteers in the nuances of Modern Art.

Patrick O'Meara sat at his desk in a downstairs room of O'Meara's Fist, plotting a raid on Tuam for medical supplies.

A knock on the door interrupted his musings.

"Are ye busy?" enquired Denny Mallon. "I'd like a word with you, Pat."

He pushed his plans up the table. "Come in, Denny."

The doctor's face was unreadable. "I have mixed news for you. Celia Larkin came to see me today."

Patrick O'Meara hadn't seen the schoolmistress for weeks. Since being appointed Military Adviser, he had been busy creating an army. He growled, "What's she been up to?"

Denny Mallon pulled out a chair, and sat down facing the sergeant. "She came to consult me in my professional capacity." He paused a moment, as though reconsidering his decision to break a confidence. Then he said, "She's had a miscarriage."

Patrick O'Meara froze.

"She's all right," the doctor assured him. "I've sent her to bed for a few days. And no one knows what's happened to her but we three."

Voice scarcely audible, he whispered, "Was it me, Denny?"

The doctor's voice was equally restrained. "Who else, Pat? Celia is not a loose woman. And, in any case, we're all sterile in Barley Cross."

Patrick O'Meara studied his palms. "What's it mean, Denny?"

The doctor leaned towards him. "It means you're unique, Pat. You are *fertile*! You may be the only fertile man in all Ireland."

Sergeant O'Meara looked up, fearfully. "What do you expect me to do?"

Denny Mallon spread his hands on the table. "I don't know yet, Pat. But we can't ignore such an opportunity. You'd better not go on any more raids . . ."

Two days later, the doctor summoned them all to his home. Pale-faced, and wrapped in a thick cardigan, Celia Larkin sat close to the fire.

The doctor rubbed his hands together briskly. "I've called us together because we have a problem. Our military adviser has discovered that he's fertile. And, since I know he has his eye on a certain young lady, I feel he should be dissuaded from his honourable intentions."

Celia Larkin marvelled at the neatness of it. Perhaps the others wouldn't be too curious . . .

General Desmond looked up from the glass he was filling with the doctor's poteen. "Why should we object to his marrying, Dinny? Is it any business of ours what the lad does in private?"

Celia Larkin blessed the old fool.

Kevin Murphy ahemmed. "Might I ask how you can be sure of what you claim?"

Denny Mallon pursed his lips. "Would you expect me to ignore my Hippocratic Oath? You know the secrets of the surgery are inviolate, Kevin. But, rest assured—I have examined Pat, and I confirm what he says."

"And who's he fancying to marry?" demanded the general. "I'd like to keep out of the lady's way for a while."

The doctor frowned in mock reproof. "Hold on now, Larry.

229

Who Pat fancies is his own business. I just feel he ought not to marry at all."

"All right, I'll buy it," agreed the general. "Tell us why he shouldn't wed."

The doctor steepled his fingers. "If our military adviser is fertile, shouldn't he be encouraged to spread his gift as widely as possible? Wouldn't we all be happy to see a few childer around the village?"

The general showed interest. "But that would mean polygamy—or its equivalent!"

"I hope not," interpolated Patrick O'Meara. "I'm no performing ram."

"There's our problem," said the doctor. "How can we fix it so that the O'Meara genes are distributed all over the village?"

"It would help if he was a ram," grunted the vet.

Denny Mallon rolled the title on his tongue. "O'Meara the Ram. Now that has a fine ring about it!"

"Even if Pat is willing—" began Celia Larkin.

"Who said he was willing?" interrupted the military adviser.

"—what about the women's feelings? He can't marry them all. And, if they were not willing, it would be rape. And, if they were, he would be committing adultery. Or fornication, if the lady were single."

General Desmond turned round in surprise. "I'm astonished to hear such talk from you, Celia!"

She snuggled deep in her cardigan. Was Larry Desmond really astonished? Or did he just want to see which way the only woman present would jump?

She said, "You're thinking with your stomach, General. What Denny has just told us means that Barley Cross could have children playing in its streets again. The village might possibly survive the demise we all fear. In a few years, I could reopen your school. But we have to work out a way to bring it about."

The general grunted. "That's easy. Line 'em up, and send 'em in by numbers. Shoot them that won't toe the line!"

The military adviser seemed about to speak. Instead, he closed his mouth, and began to think.

Celia Larkin was laughing. "We don't live in Soviet Russia, General—or wherever it is they do that sort of thing."

"Nothing wrong with Soviet Russia," grunted Kevin Murphy. "If they found a ram there, the women would have more sense than to turn their backs on him."

The general grinned. "But that's exactly what—!"

"Please, gentlemen!" Denny Mallon intervened. "Let's avoid lewd talk. We have a lady present."

Celia Larkin spread her hands before the fire. There was a way it could be done, if a certain person was prepared to forget her hopes. Did the future of a community rate higher than personal happiness? Silently, Celia Larkin made her own sacrifice.

She said, "There used to be a custom called *jus primae noctis* . . ."

Kevin Murphy choked on his poteen. "That's bloody medievalism. Pandering to a depraved aristocracy!"

She smiled sweetly. "Can you think of a better way to spread a survival gene?"

The vet conquered the politician. Kevin Murphy muttered, "Bejasus, I never looked at it in that light!"

Larry Desmond poured himself another drink. "Do you think our Barley Cross women would accept that solution?"

Celia shrugged. "It would only concern brides. *Jus primae noctis* means the 'right of the first night.'"

"Ah!" exclaimed the general sapiently.

"He would need a high rank," she went on. "If we made him Lord of Barley Cross—?"

"Duke of Connaught would be more impressive," snorted the general.

"I could fancy King of Connemara, meself," the doctor mused.

"You can't make kings," pointed out the vet. "Thrones are inherited through the blood. But you can create a lord or a duke."

"Let's make him both," suggested the general. "What the hell—they're only titles!"

The military adviser woke up. "Hey, no way! If you make me boss—I've got to be a real boss!"

"For goodness' sake, Patrick—!" began the doctor irritably.

"He's right," Kevin Murphy intervened. "We daren't fool the village with a dummy lord. If we make Pat top man, that's what he'll have to be. And he can live up at his Fist and boss us for ever more."

231

"That's agreed, then," said the doctor hastily. "When, and how, do we bring it off?"

"Soon as possible," grunted the general.

"We need a peg to hang his promotion on," sniffed the vet. "A victory of some kind—like Napoleon after Austerlitz."

"Napoleon was emperor before Austerlitz," corrected the schoolmistress.

"Would I crown myself?" queried Patrick O'Meara, betraying an acquaintance with recondite matters.

Denny Mallon tugged at his chin. "Perhaps you'd better go on that Tuam raid, Pat. But don't get yourself killed! Come back victorious, and we'll give you a triumph, like a Roman general."

Larry Desmond slapped his knee. "Bedamn—I never knew I was acquainted with so many scholars!" He turned to the sergeant. "How would your Coldstreams react to that, Pat? From deserter to Lord of Barley Cross in a couple of leaps!"

Patrick O'Meara scowled. "*Grenadiers,* not Coldstreams," he corrected. "And they'd still crucify me for it—but probably between a couple of rogues." The military adviser stared pointedly at the general and the vet.

Celia Larkin stirred restlessly in her hospital cot. Memories were crowding in. She watched Patrick O'Meara's tank return from the Tuam raid, and clank down Barley Cross' main street with a load of exuberant soldiers, to halt before the Old Market Hall. She saw Andy McGrath, now trusted to drive, wave from the driver's hatch under the big gun. She heard the cheers of the Barley Cross volunteers, as they shook their rifles to the applause of the crowd. And she saw Patrick O'Meara perched on the cupola of the Chieftain's turret, face grave, as he waited for the planned ceremony.

Denny Mallon stepped forward.

Flinty Hagan, astride the gun barrel, beat him to the punch. "Hi, Doc! We've captured enough pills to cure the plagues of Egypt—and not a man among us so much as scratched!"

Denny Mallon swallowed his prepared text, and started over. He flourished a clenched fist. "Well done, Flinty! We're proud of ye all!"

Larry Desmond pushed through the crowd to stand beside the

232

doctor. The crowd fell silent, expectant. The general shouted, "We ought to promote Pat for this, Dinny!"

Denny Mallon shrugged. "We don't need two generals."

"Och—I mean higher than a gineral," protested the old soldier. "He ought to be our top man, after today."

Well coached, Tessie Mallon called, "Why not make him Lord of Barley Cross?"

Celia Larkin tried to echo her, in turn, but couldn't speak.

An unexpected ally in the crowd yelled, "Pat O'Meara, Lord of Barley Cross!"

His soldiers on the tank took up the chant.

It was done before anyone could protest. Sergeant O'Meara was Lord of Barley Cross by popular acclaim.

He slid down from the turret, and spread his arms for silence. One by one, his men jumped down, surrendering the platform.

He said, "Fellow citizens—you have proved you can stand on your own feet! I'm willing to go on leading you, but it might not always be victories. I might ask you for sacrifices."

"Ask away!" shouted his men, from the crowd, drunk with success.

He grinned. "I know what *you* can do—I trained you!" He waved his arms. "I mean every man and woman in Barley Cross!"

"Ask!" they yelled back.

He stared down at them. They fell silent. He said, "You win—I accept the honour. I hope you won't be—"

His words were drowned by a roar of approval. There hadn't been a day like this since Barley Cross reached the quarter finals in the All-Ireland Hurley Championship.

Mick McGuire, miller and distiller, lost his head. "Into Mooney's with ye all!" he called. "The drinks are on McGuire!"

Celia Larkin watched, dry-eyed. She had lost him now. Pat O'Meara belonged to the village.

He caught her eye, and grinned. He pulled a pair of leather gloves from inside his flak jacket. "A lady left these in my turret. I carried them into battle, like a knight's favours. I hope she'll leave them with me, to bring us luck in the future."

She recognised her best navy-blue gloves. She flushed. The new Lord of Barley Cross was tucking them back inside his jacket. Celia

Larkin abandoned modesty. Placing one foot on a towing eye, she gripped the lamp bracket, and pulled herself onto the armoured deck.

She held out a hand. "I'll take *one* of those, my lord."

He gave her the glove. Bending forward, he whispered, "Goodbye, Cee."

She took the glove. Mouth quivering, she kissed him on the cheek. "Wish you good luck."

Briefly, his arms tightened around her. She heard the crowd's applause. He murmured, "I'll need it. Especially with that idea of yours."

She said, "You've won the women's hearts already. There'll be a queue."

He turned to wave to the crowd. "It's not them I fear—it's their husbands. I'm training them to be killers!"

One last memory to torment a failing mind. A church bell tolling in the night. Celia Larkin throwing a mac over her nightdress, hurrying through dark streets to O'Meara's Fist. The shuttered front door wide open, an oil lamp flickering in the hall. And the Lord of Barley Cross lying on the bottom stair, head cushioned by a servant's jacket.

When Celia entered, Michael stepped back. "Don't try to move him, ma'am."

She bent over him. Patrick O'Meara was still conscious.

"Pat—it's me, Celia."

He recognised her, and smiled. "I went dizzy on the top step. I think my back's broke."

Footsteps were pounding up the hill outside. She said, "Hold on, Pat! Denny's coming. He'll help you."

His eyes rolled. "I'm not sure I can wait that long, alanna. Hold my hand."

She took his cold fingers between her palms. Tears blurred her sight.

He whispered, "I never loved anyone but you, Larkin."

She held his hand until they took him away from her.

In her hospital cot, Celia Larkin wondered if it had all been worth while. She had given him up, so they could make a tyrant out of him. And they had repeated their presumption with poor Liam McGrath. Then, through the open window she heard the shouts of

234

children at play—children no one had ever expected to see. The sounds were vindication enough. If she had her chance, she would do it all over again, willingly.

In her mind, she heard the phantom voices of Larry Desmond, Kevin Murphy, Denny Mallon, and Pat O'Meara grunting in agreement, as was often their wont.

"Amen . . . amen . . . *amen* . . . *AMEN*!"

TRIGGERMAN
Jesse F. Bone

EDITOR'S INTRODUCTION

Sometimes in these days of high technology we forget about the men behind the weapons. There are times when the "The Triggerman" may prove to be more crucial than the weapons he controls.

———————'''———————

GENERAL ALASTAIR FRENCH WAS PROBABLY THE MOST IMPORTANT man in the Western Hemisphere from the hours of 0800 to 1600. Yet all he did was sit in a windowless room buried deeply underground, facing a desk that stood against a wall. The wall was studded with built-in mechanisms. A line of twenty-four-hour clocks was inset near the ceiling, showing the corresponding times in all time zones on Earth. Two huge TV screens below the clocks were flanked on each side by loudspeaker systems. The desk was bare except for three telephones of different colors—red, blue, and white—and a polished plastic slab inset with a number of white buttons framing a larger one whose red surface was the color of fresh blood. A thick carpet, a chair of peculiar design with broad flat arms, and an ashtray completed the furnishings. Warmed and humidified air circulated through the room from concealed grilles at floor level. The walls of the room were painted a soft restful gray, that softened the indirect lighting. The door was steel and equipped with a time lock.

The exact location of the room and the Center that served it was probably the best kept secret in the Western world. Ivan would probably give a good per cent of the Soviet tax take to know precisely where it was, just as the West would give a similar amount to know where Ivan's Center was located. Yet despite the fact that its location was remote, the man behind the desk was in intimate contact with every major military point in the Western Alliance. The red telephone was a direct connection to the White House. The blue was a line that reached to the headquarters of the Joint Chiefs of Staff and to the emergency Capitol hidden in the hills of West Virginia. And the white telephone connected by priority lines with every military center and base in the world that was under Allied control.

General French was that awesome individual often joked about by TV comics who didn't know that he really existed. He was the man who could push the button that would start World War III!

French was aware of his responsibilities and took them seriously. By nature he was a serious man, but, after three years of living with ultimate responsibility, it was no longer the crushing burden that it was at first when the Psychological Board selected him as one of the most inherently stable men on Earth. He was not ordinarily a happy man; his job, and the steadily deteriorating world situation precluded that, but this day was a bright exception. The winter morning had been extraordinarily beautiful, and he loved beauty with the passion of an artist. A flaming sunrise had lighted the whole Eastern sky with golden glory, and the crisp cold air stimulated his senses to appreciate it. It was much too lovely for thoughts of war and death.

He opened the door of the room precisely at 0800, as he had done for three years, and watched a round, pink-cheeked man in a gray suit rise from the chair behind the desk. Kleinmeister, he thought, neither looked like a general nor like a potential executioner of half the world. He was a Santa Claus without a beard. But appearances were deceiving. Hans Kleinmeister could, without regret, kill half the world if he thought it was necessary. The two men shook hands, a ritual gesture that marked the changing of the guard, and French sank into the padded chair behind the desk.

"It's a beautiful day outside, Hans," he remarked as he settled his stocky, compact body into the automatically adjusting plastifoam. "I envy you the pleasure of it."

"I don't envy you, Al," Kleinmeister said. "I'm just glad it's all over for another twenty-four hours. This waiting gets on the nerves." Kleinmeister grinned as he left the room. The steel door thudded into place behind him and the time lock clicked. For the next eight hours French would be alone.

He sighed. It was too bad that he had to be confined indoors on a day like this one promised to be, but there was no help for it. He shifted luxuriously in the chair. It was the most comfortable seat that the mind and ingenuity of man could contrive. It had to be. The man who sat in it must have every comfort. He must want for nothing. And above all he must not be irritated or annoyed. His brain must be free to evaluate and decide—and nothing must distract the functioning of that brain. Physical comfort was a means to that end—and the chair provided it. French felt soothed in the gentle caress of the upholstery.

The familiar feeling of detachment swept over him as he checked the room. Nominally, he was responsible to the President and the Joint Chiefs of Staff, but practically he was responsible to no one. No hand but his could set in motion the forces of massive retaliation that had hung over aggression for the past forty years. Without his sanction no intercontinental or intermediate range missile could leave its rack. He was the final authority, the ultimate judge, and the executioner if need be—a position thrust upon him after years of intensive tests and screening. In this room he was as close to a god as any man had been since the beginning of time.

French shrugged and touched one of the white buttons on the panel.

"Yes, sir?" an inquiring voice came from one of the speakers.

"A magazine and a cup of coffee," said General French.

"What magazine, sir?"

"Something light—something with pictures. Use your judgment."

"Yes, sir."

French grinned. By now the word was going around Center that the Old Man was in a good humor today. A cup of coffee rose from a well in one of the broad arms of the chair, and a magazine extruded from a slot in its side. French opened the magazine and sipped the coffee. General Craig, his relief, would be here in less than eight hours, which would leave him the enjoyment of the second best part of the day if the dawn was any indication. He hoped the sunset would be worthy of its dawn.

He looked at the center clock. The hands read 0817 . . .

At Station 2 along the Dew Line the hands of the station clock read 1217. Although it was high noon it was dark outside, lightened only by a faint glow to the south where the winter sun strove vainly to appear above the horizon. The air was clear, and the stars shone out of the blue-black sky of the polar regions. A radarman bending over his scope stiffened. "Bogey!" he snapped, "Azimuth 0200, coming up fast!"

The bogey came in over the north polar cap, slanting downward through the tenuous wisps of upper atmosphere. The gases ripped at its metallic sides with friction and oxidation. Great gouts of flaming brilliance spurted from its incandescent outer surface boiling away to leave a trail of sparkling scintillation in its wake. It came with enormous speed, whipping over the Station almost before the operator could hit the general alarm.

The tracking radar of the main line converged upon the target. Electronic computers analyzed its size, speed and flight path, passing the information to the batteries of interceptor missiles in the sector. "Locked on," a gunnery officer announced in a bored tone, "Fire two." He smiled. Ivan was testing again. It was almost routine, this business of one side or the other sending over a pilot missile. It was the acid test. If the defense network couldn't get it, perhaps others would come over—perhaps not. It was all part of the cold war.

Miles away two missiles leaped from their ramps flashing skyward on flaming rockets. The gunnery officer waited a moment and then swore. "Missed, by damn! It looks like Ivan's got something new." He flipped a switch. "Reserve line, stand by," he said. "Bogey coming over. Course 0200."

"Got her," a voice came from the speaker of the command set. "All stations in range fire four—salvo!"

239

"My God what's in that thing! Warn Stateside! Execute!"

"All stations Eastseaboard Outer Defense Area! Bogey coming over!"

"Red Alert, all areas!" a communications man said urgently into a microphone. "Ivan's got something this time! General evacuation plan Boston to Richmond Plan One! Execute!"

"Outer Perimeter Fire Pattern B!"

"Center! Emergency Priority! General, there's a bogey coming in. Eastseaboard sector. It's passed the outer lines, and nothing's touched it so far. It's the damndest thing you ever saw! Too fast for interception. Estimated target area Boston-Richmond. For evaluation—!"

"Sector perimeter on target, sir!"

"Fire twenty, Pattern C!"

All along the flight path of the bogey, missile launchers hurled their cargoes of death into the sky. A moving pattern formed in front of the plunging object that now was flaming brightly enough to be seen in the cold northern daylight. Missiles struck, detonated, and were absorbed into the ravening flames around the object, but it came on with unabated speed, a hissing roaring mass of destruction!

"God! It's still coming in!" an anguished voice wailed. "I told them we needed nuclear warheads for close-in defense!"

More missiles swept aloft, but the bogey was now so low that both human and electronic sensings were too slow. An instantaneous blast of searing heat flashed across the land in its wake, crisping anything flammable in its path. Hundreds of tiny fires broke out, most of which were quickly extinguished, but others burned violently. A gas refinery in Utica exploded. Other damage of a minor nature was done in Scranton and Wilkes Barre. The reports were mixed with military orders and the flare of missiles and the crack of artillery hurling box barrages into the sky. But it was futile. The target was moving almost too fast to be seen, and by the time the missiles and projectiles reached intercept point the target was gone, drawing away from the fastest defense devices with almost contemptuous ease.

General French sat upright in his chair. The peaceful expression vanished from his face to be replaced by a hard intent look, as his eyes flicked from phones to TV screen. The series of tracking stations, broadcasting over wire, sent their images in to be edited and projected on the screens in French's room. Their observations appeared at frighteningly short intervals.

French stared at the flaring dot that swept across the screens. It could not be a missile, unless—his mind faltered at the thought— the Russians were farther advanced than anyone had expected. They might be at that—after all they had surprised the world with sputnik, and the West was forced to work like fiends to catch up.

"Target confirmed," one of the speakers announced with unearthly calm. "It's Washington!"

The speaker to the left of the screen broke into life. "This is Conelrad," it said. "This is not a test, repeat—*this is not a test*! The voice faded as another station took over. "A transpolar missile is headed south along the eastern seaboard. Target Washington. Plan One. Evacuation time thirty seconds—

Thirty seconds! French's mind recoiled. Washington was dead! You couldn't go anywhere in thirty seconds! His hand moved toward the red button. This was it!

The missile on the screen was brighter now. It flamed like a miniature sun, and the sound of its passage was that of a million souls in torment! "It can't stand much more of that," French breathed. "It'll burn up!"

"New York Sector—bogey at twelve o'clock—high! God! *Look* at it!"

The glare of the thing filled the screen.

The blue phone rang. "Center," French said. He waited and then laid the phone down. The line was dead.

"Flash!" Conelrad said. "The enemy missile has struck south of New York. A tremendous flash was seen fifteen seconds ago by observers in civilian defense spotting nets . . . No sound of the explosion as yet . . . More information—triangulation of the explosion indicates that it has struck the nation's capitol! Our center of government has been destroyed!" There was a short silence broken by a faint voice: "Oh my God!—all those poor people!"

The red phone rang. French picked it up. "Center," he said.

The phone squawked at him.

"Your authority?" French queried dully. He paused and his face turned an angry red. "Just who do you think you are colonel? I'll

241

take orders from the Chief—but no one else! Now get off that line! . . . Oh, I see. Then it's my responsibility? . . . All right I accept it—now leave me alone!'' He put the phone gently back on the cradle. A fine beading of sweat dotted his forehead. This was the situation he had never let himself think would occur. The President was dead. The Joint Chiefs were dead. He was on his own until some sort of government could be formed.

Should he wait and let Ivan exploit his advantage, or should he strike? Oddly he wondered what his alter ego in Russia was doing at this moment. Was he proud of having struck this blow—or was he frightened. French smiled grimly. If he were in Ivan's shoes, he'd be scared to death! He shivered. For the first time in years he felt the full weight of the responsibility that was his.

The red phone rang again.

"Center—French here . . . Who's that? . . . Oh yes, sir, Mr. Vice . . . er Mr. President! . . . Yes sir, it's a terrible thing . . . What have I done? Well, nothing yet, sir. A single bogey like that doesn't feel right. I'm waiting for the follow up that'll confirm . . . Yes sir I know—but do *you* want to take the responsibility for destroying the world? What if it wasn't Ivan's? Have you thought of that? . . . Yes, sir, it's my judgment that we wait . . . No sir, I don't think so, if Ivan's back of this we'll have more coming, and if we do I'll fire . . . No sir, I will not take that responsibility . . . Yes, I know Washington's destroyed, but we still have no proof of Ivan's guilt. Long-range radar has not reported any activity in Russia. . . . Sorry, sir, I can't see it that way—and you can't relieve me until 1600 hours . . . Yes, sir, I realize what I'm doing . . . Very well, sir, if that's the way you want it I'll resign at 1600 hours. Good-by.'' French dropped the phone into its cradle and wiped his forehead. He had just thrown his career out of the window, but that was another thing that couldn't be helped. The President was hysterical now. Maybe he'd calm down later.

"Flash!'' the radio said. "Radio Moscow denies that the missile which destroyed Washington was one of theirs. They insist that it is a capitalist trick to make them responsible for World War III. The Premier accuses the United States . . . hey! wait a minute! . . . accuses the United States of trying to foment war, but to show the good faith of the Soviet Union, he will open the country to UN inspection to prove once and for all that the Soviet does not and has

242

not intended nuclear aggression. He proposes that a UN team investigate the wreckage of Washington to determine whether the destruction was actually caused by a missile. Hah! Just what in hell does he think caused it?''

French grinned thinly. Words like the last were seldom heard on the lips of commentators. The folks outside were pretty wrought up. There was hysteria in almost every word that had come into the office. But it hadn't moved him yet. His finger was still off the trigger. He picked up the white phone. ''Get me Dew Line Headquarters,'' he said. ''Hello Dew Line, this is French at Center. Any more bogeys? . . . No? . . . That's good . . . No, we're still holding off. . . . Why? . . . Any fool would know why if he stopped to think!'' He slammed the phone back into its cradle. Damn fools howling for war! Just who did they think would win it? Sure, it would be easy to start things rolling. All he had to do was push the button. He stared at it with fascinated eyes. Nearly three billion lives lay on that polished plastic surface, and he could snuff most of them out with one jab of a finger.

''Sir!'' a voice broke from the speaker. ''What's the word—are we in it yet?''

''Not yet, Jimmy.''

''Thank God!'' the voice sounded relieved. ''Just hang on, sir. We know they're pressuring you, but they'll stop screaming for blood once they have time to think.''

''I hope so,'' French said. He chuckled without humor. The personnel at Center knew what nuclear war would be like. Most of them had experience at Frenchman's Flat. They didn't want any part of it if it could be avoided. And neither did he.

The hours dragged by. The phones rang, and Conelrad kept reporting—giving advice and directions for evacuation of the cities. All the nation was stalled in the hugest traffic jam in history. Some of it couldn't help seeping in, even through the censorship. There was danger in too much of anything, and obviously the country was overmechanized. By now, French was certain that Russia was innocent. If she wasn't, Ivan would have struck in force by now. He wondered how his opposite number in Russia was taking it. Was the man crouched over his control board waiting for the cloud of capitalist missiles to appear over the horizon? Or was he, too, fingering a red button debating whether or not to strike before it was too late.

"Flash!" the radio said. "Radio Moscow offers immediate entry to any UN inspection team authorized by the General Assembly. The Presidium has met and announces that under no circumstances will Russia take any aggressive action. They repeat that the missile was not theirs, and suggest that it might have originated from some other nation desirous of fomenting war between the Great Powers . . . ah Nuts!"

"That's about as close to surrender as they dare come," French murmured softly. "They're scared green—but then who wouldn't be?" He looked at the local clock. It read 1410. Less than two hours to go before the time lock opened and unimaginative Jim Craig came through that door to take his place. If the President called with Craig in the seat, the executive orders would be obeyed. He picked up the white phone.

"Get me the Commanding General of the Second Army," he said. He waited a moment. "Hello George, this is Al at Center. How you doing? Bad, huh? No, we're holding off . . . Now hold it, George. That's not what I called for. I don't need moral support. I want information. Have your radiac crews checked the Washington Area yet? . . . They haven't. Why not? Get them on the ball! Ivan keeps insisting that that bogey wasn't his and the facts seem to indicate he's telling the truth for once, but we're going to blast if he can't prove it! I want the dope on radioactivity in that area and I want it now! . . . If you don't want to issue an order—call for volunteers . . . So they might get a lethal dose—so what? . . . Offer them a medal. There's always someone who'd walk into hell for the chance of getting a medal. Now get cracking! . . . Yes, that's an order."

The radio came on again. "First reports of the damage in Washington," it chattered. "A shielded Air Force reconnaissance plane has flown over the blast area, taking pictures and making an aerial survey of fall-out intensity. The Capitol is a shambles. Ground Zero was approximately in the center of Pennsylvania Avenue. There is a tremendous crater over a half mile wide, and around that for nearly two miles there is literally nothing! The Capitol is gone. Over ninety-eight per cent of the city is destroyed. Huge fires are raging in Alexandria and the outskirts. The Potomac bridges are down. The destruction is inconceivable. The landmarks of our—"

French grabbed the white phone. "Find out who the Air Force commander was who sent up that recon plane over Washington!" he barked. "I don't know who he is—but get him *now*!" He waited for three minutes. "So it was you, Willoughby! I thought it might be. This is French at Center. What did that recon find? . . . It did hey? . . . Well now, isn't that simply wonderful! You stupid publicity crazy fool! What do you mean by withholding vital information! Do you realize that I've been sitting here with my finger on the button ready to kill half the earth's population while you've been flirting around with reporters? . . . Dammit! That's no excuse! You should be cashiered—and if I have any influence around here tomorrow, I'll see that you are. As it is, you're relieved as of now! . . . What do you mean I can't do that? . . . Read your regulations again, and then get out of that office and place yourself under arrest in quarters! Turn over your command to your executive officer! You utter driveling fool! . . . Aaagh!!" French snarled as he slammed the phone back.

It began ringing again immediately. "French here . . . Yes, George . . . You have? . . . You did? . . . It isn't? . . . I thought so. We've been barking up the wrong tree this time. It was an act of God! . . . Yes, I said an act of God! Remember that crater out in Arizona? Well, this is the same thing—a meteor! . . . Yes, Ivan's still quiet. Not a peep out of him. The Dew Line reports no activity."

The blue phone began to ring. French looked at it. "O.K., George—apology accepted. I know how you feel." He hung up and lifted the blue phone. "Yes, Mr. President," he said. "Yes, sir. You've heard the news I suppose . . . You've had confirmation from Lick Observatory? . . . Yes, sir, I'll stay here if you wish . . . No, sir, I'm perfectly willing to act. It was just that this never did look right—and thank God that you understand astronomy, sir . . . Of course I'll stay until the emergency is over, but you'll have to tell General Craig . . . Who's Craig?—why he's my relief, sir." French looked at the clock. "He comes on in twenty minutes . . . Well, thank you, sir. I never thought that I'd get a commendation for not obeying orders."

French sighed and hung up. Sense was beginning to percolate

245

through the shock. People were beginning to think again. He sighed. This should teach a needed lesson. He made a mental note of it. If he had anything to say about the make-up of Center from now on—there'd be an astronomer on the staff, and a few more of them scattered out on the Dew Line and the outpost groups. It was virtually certain now that the Capitol was struck by a meteorite. There was no radioactivity. It had been an act of God—or at least not an act of war. The destruction was terrible, but it could have been worse if either he or his alter ego in Russia had lost control and pushed the buttons. He thought idly that he'd like to meet the Ivan who ran their Center.

"The proposals of the Soviet government," the radio interrupted, "have been accepted by the UN. An inspection team is en route to Russia, and others will follow as quickly as possible. Meanwhile the UN has requested a cease-fire assurance from the United States, warning that the start of a nuclear war would be the end of everything." The announcer's voice held a note of grim humor. "So far, there has been no word from Washington concerning these proposals."

French chuckled. It might not be in the best taste, and it might be graveyard humor—but it was a healthy sign.

AN OLD BANKRUPTCY,
A NEW CURRENCY
Jerry Pournelle and Dean Ing

EDITOR'S INTRODUCTION

This essay originally appeared as part of *Mutually Assured Survival*, a book I wrote with Dean Ing in 1983. Although Possony and I devised the strategy of "Assured Survival," Ben Bova was first to use that phrase as the title of a book; hence our title. The book was based on the Executive Summary Report of the Citizens Advisory Council on National Space Policy. Our conclusions were:

1. The President's proposal to change the defensive posture of the United States from Mutual Assured Destruction to Assured Survival is morally correct, technologically feasible, and economically desirable.

2. Significant improvements to national security can be made before the end of the decade.

3. Defense of the nation will require direct Presidential action and support.

How far have we come to reaching these goals in the past five years?

Unfortunately, not very far; certainly nowhere near as far as we need to go. There have been some results: SDI has brought the Soviets scurrying to the negotiating tables and there have been a number of promising technological spin-offs, advances in computer miniaturization, food irradiation, power storage, and fired-reinforced ceramics. We know a lot more about beams and particle physics; and we know about six ways we can intercept ICBMs headed for the U.S.A.

Yet, with the Congress paring expenditures every year, the program remains tentative, and research only. We have deployed nothing; we are no closer to being able to shoot down even a single missile headed for the U.S. than we were in 1980.

There have been obstacles from every side of the moral and political spectrum; from the National Conference of Catholic Bishops, who have decried SDI as morally questionable, to the Soviet scientists who have warned that SDI experiments could litter space with so much junk that it could block the sun and bring forth "Space Winter."

The Pentagon bureaucrats fear that SDI might bring about a rearranging of defense expenditures, and priorities. Congress alternately views SDI as either a giant pork barrel or a tar baby. President Reagan, his administration under attack by the media and Congress, has not been able to give the program the leadership it has needed.

Alas, despite overwhelming public support and new technological advances demonstrating the feasibility of Strategic Defense, we have yet to deploy anything real. There is a movement to put in a limited system called ALS: Accidental Launch System which would stop a limited attack. That's better than nothing, which is what we have now.

––––––––––––––––––––––'ı'––––––––––––––––––––––

THE SO-CALLED "MISSILE GAP" WAS A DECISIVE FACTOR IN THE election of 1960. Now we know that it was illusory; the Soviet Union not only did not have a lead in strategic missiles, but in fact had no real missile capability whatever. After the Cuban missile crisis of 1962 was resolved in U.S. favor largely because of U.S. strategic missile superiority, the Soviets determined never again to allow that to happen. From the early 1960s on they concentrated on developing a commanding lead in intercontinental strategic nuclear power.

By 1970 they had installed four different ICBM assembly lines, and by 1972 these were running three shifts, twenty-four hours a day. Today, in 1984, they continue to operate full time.

By 1978 (and possibly before) the Soviets had achieved strategic superiority, at least in numbers of missiles and deliverable warheads. Superiority is a problematical thing in the nuclear era. There is no point in having an overwhelming capability for destruction if your own nation will also be destroyed. Translating strategic superiority into international political advantage is no simple matter—until you achieve overwhelming superiority, enough to destroy the opponent's ability to strike back.

For a number of years strategists considered a "clean win" to be impossible. Hawks and doves could agree: the best way, the only way, to survive a nuclear war is not to have one.

This is still true, but the situation is changing. As technology develops there could come a time when one side can destroy the other's strategic nuclear forces so thoroughly that no retaliation would be possible. If the Soviet Union ever achieves such superiority, their past actions indicate they will try to translate that capability into strategic power. That will not be a stable world.

The debate over national strategic doctrine has profound implications for the future of the human race. George Orwell said, "If you want a picture of the future, imagine a boot stamping on a human face—forever." If we are to avoid that fate; if we are to preserve freedom and Western Civilization in an era in which the Soviet Union has strategic superiority, we must use every possible advantage. This includes properly exploiting our technologies, and developing superior strategies.

This is difficult but not impossible. The United States holds numerous advantages. We must develop strategies to take advantage of them.

The Origin of MAD

During the Eisenhower Administration, the official doctrine of the United States was "massive retaliation." President Eisenhower defined this as a determination to meet any attack on the U.S. or our allies "with massive retaliation at a time and place of our own choosing." At that time we had the strategic power to make good such a threat.

Shortly after taking office in 1961, Secretary of Defense Robert S. McNamara attended a briefing by the Commander-in-Chief of the Strategic Air Command (SAC). The general showed the Secretary the SIOP—the Single Integrated Operational Plan which would control U.S. strategic weapons in the event of all-out war with the Soviet Union. The SIOP consisted of a target list based on the best intelligence information available to SAC, and a schedule for the elimination of those targets. Every weapon in the U.S. inventory was allocated, and all would be launched within 36 hours.

When the briefing was completed, McNamara expressed horror. "General," he said, "you don't have a war plan. All you have is a kind of horrible spasm."

McNamara was determined to reform the U.S. strategic doctrines, and to give the President a series of options. The new policy was to be called "Flexible Response." Soon, however, McNamara found that "flexible response" would require great skill, sophisticated new weapons, and a lot of money which would have to be extracted from Johnson's "Great Society." While the Congress might then have been willing to pay the price, Johnson and McNamara were not. In part on the advice of a new school of "civilian strategists" trained mostly in Eastern university schools of social science, McNamara opted for a new doctrine.

This was called "Assured Destruction" and was based on the hostage theory. If both the U.S. and Soviet populations would inevitably be destroyed in any nuclear war, then that war would never happen. The United States need not try to retain strategic superiority, because superiority was impossible. "Sufficiency" would be enough. Moreover, the Soviets would soon come to agree. According to the new theory, the only reason the Soviet Union built strategic weapons was from fear of the U.S. weapons; if we stopped building nuclear-tipped ICBMs, so would the Soviets. Given sufficiency on both sides, we would have a highly stable world; a world of Mutual Assured Destruction, or MAD.

This theory was made the basis of U.S. doctrine: after we

deployed 1000 Minuteman missiles, we built no more. The Soviets would now be given a chance to catch up, after which we would negotiate an arms control agreement to stabilize the situation.

They caught up.

They passed us.

They continued to install new missiles. They ringed Europe with their mobile SS-20 missiles, and while developing the capability to reload their existing strategic silos to allow multiple salvoes. Note that this capability can *only* be used for first strikes, since the "reload" missiles are very vulnerable.

To this day they halt not, neither do they slow: their four production lines continue to turn out new nuclear-armed ICBMs 24 hours a day. They have achieved strategic superiority; we must now live with that.

After the election of 1980, President-elect Ronald Reagan asked a number of private citizen groups to provide briefing papers for the new administration. Some of those groups continued after the inauguration. One such group was the Citizens Advisory Council on National Space Policy. Originally sponsored by the Presidents of the American Astronautical Society and the L-5 Society, the Council is largely made up of experts in space science and engineering; but it also includes enthusiasts, home makers, writers, students, and other interested citizens.

The Council is interested in space policy. All members of the Council have agreed that without a rational U.S. defense policy, there can be no U.S. space program. Although all the Council members believe in the defense of the United States, there were considerable disagreements about the nature and feasibility of defensive weapons systems. Many scientists and technologists did not believe defense was possible at all.

The Council was therefore expanded to include several of the nation's foremost experts in laser systems, as well as military planners, computer scientists, and nuclear physicists. The third meeting of the Council was devoted to investigating defense feasibilities and reconciling differences among experts. The goal was to produce a detailed report on defense of the U.S. After long discussion, a report that every member could adopt was drafted. The Council Report, available in its original form from the L-5

Society, was read by the President, and received a letter of commendation from him.

The Citizens Advisory Council is nearly unique in that it includes not only some of the top scientific and technical talent in the nation, but also a number of technically oriented science fiction writers. Their value is highlighted by the results of a recent national news service poll. Of more than a dozen categories of "noted Americans" ranging from chief executives of Fortune 500 companies to politicians, only science fiction writers perceived the *political* importance of space research. The writer members of the Council could hardly fail to see this importance, because most of them were initially trained as physicists and engineers.

Throughout that long July weekend, while discussions spilled out of the spacious Niven home into the warmth of the California evening, members traded good-natured political jokes along with information and expert insights. Several members remarked on their heightened awareness that the goal of the Council transcended ordinary political labels. A conservative could rebel against a policy that maximizes threats against innocent Russian children, yet remain conservative. A liberal could recognize the crucial importance of a *defensive* presence in space, and still be a liberal.

Many of the Council members had special views to impart—a favorite system of hardware, or a particular set of priorities toward the national good. Some of these views were bound to meet head-to-head in committee sessions, and those sessions were always lively (occasionally acrimonious). But narrow vested interests were always subordinated to the single, overriding vested interest of the Council: to outline a specific and complete alternative to this nation's declared nuclear strategy of Mutually Assured Destruction (MAD).

The original arguments for MAD could have had some validity when then-Secretary of Defense Robert McNamara espoused them in the 1960s. They could have, that is, if the Soviet Union had accepted them. MAD always depended on the *mutual* belief that whichever of the superpowers initiated a nuclear war, both nations would be utterly annihilated: Mutual Assured Destruction. Mutual MADness, if you will.

Now, a generation later, we see overwhelming evidence that the

252

Soviets do not now and never did believe in MAD. They have, however, profited enormously from *our* belief in it. We dismantled our fledgling antiballistic missile (ABM) system and we largely abandoned our Civil Defense plans which might (still!) save a hundred million American lives. We openly admitted that our cities were hostage to the Soviets. To this moment we are hostages still.

As for the Soviet strategy: they have an upgraded ABM system protecting Moscow, and they have a vigorous, continuing C D establishment which directly involves over twenty *million* Soviet citizens trained as a nuclear survival cadre. In addition, they have tested advanced antisatellite weapon systems that might make us incapable of responding to a nuclear first strike. In short, the Soviet Union clearly plans to survive nuclear war. This isn't to suggest that Soviet planners envision a holocaust without damage to themselves, nor that they necessarily plan to start such a war. It *does* show that, unlike us, they do not despair of surviving that war; if it comes, they intend to win it. That, they proclaim and believe, is the very purpose of governments.

Since MAD always depended on both sides believing in it, our MAD strategy has not bought us a stable, peaceful future. It cannot even purchase parity in weaponry when our opponent is developing offensive orbital weapons. MAD is not merely threadbare; it is bankrupt.

This conclusion was the cement binding Council members toward a common goal. The U.S. doesn't need more nuclear warheads with more terrifying offensive capability. Nor can we match the Soviets in their huge conventional armaments without severe economic problems. Instead, we need an alternative to MAD; a less provocatively offensive, more prudently defensive strategy. For maximum effectiveness, the new strategy must be based on our strengths and its validity must *not* fundamentally depend upon unverifiable and unenforceable agreements. Finally, an optimum U.S. strategy will provide hope for a future that escapes the gloomy prediction of groups like the Club of Rome and their well-known report, *The Limits To Growth*. It's not enough that we abandon the bankruptcy of MAD; we must generate a vital new currency.

Even in the 1950s a few far-sighted strategic theorists understood that the Intercontinental Ballistic Missile (ICBM) was not necessarily an ultimate weapon, and that alternatives to MAD were possible. Some were military officers who understood that MAD was not truly mutual, because the Soviet Union would never accept the doctrine. They argued persuasively for their views; but true to their oaths, when decisions were made by civilian political authorities, they obeyed orders.

Others were civilians: strategists, scientists, engineers, systems analysts in the aerospace industry, who had been involved in long range planning studies. Their research showed new technologies not yet available, but which when they came on line would negate the power of the ICBM. These far-sighted planners urged development of these systems, including ways to intercept missiles in flight. All of the best strategists, military and civilian, understood that the ICBM was no "ultimate weapon," that indeed there can be no ultimate weapons. It is the nature of the technological war that there are no final answers. Every new development has within it the seeds of a counter weapon. The technological war will never end. Fortunately, the battles in that war are generally bloodless.

By the 1960s both the U.S. and the Soviets had proof that an ICBM could be intercepted. The United States worked from theoretical analysis of weapons effects. The Soviets moved rapidly to actual tests. In one test they launched three ICBM re-entry vehicles (RV's) and detonated a nuclear interception weapon near the first. This gave them considerable data on the effects of nuclear weapons in space and the upper atmosphere. Before the United States could repeat those tests, the Soviets agreed to an atmospheric Test Ban Treaty. This gave the Soviets a considerable lead in ICBM defense technology.

In 1964 the Soviets paraded their newest ICBM interceptor, which NATO gave the code name "GALOSH". This interceptor missile used a nuclear warhead designed to detonate above the atmosphere. The presumed kill mechanism was a surge of hard X-rays which would disrupt an incoming RV and its nuclear warhead.

The U.S. system was designated "SAFEGUARD" and employed both the Spartan, which was designed for very high altitude intercept much like the Soviet Galosh, and the Sprint. Both employed nuclear warheads; the Sprint used a comparatively low yield weapon. The Sprint, a two-stage solid propelled rocket, boasted an acceleration so high that, two seconds after launch, it was a mile above the launcher. Of course the Sprint was intended to intercept its target much higher (its range was twenty-five miles). But by this time we had discovered some of the subtler effects of a nuclear detonation. We had seen how a nuclear airburst could generate an electromagnetic pulse (EMP) that could devastate communication and computer equipment thousands of miles away. U.S. nuclear warheads detonated over our own soil, even many miles high above our soil, were, to put it mildly, not an attractive proposition. Many on this Council would argue that even the most devastating EMP pulse would be cheap compared to a groundburst, but that is an issue for another book.

Some designers pointed out that ballistic missile warheads travel at such enormous speeds (several miles per second) that they could be destroyed by "kinetic energy kill," meaning impact with a hunk of material no larger than a bullet, or even a small stone. If we could hurl a device into the path of an incoming warhead and then distribute tiny pieces of material, shotgun style, so that the warhead could not avoid them all, we would destroy that warhead. This kinetic energy kill scheme was relatively simple, it was non-nuclear, and particles that missed their targets would burn up harmlessly, high above our soil.

Other kill mechanisms, including directed nuclear debris, were also possible. In a series of papers published in 1968, and later in their book *The Strategy of Technology*, Stefan T. Possony and Jerry E. Pournelle argued that the United States should abandon the doctrine of Assured Destruction, and instead adopt a strategy of Assured Survival. Specific proposals included conversion of a portion of the existing Minuteman missiles to defensive systems, together with deployment of sufficient offensive Minuteman systems to bring the force back to strength.

Defensive systems included both "pop-up" area protection missiles designed to foil a massive Soviet strike, and hardened command, communications, control, and intelligence (C3I) systems to allow damage assessment and precision employment of the surviving Minuteman force.

The debate over U.S. grand strategy—Assured Destruction vs. Assured Survival—was carried out at high levels in the government, but never became part of public or Congressional debate.

Most of the arguments were technical. Many engineers and scientists doubted our ability to detect and track intercontinental missiles. There were more misgivings about the ability to place an interceptor missile precisely in the path of an incoming warhead. Although many highly qualified members of the technical community were convinced that the United States would be able to develop reliable non-nuclear kill mechanisms sufficient to protect the Titan and Minuteman bases, the conventional wisdom of the time was that "we cannot hit a bullet with a bullet."

Instead, the MAD strategy was adopted. The iron logic of MAD required that all defensive systems, including civil defense, be abandoned. The original plans for the Interstate Highway System included fallout and blast shelters to be constructed within many of the freeway on-ramps. This plan had already suffered under McNamara and Johnson; it was now abandoned. Meanwhile, negotiators were sent to procure by Arms Control agreements the security the United States refused to provide itself through technology.

Under the terms of the Ballistic Missile Defense Treaty (separate from, but signed on the same day as the Strategic Arms Limitation Treaty or SALT), the U.S. and the Soviet Union could each retain one Anti-Ballistic Missile (ABM) system. For a short period of time we experimented with such a system to protect the missile bases in Montana. The Soviets chose to protect missile sites in the suburbs of Moscow.

The Soviet Union has recently begun to expand their Moscow ABM system, and are now upgrading it with hypervelocity Sprint-type rockets. They have also deployed long range radar arrays suitable for nuclear battle-management far from their borders, in clear violation of the ABM Treaty. Our only ABM system was dismantled nearly a decade ago.

Two arguments were given for discarding ABM. First, the most influential technical analysts discarded the concept of non-nuclear interception as infeasible, not recognizing that research and development would soon produce new means (such as on-board micro computers) for greatly increasing intercept accuracy. Secondly, it was argued, defensive systems are illogical, since the doctrine of MAD demands that both sides remain perfectly vulnerable. If both U.S. and Soviet populations are hostage, then peace is assured; and anything which mitigates the horrors of war paradoxically increases the chances that war will begin. The Soviets have never accepted this argument.

Moreover, when lasers were first developed, a number of laser scientists argued that lasers would never be powerful enough to destroy or damage aircraft and missiles. Certainly early laser systems were insufficient; the early lasers were both low power and inefficient. However, a decade later, the United States openly demonstrated an airborne antimissile laser that can and does destroy not only aircraft, but also small air-to-air missiles in flight. Beam technologies are still in their infancy, and even more dramatic advances can be expected.

During the 1970s, advances in semiconductors, infrared sensors, and radar provided very much better target acquisition. It began to look as if impact weapons might indeed be able to stop a bullet with a bullet. But it looked that way only to a few who bothered to plug in the new advances, and to consider some fresh conclusions. By the mid-1970s, those few were already working to convince others that MAD was fatally flawed; not only was it now feasible to defend against ICBMs, but the Soviets appeared to be working feverishly toward that very goal. Indeed, in some of the most promising areas of research the Soviets were ahead of us even then. During the late 1970s, some Council members were arguing that MAD was obsolete, and that with its new technologies the U.S. could devise strategic defense worthy of the name. Such a system would at worst save many millions of lives by protecting our population and, by its very presence, lessen the attractiveness of a first strike.

The deterrence of a defense system that is only somewhat effective is absurdly underrated by critics. Professor William Baugh (both a physicist and political scientist) has explained it succinctly in his evenhanded new textbook, *The Politics of Nuclear Balance*. As Baugh puts it, "The intent in building such a defense is not to achieve perfection in the form of zero enemy penetration, but to reduce enemy penetration to the point that any attack is deterred by uncertainty about its effects." In other words, if your enemy's missile farms might survive it, the attractiveness of a first strike is much reduced.

By mid-1983, Council members had already shown that such strategies could be developed. But could the heartfelt views of thirty experts be abraded down to something approaching a unanimous opinion without erasing all detail in the process? A man who has spent thirty years cursing experimental devices that determinedly resist translation into foolproof, mass-producible hardware has a natural inbred reluctance to bet on an unproved technology—just as a scientist who has seen his experimental hardware perform several orders of magnitude better than older gadgetry, is unlikely to opt for yesterday's systems.

It was Jerry Pournelle who kept the various committees, deliberating in separated portions of chez Niven, aware of developments elsewhere in the house. Sometimes a committee member would be invited by the Chairman to take a half-hour sabbatical with another group. Almost as often the roving Chairman, upon finding that a committee had reached consensus on some detail, passed the datum on to the other committees. There are times when the timbre and decibel level of Chairman Pournelle's voice are sorely needed; the July Council meeting was one of those times. In this way, the various groups managed to avoid the false starts and reiterations that plague so many large councils.

The findings of the Systems Assessment Group were particularly crucial for several reasons. Its members included top-ranked experts in several areas of defense technology (although the discussions remained on an unclassified level); and it was their task to decide which systems proposed by the other groups would be most effective in defending against nuclear attack.

For an example, some defensive weaponry would not require a continuing human presence in space. Those that did might require manned space stations, a longer development time, or a lunar settlement. Clearly, the report of the Systems Assessment Group would figure in the deliberations of the committees on strategy and economics. But information flowed in all directions; there was no advantage in recommending a system which had inferior strategic value, or which was inordinately expensive even if it did fry the proposer's fish particularly well.

On the evening of Saturday, 30 July 1983, the Systems Assessment Group drafted a set of recommendations that was read in plenary session. The other committees, already provided with "leaks" as to the general nature of those recommendations, were also ready with portions of a letter to the White House stating the findings of the Council.

Inevitably, the plenary session unearthed minor disagreements which required resolution. It was the intent of the Chairman to extract, somehow, a letter draft that was unanimously acceptable to attending members. Perfect unanimity still escaped us at the end of the Saturday session, but by then we were all satisfied with the content of the letter. The only remaining problems lay with the phrasing. One engineer, easing into the Niven Jacuzzi that night, wryly voiced a consensus opinion: "We don't have many writers," he grinned, "but every s.o.b. with a pencil thinks he's an editor. . . ."

On Sunday, 31 July 1983, another plenary session yielded phrasing that was acceptable to every member present. Since the letter emanated from the Systems Assessment Group, it was quite brief, addressing only the imperative of specific defenses against ballistic missiles. MAD was not even mentioned; it was simply superseded by implication. Other Council recommendations were collated for inclusion in a 135-page summary report, which was submitted to the White House later. They range from the industrial exploitation of space to the strategic question of stability and our belief that the Soviets and others should be invited to develop space-based ballistic missile defenses of their own. Also, the findings provided a data base for subsequent meetings of the Council. They gave us reason for optimism, not only for citizens under the shadow of nuclear weapons, but for generations yet unborn in every nation on Earth and, we believe, beyond Earth. They gave us, in brief, a glimpse of Mutually Assured Survival.

To deprive our more tendentious critics of a straw man to knock over, we emphasize once again, what Assured Survival does not and cannot mean. While it does, once implemented, assure the continued existence of all peoples, and increase the chance of that existence being a peaceful one, it does not—no strategy can—provide perfect assurance of the survival of everyone, or of any one person. Terrorists might one day detonate a nuclear weapon inside a city; it is also conceivable that a missile, or several missiles, might be fired through error or insanity on the part of some local commander; nuclear-tipped ballistic missiles might still be unleashed in general warfare—but with Assured Survival in place, most of these dreadful weapons, perhaps almost all, would be intercepted. The casualties of such a war would probably be unequalled in human history—but at *the very least, scores of millions of people would survive who, without a defensive umbrella, would have died.* What is the dollar value of fifty million lives?

It is absurd to demand that a system save 100% of the people in its care, to demand that no defensive umbrella be developed unless it be guaranteed to intercept *every* hostile weapon. No rational physician would claim 100% certainty that an operation would be successful for every patient; no rational designer of automobile restraint systems would claim that his system assures the survival of every user. The operation and the restraint system should, however, assure the survival of many, and better the chances of all.

Strategists ignore the defensive aspects of war at their peril. From Sun Tzu to Clausewitz, the best strategy analysts have always regarded the defense as "the stronger form of war." Hannibal was a master at combining defense with offense. The French won at the Marne through counter-offensive strategy.

Stalin regarded the counter-offensive as the most significant form of war, and to this day the Strategic Defense Forces are a separate branch of service in the Soviet Union, taking precedence over the Soviet Air Force and the Soviet Navy. The Defense Forces are a separate and unified combat organization, reporting directly to the Supreme Commander. They are always commanded by a Marshal of the Soviet Union. The Soviet Army (Land Forces) is five times the size of the Strategic Defense Force, but is headed only by a General of the Army.

It is high time that U.S. strategists, including academic theoreticians, rediscover strategic defense; to reject defensive systems on the grounds that they are imperfect is absurd. Assured Survival cannot assure the survival of any particular individual, but it can provide assurance that many more individuals, and society itself, will survive. To demand absolute perfection from fallible humanity is to demand the unattainable, and those who demand the unattainable are not to be taken seriously.

Once it was popular to characterize an impossible demand as "asking for the Moon." Now, Americans have landed on the Moon, and we stand ready to return. With clearer vision we could have gone from our lunar demonstrations to more practical developments.

THROUGH ROAD NO WHITHER
Greg Bear

EDITOR'S INTRODUCTION

Greg Bear is married to Astrid Anderson, whom I literally watched grow up. Sometimes that makes me feel old.

Greg needs no help from his father-in-law; if he collects any more awards they'll have to retire the trophies. He's also currently the President of Science Fiction Writers of America, a post I held more years ago than I care to remember.

We are told that all tyrannies mellow. Perhaps.

―――――――――――"ǀ"―――――――――――

THE LONG BLACK MERCEDES RUMBLED OUT OF THE FOG ON THE road south from Dijon, moisture running in cold trickles across its windshield. Horst von Ranke carefully read the maps spread on his lap, eyeglasses perched low on his nose, while Waffen Schutzstaffel Oberleutnant Albert Fischer drove. "Thirty-five kilometers," von Ranke said under his breath. "No more."

"We are lost," Fischer said. "We've already come thirty-six."

"Not quite that many. We should be there any minute now."

Fischer nodded and then shook his head. His high cheekbones

261

and long, sharp nose only accentuated the black uniform with silver death's heads on the high, tight collar. Von Ranke wore a broad-striped gray suit; he was an undersecretary in the Propaganda Ministry. They might have been brothers, yet one had grown up in Czechoslovakia, the other in the Ruhr; one was the son of a coal miner, the other of a brewer. They had met and become close friends in Paris, two years before, and were now sightseeing on a three-day pass in the countryside.

"Wait," von Ranke said, peering through the drops on the side window. "Stop."

Fischer braked the car and looked in the direction of von Ranke's long finger. Near the roadside, beyond a copse of young trees, was a low thatch-roofed house with dirty gray walls, almost hidden by the fog.

"Looks empty," von Ranke said.

"It is occupied; look at the smoke," Fischer said. "Perhaps somebody can tell us where we are."

They pulled the car over and got out, von Ranke leading the way across a mud path littered with wet straw. The hut looked even dirtier close-up. Smoke curled in a darker brown-gray twist from a hole in the peak of the thatch. Fischer nodded at his friend and they cautiously approached. Over the crude wooden door, letters wobbled unevenly in some alphabet neither knew, and between them they spoke nine languages. "Could that be Rom?" Fischer asked, frowning. "It does look familiar—Slavic Rom."

"Gypsies? Romany don't live in huts like this, and besides, I thought they were rounded up long ago."

"That's what it looks like," von Ranke repeated. "Still, maybe we can share some language, if only French."

He knocked on the door. After a long pause, he knocked again, and the door opened before his knuckles made the final rap. A woman too old to be alive stuck her long, wood-colored nose through the crack and peered at them with one good eye. The other was wrapped in a sunken caul of flesh. The hand that gripped the door edge was filthy, its nails long and black. Her toothless mouth cracked into a wrinkled, round-lipped grin. "Good evening," she said in perfect, even elegant German. "What can I do for you?"

"We need to know if we are on the road to Dôle," von Ranke said, controlling his repulsion.

262

"Then you're asking the wrong guide," the old woman said. Her hand withdrew and the door started to close. Fischer kicked out and pushed it back. The door swung open and began to lean on worn-out leather hinges.

"You do not regard us with the proper respect," he said. "What do you mean, 'the wrong guide'? What kind of guide are you?"

"So *strong*," the old woman crooned, wrapping her hands in front of her withered chest and backing away into the gloom. She wore colorless, ageless grey rags. Worn knit sleeves extended to her wrists.

"Answer me!" Fischer said, advancing despite the strong odor of urine and decay in the hut.

"The maps I know are not for this land," she sang, stopping before a cold and empty hearth.

"She's crazy," von Ranke said. "Let the local authorities take care of her later. Let's be off." But a wild look was in Fischer's eye. So much filth, so much disarray, and impudence as well; these things made him angry.

"What maps do you know, crazy woman?" he demanded.

"Maps in time," the old woman said. She let her hands fall to her side and lowered her head, as if, in admitting her specialty, she was suddenly humble.

"Then tell us where we are," Fischer sneered.

"Come," von Ranke said, but he knew it was too late. There would be an end, but it would be on his friend's terms, and it might not be pleasant.

"On a through road no whither," the old woman said.

"What?" Fischer towered over her. She stared up as if at some prodigal son, returned home, her gums shining spittle.

"If you wish a reading, sit," she said, indicating a low table and three tattered cane and leather chairs. Fischer glanced at her, then at the table.

"Very well," he said, suddenly and falsely obsequious. Another game, von Ranke realized. Cat and mouse.

Fischer pulled out a chair for his friend and sat across from the old woman. "Put your hands on the table, palms down, both of them, both of you," she said. They did so. She lay her ear to the table as if listening, eyes going to the beams of light coming through the thatch. "Arrogance," she said. Fischer did not react.

263

"A road going into fire and death," she said. "Your cities in flame, your women and children shriveling to black dolls in the heat of their burning homes. The camps are found and you stand accused of hideous crimes. Many are tried and hung. Your nation is disgraced, your cause abhorred." Now a peculiar light came into her eye. "And many years later, a comedian will swagger around on stage, in a movie, turning your Führer Into a silly clown, singing a silly song. Only psychotics will believe in you, the lowest of the low. Your nation will be divided between your enemies. All will be lost."

Fischer's smile did not waver. He pulled a coin from his pocket and threw it down before the woman, then pushed the chair back and stood.

"Your maps are as crooked as your chin, hag," he said. "Let's go."

"I've been suggesting that," von Ranke said. Fischer made no move to leave. Von Ranke tugged on his arm but the SS Oberleutnant shrugged free of his friend's grip.

"Gypsies are few now, hag," he said. "Soon to be fewer by one." Von Ranke managed to urge him just outside the door. The woman followed and shaded her eye against the misty light.

"I am no gypsy," she said. "You do not even recognize the words?" She pointed at the letters above the door.

Fischer squinted, and the light of recognition dawned in his eyes. "Yes," he said. "Yes, I do, now. A dead language."

"What are they?" von Ranke asked, uneasy.

"Hebrew, I think," Fischer said. "She is a Jewess."

"No!" the woman cackled. "I am no Jew."

Von Ranke thought the woman looked younger now, or at least stronger, and his unease deepened.

"I do not care what you are," Fischer said quietly. "I only wish we were in my father's time." He took a step toward her. She did not retreat. Her face became almost youthfully bland, and her bad eye seemed to fill in. "Then, there would be no regulations, no rules—I could take this pistol"—he tapped his holster—"and apply it to your filthy Kike head, and perhaps kill the last Jew in Europe." He unstrapped the holster. The women straightened in the dark hut, as if drawing strength from Fischer's abusive tongue.

Von Ranke feared for his friend. Rashness would get them in trouble.

"This is not our fathers' time," he reminded Fischer.

Fischer paused, the pistol half in his hand, his finger curling around the trigger. "Old woman—" Though she did not look half as old, perhaps not even old at all, and certainly not bent and crippled. "You have had a very narrow shave this afternoon."

"You have no idea who I am," the woman half-sang, half-moaned.

"*Scheisse*," Fischer spat. "Now we will go, and report you and your hovel."

"I am the scourge," she breathed, and her breath smelled like burning stone even three strides away. She backed into the hut but her voice did not diminish. "I am the visible hand, the pillar of cloud by day and the pillar of fire by night."

Fischer laughed. "You are right," he said to von Ranke, "she isn't worth our trouble." He turned and stomped out the door. Von Ranke followed, with one last glance over his shoulder into the gloom, the decay. *No one has lived in this hut for years*, he thought. Her shadow was gray and indefinite before the ancient stone hearth, behind the leaning, dust-covered table.

In the car, von Ranke sighed. "You *do* tend toward arrogance, you know that?"

Fischer grinned and shook his head. "You drive, old friend. *I'll* look at the maps." Von Ranke ramped up the Mercedes' turbine until its whine was high and steady and its exhaust cut a swirling hole in the fog behind. "No wonder we're lost," Fischer said. He shook out the Pan-Deutschland map peevishly. "This is five years old—1979."

"We'll find our way," von Ranke said.

From the door of the hut, the old woman watched, head bobbing. "I am not a Jew," she said, "but I loved them, too, oh, yes. I loved all my children." She raised her hand as the long black car roared into the fog.

"I will bring you to justice, whatever line you live upon, and all your children, and their children's children," she said. She dropped a twist of smoke from her elbow to the dirt floor and waggled her finger. The smoke danced and drew black figures in the dirt. "Into the time of your fathers." The fog grew thinner. She brought her arm down, and forty years melted away with the mist.

High above, a deeper growl descended on the road. A wide-winged shadow passed over the hut, wings flashing stars, invasion stripes and cannon fire.

"Hungry bird," the shapeless figure said. "Time to feed."

LOGAN
Paul Edwin Zimmer

EDITOR'S INTRODUCTION

In these days of blank verse and random word patterns the epic poem is almost a lost art form. Yet, in times past it was the prince of poetry. Much of our knowledge of the Sumerians, the Greeks, and other ancient cultures comes from surviving epic poems, such as *Gilgamesh, the Iliad, Beowulf,* and the *Guillaume d'Orange.*

The decline of the epic in our culture may well be related to the rise of the "common man" ethos. In the Homeric epics there was a celebration of the *heros,* or hero; the superior man who excelled in war and adventure. The Greeks admired above all the virtues of courage and loyalty. In our culture we are told to prize the anti-hero—the man who stands aloof and above such lesser values as duty or love of community. True, the anti-hero may have a sense of personal courage or family loyalty, but it is the bravery of the outsider, one who has nothing to lose; there is no sacrifice here.

Some scholars believe that the Homeric and other early epic poems reflect the values of cultures dominated by a warrior or feudal aristocracy. The hero's exploits were celebrated in songs and ballads by wandering bards. Thus, they exemplified the ideals of early civilizations; I doubt such could be said of much of the body of modern poetry.

Here in "Logan" we find a rare exception as Paul Edwin Zimmer, younger brother of Marion Zimmer Bradley, tells of the trials of James Logan—"The White Man's Friend"—as he attempted to work out a lasting peace between the early American settlers and the Indians who had formed the League of Five Nations. It was a conflict doomed to end in Armageddon.

———————————'ı'———————————

We are met upon the gravesite
Of a million murdered children;
We are met beneath the shadow
Of slaughtered women, children.
But who can count a million,
Or can mourn a hundred thousand,
When the Earth we walk is made up
Of the bones of many millions?
A multitude is faceless, and one cannot mourn
A cipher.
All statistics of destruction are as empty
As the sorrow that is given by convention.
Yet—
Who is there to mourn for Logan?

Now listen, ye who established the Great League!
Now it has grown old.
Now it is nothing but wilderness.
Ye are in your graves,
Ye who established it.

Deganoweda and Hayenwatha
Comb the snakes
From Atotarho's hair.
The Long House reaches

268

From the Great Lakes to the Hudson:
Five tribes shelter
Beneath the Great Peace.
The Senecas sit at the
Western Gate;
The Cayuga between them
And the fire.
At the Eastern Gate
The People of the Flint
The Canienga,
Gaze towards the ocean
Over those who call them Mohawks.
Between them and the fire
The Oneida sit.
Between the Cayuga and the Oneida
The Onandaga keep the Council fire—
That was the roll of you—
You that combined in the work,
You that completed the work,
The Great Peace.

But the sea has coughed up thirteen tribes,
White-skinned outlaws from beyond the dawn.
Heretics and traders, convicts and slavers,
They sit themselves down by the Eastern Gate.
They trade guns for beaverskins,
They bring beads and whiskey—
Whiskey! Whiskey!
They eat up the land
Of the lesser tribes
(Broken peoples flock to the Long House).
The forest echoes to the drum of their axes,
And trembles to the tale of toppling timber.
Dutchmen and English,
Puritans and rogues—
They trade guns for beaverskins,
They bring beads and whiskey—
Whiskey! Whiskey!
They prey on the lesser tribes

And quarrel among themselves.
Catholics in Maryland,
Puritans in Plymouth,
Quakers in Penn's Woods.
Dutch, Scots, and English,
Rich men and poor—
Convicts, landed gentry—
How they hate each other!

Etho! They have no Hayenwatha:
The serpent locks of hatred
Must writhe and hiss uncombed.
No Deganoweda speaks to still
The ancient feuds, covering old corpses;
Singing spilled blood to silence.
They quarrel over the land
Of the lesser tribes—
For *they* lock up land in little boxes,
Plowing up their Mother
With the labour of black brother.
They disagree about the nature
Of a single, distant, god.
Barbarous and bloody,
Divided by hatred;
They watch and wait
By the Eastern Gate.
No Council governs them,
Keeps peace between them,
No Council speaks for them all . . .
But—
They have a King across the sea . . .

The King he sits in London Town,
Planning his long French war:
Saying: "Indian allies we must have
To defend the American Shore.
The Hurons with the French have joined
To drive us into the sea:
We must send gifts to the Iroquois
To bind their League to me."

Messengers now come to the Long House;
Bearers of gifts from the English King.
Old men listen to promises of peace,
While young men listen to words of war.
Ten pounds sterling for each Huron scalp;
Paid in bright cloth and beads,
In powder and in lead, and in sharp steel hatchets.
Huron scalps are better than beaverskins!

White belts are given to the English King,
And peace, and war both made.
Frenchmen are good in stew.
Huron scalps are better than beaverskins:
They bring guns and hatchets,
Woven cloth and beads,
Powder, lead, and whiskey
Whiskey! Whiskey!
The Hurons are broken,
Eries and Attiwandaronks crushed.
Broken bands fly westward,
And prisoners and orphans
Absorbed by the League,
Adopted into the Clans:
New sons and daughters
Swell the ranks of the Five Nations—
And the League stands
More strongly than before.

Up from the south
Tuscaroras come flying—
Slavers have been hunting them,
The supply of blacks is low.
Beaded wampum figures
On a white wampum belt
Link hands to hold up the tree.
The youngest brother
Takes his place by the fire
To live in peace upon Oneida land:
Six Nations now, instead of Five,
The League stands

More strongly than before.
Sheltered by their treaty
With the English King,
Rich and powerful, strongest
Of all the tribes,
Allies now with the white-skinned folk
Who trade guns for beaverskins
And bring beads and whiskey—
Sheltered by their treaty with the English King
The League stands more strongly than before. . . .

The seasons came and went, the years whirled by;
Wind Keeper drove his creatures across the land.
Dead leaves scattered: so did the foes of the League.
Into Ireokwa hands
The Northern nations give belts of peace,
To intercede with the English King,
And stand between the White Man and the Red.
Ojibway and Chippewa,
Delaware and Shawnee,
Miami and Illinois—
All listen in silence
When Six Nations meet.
The League forbids them war;
Bids them grow
Three Sisters,
Corn, Squash and Beans.
Nor may they sell their land to whites
Unless the League gives leave.

Between White Man and Red, the Great League stands:
The treaty belts for all the North gathered in their hands.

But listen, ye who established the Great League!
Now it has grown old.
Now it is nothing but wilderness.
Ye are in your graves,
Ye who established it!

Thus it began.
The Shawnee shelter in the shadow of the Long House;

Swatana is sent, the staunch Oneida,
Legate from the League to the lesser tribes
To represent as regent Ireokwa rule
And shield the Shawnee from shady dealings,
As accredited Ambassador to the English.
With him his children came,
Cayugas, of their mother's clan and tribe:
Tagnegtoris was the eldest;
White men called him John Shikellimy.
Sagoheyata was the youngest;
John Petty was easier on the English tongue.
And thus their brother, Soyegtowa,
Was called James Logan,
The "White Man's friend."

Upon the Ohio, old and honored,
Worn out with work for White Man and Red,
The ageing Oneida his ancestors met:
Swatana sought strawberries on the skybound trail.
Sing the Karenna
White Man and Red!
Raise the praise
Of the honoured dead.
Sing to greet and thank the League,
Sing to greet and thank his kinsmen.
Thank the men and thank the women;
Lay the wampum on the grave.
Swatana's sons now sorrow with the Shawnee.

Wind Keeper's wind creatures wander across the land,
Driving years before them in a whirl of leaves.
White Bear Wind breathes winter through the trees,
Harrying wolves and bobcats south with swirling snow.
Timid Fawn Wind from the South
Breathes Spring into the green buds.
Thus seasons pass, and the selfless brothers,
The Oneida exile's offspring among the Ohio Shawnee
Fulfill their father's mission freely for the League.
But Logan is lonely: the League far distant.
From his Cayuga kinsmen he is cut off.

His youthful years filled with the usual yearnings
The lonesome Logan longs for love.

Unlock your legs to Logan, lovely maid.
Let the sachem's seed inside you
Fill you full; feel not afraid
But widen your womb for the wise and true.

Lonely no longer, let the Cayuga
Conceive him kin in your kind embrace
Found a family, far from Ireokwa,
Rejoice in the renewal of his race.

Babies are born of the blood of Logan,
Lonely no longer along the Ohio;
Cherished by the chieftain, his children grow,
To play in the peace his prestige has brought—
For the father never falters in his fight for peace.

Though shrewdly shielding his Shawnee charges,
He wins White friends by the wisdom of his counsel:
Wars were averted, and once, when words failed,
And death and destruction by deaf ears wrought,
Calm in his cabin, the Cayuga chief
Sorrowed for the slaughter and sought for peace;
Well was he famed as "the White Man's friend."

Where Logan dwells along the Ohio
Peace is preserved by his prestige alone.
Peacekeeper's prize is not praise from the Council,
But the laughter of little ones who live free from war.
The Cayuga keeps peace from his care for his children.
A fond father, he forges them joy
Telling old tales by the twilight fires;
A legacy of legend for Logan's children,
Of husk masks and false faces,
Of stonish giants and flying heads.
He tells how He-noh, the Thunderer
Fills thirsty fields,
How gladly the Three Sisters drink rain.
Of Wind Keeper's wind creatures, and when
    and why they come,

Of Onestah, corn spirit, who feeds us all.
Closely clutching their cornhusk dolls,
Little ones listen, alight with joy
Their wondering faces watching their father.
Old Logan lives in his children.

Ohio River, flow with tears,
For after years the blow
Will fall, and Logan sorrow know.

White Bear Wind brings winter many times,
Stalking in snowstorms the silent ice river.
Winters have whitened the warrior's locks,
and long-lived Logan, who loves his children,
And shields the Shawnee on the shores of the Ohio,
Their gray-haired guardian: is a grandfather now.

The Virginia governor, Lord Dunmore,
Casts covetous eyes on Ohio land.
The vastness of the West impels his dreams,
And bends his mind to Westward rulership.
To rule a tract stretching from sea to sea,
Would be a post more fit for belted Earl.
What though the King has treaties made with tribes
Of red-skinned savage pagans in the North?
His Colonials would gladly drive them forth,
And the Crown would gain thereby. These jailbirds
With whom the King had charged him were scarce fit
To be called men: disloyalty was rife.
Already tea was floating in Boston Harbour;
Rabble-rousers ranted in the taverns
And public streets of Williamsburg itself.
Indian war would keep them occupied.
Rebels and red niggers could kill each other.
The King would come to recognize his worth.

That scoundrel Greathouse was the tool to use,
And that fool, Cresap—needless more to choose,
The common mob would follow common ways.

Long has Logan laboured for peace,
Following his father, fulfilling his work.

As age approaches, after thirty autumns
He seems to see success surrounding him.
With English aid, an era of peace appears:
Even the Iroquois' ancient enemy sends envoys,
Cherokee chieftains, whose champions have
Long scoured for scalps the southern trails
Come to the Council to cover the old feud,
Singing spilled blood to silence.

Since Iroquois slew Erie on the Ohio,
Crushing the Cat-people for the King,
The Shawnee's shelter in the shady forest
A bloody battleground has been, the border of warring
    tribe
With English aid the old enmity ends,
In the Western wilderness no war-band prowls.
Worn out with work for White Man and Red,
The diplomat Logan dreams of a dawn of peace.

Greathouse; fat, nervous, a toady born.
Dunmore hides his sneer, thinking of return
And triumphant entry into London Town.
"I thought to buy land from the Shawnee, but—"
A civilized shrug of well-bred indifference,
"They cannot sell land: the League forbids it.
No matter. The charter of the Colony
Sets our borders to North and South, but West
Our claim runs to the shores of the Spanish sea.
The Shawnee are but squatters on our land,
Refugees, fled from slavers further south."

With trembling voice, Greathouse dares to demur.
"But the Council claims the land by conquest,
And both Crown and law support the League!
Royal edict forbids settling their land."

The vicious, low-born dog was insolent!
Nevertheless—the perfect instrument.

"The Crown will not prefer the League to me!
I am His Highness' rightful deputy—

But we speak not of the League, but the Shawnee.
If they rise to contend with us in war,
Then we must defend ourselves—no more
Is needed; for surely then, we must provide—
For our defence—forts by the riverside.''

Greathouse's fat face swung denial back and forth.
''No war on Whites will the Shawnee wage while,
Loyal to the League, Logan keeps the peace.
He'll complain, through the Council, to the King.
His Majesty will take the Shawnee's part,
And end your war before it is begun.''

''*If* Logan holds them back,'' Lord Dunmore said,
And laughed. Why such as this was simple sport!
He would yet return in triumph to the Court.

West through the mountains march the pioneers,
Despite Royal edicts and their own fears.
A flood of White Men on Allegheny trails,
Into the vast and virgin forest home
Of bears, wolves and Indians, dreaded vermin all.
Rifles ready, settlers watch each shadow,
Haunting the woods with ghosts of their fears.
Greathouse, with his wagonloads of whiskey,
And Michael Cresap with his militiamen,
And land-hungry settlers from Virginia,
Seek out and cross the ford of the Ohio.
Axes resound like thunder in the woods,
As they clear away the land for cornfields.

Ohio River, sing your song,
Nor right nor wrong you bring;
Water wants not any thing.

Men fell trees that have stood for a hundred years.
They fear the woods; its shadow haunts their dreams.
The devils in their minds take human form,
Red-skinned, and dressed in buckskins and war paint.
Greathouse feeds their fears with tales of torture;
Of captives writhing for hours at the stake.

277

The vastness of the West troubles their dreams,
Women and children grow gaunt and hollow-eyed;
In the vast and virgin forest they can hear
Wind Keeper's wind creatures wander in the trees.

The East wind comes as a gigantic moose,
Crashing with his antlers through tangled trees.
Blowing in fury from the lands of the League.
Their eyes dart rapidly about the forest
Their fears have haunted with a thousand shapes;
Children start and sob at the slightest sound.
And even brave men remember tales of terror
When the black wind panther howls out of the West,
Eerily in the air among the endless trees.

Cornstalk comes to the cabin of Logan,
Talking of treachery, and treaties broken.
(On the Cayuga's wise counsel, Cornstalk,
Chief of the Shawnee, charts his people's way.)
"When White Men come, they cut down the woods!
The deer decrease, driven from the land!
Deserted beaver dams dry up;
And the folk who fill the forest vanish too.
We slew many slavers in the South, yet
Were forced to flee and find homes here.
Must we now wander wearily into the West,
Hungry and homeless, our hunting-grounds destroyed?
Where, Logan, is the Law of the League?
Colonists have come across the Ohio,
To the North Shore treaties ensured as Shawnee land.
Surely the Shawnee are shielded by the League?
Let the League help its loyal allies,
To defend our domain and drive out the Whites!
Or does the Cayuga still call, like a coward, for peace?"

"Choose, Shawnee Chief, your words: Cherokee scalps
My bravery in battle show beyond question.
Calm yourself, Cornstalk: comfort your people.
Leave to Logan, and the League, these Whites.
The power of my people will prevent further inroads.

As for these ones—these woods are wide: White Men
   few.
Surely the Shawnee could share a *little* land?''

''With perfidy there is no peace,'' the proud Shawnee
   replied.
''But long has Logan, and the League,
Pursued peace for my people.
Visit the Whites, vanquish them with your voice.
Yet walk, wise one, warily among them.''

''Who is that white-haired Indian, who stands,
Palm upraised in peace, by the palisade?''
''Surely, that is Logan, the 'White Man's Friend'?''
''Shouldn't we shoot him? He leads the Shawnee.''
''Not yet, you fool! Let the Captain talk first!''
''Welcome him with whiskey!'' comes Greathouse's voice,
''A welcome with whiskey for the White Man's friend!''
With childish glee the chieftain takes the cup,
Drinking while he confers with the Captain,
Drowning his wisdom in welcome whiskey.
Nervous wide-eyed women watch, picturing
Their children scalped; their cabins smouldering ash;
Themselves tied screaming to the torture-stake.
Logan drinks, and babbles, and goes home sure
That the Whites are friendly, and there'll be no war.

Even the nervous, watchful women that winter became
Inured to Indians, as, again and again,
Logan returned; they learned to laugh, saying, ''Look,
Back for another bottle!'' Before long,
His wife comes with the wise one, wanting whiskey,
Bringing her younger boy beside her, and
Big with child, a baby on her back, Logan's daughter.
At last a time when Logan cannot come:
To his Shawnee charges the chief has duties:
Without the father, his family goes to the fort.
Hurrying off happily, knowing there'll be
A welcome with whiskey for the women of Logan.
Even the babe at the breast imbibes the liquor,

His mother's milk mingled with alcohol.
Dozing, drunk in a ditch, Death comes on them.
Greathouse has taken Lord Dunmore's bright gold,
And now his men to earn their pay are told.
Women and children lie helpless in mud,
Hatchets and skinning-knives are stained with blood.

Ohio River, flow with tears,
For after years the blow
Has fallen. Who is the foe
Of children? Who knows why their death,
Their failing breath and cry
Should be a thing gold could buy?

While women's wailing wounded the silence,
Cornstalk called the Cayuga Peacemaker.
He came from his cabin, and questions died on his lips.
All Logan's loved ones were laid in a row:
Bloodied bodies of babes and women.
Cornstalk cursed Cresap while the Cayuga stared.
The Chieftain's face changed with his children's death.

Ohio River flow with blood!
A raging flood to show
What seed fear and greed can sow!

April, seventeen seventy-four.
The beginning of Dunmore's War.
The flowers that bloomed that Spring
Fed on the blood of Logan's children:
Fed on the blood of Red and White Men:
Blood of innocence, blood of guilt—
To the flowers it tasted the same.

Who could hold back the howling avengers
When Logan leads them; no longer the White Man's
    friend?
Well-loved is Logan along the Ohio:
To Cresap's camp the crazed Cayuga
Brings torch and torture—and triumph for Dunmore.

With all Virginia's power riding to war,

This is Lord Dunmore's hour! Proud and cocksure,
He leads his soldiers through the Western hills,
To the border, where Logan kills and kills,
Mourning in madness his murdered children,
Burying in butchery and blood his grief.
Colonel Cresap's tired troop finds no relief
On their grim retreat through the tangled wood.
Six Nations meet in Council at Thendara:
Settlers writhe screaming at the torture-stake.
Lord Dunmore swells with pride. This day is his!
Naked savages must face cannon and steel:
(He thinks of the Charter, with its great seal,
And all the wealth he could expect to flow
As soon as the valley of the Ohio
Virginian land became—and *his* domain.)
Sweeping down on the bloodstained savage hordes,
The Virginian followers of Lord Dunmore
Bring sabre and musket and cannon's roar.

The flowers feasted well.
Rifles and roaring cannon wreak destruction
Among charging Shawnee, and shattered they retreat.
Fallen on the field, the father of Tecumseh
Leaves hate as legacy to a later generation:
The wailing of his widow much woe shall cause.

Between White Man and Red, the Great League stands;
The treaty belts for all the North gathered in their hands.
The Onondaga call the Council at Thendara:
Wild Seneca come from the Western Gate,
With concerned Cayuga, the kin of Logan,
And the Youngest Brother, the Tuscarora.
From their rocky homes the Oneida bring
The hymns that settlers have taught them to sing:
And from the Great League's eastern wing
Come Anglican Mohawks, loyal to the King.
Messengers now leave the Long House,
Bearing belts of peace over forest trails.

Shattered by the shells, the Shawnee gather

Cheerless while their chieftains choose their path.
Cornstalk comes to the Cayuga peacemaker,
Lonely old Logan, lamenting his children,
Proposing a parley for peace.
"What purpose peace with perfidy?"
The chieftain's face changed at his children's death;
Now fiercely flashes fire in his eyes.
"*I* was not at war with the White Man!
Through thirty years their throne I served
Persuading to peace the peoples of the forest.
Now thirty scalps I've seized to soothe my heart's aching:
But thrice thirty scalps will not thaw out my hatred!
Let us fight on forever, until fear of us
Wakes in the White Man such wailing and terror
That they board their boats, and back over the ocean go.
There is no peace with perfidy. Let us paint for war."
Cornstalk confronts the Cayuga's raving eyes.
"What, Wise One, would you have us do?
The big knife is before us.
It can kill us all.
Shall we *all* kill
Our women and children,
And fight on till we fall?
         No.
I shall go make peace."

Ohio River, flow with tears
For all the years that no
Child of Logan's line may know.

Now messengers from the Long House come running,
With White Men, agents of the English King.
White wampum belts of peace are in their hands.
Between White Man and Red the Great League stands.
The royal envoys seek out Lord Dunmore
To bid him cease his cruel and bloody war.
The League looks now to Logan peace to bring:
Along the blazing border war must cease
Because the League has treaties with the King.

All his life long Logan has served that peace.
White Men have come to bring the "White Man's
  Friend"
To Council, so their king may deal with these
Troubles, and bring all warfare to an end.
To treat with Lord Dunmore is Logan's task—
Such is the message that the Sachems send:
Terms of peace he must at the parley ask.
While White Men wait, the weary chief replies:
Like moaning wind they hear his voice arise.

"I ask if ever any White Man
Hungry came to the cabin of Logan,
And found not food,
Or who came naked and cold, and clothing was denied
  him?
For the length of the last long and bloody war,
Logan calmly stayed in his cabin, calling for peace.
So loyal was Logan's love for the whites
That my people pointed as they passed,
Saying, 'See, there is the friend of the White Men.'
I had thought to have lived in friendship forever,
But for the cruel deed of one man. Colonel Cresap
This last spring, in cold blood and unprovoked,
Murdered *all* of the family of Logan;
Not even sparing my women and little children.

There runs not a drop of my blood
In the veins of any living creature.
This called on me for revenge.
I have sought it. I have killed many:
I have thoroughly glutted my thirst for vengeance.
For my people, I rejoice at the promise of peace:
But do not think my joy the joy of fear.
Logan never felt fear.
He will not turn on his heel
To save his life.
Who is there to mourn for Logan?
Not one!"

Some say
That Patrick Henry wept:
And that Thomas Jefferson dabbed at his eyes
Where he sat taking notes in a corner.
To have killed the Cayuga a kindness had been:
But lonely old Logan must live six more years.

But the deed went on.
Surly Shawnee gather,
Refusing belts of peace
When the Onandaga call the Council at Thendara:
Demanding with red belts
A hatchet to strike the English.

Angrily the Sachems
Hurl back their belts,
And bid them till the soil.
But the Shawnee defy the League;
To seek white scalps by the side of the river.
But now the White Man's war is blooming:
The settlers rise against the King in war.
Virginian rebels drive out Lord Dunmore,
Who leaves, as he flees from the rioting bands,
All his gold invested in Ohio lands—
And thus fade into nothing all his plots.
Lexington farmers fire their famous shots.
Between English settler and English King
The war-belt lies, to fill the land with pain;
Partisan cries across the land loud ring.
The Onandaga call for peace in vain.
The almost-English Canienga bring
The red belt of war sent them by the King.
Cayuga and Seneca stalk coldly from the Council,
Vowing vengeance for Logan.
Rebel preachers have taught the Oneida well:
Who stands for the King takes the road to Hell.
He who desires to become a saint
Must fight for the Congress in his warpaint.
Thus, torn apart by the partisan calls,
Drawn into a White Man's war;

The League is split, the Long House falls:
The Council shall meet at Thendara no more.

A new Deganoweda and Hayenwatha,
Franklin and Jefferson,
Unite the Thirteen Tribes,
To build a second Great League,
In imitation of the first . . .
But listen, ye who established the Great League!
Now it has grown old.
Now it is nothing but wilderness.
Ye are in your graves,
Ye who established it!

We are met upon the gravesite
Of a million murdered children.
Unknown, unnamed, unnumbered,
Their bones make up our soil.
It is their flesh that fills our gardens,
We drink the tears shed for them:
The air we breathe—their laughter!
But who can mourn an abstract?
Truly sorrow for the nameless?
All statistics of destruction
Are as empty as the sorrow
That is given by convention.
A multitude is faceless,
One cannot mourn a cipher, yet—

Who are *we* that mourn for Logan?

THE WORLD NEXT DOOR
Brad Ferguson

EDITOR'S INTRODUCTION

The total destruction of the human race by nuclear war or by any other means is too horrible for any sane person to truly contemplate. Even in *Lucifer's Hammer* and *Footfall,* we only touched upon the disasters that *threatened* mankind's continued survival. The science fiction writer who's probably come closest to touching the heart of this tragedy is Greg Bear in his novel *Psyclone,* where the residual "souls" of the Hiroshima/Nagasaki dead collectively pass over the Pacific Ocean to seed their revenge upon the victors of World War II.

I don't read many horror stories, but I do not remember another as chilling as *Psyclone;* yet, it only touched upon the fringe of nuclear annihilation. In "The World Next Door" Brad Ferguson takes a different tack; he shows how the death of an entire civilization might well move through time as well as space . . .

———————————————— ¶ ————————————————

September 15

JESS TOLD ME TODAY HIS SUGAR BEET CROP SEEMS TO BE DOING pretty well. Time was when nobody could get anything at all to grow, much less something as tricky as sugar beets, so Jess deserves a lot of credit . . . and it'll be awful nice to have real table sugar again, the white, grainy stuff you could buy at the store. (What was it called? Dominoes? Something like that.) We're all sick of maple sugar, and the women say you can't cook with it, except for ham—and we don't have any pigs around here anymore. It surprised me a little last spring, when the town decided it wanted real sugar so bad, it allowed Jess to turn two acres over to it. Jess raises some of the best corn in the county, and we need all we can get—the eating kind and the drinking kind, both. But sugar is calories, too.

More dreams last night, the crazy kind a lot of people around here have been having. Didn't sleep all that well myself. Doc says it's more wish-fulfillment stuff than anything else, like right after the war. I don't know; these seem different. I remember them better, for one thing. I hardly ever remember dreams at all; now I can remember whole bits of them—colors and smells, too. In fact, in last night's dream I was watching color television, but I forget what was on.

September 18

A singer named Wanderin' Jake came through today; he's from the Albany area. I wrote his news on the chalkboard at Town Hall, and the mayor's wife fed him well. The news: There were floods in Glens Falls last month, eleven people dead; there's a new provisional state government in Rensselaer (that makes four that I know of, if that preacher in Buffalo hasn't been assassinated yet); the governor in Rensselaer wants to send a state delegation to next year's American Jubilee at Mount Thunder; and there's been no word from an expedition that set out six months ago from Schenectady, bound for the atomic power plant at Indian Point to see if it can be made useful again. The party is presumed dead.

Wanderin' Jake led a sing-along in the square just after sunset tonight, and we had a good time, even though there wasn't much on hand to picnic with and won't be until we get the crops in. With this climate, we can't harvest until maybe late October, and only then if we're lucky and there's been no rain from the south.

Today I remembered that it was Domino sugar, singular. There was a jingle about how grandmothers and mothers know the best sugar is Domino, which is how I remembered it. It's strange how those jingles come back to haunt you. Twenty-one great tobaccos make twenty wonderful Kings. Let Hertz put you in the driver's seat. I like Ike, you like Ike, everybody likes Ike. And you get a lot to like with a Marlboro.

September 25

The town got together tonight to discuss what, if anything, we're going to do about the American Jubilee. No decision, of course—we've only talked it over once—but the thrust of tonight's meeting was, the hell with Rensselaer and the governor there, just like we said the hell with the governors in Buffalo, Syracuse, and Watertown. What if Rensselaer decides to tax us? We don't have the crops to spare for taxes, and our town has been doing a good job of hiding away nice and quiet in these mountains.

I also asked if we were going to be doing something about getting me a new typewriter ribbon. The mayor says he wants typed minutes—he says they mean we're still civilized and a going concern, and he's not wrong about that—but I've been reinking this same damn ribbon for more than ten years, and it's got big holes in it, especially at the ends where the keys hammer away before the typewriter catches its breath and reverses the ribbon. I'm also running out of ink. I said I'd be willing to go with some people into a big town like Tupper Lake to see if there's a few ribbons left in the stores there, but the mayor said he can't spare the people; there's bandits all over the place and it would be dangerous to go into a big, empty town like Tupper. He said maybe somebody could make a new ribbon for me. I said fine, but where are you going to get a *long* piece of cotton that's not falling apart? If I'm going to be town scribe, I told him, I have got to have something to scribe with.

At least we don't have to try and make paper, which I think would be impossible. The old school's still got a lot of paper in it. The Hygiene Committee's been doing a good job of keeping the building free of vermin, so the paper should last. If I don't have a newspaper anymore, at least I have this journal and the Town Hall chalkboard, so I'm still a newspaperman.

September 30

Another meeting on that Jubilee. Half the town now seems to want to do something—send a representative, hold a picnic, whatever. Maybe they think Camelot's going to come back. The other half agrees (with me) that the Jubilee is just an excuse to blow the President's horn for him, and that if it hadn't been for the war, the President would have been out of office in '68, maybe even '64. Giving him a toot for still being in office is an unnecessary reminder of the war, and maybe even a reward for having half-caused it.

I wonder who the ass-kisser was that came up with the idea for the Jubilee? Some general in charge of public relations? At least we know it wasn't a congressman. If we've lost a lot, we at least got rid of the goddamn congressmen.

October 2

Jess, the fool, went out in a pouring rain today to check on his beet crop. The poor idiot. At least the winds were from the northwest, up Montreal way. It's pretty clean up there; maybe Jess is okay, but we've got no way to check. Jess' wife is frantic. I don't blame her. I also wonder if we've lost that beet crop, not to mention his corn and everyone else's crops, too. Damn, damn, damn.

October 5

Funny thing happened. I was talking to Dick LeClerc this morning, just passing the time at his trading post. Dick mentioned he hasn't been sleeping well lately. He says he had a dream last night in which he's in his store, but it's not the trading post. It's bigger and cleaner, for one thing, and there are electric lights and freezers and shopping carts, like in those city supermarkets from before the war. The thing he remembers best from the dream is his cash register. It's a little white thing, he says, but it had funny numbers on it . . . green, glowing ones, made up of sharp angles. The thing hardly made any noise at all, except for some beeping whenever you hit a key—and you really didn't hit keys, but numbers on a pad that felt like a thin sponge. Dick says when he woke up, he was real disappointed that he didn't still have the cash register to play with. That's just like Dick; I've seen him fool with a rat trap for hours, trying to make it work better. He's always been one for a gadget.

October 13

Another weird dream. (I feel a little guilty about using up ribbon and ink recording all these dreams, but I think it's important.) This time I wrote down what I could of it before I forgot. Couldn't remember much, anyway. I was back at the paper and there were a lot of people around, people I'd known for years (but haven't ever met, waking). There was all kinds of stuff around the office. Electric lights (no, *fluorescent* lights; they were different) and a few desks had typewriters better than this one, but most of the desks had little TVs on them—except the TVs didn't show pictures, but words . . . hundreds of little green words on a dead black screen. Maybe Dick LeClerc planted this in my head with his tale of the cash register with the little green numbers on it. Crazy how your mind works.

Jess is still okay, his wife says. His gums look good, and bleeding's one of the first signs. He didn't get the shits, either, and he hasn't been particularly tired.

October 20

Another singer showed up today, and getting two in just over a month is really unusual, because we're so hidden away here. His name is Elvis Presley, and he came into town this afternoon with a couple of what he called "backup men"—a guy with a guitar and another guy with a small set of drums that didn't look too easy to carry through these mountains. The drummer's a Negro. We haven't seen one of those around here in maybe twenty years.

Some of the folks remember Elvis pretty well from the old days. He was a big deal back then, always being on television and making records; he even made some movies. Now he makes a living on the road, singing. He looks good . . . maybe a little thin, but we all are. Some of his hair's gone, too; whether it's from radiation or because he's, what, fifty?—I don't know. He'll do a set for us tomorrow. I think it'll help take our minds off the anniversary of the beginning of the war.

We've got Elvis and his people boarded with the mayor. Elvis says he's just happy to get in out of the weather. He also says he's got a lot of news from faraway places, which he'll tell us about just as soon as he and his group get themselves some food and rest.

October 21

Elvis did a nice set, all right. Led it with a song I remembered about loving him tender. I liked it; we all did.

I got his news at the shindig after the performance. Elvis says there's not much of the country left, as much as he's seen of it. The war caught him in Nashville, where he was making one of his records. The Russians didn't bomb Nashville, but the city was abandoned after the Fidel flu hit in '69 and most people died. Elvis caught it but recovered, and he's been on the road ever since.

Elvis says he walked most of the way here, taking his sweet time; he and his backup men only rarely find a ride. Sometimes they settle in a place for months; right now, they're going to Montpelier to see how things are there. (I told him there's been no news from that part of New England for years.)

Elvis says he no longer bothers to go near big cities. He says the cities they didn't get with the bombers have been deserted—no food supply, no law and order, and loads of disease and misery did the job. We knew New York was bombed, and Boston and Washington and Cleveland, too, but we weren't sure about Columbus, Chicago, Gary, Indianapolis, and about twenty others Elvis mentioned. All gone. Where the hell was the Air Force that October? For Christ's sake!

Elvis says he thinks the population is headed back up again, but he admits that it might just be wishful thinking on his part. Elvis also says he met the President at Mount Thunder a couple of years ago, and he looked all right—but gray and lined, not nearly the young man we remember, and he's sick to boot . . . something to do with his kidneys. He never did get married again, either, although Elvis understands that the President still takes his pleasures with any of the couple of hundred women who live in the mountain's government complex, which is no less than I'd expect from a scoundrel like him.

October 22

Today was the anniversary. We all stood up at the end of Elvis's performance and sang the Banner, him leading us along on his guitar. Most of us cried a little. The mayor made a speech, said an Our Father, and raised the anniversary flag his wife made back in '78. The flag looks odd like that, the red and blue parts replaced by black, but it's appropriate. After the Pledge, the mayor hauled the flag down for another year.

Elvis did a bunch of his old songs and also some that his drummer wrote. His drummer's really quite a songwriter. One was a happy thing called "Girls Just Want to Have Fun"—the lyrics weren't much, but the tune was good and the whole thing made us laugh, which we needed—and the other was one that made me get all teary. Elvis called it "Let It Be." That man can sing a little, all right. I asked the drummer afterwards where he'd gotten the songs. He shrugged and said he'd just dreamed 'em, woke up and wrote 'em down. He says he's been dreaming recently that he's an executive with some big record company in New York. Big office, too, with air conditioning. I remember air conditioning.

Elvis was interested that I've been keeping a journal of our times here, and I've let him read some of it. He says that while he hasn't been having any dreams at all, he's interested in ours.

October 23

Elvis gave his last performance here tonight, finishing with a song called "The World Next Door." He says he wrote it himself just this morning. It's about the world we could have had without the war. He says he was inspired to do it by all the dream entries in this journal of mine. I'm proud of that, inspiring a song and all.

I had another one of those dreams last night. I was on a big airplane—I mean a *big* one. People were seated maybe ten across. They showed movies. I was having a real liquor drink—Jack Daniel's, and I can almost taste it now—and on the little napkin that came with the drink was printed AMERICAN AIRLINES LUXURYLINER 747. I wonder where I was supposed to be going? Maybe Elvis can work the dream into his song somehow, the next time he does it somewhere.

November 1

Winter's here with a vengeance. It's warmer the year 'round than it used to be, but the first snow fell today. It'll melt off, but we should be doing more than we are to prepare for the winter.

Jess, who still feels good, finished hauling in his beet crop today, with the help of a bunch of kids from Mrs. Lancaster's school. We're all looking forward to the sugar.

Last night was Halloween, and the kids still do dress-up, although trick-or-treat is out of the question. Strange thing, though: One of the kids—Tommy Matthews—went around town wrapped in a charcoal-colored Navy blanket and an old Army helmet his dad's had since Korea. He also had a pair of swimming goggles and a broomstick handle he held like a sword. The costume made no damn sense, so I asked him who he was supposed to be. Darth Vader, he said. Who's that? I asked him. A bad man, Tommy said. He says he dreamed him. He breathes like this, Tommy added, noisily sucking in air and blowing it out again.

Jesus. The kids are beginning to dream, too.

November 10

More and more dreams. Everybody's beginning to talk about them now. No one understands what's going on.

We had a town meeting tonight, at which it was decided to forget about doing anything for the Jubilee. We've got our own problems.

Nobody's sleeping very well. They wake up in the middle of the night with such a profound sense of loss, there's no getting any rest. Everybody's tired and cranky.

After the Jubilee vote was taken, we suspended regular business so everyone could talk about the dreaming. I was asked to write down some of the things people remember from their dreams. Here are some of the clearest:

Men land on the moon in a black-and-white spaceship that looks like a spider. There's another kind of spaceship that looks more like an airplane. Both have American flags painted on them.

A guy named Sylvester (or maybe Stephen) Stallion is in a movie about a guy who rescues people—prisoners of war?—from a place called Vietnam. (I remember Vietnam, and so I'm putting that one

293

down.) Also, there's a big, black monument in Washington to servicemen who died in Vietnam . . . thousands and thousands of servicemen.

Watches that show numbers to tell time.

Seat belts in cars.

Telephones with little buttons on them instead of dials. The buttons make music.

Something called Home Box Office. Something else called *People* magazine. Somebody named Princess Di.

A man named Jerry Falwell who's either a preacher or a politician.

Young men with purple and orange hair wearing earrings in pierced ears.

Radios so small you can wear them on your head, so people can listen to them as they walk around.

A government program called Medicare, for old people.

There were others, but these are representative. Doc spoke up about wish-fulfillment fantasies again, and theorized that Elvis being here recently might have reminded us too much about the old world. He pointed out that while everyone seems to be having dreams, no two people are having exactly the same dreams about the same things. He says not to worry, that it will pass. The mayor said that while people aren't having *exactly* the same dreams, they're close enough to make him suspicious; he called it a psychic event. Doc's answer to that was that since people have been doing nothing else but talk about their dreams, the dreams they have are being influenced by those conversations.

In other business, Jess said he'd have the sugar ready in a week or two; the grinding and drying is taking him longer to do than he thought it would, but he says he doesn't need any help. We're all looking forward to the sugar. Since Jess is still okay, we're assuming the crop is. Now if we could only grow coffee . . .

November 12

Big snow last night. Twelve inches on the ground, and this one won't melt off. But we've gotten the crops and firewood in.

The temperature's taken a plunge, too. We'd probably have lost some field hands if they'd still been working out in the open. Doc says with the winds still coming out of the northwest, the snow's safe enough, since the early October rain was. That's a relief; it means we'll have a healthy soil for next spring's planting.

November 15

The dreams got very sharp, very real last night. I saw superhighways with thousands of cars on them. I was reading a thick paperback book by somebody named Jackie Collins. My wife and daughter were still alive and with me. There was a nice little house I lived in, right in this town. There was a color TV set in the living room and another one in our bedroom; both were showing the news, but I don't remember any, except that the announcer seemed excited and worried, maybe scared. And there was a wonderful, luxurious indoor bathroom with all the hot water you could want. It was so real I could touch it. I woke up suddenly in the night and I cried for my family—gone all these years, since the first, worst days.

November 16

No dreams last night at all. Slept well for the first time in weeks.

I tried Jess' sugar. Wonderful! I'd forgotten how good real sugar could be. I sprinkled some of my share on wild blueberries I picked a couple of days ago.

November 18

Everybody in town is saying their dreams are gone. Doc says we've all had a psychic trauma, but it's over now.

Big topic in the meeting tonight was how to ration out the meat supply. The dairymen think it's time to rebuild their milking stock; the townies say they're hungry for real, red meat, and since the rain's been good, the meat will be good, too. We'll probably compromise on this again; a lot of those bossies aren't going to make it through the winter anyway. And it snowed like hell again today.

November 19

Jess came in from his farm to say he'd found a body by the side of the road on his way in. It was a stranger, shot dead where he stood; there was dried blood under him and nowhere else. Doesn't look like a bandit attack, though; the kid still had his wallet on him. Maybe it was a hunting accident, but the mayor's posted extra patrols, just in case it was bandits after all. We'll go out and get the body tonight.

November 21

Nobody can figure it out.

The body's the damnedest thing anyone's ever seen. Doc went through the kid's ID and came up with all sorts of stuff that didn't make any sense.

First off, there was a lot of ID, and no one here has any anymore. The kid's name was John David Wright. He was just about to turn twenty. There was a New York State driver's license dated this year; the kid's picture was on it. It's a good sign things are returning to normal, if they've begun issuing those again. Only problem is, it doesn't say where the seat of government was that issued it. Was it in Rensselaer or Syracuse or what?

Wright's home town is given as this one, but he's a complete stranger to us. The address on his driver's license is for a big house on Bates Road that burned down right after the war. Jess says he thinks he remembers a family named Wright who lived there around the time the war started, but they all died in the fire.

The kid was wearing a wristwatch with numbers on it instead of hands; Fred Crawthers says it looks a lot like the watch he saw in one of his dreams. He had money, too—bills and change both—all with recent dates. I was pleased to see the mint is back in business . . . but there was a half-dollar coin that bore the President's picture, which I think is overdoing it. There were also a couple of credit cards called Mastercard and Visa; it took me a while to recognize a credit card when I saw one.

Wright also had a receipt, dated three days ago, from a Howard Johnson's restaurant. I remember those. They were on highways and had orange roofs. But there aren't any around here and there never were.

Young Wright was wearing eyeglasses, but they weren't made of glass. They had plastic lenses that scratch easily; Doc showed me. Doc's been through the kid and reports nothing physically unusual except for his teeth. He's got the usual fillings, but one of his front teeth was covered by a tough white plastic. Doc says it covered a bad crack and looked convincingly good. (I wish I knew where they were doing dental work these days. Everybody in town needs some.)

The only other thing Doc said was that the kid was maybe too healthy. He had good weight on him, no obvious signs of radiation impairment, no nothing. About like we all were, before the war.

Well, the kid may be one of ours; we don't know. We'll treat him right, anyway. We'll bury him tomorrow as best we can, with all this damn snow on the ground.

November 23

Doc came by the house this morning, red-eyed and sleepless. He says he didn't tell all he knew about the Wright boy, but he decided to tell me and give me the proof. I can write it down and hide the proof, as long as I don't show it to the mayor or anyone else right away. Doc's afraid people might panic or something. I think the people around here are stronger than that, but I'll respect Doc's wishes.

Anyway, I'm not sure I believe it myself, although I've got it all right here in front of me. When Doc began undressing Wright's body for autopsy, he found that the kid had wrapped himself in newspapers. It's an old Boy Scout trick, for insulation. The kid had used six sheets from the Albany *Times-Union* from the 13th of November, this year. Now there is no Albany and that area sure isn't in any shape to print newspapers . . . but this paper was fresh and white. The sheets covering the kid's chest are full of buckshot holes and covered with blood, but the rest of the sheets are okay.

We have the front page, and it's clean. The headline tells about a SOVIET ULTIMATUM. Another story says PRESIDENT URGES CIVIL DEFENSE MEASURES. A third reads POPE FLIES TO MOSCOW TO MEDIATE CRISIS. There's also what we used to call a think-piece about the number of weapons the U.S. and the Soviet Union have and the damage they could do. The story is a horror of thousands of intercontinental missiles that carry ten or more warheads each, and there are germ bombs and chemical bombs and orbital bombs and things that carry radioactive dust.

None of this is anything we know about, none of it. I read the ULTIMATUM story. It said the presence of missile-carrying Soviet nuclear subs off the Atlantic coast had caused the worst breach in relations between the superpowers since the Cuban missile crisis, which almost caused a war back in '62.

Almost. My dear sweet Jesus. Almost, it said.

Doc says he thinks he knows what happened. The world next door, Elvis called it, and Doc says he was right.

Doc thinks the next-door world was the one we'd be living in if there hadn't been a war about Cuba. He says it's a real place, or it was. Now Doc thinks it's gone, because the dreams stopped; Doc no longer thinks the dreams were mass hysteria or any of the other things he called them. He says the next-door world must have had an even worse war than we did, because of those weapons in the paper. He thinks everybody died, and maybe the impending death of a whole, entire planet is enough to open a door wide enough so that dreams, and even a kid, start coming through. Maybe we were on the receiving end because we're a nearly dead world . . . not quite dead, and maybe we'll pull through, despite everything. But that other world, with those fearsome weapons, must be gone, just like the dreams it sent us.

We don't know who shot John David Wright, but Doc figures it was Jess himself, startled when the kid came out of nowhere without hailing Jess first.

We could probably prove it, if it's true, but that would only get Jess hanged, and we need him and his farm. Besides, Jess was decent enough to report the body and make sure we'd bury it with proper respect. The poor kid is dead, and we can't bring him back. Let it lay.

November 28

We all got together and ate as much as we'd put aside for the feast—it turned out to be a fairly good year. All in all, it was a pretty nice Thanksgiving . . . except the kid's watch won't show any numbers anymore, and I can't make the thing work. I guess the battery or whatever must be dead. That was the best goddamn watch I ever had, even counting the old days. It's a shame it gave out so soon.

SIEGE AT TARR-HOSTIGOS
Roland Green and John F. Carr

EDITOR'S INTRODUCTION

H. Beam Piper could easily be called the Robert Louis Stevenson of science fiction; his stories were strong and his narratives thought-provoking and spare. Piper's classics— *Space Viking, Cosmic Computer, Little Fuzzy,* and *Lord Kalvan of Otherwhen*—still rank among the finest adventure sf novels ever written. John W. Campbell—the great golden-age editor of *Astounding/Analog*—said, "*Space Viking* itself is, I think, one of the classics—a yarn that will be cited, years hence, as one of the science fiction classics. It's got solid philosophy for the mature thinker, and bang-bang-chopp-'em-up action for the space pirate fans. As a truly good yarn should have."

In the *Complete Index to Astounding/Analog* by Mike Ashley, Piper ranked third in overall cumulative Analytical Lab voting (A regular feature in Campbell's *Astounding/ Analog* where each month the readers voted for their favorite stories.); finishing right behind number one vote getter Robert A. Heinlein and number two, C. L. Moore.

H. Beam Piper's writing was probably the single greatest

influence on my own career and that of my associate, John F. Carr. John is a recognized authority on the life and works of H. Beam Piper; he edited the Piper short story collections: *Federation, Empire, Paratime,* and *The Worlds of H. Beam Piper.* I myself was fortunate enough to help Beam work out a few knots on his History of the Future in the last decade of his life.

For these and other reasons, we were both invited to be co-Guests of Honor at the first Hostigos Con; dedicated to the memory and works of H. Beam Piper and put on by the Pennsylvania State College SF Society. This was more than just another convention. Penn State is only eight miles away from Tarr-Hostigos, the center of Piper's *Lord Kalvan of Otherwhen.* We were both promised a guided tour of Hostigos (most of Centre and Lycoming counties) and Williamsport, Beam's last place of residence.

A little background: *Lord Kalvan of Otherwhen* is one of the most beloved of alternate history yarns. It begins when a Pennsylvania State trooper, named Calvin Morrison, is picked up unwittingly by a passing Paratime conveyer and dropped off accidentally on an alternate time-line. Instead of Indians, Kalvan runs into Indo-Europeans who have migrated across the Aleutian Islands and settled into most of North America. They have developed a fifteenth-century late-Medieval society with both armor and gunpowder weapons.

Only in the Five Kingdoms the manufacture of gunpowder is a religious *miracle* zealously guarded by Styphon's House, a nasty theocracy with delusions of grandeur. Kalvan arrives just as Styphon's allies are about to attack the small princedom of Hostigos; Kalvan meets the Prince's daughter, falls in love, and decides he has to do something to help these people. Then things begin to get really interesting . . .

Lord Kalvan of Otherwhen was a strong influence on my own *Janissaries* series and over the years I've reread it many times. The tour of Hostigos began on a lovely Friday morning and, as we traveled across some of America's most beautiful landscape, it was obvious why Piper had centered his mythical kingdom in this part of Pennsylvania. We passed through Bellefonte (Hostigos Town) and then on to Hostigos Gap, which separates the Bald Eagle Mountains, and where the castle of Tarr-Hostigos rises to guard the pass.

It was easy to see where the castle sat; there were two large kettle-shaped mountains, joining at about 700 feet. The keep would have perched on the lower mountain, with the tower and outer walls atop the higher crown. The mountains were much higher and more massive than I'd ever imagined—or John and Roland, for that matter.

A few years earlier they had written *Great Kings' War*, the authorized sequel to *Lord Kalvan of Otherwhen*. They had been working on the next book in the series and both of them were excited about finally seeing the area they had been writing about for so long. It was probably a good thing.

On Saturday night, Roland was scheduled to do a reading from the new book, *Gunpowder God*. Unfortunately, due to scheduling problems, Roland didn't arrive until late Friday afternoon; thus missing the Hostigos tour. Roland read from a section of the book titled "Siege at Tarr-Hostigos." After the reading I pointed out several factual errors in the description of Tarr-Hostigos and environs. They made the necessary corrections and I'm pleased to be able to offer you this story for your own enjoyment.

ONE

I

PARATIME POLICE CHIEF VERKAN VALL TRIED TO SORT HIS atypically jumbled thoughts as the transtemporal conveyor carried him toward Fourth Level Aryan-Transpacific, Kalvan Subsector. The civilized Second and Third Levels were behind him now. Once in a while he caught flickering glimpses of Fourth Level—buildings, airports, occasionally a raging battle.

Fourth Level was the high-probability one of the inhabited Paratime Levels. There the human First Colony had come to complete disaster, in the past fifty thousand years losing all knowledge of its Martian origins.

It was the most barbaric level, as well as the biggest. Its cultures ranged from idol worshippers to the technological sophistication and social backwardness of the Europo-American, Hispano-Columbian Subsector.

It was from one of these Europo-American lines that Corporal Calvin Morrison of the Pennsylvania State Police had accidentally traveled in a conveyor to Aryan-Transpacific, Styphon's House Subsector. Thrust into a ruder and deadlier culture, Calvin (or Kalvan, as the inhabitants of that time-line called him) not only

303

survived, he prospered—until just a few days ago. In less than four years he'd married a princess, founded an empire, broken Styphon's House's monopoly of gunpowder, and more than held his own against the worst that band of priestly tyrants could do.

No more. Styphon's House assembled their Grand Host, and at the Battle of Ardros Field broke the outnumbered army of Hos-Hostigos.

Verkan had been tied to his desk on First Level at that time by piles of routine business and some non-routine schemes by his political enemies. To put it mildly, his conscience was nagging him that he hadn't been there when his friend needed him. He refused to think about what the Bureau of Psychological Hygiene would say, if they discovered that the top Paracop was suffering from Outtime Identification Syndrome. He already had enough headaches for one day.

The biggest of those headaches was the Dhergabar University Study Team caught in the rout of the Hostigi. Like all outtime researchers, they worked under Paratime Police protection. That might not be enough, on the kind of Fourth Level time-line where civilians were likely to end as part of the body count when a victorious army swept through hostile territory. Too many of the University Team were still unaccounted for; every casualty among them would be a gift to the Opposition Party.

Kalvan would have to fight his own battles for a while, against even longer odds than before. He'd need skill as well as luck to save his own life and Queen Rylla's, never mind refounding his empire.

Already the Grand Host's cavalry scouts had raided almost to the outskirts of Hostigos Town. Its main body could hardly be more than a day behind. Kalvan's father-in-law, Prince Ptosphes, might be able to hold Tarr-Hostigos for a few days. If the Grand Host had to stop and lay siege to the castle, Kalvan still might never rule a kingdom again. He and Rylla might at least escape westward, to sell the services of their army somewhere in the Middle Kingdoms, menaced by barbarians and now by the Mexicotl.

The conveyor dome shimmered into material existence. They had reached Kalvan's Subsector. Verkan checked his personal equipment and headed for the hatch. Somehow four Paracops reached it before him, all with drawn Fourth Level pistols and palmed First Level sigma-ray needlers.

"Sorry, Chief," one of them said. He didn't sound sorry. Verkan looked behind and sighed. The other eight men of his personal guard had closed tightly around him from the rear. Swaddled in bodyguards like a baby in cloth, Verkan stepped out into a large storeroom. The rest of the conveyor-load of Paracops followed, lugging equipment or pushing lifter pallets.

From the outside, the Subsector's conveyor-head was disguised as one of four large storehouses attached to the Royal Foundry of Hos-Hostigos. The room before them held a desk, some First Level monitoring equipment, racks of muskets, two field-gun carriages, and hundreds of sacks of oats and corn.

No good to anybody except maybe the Grand Host was Verkan's thought as he strode across the room. Like the other Paracops, he held a flintlock pistol nearly two feet long, loaded and cocked. On his head he wore a high-combed morion helmet; his clothes were a sleeveless buff jack, dark blue breeches, a bright red sash, and thigh-high boots. Nobody from Kalvan's Subsector would have thought him anything but a Hostigi light cavalry officer.

As he'd expected, the storehouse was empty of anything except mice and rats. He opened the keyed magnetic lock, stepped back, let the four point men go first, then followed at their hand signals of "All clear."

The door was intact, as he had expected. Under local oak planking, it had a collapsed-nickel core. Nothing local could even dent that, not even a two-hundred-pound stone ball from a siege bombard.

Nothing else in sight had been as lucky. The main Foundry buildings had all burned; some had collapsed. Most of the outer buildings also showed battle scars, and bodies lay everywhere.

Smoke still rose from most of the buildings. That confirmed Verkan's guess that the attack had come only hours before. The half-dozen survivors of the University Team who'd reached First Level's Kalvan Subsector Depot had been incoherent with fright, except for Baltov Eldra, who was unconscious from a head wound.

"Too many tourists," a Paracop said.

Verkan nodded. The University had insisted on doing their own investigation of Kalvan's time-line. Short of imposing a quarantine, there'd been no way to stop them. For a moment Verkan wished himself back as Chief's Special Assistant, where he could do the sensible thing without having a dozen political potentates baying at his door.

The Paracops spread out, leapfrogging from building to building, covering one another until they'd reached the edge of the Foundry on all sides. Then they posted sentries, sent a miniature spyball to hover a thousand feet up, and began the grisly task of recovering the bodies.

Verkan turned over the nearest civilian casualty with his sword. It was the Team's expert on pre-industrial sociology, Professor Lathor Karv. He had a gaping hole in his forehead and several stab wounds in his torso, but no signs of torture.

First good news all day.

No signs of torture meant that none of Archpriest Roxthar's "Holy" Investigators had ridden with the cavalry. Hypno-mech conditioning or not, it was asking a lot of anyone to resist the kind of torture the Investigators handed out. Not that they were as efficient as the priests of Shpeegar or some Europo-American secret police agencies, but they would improve with time and practice. The Grand Host's victory had bought them the time, and Roxthar's fanatical determination to find and extirpate heresy everywhere would guarantee the practice.

Of the fifty-odd bodies in the open, some were here-and-now Foundry workers, the proverbial innocent bystanders. About twenty were mercenaries of various persuasions or undercover Paracops, and the rest members of the University Team.

"Fiasco" is a mild term for this was Verkan's thought. *Nobody is going to be happy about it.*

"Chief!" the head guard called. He ran up and lowered his voice. "We've found Investigator Ranthar Jard."

Nobody, starting with me.

Ranthar Jard's dead mouth was twisted into the parody of a smile, but it looked as if he'd fought as well as he'd lived. Five troopers in yellow Harphaxi sashes lay dead and bloody around him.

Verkan cursed out loud. There went an old friend and one of the few Paracops he could still trust absolutely.

The lifter teams started loading bodies for shipment back to First Level, while the rest began the house-to-house (or ruin-to-ruin) search. In spite of the danger from smoldering embers and falling beams, they turned up twelve more Paratimer bodies, three of them Paracops. Seven skeletons too badly burned for field identification made the last load before the conveyor headed back to First Level. Paratime Police Headquarters had a full medtech team on standby, for DNA identification.

Verkan spent most of the time before the conveyor's return wandering aimlessly among the ruins. Every Paracop on this team knew when to steer clear of the Chief; Verkan knew he was being guarded but so tactfully he couldn't complain.

One thought dominated Verkan's mind. He'd thought he had a crisis, with an alliance of Opposition Party chiefs and outtime traders after his scalp over closing Fourth Level Europo-American. He had a case—too many nuclear and chemical weapons in the hands of national governments. However, he and Dalla would live through it even if he couldn't persuade anyone else.

Kalvan and Rylla were running for their lives, which might not be very long if Ptosphes's garrison of the lame and the halt couldn't hold Tarr-Hostigos for at least a few days.

As the day wore on, Verkan began to hope that the Grand Host's scouts would reappear. It was out of the question to seek the main body and tear it apart with First Level weapons. A few hundred dead cavalry troopers, however, could be labeled "non-contaminating self-defense" in an Incident Report. Their demise would make the Grand Host only a little less strong but a lot more cautious.

Or it might make people genuinely believe that demons fought for Kalvan, and create enthusiastic support for Roxthar's fifty-times-cursed Investigation! That was the problem with contamination—you couldn't control how people would interpret your intervention. Good Paracops always remembered that.

Verkan Vall gritted his teeth and decided to be a good Paracop again. He hoped his present set of teeth would survive the experience—

"Vall?"

He started to glare at the interruption, then recognized Kostran Garth, his wife Dalla's brother-in-law, and another of that handful of good friends and reliable Paracops. The conveyor must have returned with the lab test results—although from the look on Kostran's face, he was not the bearer of good news.

"I'm sorry, if that helps any," Kostran said.

"Some. Better security would have helped more. Dralm-dammit, we could have had it!"

"By Xipph's mandibles, Chief, you did all you could!" He added several more curses from a particularly vile Second Level time-line where spiders and beetles were sacred fetishes. "They sabotaged everything you and Ranthar tried to do."

"They paid for it, too. But keeping that from happening was ultimately the Chief's responsibility. *My* responsibility." Verkan managed a wry grin. "Wasn't it Kalvan's own—'Great King Truman'—who said, 'The buck stops here'?"

The grin faded, but Verkan managed not to sigh. "All right. Who did we find?"

"Five locals, Gorath Tran, and Sankar Trav, the Team medic."

"That leaves Danar Sirna and Aranth Saln unaccounted for." The two Paracops' eyes met. If the two missing people were prisoners, they were probably on their way into the hands of the Investigation. Then they'd soon wish they had burned to death instead.

"Danar Sirna. Doctoral candidate in history?"

Kostran nodded. "Right. Tall woman, auburn hair. Great figure too."

"Let's wish her better luck in her next incarnation. The soldiers here-and-now have rough-and-ready notions about dealing with enemy civilian women. What about Aranth Saln?"

"He's ex–Strike Force, one of the few Team people with survival skills. He was their expert on pre-industrial military science." Kostran hesitated. "I wonder if he was forced to try putting some of his theories into practice?"

"You mean, take an unscheduled field sabbatical?"

"Exactly. His cover is an artillery officer from Hos-Agrys and you can bet he won't break it by accident. If he catches Phidestros's eye, he may even be safe from the Investigation!"

It rubbed Verkan the wrong way, to possibly owe anything to the man principally responsible for Kalvan's defeat. Still, if under the circumstances Aranth had succumbed to the temptation that most outtime workers felt every so often—Verkan could only wish him luck.

Now, to interrogate the surviving Team members thoroughly.

Verkan wasn't looking forward to the job, but maybe it would turn up some clues. He decided to start with Baltov Eldra, if she was ready; she had the reputation of both a cool head and a keen talent for observation.

II

The climb to the gun platform on top of the north tower of Tarr-Hostigos left Prince Ptosphes unpleasantly short of breath. Old age had been pursuing him for a long time. Now it had finally caught him. Under other circumstances he would have been angry at the prospect of not seeing his grandchildren grow up, but that matter had been taken care of four days ago at Ardros Field.

"Should we summon Uncle Wolf for you, my Prince?" the gun captain asked.

Ptosphes shook his head. "No. Just let me sit down and catch my wind."

He lowered himself on to an upended powder barrel and was about to light his pipe when he remembered what he was sitting on. The gunners and sentries, he noticed, had returned to their work as soon as they knew he needed no help.

Good men, and more than ever a pity that they had to stand here and face certain death even if most of them were like him, a bit long in the tooth. At least they were the last good men he'd be leading to their doom. No more battles like Tenabra, to haunt him during the long winter nights. Kalvan and Rylla wouldn't be so lucky, and Kalvan at least liked such work even less than Ptosphes. Kalvan would just have to endure Rylla's tongue on the subject, as Ptosphes had endured Demia's.

Ptosphes chuckled, as he thought of Rylla's mother for the first time in nearly a moon. Rylla had much of her mother in her, both the strengths and the tongue and temper. Ptosphes remembered Demia asking (at the top of her lungs) whether he hated war too much to hold even the little Princedom of Hostigos.

Well, she'd been right in a way. He would have lost even that to Gormoth of Nestor, for not wanting to fight the battles of Styphon's House, if the gods hadn't sent Kalvan. Why, then, had those same gods turned their faces away when he needed their help most? What had he or Kalvan done to earn their wrath?

309

Great Dralm, I ask nothing for myself. Let your wrath fall on me, and spare Kalvan, Rylla, and my granddaughter Demia.

Ptosphes's breath came more easily now, and he badly wanted that pipe. He rose and was turning toward the stairs when he saw a horseman riding uphill toward the castle. He wore armor but no helmet, and a sash with Prince Phrames's colors. Probably one of Phrames's loyal Beshtans.

"Ahoooo! Prince Ptosphes! Prince Phrames has sent me back to warn you. The Styphoni are on the march once more. Their scouts are barely a candle from Hostigos Town!"

"Thank you, and carry my thanks to Prince Phrames." *So the siege begins even sooner than we expected.*

The trooper made no move to turn his mount. Ptosphes glared down at him. "No, you can't come into the castle. Your Prince and your Great King need you more than I do."

"Prince—"

"Now, Dralm-damn you, turn that horse around and get it moving! If you're not gone before I count to ten you'll be the first casualty of the siege of Tarr-Hostigos."

Ptosphes drew his pistol but his roar had already startled the horse into movement. It wheeled, nearly losing its footing on the steep slope, then broke into a canter. By the time Ptosphes had counted to five, it was out of pistol range. The Beshtan was still looking back at the castle. Ptosphes hoped he would turn around and look where he was going before he rode into a ditch.

Once his pipe was drawing well, Ptosphes walked around the walls to where he had a good view to the southeast. That was the likely direction for the Grand Host, or at least where he hoped most to see them. Anyplace else would mean they had a too-godless-good chance of cutting off at least Kalvan's rearguard.

The southeast was empty of smoke clouds, and so were all the other directions. Were the Styphoni advancing along roads where there was nothing left that even a fanatical believer would consider worth burning? Or was the vanguard mercenaries, who would be thinking of having roofs over their heads and food in their bellies during the siege?

Tarr-Hostigos should have a bit of time before its walls *had* to be manned and kept manned until the Styphoni stormed them. Plenty of time, for what Ptosphes intended.

He pointed the stem of his pipe at the nearest sentry. "Take a message to Captain-General Harmakros. Summon everyone in the castle except the sentries to the outer courtyard."

"Every—?" the man began, then broke off at Ptosphes's look. "Everyone. Captain-General Harmakros. Yes, my Prince."

The soldier hurried off, as if he wanted to open the distance between himself and his Prince before Ptosphes showed any more signs of madness.

Ptosphes followed at a more leisurely pace.

III

By the time the garrison was gathered in the outer courtyard, the sun was high overhead. Even the twenty-foot walls cast short shadows. Ptosphes sweated in his armor, wishing the laggards would hurry and resting his hand on the hilt of his sword.

It was a newly forged Kalvan-style rapier, balanced for fighting on foot but quite long enough for his purposes now. The Great Sword of Hostigos, which he'd belted on the day he was proclaimed Prince, was on its way westward with Kalvan and Rylla. His grandson would need that Sword some day, when he ruled a realm so huge that Old Hostigos would barely rank as a respectable Princedom.

If the gods are merciful.

Ptosphes saw no more men joining the crowd. He drew the sword and raised it overhead in both hands. Sunlight blazed from the steel.

"Men of Hostigos. You all know why you are here. You all were told, when you offered to hold Tarr-Hostigos until our Great King and his family might reach safety. Every one of you has already earned honor in the eyes of Dralm Allfather, Galzar Wolfshead, and the other true gods, the gratitude of your Prince and Great King, and the goodwill of your comrades.

"Styphon's Grand Host is approaching faster than we thought. Within a candle, two at most, this castle will be surrounded by the mightiest army in the history of the Great Kingdoms. For every one of us, there will be a hundred of the enemy. When they camp, a mouse won't be getting out of this castle.

"Any man who wants to leave can still do so. I'll say nothing against him nor let anyone else say a word. He'll have to hurry, to catch up with our rearguard before nightfall, but there's an open road for any who want to take it." He pointed toward the castle gate with his sword.

"For those who stay—you all know what kind of quarter Styphon's dogs gave us at Ardros. The lucky ones will have a quick death. The rest will have an appointment with Roxthar's Unholy Investigation."

A few hollow laughs sounded from the ranks; most faces were set and pale. All knew what had happened to the Hostigi prisoners after Ardros Field; few had not lost kin or friends in that butchery. Most of the prisoners not slaughtered outright were in the hands of the Investigation, doubtless envying their dead comrades.

Ptosphes lowered his sword and strode to the door of the woodshed on one side of the courtyard. Then he drew a line with the sword's point, through the dirt and straw covering the flagstones of the courtyard, from the woodshed to the blacksmith's forge on the other side. He then took a deep breath, sheathed his sword, and turned to face his men.

"All who want to stay—cross over this line and join me. Those who want to die somewhere else—stay where you are!"

Silence. Ptosphes could hear the stamping of horses from the stables on the far side of the courtyard. An unnaturally complete silence to be hanging over five hundred men. No one coughed, no one shuffled his feet. Ptosphes could have sworn some had ceased to breathe.

A thickset man in battered armor pushed his way from the rear into the open. Ptosphes tried not to stare too hard. It was Vurth.

Vurth, the peasant who'd been Kalvan's first host in this land, who owed his life and his family's to Kalvan's fighting skill. Who'd sent word of the Nostori raiders to Tarr-Hostigos, so that Rylla could lead out the cavalry who cut off the raiders and found Kalvan.

Vurth, a peasant who might really be called Dralm's first chosen tool for bringing about everything which had happened since that spring night almost four years ago. Ptosphes wondered briefly what Patriarch Xentos would have to say about the theological propriety of that notion—if presiding over the squabbles of the League of Dralm in far-off Agrys City left him any time for such matters.

Much good may that do Xentos in the eyes of the gods, when the League sends only words of condolence instead of soldiers and muskets to those who fight its battles against Styphon.

Ptosphes examined the gray-haired peasant. His clothes and face

312

were caked with mud and powder smoke, one shoulder was bandaged, and he limped. He wore the breastplate of some Harphaxi nobleman, once etched and gilded, now hacked and tarnished, over his homespun smock. On his head was a battered morion helmet, on his feet cavalry boots from two different corpses. He still carried the cavalryman's musketoon he'd acquired the night of Kalvan's coming, and both it and the powder flask at his belt were clean.

"First Prince, Captain-General Harmakros, people," Vurth began. "This isn't really a Council, so maybe I don't have the right to start off, as if I was Speaker for the Peasants like Phosg, Dralm keep him. I think I've a right to be heard, though."

Ptosphes would have cut down anyone who disagreed. The men saw this, and Vurth went on.

"Prince, most of us here either can't run, don't want to run, or don't have anywhere to run to. My farm has burned, my wife is dead, and one son too. The other son's off with King Kalvan, in the Royal Dragoons, and my son-in-law Xykos is Captain of Queen Rylla's Lifeguards. Dralm keep all the daughters who ran off with mercenaries.

"Styphon's taken or chased off everything I had except my life. All I want to do with what's left of it is kill Styphon's dogs until they kill me. I'm too old to go climbing trees or hide in caves like a thief, even for that. I'd rather sit here and kill the bastards in comfort!"

Vurth shouldered his musketoon and stepped forward across the line before anyone could cheer.

Ptosphes felt his eyes burn and quickly blinked back the threatening tears. He stepped up beside Vurth and put his arm around the peasant's shoulders. Any land that bore men like this would be barren ground indeed for Styphon's House. Such men could be killed; they could not be frightened.

Harmakros's voice cut through the new silence.

"Lift that litter, you fools! You don't have to stay yourselves!"

The bearers' reply was nearly inaudible and totally disrespectful. They had the Captain-General across the line before Ptosphes stopped grinning.

Another man stepped out, then two more, then five, then a band of ten, then a band too numerous to count, and after that it was a steady stream. Ptosphes saw one gray-haired man telling a club

313

footed boy no more than ten to stand where he was, then step out. The boy looked sullenly after his grandfather until he was sure the man couldn't see him, then slipped across the line.

Ptosphes turned his back on the men. He didn't want them to see his face until he could command it as a captain and a Prince ought to.

By the time he turned around, the space on the other side of the line was empty.

Ptosphes ran his eyes over the garrison, with the care of a man trained at the quick counting of large masses of men. There'd been just over five hundred before. No doubt a few had slipped off, perhaps as many as a man could count on his fingers and toes. Call it four hundred and eighty left behind, quite enough to do all the work Styphon's Grand Host would allow.

Ptosphes was fumbling for words of thanks when a sentry on the keep shouted. "Prince Ptosphes! Enemy scouts in Hostigos Town! On the east side, cavalry with two guns."

Guns up with the scouts meant they had orders to fight instead of hit and run. Who would have such orders? Perhaps the Zarthani Knights . . .

Ptosphes swallowed; the lump in his throat twitched but remained where it was. "What colors?" he managed to shout.

"King Demistophon's and a mercenary company's. Looks like a rearing white horse on a blue field."

The lump shrank. Mercenaries wouldn't burn a town they expected to provide them with dry beds and hot food, unless they had other orders. Such orders might not be obeyed, either, unless the man who gave them was watching.

With Grandbutcher Soton not up yet and Phidestros himself a mercenary, there might be no such man here. If Soton arrived after the Grand Host's advance guard had settled in—well, making mercenaries in another king's pay burn their own shelter and food was a task Ptosphes wouldn't wish even on Soton.

IV

Grand Captain-General Phidestros of Hos-Harphax felt his guts twist as the vanguard of his Iron Band rode by a burning farmhouse. A child lay on the steps, skull split.

In the farmyard itself, three of Roxthar's Holy Investigators were "questioning" a Hostigi woman, no doubt the child's mother. The Investigators wore hooded white robes with a red sun-wheel over the breast. The robes were well stained with mud and blood, some of the blood long dry.

"They can fight women and children well enough!" growled Grand Captain Kyblannos, commander of the Iron Band. "Where were Styphon's swine when we charged Kalvan's artillery at Ardros Field!"

Phidestros leaned out of his saddle to grip his friend's hand before he could draw a pistol and do something foolish. Not that half the Iron Band and Phidestros himself didn't feel the same . . .

Phidestros shut his ears against the woman's screams. Why in the name of every god couldn't the Styphoni at least find more private places to torture and maim? It was Roxthar, of course—Roxthar, with the fanatic's blindness to the opinions of others and total sense of his own rightness. He'd still better learn discretion, before half the Royal Army of Harphax and more than half the mercenaries started hunting Investigators instead of Hostigi.

Phidestros led veterans, men accustomed to danger, wounds, and death, for themselves and for others. He didn't lead butchers who reveled in killing like weasels among turkey chicks!

Curse and blast the Holy Investigation and all its works! They were dragging honorable soldiers down into the same kind of sty they enjoyed, without doing Styphon's House on Earth all that much good. These priests seemed to forget too easily what soldiers learned young if they wished to grow old: men made desperate by fear will fight to the last.

Phidestros twisted his head and flexed his shoulders as much as his armor would allow, to ease the tautness. He should be the happiest man in the Great Kingdoms, yet he felt more fear of the future than he had ever felt of Kalvan.

Kalvan was not invincible. Ardros Field proved that. The greatest victory since Erasthames the Great defeated the Ruthani Confederation at Sestra more than four centuries ago, and won by a man who three years ago was lucky to count two hundred soldiers following his banner! A victory so great that the Grand Host had

already released some of its mercenaries and set others to garrison-
ing captured castles. Five thousand of the best were hard on the
heels of the fleeing Royal Army of Hos-Hostigos.

Phidestros knew he should be riding with those men, instead of
playing steward to Archpriest Roxthar and his Investigators. Let
Grand Master Soton invest Tarr-Hostigos while Phidestros pressed
the pursuit until Kalvan was no more! As long as Kalvan was alive,
he might rise again. A man who could conjure a Great Kingdom
out of not much more than the gods' own air was no ordinary foe.

But try telling that to anyone else, including Grand Master
Soton, who ought to know better! Phidestros could not understand
why Soton deferred so much to Roxthar. The Grand Master was not
only the highest-ranking soldier of Styphon's House, he was an
Archpriest in his own right, the Investigator's equal in priestly
rank.

A mystery, and one that demanded an answer soon. Otherwise
they'd never run that wily fox Kalvan to earth before he found
another burrow.

It would not be an answer easily come by, either. Undue
curiosity about the affairs of the Investigation was a short road to a
charge of "heresy."

The Iron Band started down the last slope into Hostigos Town,
laid out on its alternating hills and dales. In the distance, Phidestros
saw the Kettlepot Mountains and Hostigos Gap, with Tarr-Hostigos
perched atop two formidable mountains to the right of the Gap.

The first mountain held the main castle with its great keep
surrounded by walls and gun towers. The second and higher peak
held a tower with its own walls.

Removing Tarr-Hostigos from the path of the Grand Host was
not going to be as simple as taking a splinter from a child's foot,
regardless of what Roxthar thought. If Phidestros had his choice, he
would leave a detachment to blockade the castle and let starvation
do the rest.

But he was merely a Grand Captain-General, in a war run by
priests. Also a Captain-General who answered to a Great King
who'd mortagaged everything but his concubines' shifts (if they
had any) to Styphon's House!

It was time to send the priests back to their temples and the counselors back to their castles so the soldiers could go on with finishing off Kalvan.

As they rode down toward Hostigos Town, Phidestros was pleased to see only two columns of smoke rising from it. There'd be dry beds at least for the next quarter-moon.

A rider galloped up, shouting for Phidestros. From his silvered armor and black-caparisoned horse with a silver sun-wheel on each quarter, he was a Knight of the Holy Lance.

"Hail, Grand Captain-General Phidestros! I am Commander Rythar of the Holy Lance, with a message from Grand Master Soton."

"Greetings, Commander Rythar. What is your master's pleasure?"

"The Grand Master requests your presence upon yonder hill."

The Commander raised his visor and pointed to a nearby hill. A Blade of sixty Knights stood in attendance on the diminutive figure of the Grand Master, whose blackened armor made a stark contrast to their polished finery.

Phidestros nodded to Kyblannos. The Grand Captain told off sixty of the Iron Band and placed them around his Captain-General until Phidestros felt like a babe in its nurse's arms. He held his peace; Kyblannos would be like a she-wolf with one cub toward his old captain until the day he died.

It took a few moments for the horses of Phidestros's party to get used to rough ground again, after several candles on the smooth paving of Kalvan's Great King's Highway. *Kalvan is a hard man not to respect, even in defeat,* was Phidestros's thought. *Many saw the wisdom of such roads. None were built, until Kalvan came.*

A quarter-candle took Phidestros up the hill to Soton's outpost. Phidestros dismounted and advanced to greet Soton, as Banner-Captain Geblon arrayed the Iron Band facing the Knights.

The two commanders clasped hands. Soton pointed to Tarr-Hostigos.

"A hard nut to crack, aye, Captain-General?"

"One to give any squirrel a bit of work. It's big enough to hold two thousand men and supplies for a year, if they don't mind horseflesh. We may see snow before we see a breach in those walls!"

317

"Rest easy, Captain-General. We've interrogated some prisoners—*not* as the Investigation does it, by the way. Kalvan's left only a skeleton garrison, five hundred men and some of those wrinkled like crab apples. We should have the castle invested in a few days. Then we can see about tracking Kalvan all the way to the Great Mountains if we must!"

Phidestros wanted to sing, dance, and embrace Soton, but dignity and caution shaped his tongue to a question. "Will His Bloodiness let us show such wisdom?"

"Guard your tongue, Phidestros. You are not so high that you cannot be made to lie down on the rack!" Soton's look would have stopped a charging bull.

This time frustration and disgust kept Phidestros altogether silent. Just how far into Roxthar's pocket *was* Soton? Before this year he would not have believed a man lived who could bind Soton to his will. Surely the mystery of Soton and Roxthar demanded a solution, before it threatened the victory so dearly bought with the blood of men Phidestros had led to battle!

When Phidestros found his tongue again, his voice was cold. "Yes, Grand Master. I have seen the fate of women and children who defy the Holy Investigator."

Soton's face paled and he looked away. "It is our duty to obey the Temple's will," he muttered. "This war against women and babes is not my choice, either, Phidestros. But when the Hostigi heresy is scourged from the land, the Investigation will be ended."

If you believe that, Phidestros thought, *you aren't half the man I'd thought.*

"The commanders are to be billeted at Ptosphes's new palace in Hostigos Town," Soton continued. "I'll be going there myself, as soon as we finish this drawing of Tarr-Hostigos."

He pointed at a Knight sitting on a stump with a slate and charcoal in hand. Phidestros peered over the man's shoulder, to see a fine rendering of the castle, with every tower and gate clearly shown.

Best round up Kalvan's mapmakers as soon as we're settled in. Some may have fled, and doubtless Soton will want his share. But this, please Galzar, is something soldiers can settle between them without listening to priests' babbling!

A hundred petty matters kept Phidestros and his Iron Band out of

Hostigos Town for much of the morning. By the time they'd covered the last furlongs of Old Tigo Road, the few fires were out. The streets were deserted, except for soldiers and chain gangs of prisoners, led by Roxthar's Investigators and Styphon's Own Guard, resplendent in their silvered armor and red capes.

Phidestros was hardly surprised to see the Guard acting as the Investigators' allies. The Temple Bands had a reputation as stout fighters, who neither asked nor gave quarter. That last habit had given them the nickname of "Styphon's Red Hand."

The chain gangs all seemed bound for Hostigos Square, which Phidestros found already half-filled with slave pens of Hostigi prisoners. The palace itself was garrisoned by Guardsmen standing practically shoulder-to-shoulder, and Investigators darted in and out like rats from a half-eaten corpse. Phidestros led the Iron Band toward the palace, ignoring the curses and threats of Styphoni brusquely pushed aside.

The Iron Band replied only with silence, and occasionally with a hand rested lightly on a pistol butt. Before it reached the palace, the Styphoni were giving way without protest.

As Phidestros dismounted, he knew one thing. He'd be cursed if he billeted any of his men in this nest of temple-rats! He'd say that the siege demanded all his attention and find quarters elsewhere! Otherwise the Iron Band would start the war against the Investigators here and now, and he'd be lucky to end up back commanding a company of every other captain's leavings!

TWO

I

Danar Sirna's first thought on waking up was to wish that she hadn't. Being dead or at least asleep seemed the best solution to quite a number of her problems, starting with her crashing headache.

The first thing Sirna saw clearly was a dead man. Beyond him lay two more dead men, one with half of his face blown away. Was she in what passed for field hospitals here-and-now?

She was lying on a straw pallet, with a wood-beamed roof over her, whitewashed plaster walls around her, and a window in one of those walls. The warped wooden shutter was ajar; through the gap she could see what looked like a cobblestone street in Hostigos Town.

She must have been picked up and brought in by one side or another, and put in here because she looked dead or dying. The whole left side of her head not only throbbed horribly but felt caked and stiff with dried blood. A scalp wound like that could make you look dead to people in a hurry.

Sirna had just decided that sitting up was a bad idea when a board creaked behind her. She decided to face her visitor sitting.

320

She struggled up, groaned, and turned to see a woman well past middle age, made up in a fashion that would have announced her profession on many other time-lines besides this one.

"So you're alive," the painted lady said. "They call me Menandra. What's your name, sweetheart?" The voice was gruff and coarsened by alcohol, but not unfriendly.

Better say something. Sirna didn't dare nod, but her mouth was so dry that only a croak came out.

Menandra bawled something in a voice that would have rallied a cavalry regiment. Sirna winced. One of the house women appeared with a jug and a cup.

"Drink this."

Sirna rinsed her mouth out, then swallowed. It went down, heavily watered wine with some herbs in it. When she thought it was going to stay down, she asked, "What's been happening since—Ardros Field?" She realized she didn't know how long she'd been unconscious.

Menandra looked at the ceiling as she spoke. "Well, King Kalvan is on his way west with what's left of the—his men. Prince Ptosphes is holding the castle, to let him get away. We're playing host to Captain-General Phidestros's Iron Band. Does that answer you, girl?"

"What's Phidestros doing here?" Sirna asked.

Menandra's reply was a hoarse whisper. "I hear that the Captain-General's not too pleased with how Roxthar's Investigators are tearing up this town. He's supposed to be staying over there at the big headquarters, in what used to be Ptosphes's palace. But he spends most of his nights here or over by the siege works." She grinned. "Once he sets eyes on you, he won't be staying anywhere else."

Sirna strangled another groan. Menandra shrugged. "War's like that. Now, the next question is, what do we do with you now? Some peasants picked you up, thought you fit for ransoming. They had you in a cart when the Iron Band passed by. They ran you into town in the cart, facedown on top of a load of squash with your skirt up to your arse."

"With my skirt—?"

The picture made Sirna giggle, then laugh. Once she started laughing she couldn't stop, although it made her head hurt worse. It also shook her stomach, which finally rebelled.

When Sirna stopped retching, Menandra was still standing over her, trying to look stern but not entirely succeeding. "As I said, what about you, girl? You're a long way from home and your friends at the Foundry are either dead or run off, the true gods alone know where."

"Run off?"

Menandra couldn't give many details, but what she said told Sirna very clearly that the survivors of the University Study Team had left her for dead. It took all her self-control not to cry. She not only felt sick, she was frightened.

"Not good for you, the more so since the Styphoni will be looking for people from the Foundry. Outlanders especially. I can probably protect you here at the Gull's Nest, if you're willing to work."

This was more than Sirna could digest in one gulp. Clearly Menandra was the owner and madam of the Gull's Nest (and why that name, this far from the sea?) and was quite willing to let her earn her keep, sick or not.

"No!"

"It's how I started out in Agrys City, girl. More years ago than either of us wants to think about. There's worse things than making a living on your back. Gives you a new view of the world, you might say."

There probably were worse things here-and-now than making a living as one of Menandra's whores. Right now Sirna couldn't think of them. She shook her head slowly.

"Well, you're handsome enough for it, and to spare."

Sirna shook her head again.

"I'll leave it be, then. Just remember, though—anything you make in the house, half goes to me. Or you go to the soldiers!"

Sirna closed her eyes and wished it all away. The smoke-blackened timbers were still there when she opened her eyes. She really was in a situation where she could be turned over to a band of mercenaries and passed from man to man until she died or they got tired of her. It was a long way from reading or even writing about "the inferior position of women" to experiencing it.

Deliberately, she closed and locked a door in her mind, on First Level and all the pleasures and privileges she had there, even on her chances of ever seeing it again. (Which were slim enough at best, with Kalvan defeated and her left for dead.) She would look forward, look this Styphon-cursed time-line squarely in the eye, and dare it to do its worst.

Not that it hasn't already given me its best shot—

She came back from this mental exercise to see Menandra looking positively concerned. "That crack on the head didn't addle your wits, did it?"

"I—don't think so. I must have slept off the worst of it. I was just thinking—what I'm going to do to those sons of the gods only could count how many fathers who ran off and left me."

That was no lie, either. She now understood emotionally as well as intellectually the concept of the blood feud. If she ever caught Outtime Studies Director Talgan Dreth alone in a dark place—

"By Yirtta's dugs, girl, I can't give charity! Phidestros's men may pay me if Styphon's House ever pays them. Then again they may not. If they don't want to and I ask, they may burn the place down!"

And pass the women around among themselves, Sirna added mentally. Somehow the idea was no longer so paralyzingly frightful, now that she'd closed that door to First Level.

"If you know anything about healing, even the smallest bit, you might make yourself useful. Phidestros is going to be sending his sick and hurt here. The Iron Band's Uncle Wolf was killed in the battle, and there aren't so many priests of Galzar that even a Captain-General can conjure them up. You help patch and purge Phidestros's men, and there won't be any trouble keeping you."

"Help those damned filthy Styphon's sons of—?" Sirna began.

Gently but emphatically, Menandra slapped her. At least it was probably intended as a gentle slap. Sirna had to shake her head a couple of times, to make sure her neck wasn't broken. Through the ringing in her ears, she heard Menandra warning her against saying anything less than complimentary about Styphon.

"Archpriest Roxthar's here with his Investigators. Anyone who blasphemes Styphon within a day's ride of him will wish she *had* been turned over to the soldiers. Yes, and the stallions and the draft oxen too!"

From what she'd heard of Roxthar, Sirna saw no reason to argue the point. "I'm sorry, Menandra. I'm still a little confused."

323

"Well, unconfuse yourself, girl. You might start with that head wound. Clean it up, and I'll think you're good enough to turn loose on Phidestros's men."

Menandra bawled for scissors, a mirror, hot water, and bandages, while Sirna took off her mud- and blood-smeared clothes and examined her body for other injuries. A prize collection of black-and-blue marks was all she turned up. Her anger toward the people who'd abandoned her grew. If they hadn't been too panic-stricken to spend ten seconds examining her, they'd have learned she was alive and fit to be moved.

The head wound was a long shallow gash, probably a sword cut. She must have picked up the concussion when she fell. No signs of infection, but she made a thorough job of cleaning the wound, starting with cutting off the hair all around it. It was bleeding again by the time she was finished, and so was her lower lip where she'd bitten it. She finished by trimming her hair all around.

"You're cutting off one of your best parts, you know that, girl?" Menandra said.

Persistent, aren't you? "I'll be hard to recognize with my hair short. Maybe they'll even think I'm too ugly to bother."

"With a figure like yours? You've got a lot to learn about men, girl. Somebody's going to want what you've got if you shaved yourself bald! Best arrange to give it to a man big enough to fight off the rest. Or else you'll wish you'd taken my first offer."

What am I, a mare to go with the strongest and fiercest stallion in the herd?

Exactly.

Sirna sighed and stood up, swaying slightly but not really wanting to lie down again. That was one good sign. Another was that she was hungry.

"Is there anything to eat around here?"

Menandra chuckled. "You'll do, girl. Come on down to the kitchen and I'll see if the bread and tea are ready."

II

Tiny clouds of white smoke rose three times from the Styphoni siege battery. Ptosphes started counting. At "five" the three shots crashed into Tarr-Hostigos. One struck the face of the outer wall, the others hit the left side of the breach. Rock dust as white as the

324

powder smoke whirled up, carried down toward Ptosphes on the morning breeze. He tasted the grit on his tongue and teeth. It was a familiar taste by now, with the siege into its tenth day.

The men working on the barricade rising inside the breach barely looked up from their work. The barricade was made of heavy timbers from the buildings of the outer courtyard, flagstones from the courtyard itself, and stones from the breach itself. The men at work were lacing the timbers together with ropes and strips of leather, while others stood by, ready to haul a cannon on to the top of the barricade.

"Pretty old-fashioned way they have of doing things," said Master Gunner Thalmoth, who was standing beside Ptosphes. "'Thout those captured guns and the slaves to haul 'em up, they'd be sitting down on the level making faces at us."

Thalmoth was old enough to remember standing in the crowd with his father to see the newborn Ptosphes presented to the people of Hostigos as their future Prince. Too old to take the field, he'd taught at the University as well as lending a lifetime of artillery experience to testing the new Hostigi guns.

Ptosphes wondered if Thalmoth had volunteered to remain behind entirely because of his age. (He'd been seen to lift powder barrels and wield handspikes on balky guns.) Did he perhaps hold himself responsible for the prooftesting explosion that killed four men and took off Captain-General Harmakros's leg on the eve of the campaign that led to Ardros Field?

Thalmoth owed an answer to that question only to Dralm or Galzar, not to an overcurious Prince.

"It's their first big siege," Ptosphes said tolerantly. "No doubt they'll do better next time."

This morning he felt almost benign even toward the besieging Styphoni. It was a beautiful day, and not too hot. He'd eaten a good breakfast. The garrison's wounded were doing as well as could be expected. Best of all, the men of Tarr-Hostigos now knew they'd won the victory they *had* to win.

Last night a party of picked men had slipped into the besiegers' forward positions. Their score was twenty-eight taken prisoner, more than fifty killed, a magazine blown up, and three bombards spiked, all for the price of one man dead and four wounded.

All the prisoners said that Kalvan hadn't been overtaken. Some added that the men chasing him had been ordered back to join the siege. One said he'd heard a whole band was wiped out in an ambush by Kalvan's rearguard. (Ptosphes suspected that the last man was trying to please his captors, who had nothing to lose by blowing him from a gun.)

The last stand at Tarr-Hostigos was *not* going to be a waste of lives. If that wasn't worth celebrating, then nothing was.

Of course, the odds against the besieger would rise still higher now that the Grand Host was bringing back their vanguard. Since those odds were already close to a hundred to one, who cared? Ptosphes rather liked Harmakros's way of putting it:

"Aren't we lucky? We'll *never* run out of targets now!"

That might have been Harmakros's fever speaking. In spite of his stump having been cleaned to drive out the fester-demons, Harmakros had been working far too hard for a man so badly hurt. However, most of the rest of the garrison seemed to feel the same way.

Ptosphes continued his walk around the castle walls, Thalmoth following ten paces behind. The riflemen in the towers encouraged enemy musketeers to stay beyond accurate range, and the besiegers didn't waste cannon shot on single men. Ptosphes suspected that they were short of fireseed and saving what they had for the storming. No trouble of that kind for his people, even without the reserve of twelve tons of Styphon's Best in the cellar of the keep.

He inspected the gunners at the main gate and the siege battery at the bottom of the draw leading up to the gate. The battery had been laid out by someone who knew his business, which was also why it had no guns in it as yet. They would be needed for the storming, to keep the Hostigi on the gates from having target practice on the men coming up the draw. Until then, they would simply be on the wrong end of plunging fire from the gate towers.

Another hundred paces along the walls, and some of Ptosphes's good mood evaporated. On this side Archpriest Roxthar had his prison—really more of a stock pen—for the people he was Investigating. Like most of the besiegers' works, it was walled in timber and stone carted by slave gangs from Hostigos Town, but lacked their roof of old tents. At the rate the besiegers' works were swallowing the town, it soon wouldn't matter if they burned it or not.

A long line of gallows rose by the gate of the prison pen, most of them dangling bodies, and continued on down the road halfway to

326

Hostigos Town. Ptosphes could smell the bodies who'd been dangling more than a couple of days, even over the stable-and-powder-smoke reek of the siege.

The gallows seemed to be more burdened now than even a few days ago. No doubt the Styphoni had finished with their Hostigi slaves after they'd sweated and bled to haul the captured sixteen-pounders up the slope to the siege battery.

That whole affair had been as bloody in itself as some of the battles of the days before Kalvan. The Styphoni had killed a fair number of their own men, mining the places where Ptosphes' grandfather had carved the slopes into vertical faces. The Hostigi had also had to kill some of their own folk, weeping and cursing as they flailed at the gun teams with case shot and rifles.

The end of it was what had to be, when one side could spend men like water. The guns were in place and hammering at the walls of Tarr-Hostigos in a way even those ancient stones could not endure forever. Hostigi guns, Alkides's prize sixteen-pounders. No surprise that, considering that all of them except "Galzar's Teeth" had been lost at Ardros Field.

No surprise, and therefore something Ptosphes *should* have been able to do more about. He'd forgotten Kalvan's advice, given late one night when they'd all been emptying a jug of Ermut's brandy.

"Always plan against the worst thing your enemy can do. That way you'll be safe, no matter what he does. If he doesn't do his worst you'll win more easily."

Wise words. Clearly the army of the Great King Truman taught its captains well.

Ptosphes shook his head and lit his pipe. There was no call to feel sorry for himself. He had done too much of that. Besides, while he might not be fit for service in the hosts of Great King Truman, he was no bad captain for Tarr-Hostigos when every day it held was another victory over the Styphoni.

III

The man on what had been Menandra's best table writhed and twisted, and almost but not quite screamed. The four mercenaries holding him strained to keep him still.

"Lie quiet," Sirna muttered. "You lie quiet, or I'll have to use a sandbag on you. I don't want to do that. You may have already hurt your head, when the tunnel fell on you."

The soldier on the table sank his teeth into his lower lip. Blood came, but he lay still as Sirna cut open the flesh of his cheek over the finger-length splinter there and drew out the bloody wood. More blood flowed freely. Sirna let it flow while she picked out the last bits of wood, then bound up the wound in a dressing of boiled rags. By the time she'd finished the bandaging, the soldier had fainted, but he came awake as his comrades lifted him off the table.

"Sorry to be so much trouble, girl," the soldier said between clenched teeth. "But I wanted to look at something pretty."

Sirna grinned. "With the gods' favor and no fester-demons, you'll have two eyes to look at pretty girls. And a fine scar to attract the ones you want."

The scar would be a lifelong disfigurement—no reconstructive surgery here-and-now. Still, if the soldier was able to contemplate life with it . . .

She'd thought she'd been used to what people on Fourth Level could face, after almost three years with the University Team. It still made a difference, to live alone among such people, with the nearest person who would have ever heard of First Level at least a hundred miles away—farther if they'd kept on running. Not to mention the possibility of spending the rest of her life here-and-now.

On top of everything else, Styphon's soldiers! It wasn't easy to accept that men who fought for something as silly, irrational, even barbaric, as Styphon's House could be like other men. But they fought just as bravely, cried out just as loudly for their mothers when they hurt, and made just as many bawdy jokes that could still turn her face brighter than her cropped hair.

Or rather, it hadn't been easy to accept this, ten days ago. Now it sometimes seemed that she'd never believed anything else.

No more sick or wounded seemed to be coming, so Sirna sent one of the women with the knife and the salvaged bandages off to the kitchen to boil them clean. She also made at least her twentieth mental memo:

Borrow some better instruments from a priest of Galzar, or have the Iron Band's armorers make them.

328

Another woman, face streaked with makeup, wiped down the table with a bucket of boiling water. Menandra herself brought Sirna a cup of hot turkey broth.

"You'd better eat something solid, you know," the madam said. "Even if it's only an omelet. Won't do, having you faint on top of men too hurt to enjoy it!"

"Oh, I'll eat something tonight." At the moment, the mere thought of solid food made her gag.

"Tonight . . ." Menandra began, then lowered her voice to a whisper so that none of the wounded on pallets along the other side of the room could hear.

"The talk in town is that it's tomorrow they go for the castle. So you'd *better* eat and sleep tonight, or by Yirtta I'll turn you over my knee and spank you!" She ruffled Sirna's hair with one large greasy hand.

Sirna gulped her broth with both hands clasped tightly around the cup so Menandra wouldn't see that they were shaking. Seventeen wounded men in one day was bad enough. If they stormed the castle, it could be more like seventy—or seven hundred! Although she might have more help from the priests of Galzar if the promised reinforcements came up. Had they? She was trying to think of a tactful way to ask when the door to the street opened and a suit of armor wearing dusty leather breeches and boots strode in.

The suit of armor also had a brown beard and wide gray eyes, but it wasn't until the high-crested helmet came off that Sirna realized there was a man inside. When she saw that the man had a high forehead and a long scar across his right cheek, she knew who'd come to visit his wounded.

Grand Captain-General Phidestros waved the men trying to rise back on to their pallets with his free hand, set his helmet on the table, and took off his mud-caked gloves. Then he grinned at Sirna.

"You randy bastards! You've been keeping secret the best thing this wreck of a town has to offer. Where's your loyalty to your commander, you ——?" The term would have been insulting as well as obscene in any other tone. The men replied in kind, except for Banner-Captain Geblon, on light duty today because of an attack of dysentery.

329

"She is Menandra's healer, Captain-General," Geblon said, trying to both look and sound innocent. "She has been marvelously chaste."

"I'm sure she has," Phidestros replied. "But has she been caught? If she hasn't, you aren't the men I thought you were!"

Sirna stopped blushing and started giggling. Phidestros bent down and gripped her by one arm, pulling her to her feet as easily as if she'd been a child. Seen close up, his long face showed deep lines, apparently gouged with a blunt chisel, then filled with dust.

By the time he'd led her into the hall where no one could see her, she was trying to stop giggling. Somehow she wanted to impress him favorably, and not only because he had the power of life and death over her.

"To speak plainly—what is your name, by the way?"

"Sirna."

"Speaking plainly, Sirna, I owe you for a good thirty of my men helped and at least two saved outright. Where did you learn to treat burns like Aygoll's?"

"My father had some skill in healing, and was always quick to learn anything someone else would teach. One year we lived not far from a smithy. They knew how to heal burns from molten metal."

"Curious. What you did for Aygoll is very much like what Kalvan is said to have taught, about driving out the fester-demons."

"Is it not possible that the gods can send wisdom to both good and evil men, and leave it to them how it shall be used?" She looked up to meet his eyes as she spoke, and she thought she kept her voice steady.

"It's not only possible, it happens all the time," Phidestros said. "Only don't try arguing the point with Holy Investigator Roxthar. He's threatening to purge the hosts of Styphon once he's finished with Hostigos."

"Aren't you speaking a little freely, if he's running—if he's that suspicious?"

Like most of the surviving population of Hostigos Town, Sirna had stayed indoors. Those whom urgent business or the search for food drove outside too often found themselves confronted by white-robed Investigators or squads of Styphon's Red Hand. Few of those returned. Now only rats and fools strayed outside; rumor had it that the Investigators were turning to house-to-house searches in East Hostigos Town.

"Afraid you won't be paid, Sirna?"

"That's not it at all! I just—I'm not like Menandra, you know. I'd feel sorry for a thrice-convicted rapist facing the Investigation."

"So would I, believe me." He grinned, displaying a mouthful of almost intact white teeth, which meant not only good health but good luck in battle.

"Menandra is no worse than the gods made her, but they were drunk that day and perhaps a little careless. No, Sirna. I'm in no danger. Not unless the Archpriests decide they don't need good soldiers anymore. That won't be until Kalvan's dead, and somehow I think that man is going to take a lot of killing."

Sirna would have kissed Phidestros if she hadn't known he would misinterpret the gesture. "I wouldn't be at all surprised if it did," she said.

"No. Which means that Roxthar is going to be dealing lightly with soldiers for a while. Healers who may be tainted with heresy aren't quite as indispensable. Remember that, and you may live to be paid for your work with the Iron Band.

"Oh, and I'll pay it right into your hands. If Menandra asks for a single brass piece, tell me. We'll roast our victory ox over her furniture."

The way Phidestros's voice and face changed in those last words made Sirna want to flinch away from his touch. She forced herself to stand still as he put a hand behind her back and urged her back toward the main room.

"Let's join the men, before they gamble away all their money wagering which one of us was on top!"

THREE

I

Phidestros awoke the instant a hand pressed over his lips. Instinctively his right hand snaked underneath the bedroll his head rested on, to grip the poniard there.

Now another hand gripped his right wrist. Phidestros used his left hand to reach for the single-shot widow-maker he kept in a pouch next to his heart.

"For Galzar's sake, sir! It's me, Kyblannos!"

Phidestros stopped struggling when he recognized the voice, but didn't let go of the still-undrawn widow-maker.

"What in Regwarn's Hidehole is up now?"

"A parlay, sir. Some of the mercenary captains would like a private word with you, out of Archtorturer Roxthar's hearing."

"By the Wargod's Mace, couldn't they pick a more civilized hour?" Phidestros groaned.

At least the captains had picked the right place. The tent Phidestros used when he spent the night in the siege lines was a thousand paces from the nearest other tent. Men like Kyblannos guarded it, men who had been with Phidestros in the days of the Iron Company, men who had no fear of priests or torturers. Men who had guarded him with their lives and would go on doing so.

Phidestros cursed again and sat up.

"Who wants to talk with me?"

"Grand Captains Brakkos, Demmos, and Thymestros, Captain Phidammes, Uncle Wolf Eurocles, and three other captains I could not recognize."

That was five of the best freelances in the Grand Host, leading about a sixth of its strength. Now that he was awake enough to think clearly, Phidestros found himself not altogether surprised.

The first attempt to storm Tarr-Hostigos had been a disaster. The attack up the mountainside at the breach and up the draw toward the gate had been bloodily repulsed. The Hostigi had thrown everything from barrels of fireseed to ordinary rocks at the storming parties, reducing them to bloody rags fifty paces from the walls.

In the northern work, a handful of Hostigi had slaughtered twenty besiegers for every man they lost before the scaling ladders finally reached the walls. They might have held as firmly as they had in the main castle, if it hadn't been for the newly arrived siege rifles.

Converted from the heavy boat swivels used by the Zarthani Knights against the Ruthani of the southern swamps, they could go anywhere three men could climb. Once in action, they outranged even a Hostigi rifleman perched on a tower. Ten of them had given the Grand Host the northern work of Tarr-Hostigos. Fifty might have given them the main castle.

At least they now had a place where heavy guns might play against the keep, once they were hauled up there. Given time, those guns would finish the work with no need for another attack.

Time, though, is just exactly what I won't have. If the freelance captains don't take it away, Roxthar will. He knows only one way of solving this problem, and that the bloodiest.

Does he plan to bleed the Grand Host to a shell, so it cannot turn against him after Kalvan is overthrown?

Phidestros began pulling on his clothes. "By the way, Kyblannos. What do they want? More gold?"

"I don't know, sir. Truly."

"Help me get my breastplate on, then let them in."

The captains slunk into the tent like foxes into a turkey yard. Uncle Wolf Eurocles was in the lead, chief among the Host's Uncle

Wolfs and formerly a freelance Captain-General of some note in his own right. His hair was almost white and his beard iron gray, but his face was still ruddy and his back straight as a musket barrel.

When everyone was inside, Phidestros rose. "I won't apologize for poor hospitality. It's too late for that. What can I do for you gentlemen?"

Eurocles spoke first. "In the name of Galzar, can you bring this mad siege to an end?"

"Not without putting my jewels between the blades of Roxthar's clipping shears."

Nervous laughter skittered around the tent.

Grand Captain Brakkos spoke up next. "I thought you led this army, *Grand* Captain-General, not Roxthar's regiment of bedgowns."

"I command, but only so long as I do nothing to offend Archpriest Roxthar or Great King Lysandros. Where do you think I would have been if we had lost at Ardros Field? Even now, I have Grand Master Soton, Roxthar, and would-be successors all tugging at my swordarm.

"The real commander of this Host is the one who fills your pay chests with gold—and you know it."

"Then not even you can stop this senseless assault on Tarr-Hostigos?" Eurocles asked.

"No, Uncle Wolf. Were it up to me I'd leave a blockading force with a few heavy guns, to starve the Hostigi out of their fortress or knock it down on their thick heads. I would take the rest of the Host after Kalvan until I caught him, then pickle his head as a gift for Lysandros.

"But our Holy Investigator decrees otherwise. As I would like to survive this siege, I am not going to disobey."

"May Galzar strike that blasphemer of Galzar dead!" Brakkos shouted.

"Hush, man! Even the walls have ears," a captain urged.

"Curse and blast Styphon and all his Archpriests!" Brakkos raved on. "This isn't the only gap in the mountains, for Galzar's sake! None of the others are half so stoutly defended. Let us push through one of them and fight Kalvan's fugitives, not sit here like owls in a thunderstorm!"

"Silence, Brakkos," Eurocles replied. "Your flapping tongue is a danger to us all." His steely gaze finally reduced Brakkos to stuttering.

"Captain-General Phidestros, *you* are the leader of this Host, and that is a sacred trust given by Galzar. You must stop this madness."

"If I had Galzar's hand to guide mine, I would. I do not. Only Styphon's branding iron and the headsman's ax rule here. I say again, and I hope for the last time—if I order the Host to do anything whatever that displeases Roxthar, my life will be forfeit and the Host under the command of Soton."

"Then stay and be Roxthar's slave if you will," Grand Captain Demmos snapped. "We shall do otherwise."

"Do anything else and your life won't be worth a bent phenig," Phidestros replied. "Roxthar has a memory like Galzar's Muster Book."

"Styphon's tentacles do not cover the earth," Brakkos replied. "King Theovacar is always ready to hire freelances, and I've heard there's a revolt in Wulfula and a king taking oaths. Too, there are no Investigators in Hos-Zygros or Hos-Agrys."

"Not yet, my friends," Phidestros said, wearier than even the hour and a moon of work could explain. "Leave at your own risk. The day is Styphon's and his sun burns hot and reaches everywhere.

"If you must leave, do so at night, without a word to anyone. If Roxthar hears of your plans, the Red Hand will drown you in your own blood.

"Let it also be said that this is oathbreaking and I speak against it. Uncle Wolf, what say you?"

Eurocles shook his head. "The Captain-General speaks the truth. Any of you who desert this siege without his permission will be under Galzar's ban. I have no choice."

Brakkos spat on to the ground. "Priest, you are as weak-spined as our *Grand* Captain-General! Don't you see, when Roxthar and his butchers are through with Kalvan they will next turn on Dralm, then Lytris, then Yirtta Allmother, finally on Galzar himself! Fight before it is too late! We betray Phidestros, but we do not betray our god!"

In a thunderous silence, Brakkos left the tent.

It was Eurocles who broke the silence. "He and his men will be gone before dawn," the priest said in a hushed voice. "By Galzar's Mace, they are doomed.

"Yet I fear he may well be right."

II

Ptosphes looked around him at the battle-strained faces on the keep's roof. At dawn they would face the twenty-first day of the siege; almost certainly they would face the second storming attempt.

The first one ten days ago had cost the garrison a hundred men, the Styphoni three thousand. It had gained the enemy the north tower, but shellfire from the keep had kept them from mounting guns there.

The second storming would be more dangerous. The enemy would certainly have some tactics devised to meet shells. Those heavy rifles would come into play against the Hostigi marksmen who had butchered the mercenaries' captains.

Worst of all, this time Styphon's Red Hand would be clutching at Tarr-Hostigos. Their massed columns had been gathering in Hostigos Town all day. Would they lead the assault, or bring up the rear to remind the vanguard that there was something more to be feared than Hostigi shells?

Two men carrying Captain-General Harmakros's chair set it down with a thump. The two men carrying Harmakros himself gently lowered him into the chair, arranged the cushions behind him, and stepped back.

Even in the twilight, Ptosphes could see that Harmakros's cheeks were too flushed for a man who was supposed to be healing well.

"Did you have wine at dinner?"

"Why not, Prince? It will take more wine than we have in Tarr-Hostigos to kill me before Styphon's House does."

Ptosphes sighed. With variations, he'd heard this at least twenty times today, since it had become obvious that the Styphoni were gathering again. No one expected to see tomorrow's sunset. Nobody seemed to care, either, so long as they could take a proper escort with them. To be sure of doing that, everybody had worked

336

all day as if demons would pounce on them the moment they dropped their tools or even stopped to take a deep breath.

Ptosphes looked the length of what was, for another night at least, *his* castle. The work done to protect the mortars showed most clearly. The four small ones now had stones banked around them, so that the shells bursting outside wouldn't do so much damage. The three larger mortars were back on their field carriages. They could move to prepared positions all over the courtyard as fast as the men on the ropes could pull them, then be firing again almost as soon as they stopped.

The four biggest "mortars" were still in the pit in the outer courtyard. They were really just an old twelve-pounder and three eight-pounders, with their breeches sunk into the earth and their muzzles raised. They were too heavy to move or mount anywhere else, and in any case they could reach everywhere around Tarr-Hostigos from the courtyard. Their crews were finishing a magazine of timbers covered with stones, to protect their shells and fireseed.

"Prince Ptosphes!" One of the riflemen on sentry duty was pointing toward the siege lines on the west side of the castle. "They're starting to move around before the light goes. Think they'll come tonight?" He sounded almost eager.

Ptosphes stared into the dusk, wishing for the hundredth time in the last four years that he had one of the far-seeing glasses of Great King Truman's army. But they were like Kalvan's old pistol—the Great King couldn't even teach his friends how to make the tools to make the tools to make the glasses!

Yet those skills *would* be learned. What the gods had taught once, they could teach again—and more easily, because they would be teaching men who were trying to learn and knew what power the new knowledge might give them.

If Kalvan's luck continued to hold, his children might live to look at a battlefield through far-seers, or even ride into battle aboard one of those armored wagons that moved without horses and carried guns that fired many times while a man was drawing a deep breath.

Ptosphes put aside thoughts of the future he wouldn't see and looked to where the rifleman was pointing. The man was right. Guns—heavy ones from the number of horses drawing them—

were rolling slowly along behind the lines. It was too dark to make out more, but Ptosphes suspected that the missing Hostigi sixteen-pounders had just been found.

"Should we try a few shots, just to remind them that we're awake?" Harmakros asked.

"Not with the mortars. We want to save their shells. That little rifled bronze three-pounder on the inner gate, though—it might have the range."

"Kalvan said we shouldn't use case shot with rifled guns," Ptosphes said. "It damages the rifling. With solid shot, that three-pounder will do more good up here."

Harmakros's face asked what he was too tactful to put into words: how likely is it that any gun in Tarr-Hostigos will last long enough to damage itself, once the Grand Host advances? Perhaps he was also chafing at waiting like a bear tethered in a pit, for the dogs to come down within reach.

The hoisting tackle on the keep easily hauled the three-pounder up on to the roof, but not before darkness fell. Half a dozen shots produced a satisfactory outburst of shouts and curses from the Styphoni, but otherwise they seemed to have fallen off the edge of the world. After the half dozen failed to start a fire, Ptosphes ordered the gun to cease fire.

He made a final inspection, counting with special care the torches and tarpots laid ready, in case the Styphoni came at night. It wasn't likely; the chance of hitting friends in a night attack would not please the mercenary captains. It wasn't impossible, either, and Ptosphes was determined to follow Kalvan's teachings to the end (not far away now): prepare for *everything* that isn't impossible.

At last Ptosphes returned to the Great Hall, to find Harmakros asleep in the chair of state and snoring like volley fire from a company of musketeers. Ptosphes rolled himself in his cloak without taking off his armor, on a pallet as far from Harmakros as he could find.

He'd thought he might be too tired or uneasy to sleep, but instead he was drifting off into oblivion almost as soon as he'd stretched out his legs and lowered his head on to the dirt-stiffened cloth.

Phidestros brushed the sleep out of his eyes and stared through the valley's early-morning shadows at the Grand Host's encampment. A splendid sight with its thousands of campfires—until one remembered that all these tens of thousands of men were chained to this desolate valley by a castle held by four hundred old men and walking wounded. Meanwhile, the Usurper fled into the wilderness.

Phidestros realized now that it was in some measure his own fault, that he was not free to ride on Kalvan's trail. He had not questioned Lysandros's orders that he should not go against the will of Grand Master Soton. Apart from the folly of divided command, he respected the man too much.

He had not realized how completely Soton would be in Roxthar's pocket. He had not considered the possibility with as much attention as he would have given to the effect of rain on the roads he needed to bring up fireseed! Had he done so, a few discreet questions at least might have already been asked, and the mystery closer to solution. Certainly he would have been able to do more than he had, against the Grand Master's seeming need for Roxthar's permission to break wind!

As it was, he was chief over the Grand Host only in name. In truth, he was first among equals, all of them hamstrung by Roxthar. The Investigator was utterly convinced that the root of Kalvan's heresy was to be found in Hostigos and equally determined to extirpate it if he had to Investigate every person in the Princedom! He would not allow any stone to be left unturned, including Tarr-Hostigos. Against that particular stone the Grand Host had bruised its foot for the best part of a moon, but with Galzar's favor that was about to end!

Phidestros also asked for Galzar's favor, to keep Investigators out of his promised lands of Sashta, Beshta, and Sask. A small forest of poles already held the bodies of more than a quarter of Hostigos Town's people, those who had failed the Investigation. Add to that those who fled with Kalvan, and by spring there would hardly be enough Hostigi left to bury their dead!

If the Investigation came to his lands, Phidestros resolved it would not be *his* subjects who decorated gallows. He somehow doubted that Investigators with iron pincers would do as well against soldiers as they did against women and children. It might cost his own head to take Roxthar's, but he would have the pleasure of harvesting the Investigator's first!

The shadows began to fade. From his high vantage point, Phidestros saw the camps coming to life, like kicked anthills. He'd wanted to lead the Iron Band in the first assault himself, but Soton insisted on his staying safely in the rear. Captain-Generals, Soton stated emphatically, were *not* meant to be fired off like barrels of fireseed!

Soton was right, of course. Had Phidestros been in the vanguard during the first storming attempt, he might be dead along with so many others from Ptosphes's exploding cannonballs.

He might also have kept more influence over the mercenary captains. It would have been worth risking Soton's wrath to forestall the hornet's nest Brakkos's departure had unleashed. Or would unleash, as soon as the Red Hand could be spared from the siege to go and hunt the captain down. Roxthar had somehow realized that sending away his picked troops at this moment would end the siege and might end his own existence.

It still rankled, to be leading from behind. One more thing he would have to get used to, he supposed, along with asking who had married whom *before* he swore unquestioning obedience . . .

Phidestros cupped his hands around his pipe bowl and used the tinderbox to get a spark. When the pipe was drawing, he blew out a long plume of smoke, watching the rising morning breeze chase it away.

"Please, Captain-General," Banner-Captain Geblon said. "Would you get down? Otherwise the Hostigi will aim at your smoke."

Phidestros doubted that in this breeze even a Hostigi rifleman could hit a man at this distance, but obeyed. He could see as well, and make Geblon happy to boot.

The guns newly emplaced in the battery at the foot of the draw thumped. Their shots tore masonry from a gate tower. Another salvo followed, and white smoke rose in place of the morning mist.

Phidestros puffed on his pipe and prayed to all the true gods that today's butcher's bill would be a light one.

FOUR

I

Ptosphes was leading a cavalry charge at the climax of a great battle. The guns thundered and something else was growling like a whole forestful of hungry bears.

He looked down. He wasn't riding a horse, but standing on top of one of Great King Truman's iron wagons with its strange gun. Except that the wagon wasn't quite as Kalvan had described it—it had the head and tail of a horse, the mane flying into his face. As they rode downhill toward the lines of an enemy in the colors of Styphon's Red Hand, the wagon-horse turned its head to look at Ptosphes. Its eyes glowed a sinister green, and he knew that he was riding a creature possessed by demons.

He clawed for reins he couldn't find, trying to turn the creature so he wouldn't have to look into those eyes. No matter how desperately he groped, he couldn't find the reins. At last his fingers closed on something that felt like woolen cloth, which was a strange thing to make reins out of—

"Prince Ptosphes! Prince Ptosphes! Wake up!"

Nobody should be telling him to wake up in a dream and this was still a dream. He could still hear the thunder of guns, even if he couldn't hear the bearlike growling of the iron wagon.

341

"Prince Ptosphes! The Grand Host is coming!"

"Hu-rrrupppp!" Ptosphes lurched into a sitting position before he realized that he was awake and clutching his blanket.

He also heard guns thundering and someone shouting in his ear that the Styphoni were attacking. The window showed gray instead of black. Two men ran toward it, carrying a heavy rifled musket and nearly tripping over Ptosphes as they came.

Ptosphes threw off the blanket and stood. The air of the keep already held a sodden heat. He felt obscurely resentful that so many men should have to fight their last battle on a miserably hot day.

Someone was pushing a cup of tea into his hands. He emptied it in three gulps and held it out again for more. The second cupful was half Ermut's brandy. He set the cup down on the nearest chest, retrieved his sword, and buckled it on.

Harmakros was sitting in the chair of state, wide awake and barking orders. His stump was propped up on a pillow-padded stool and two pistols hung from the arm of the chair.

"Good luck, Prince."

"The same to you, old friend."

That was all the speech Ptosphes allowed himself, even if it was probably the last time he would see Harmakros. If the riflemen were taking position before the arrow slits, there was hardly time to talk.

Chroniclers a hundred years from now will probably make up fine farewell speeches for both of us. Tutors will torment children by forcing them to learn those speeches.

As Ptosphes passed through the keep door on to the outer stairs, the gun-roar doubled, then doubled again. The mortars had opened fire. Whatever was coming at Tarr-Hostigos was now within their range.

Ptosphes hurried down the stairs as fast as he could without appearing uneasy. At the bottom he saw that the guards who saluted him were also busily piling tar-soaked brushwood under the timbers of the stairs. One torch and the easy way into the keep would go up in flames, making another line of defense for the last of the garrison.

From the tower over the gate between the courtyards, Ptosphes could see everywhere except directly behind the keep. Three large storming parties were advancing, one toward the breach made by the siege guns, one by the main gate, and one holding well back on

342

the northeastern side. At a single glance, Ptosphes knew that nearly half the Grand Host must be hurling itself at the castle.

Heavy guns were now firing from the battery at the foot of the draw, over the heads of the column climbing. Big guns, too, even if maybe not the Hostigi sixteen-pounders. Ptosphes saw half the main gate flung backward off its hinges into the portcullis, which bent ominously.

A less well aimed shot ploughed through the infantry of the storming column. They halted, giving the guns and musketeers on the gate towers an even better target. Their firing sounded like a single volley, and they fired three more times before the column moved again. It moved more slowly now, leaving behind it a trail of writhing, bloody bodies, like a dying animal dragging its guts behind as it sought to close with the hunter.

The column coming at the breach was taking most of its punishment from the mortars, whose crews were firing too fast to be much concerned with safety. Ptosphes saw one man knocked down and crushed as a mortar shifted on its base, and a shell with a fuse cut too short blew up just above the walls. A dozen defenders went down. The ones who rose again shook their fists at the mortar crews.

Now the guns beside Ptosphes were shooting. Another regiment was coming into sight behind the first one—armored men, marching under a black banner with a silver sun-wheel. Soton's Knights were fighting on foot today.

The Knights lumbered through the gaps in the first line to take the lead. Ptosphes shouted, "Change to case shot!" It wasn't going to make any difference to the fate of Tarr-Hostigos now, but the more dead Knights, the better for Kalvan.

The guns aimed at the main gate was firing higher now, trying to silence the guns in the gate tower. One of them was disabled, but the other was still hurling case shot straight into the column, inflicting hideous losses. Guns from the other towers were now hammering at the column as well, scything down entire companies like farmers scything wheat.

Smoke gushed up from the enemy battery, more than one could expect from the discharge of even the largest gun. Ptosphes saw men flying into the air and others running with their clothing on fire. He heard the double-thump of an explosion—someone careless with fireseed—as the rate of fire increased.

343

More Hostigi case shot tore the main column—then suddenly it was breaking up and the men were running back down the draw in a futile effort to escape, some of their officers beating at them with halberds and swords, others joining the rout. From the walls of Tarr-Hostigos, cheers joined the gunfire.

Ptosphes had a moment of thinking that perhaps their doom wasn't so certain after all. One column broken, and its men looking as if they would be hard to rally for another attack. Do the same with the other two columns, and at least the mercenary captains might have the same second thoughts they'd had during the first storming attempt. If they had second thoughts and let Styphon's House know them, the False God himself couldn't keep the Archpriests from having to listen. And if the Archpriests chose to turn the Red Hand loose on the mercenaries, the Grand Host's war against Hostigos would become a civil war within its own ranks—

Ptosphes's moment of hope ended as he saw the column approaching the breach suddenly sprout scaling ladders. They were going to get in or at least close; the heavy mortars had fired off all their shells and round shot wouldn't do so well even against packed men—

The twelve-pounder on top of the barricade let fly with a triple charge of musket balls. Like a volley from a massed regiment it smashed into the column. Already ragged from climbing the slope, the column now barely deserved the name.

Hard on their heels came point-blank musketry that melted away more of the column. Every musketeer within range had six or seven loaded weapons ready to hand for just this moment. For a brief space, they could fire as fast as the rifles of the Great King Truman's host, with their "magazines" of eight rounds.

These foes had their blood up, though, or maybe better captains. Then Ptosphes saw the blue and orange colors and recognized the Sacred Squares of Hos-Ktemnos, the best infantry in the Seven Kingdoms. They rose across the rubble before the breach like a blue wave, with clumps of musketeers on the flanks firing over the heads of the storming parties to keep down Hostigi fire. The crews of the useless heavy mortars drew swords and pistols and joined the mass of men struggling in the breach. Ptosphes drew his own sword, ready to join them if they showed signs of flagging.

One of the overheated four-pounders beside Ptosphes recoiled so violently that it snapped its breechings and knocked down Thalmoth. He lay with his thigh a mass of blood, white bone shining through the torn flesh, cursing the gun crew for not remembering what he'd taught them and asking for a pistol. Ptosphes gave him one of his own, as scaling ladders suddenly sprouted to either side of the breach.

The first ladder rose, then flew to pieces as a shot from nowhere split it from top to bottom. At least it came from what seemed like nowhere to Ptosphes, although he knew that what he could see and hear must be rapidly shrinking. This storming of Tarr-Hostigos was already making every other battle he'd seen sound like a mother's lullaby.

The rifled boat swivels were coming into action now. Dead men around them showed that the Hostigi riflemen weren't out of the fight yet. New gunners moved up to replace the dead, though, obviously eager to claim their share of glory. Ptosphes wondered what share of glory they would have if they hit more of their own men than the enemy's. Share of broken bones and heads, more likely.

More ladders rising now. The men on them must be some of the southern swampmen Soton had brought north—no armor, no clothing except leather leggings, and no weapons but hand axes and long wicked knives.

The mortar emplacement spewed flame, smoke, slabs of stone, and flying timbers. An enemy shot or a stray spark had touched off the remaining fireseed in the magazine. Most of the men in or around the pit went down where they stood.

Flying debris scythed into the rear of the Hostigi infantry holding the barricade at the breach. Their line wavered. Some charged forward, grappling with Styphoni and rolling down the rubble to die in the moat with them. Others gave way, and a volley of musketry cleared a path through the ones who stood. Across the dying and the dead of both sides, the Sacred Squares poured over the barricade and down into the outer courtyard.

It seemed to Ptosphes that the Styphoni reached the gatehouse where he stood in the time between one breath and the next. Bullets whistled around him; the men atop the keep were now firing on the inner wall without caring much who was there. His reluctance to turn his back on the enemy gave way to an indignant refusal to be

345

shot in the back by his own men. He ran to the edge of the gun platform, sheathed his sword, dangled from the battlements with both hands until he was sure his arms would pull out of their sockets, then dropped to the inner courtyard.

It was a long drop for an armored man no longer young. Ptosphes went to his knees and was quite sure all his bones were jarred loose from one another. Thankfully, all of them seemed intact when he stood. Smoke was rising from the base of the stairs to the keep. He sprinted for them without stopping to take a breath.

Bullets tore through his jack and glanced off his breastplate, clipped his beard, and seared one hand. At first they came from both sides, then he heard a shout from above, ''That's Prince Ptosphes, you wolf's bastard!'' and the bullets from the keep stopped. A moment later a crash like the end of the world sounded from behind, followed by screams and curses that penetrated even the ringing in Ptosphes's ears and a choking wave of fireseed smoke. Some Styphoni with more zeal than sense must have used a petard on the inner gate, no doubt blowing it open but also demolishing a good many comrades as well!

Two of the swamp warriors reached the foot of the stairs before Ptosphes. He cut one down with his sword, knocked the ax out of the other's hand, leaped on to the stairs, and dashed up them with flames rising behind him almost as fast as he climbed. By the time he reached the top, the blood pounding in Ptosphes's ears drowned out every other sound. He leaned against the wall beyond the doorway, feeling the cool stone against his forehead and not hearing the outer door being shut and bolted behind him.

By the time he'd been led to a chair and had a cup of wine thrust into his hands, Ptosphes had enough of his wits back to think about what to do next. This was no normal siege, where the garrison of the keep was always given one last chance to surrender. This one would end with the Styphoni trying to bury the Hostigi under a pile of their own dead flesh if they couldn't finish the battle any other way.

If Phidestros and Soton and their captains had the wits the gods gave to fleas, they would launch the last attack as soon as they could, before their men had time to lose their battle-rage. Otherwise those men might start thinking of the kind of fight waiting for them behind the walls of the keep.

When Ptosphes had drunk the wine and could stand, he walked over to Harmakros in the chair of state. He had to walk carefully, to avoid stepping on exhausted men catching their breaths, cleaning their weapons, or just lying staring at the ceiling. The lightly wounded were taking care of each other; the badly wounded hadn't reached the keep.

"I lost sight of the column on the ridge. What of them?"

"They started to close when the column at the main gate ran. Then the breach fell, and the ridgerunners drew back. Not without leaving a good many men behind, to be sure."

"What do we have left?"

Harmakros shrugged. "A hundred, maybe a few more."

"They'll come soon, wherever they do it." Ptosphes leaned against a stone archway and propped himself up with his sword. By the Twelve True Gods, he was getting old!

"I have men watching on the roof, and more men on the stairs relaying messages, my Prince. They won't catch us napping."

"Unless they kill the men on the roof."

"Not without shells, and maybe not even with them. Anyway, I'll wager a cask of Ermut's best brandy that they don't have any shells."

"Done," Ptosphes said. "But just in case they do . . .?"

"I've had the men on the roof build themselves a shelter with chests and rolled-up tapestries."

Some of those tapestries, Ptosphes realized, were probably part of his wife's dowry. Not that anybody except Rylla would be left to care before long, of course, and this was a better end for the tapestries than being looted or burned, eaten by vermin, or left to rot in the crumbling shell of the keep . . .

Ptosphes forced his mind away from such thoughts and climbed the stairs to the roof of the keep.

II

Seeing the Styphoni swarming over the shambles that had been his seat and home didn't improve Ptosphes's mood. It helped to see the men on the rifled three-pounder actually smiling as they carved notches in the smoke-stained oak of the gun carriage.

"The big one's for smashing the wheel of one siege gun. Didn't hit any of our people, either," the gunner added. "The four little ones are banners we knocked down. The circle is one of the swivels. We'd have got ourselves a second, but the Styphoni were too cowardly to man it again."

Never mind that the gunners probably hadn't done half the damage they thought they had. If they spent the last candle of their lives grinning and the last moments killing more Styphoni, what did anything else matter to them now?

Ptosphes had just descended to the Great Hall when a messenger followed him down the stairs. "They're moving a heavy field gun into the inner courtyard. One of theirs, though, from the number of men they've put to hauling it."

"Everyone to your places, men," Ptosphes said. He hesitated, then added, "It's been an honor to be your Prince and captain."

A ragged cheer rose, then outside the musketry began again, heavy, rapid fire. The expected message came down from the roof—bullets were mostly coming up, to keep the gun there out of action. Even a three-pound ball could wreck a gun carriage.

"Wait until they attack," Ptosphes ordered. "Then they'll have to cease fire or have spent bullets falling back on their friends." He doubted that the mercenaries or even the Knights would care to risk much of that. It had been a bad day for self-inflicted casualties on both sides; for the Styphoni it was about to get worse.

Galzar's muster-clerks are going to be working long hours today, Ptosphes thought both irreverently and irrelevantly.

Chrunngggg!

Something struck the outside of the wall—a solid shot, the report of its firing lost in the roar of musketry. "Not bad," Ptosphes said. "Sounds as if they hit just to the left of the door."

It took three more shots before the smashing of wood and the ringing of iron signaled a direct hit on the outer door. Two more shots completed the work. A rifleman crept into the doorway and peered over the wreckage.

"They're reloading, but they've lined up a storming party too. They can't be going to fire right over—here it comes—ayyyyhhhh!"

The pieces of the door flew into the Great Hall. So did the pieces of the rifleman. A cannonball rolled in after them, making the Hostigi do spritely dances to avoid it.

Harmakros unhooked his pistols from the arm of the chair of state, cocked them, and laid them in his lap, then raised an empty wine cup in salute to Ptosphes. "I'll claim that brandy, Prince. If they had shells, they'd have used one then."

"So it would seem."

Then from all the firing slits the sentries shouted that the storming party was on the way. The gun on the roof let fly, although no one bothered to tell Ptosphes if it hit anything. It fired a second time, a third.

As the fourth shot went off, the Styphoni burst into the Great Hall.

A ragged volley of pistols and muskets half-deafened Ptosphes. He saw the leading rank of the enemy stagger and go down, but realized that the men behind them now had shields of once-living flesh. He drew his own pistol and fired it over the heads of the six men who'd appointed themselves his last bodyguard. Then the Styphoni were everywhere.

Ptosphes decided that if demons ever really came into the world, they might look like Styphon's soldiers. The attackers wore every sort of armor and clothing except for those who wore little of either. They were black-faced, red-eyed, stinking, shrieking cries in no language intended for human ears, and waving strange weapons in more arms than the gods gave men.

The massed Styphoni gave Vurth a fine target for his musketoon. He shot one man, smashed in a second's face, then got a third in a wrestler's headlock and broke his neck before someone else ran him through. Vurth's diversion let Ptosphes break away from his bodyguards toward the fireplace and the concealed ladder leading down to the cellar. He had to be down there to do his last duty as Prince of Hostigos—not last Prince, the gods grant it!—and knew he might have already waited too long.

Four of the bodyguards stayed alive to reload their weapons and see that their Prince no longer needed them. They fired into the Styphoni, then closed with steel.

The first man to make a way past them, Harmakros shot in the head. The second man ran Harmakros through the stomach; the Duke returned the compliment with his second pistol. A third man wanted to either help his comrades or see if Harmakros was dead. Harmakros snatched the pistol from the man's belt, rammed the

349

muzzle up under its owner's jaw, and pulled the trigger. The chair of state fell over, spilling out Harmakros's body as Ptosphes swung himself into the chimney.

He forced himself to go down the iron rungs of the ladder one at a time. It would help nobody except Styphon's House if he failed in his last duty by falling down the chimney and dashing out what the siege had left of his brains.

By the time he reached the bottom, he knew that if he had to climb back up again his heart would burst before he finished the climb. He'd been right; he would not have lived to see his grandchildren grow up even without this Dralm-damned war! However, this way he was at least spared years of listening to old Tharses and Rylla fussing at him, making him eat and sleep and rest as they thought proper, and generally trying to turn him into a corpse while he was still alive.

The blessed coolness of the cellar revived him a little. He found that he'd brought his pipe, tobacco, and tinderbox with him, started to light up, stopped as he remembered the ironclad rules about smoking near fireseed, then laughed. It made precious little difference *what* anybody did down here now.

Ptosphes found the fireseed intact, all twelve tons of it minus a barrel or few. He also found the last of the magazine-keepers sitting at the foot of the stairs, along with his clubfooted grandson. The keeper was an old soldier past campaigning, with the grandson to support and no other kin. Ptosphes had given him the magazine by way of a pension.

"What can we do for you, my Prince?"

"If you have pistols—?"

The keeper showed an old cavalryman's matchlock. The boy produced a heavy-barreled boar-hunter's pistol.

"Good. Keep watch on the stairs."

With his pipe in his mouth, Ptosphes walked over to a row of small barrels, chose one, cracked it open, then laid a trail of fireseed a thumb wide and a finger deep to the main pile of larger barrels. Just to be safe, he borrowed one of the keeper's handspikes and knocked in the head of one of the larger barrels. Fireseed poured out, until a helmetful lay waiting at the end of the train, with the twelve tons waiting beyond.

By the time Ptosphes was finished, fists were hammering on the outside of the cellar door. Then he heard the more solid sounds of a chest or bench being swung against it. Wood cracked and metal pulling out of stone screeched, as a hinge gave way. The door half-swung, half-fell inward.

All three Hostigi fired together at the first silhouettes to appear. The answering volley sent bullets spanging around the cellar. One hit the boy in the thigh. The Styphoni drew back, except for the one who fell forward and rolled down the stairs to land at Ptosphes's feet.

He was as filthy as all the others and no more than eighteen. He was crying for his mother as he clasped his hands over a belly wound that under other circumstances would have killed him slowly over the next few days. Well, he'd be spared that, and he'd already lived longer than the keeper's grandson would, or Harmakros's son if the Grand Host overtook Kalvan.

Except that they wouldn't. Ptosphes knew this, although he couldn't have explained how he knew it. He was sure it was true knowledge, not a dead man's dreaming to make his death easier.

Since he was dead, why wait any longer, in case one of those Styphoni cursing so loudly at the top of the stairs wanted to come down and argue the point?

Ptosphes finished tamping the ball and wadding of his new load, checked the pan, then rested the pistol on one knee as he knocked the live coal from his pipe into the train of fireseed.

FIVE

I

"Damn you, Sirna! What are you using in the wound? Galzar's Mace?"

Sirna ignored Phidestros's blustering. She knew she must be causing him agony, probing his wounded thigh with her limited skills and instruments improvised by the Iron Band's armorers from Menandra's kitchen utensils. He'd refused a sandbag, though, and she had to go on and extract that last piece she felt in the wound. Otherwise he would certainly lose his leg and probably his life. Then what would happen to her? Sirna told herself that her concern was thoroughly practical and continued digging.

Finally the probe clicked on the fragment again, this time loosening it until she could grip it between two blood-slimed fingers. It was a piece of stoneware, sharp-edged but solid. It wouldn't leave any more fragments in the wound (or so she told herself, because she knew that her hands would start shaking uncontrollably if she had to burrow back into that mangled flesh).

She held up the stoneware. Phidestros managed a grin. "So that's why they didn't run out of bullets. They saved up their last moon's trash and shot it at us!" Phidestros made a face and

352

groaned. "That's not all the trash I'm going to get shot at me when Soton learns I got this kiss from Galzar rallying his swivel gunners not a hundred paces from the breach! My ears will hurt worse than this leg!"

Petty-Captain Phyllos lifted Phidestros's leg so that Sirna could bind it in the boiled remains of a shift. Phyllos's wrenched knee made him slow, but as long as he could stand he felt that he had to be on duty. Certainly he'd had more experience dealing with battle wounds than any of Menandra's girls, didn't mind taking orders from a woman who knew her business, and whipped into line any soldier who did.

At last Phidestros was bandaged. Sirna came as close as she could to offering a prayer for his recovery. She could no longer tell herself that wish was entirely practical, either. Phidestros was too good a man to die, even if he was serving a particularly murderous brand of superstition.

"Sorry to give you such a bad time," she said as four of the hastily recruited orderlies lifted Phidestros off the table. Half the Captain-General's bodyguard had escorted him to the Gull's Nest after he fell. She'd drafted most of them into helping with the wounded who'd been streaming in since dawn. And this was only one of the besiegers' hospitals! Galzar's Great Hall was going to be crammed to the rafters tonight.

"Menandra runs a fine whorehouse, but it's not much of a hospital," Sirna went on. "If I had some proper tools, or the help of a priest of Galzar—"

Phidestros sighed. "My lovely Sirna, if I knew where to find an Uncle Wolf who didn't already need two heads and six hands, I'd have him dragged to you. You're going to be all we have for today. When they carted me off I heard we already had two thousand men down."

"Two thousand!" Sirna shuddered at the implications. Phidestros had been hit early enough to reach the Gull's Nest before the storming of the keep. Two thousand men down in the time it took the Styphoni to close the walls. How many more in the fighting since—?

Thunder battered at her ears and the floor quivered. The door and all the window shutters banged wildly and dust rose until the room looked as if someone had fired a small cannon. Sirna looked frantically out the window, saw nothing but people gaping idiotically, knew she must be doing the same, and dashed out the door.

A vast cloud of gray smoke towered over Tarr-Hostigos, blotting out the whole castle and slowly swallowing the hillside below it. The top of the cloud was already several thousand feet high, spreading into something dreadfully like a fission bomb's mushroom. Sirna lived a moment with the nightmare that Kalvan had done the impossible, taking his time-line from a poor grade of gunpowder to fission bombs in four years.

The mushroom shape started to blur, and Sirna breathed more easily. The top of the cloud was simply spreading in a breeze not felt here in the lee of the hills. She watched the cloud start to trail off toward the southeast, bits and pieces of smoking debris dropping from it as it went.

Ptosphes had given himself and the last of his men over to a quick death, destroying Tarr-Hostigos and more of his enemies than anyone would ever know.

Sirna wanted to weep, scream, pound her fists against something. For a moment she even wanted to die herself. There had to be something wrong with her, if she was still alive with so much death around her. The battle, the flight, her surgery at Menandra's, Roxthar's Investigation, and now the storming of Tarr-Hostigos— dead men (and women, and children) were everywhere.

Sirna didn't die. She didn't even have hysterics. Instead she gripped the porch railing until she knew she could stand without help. Around her Hostigos Town awoke from a stunned silence into a hideous din of bawled orders, howling dogs, shrieking women and children, horses neighing or galloping wildly about in panic, and an occasional pistol shot.

Menandra was standing in the doorway when Sirna turned. "Better come in quick, girl," she said. "The soldiers who lost comrades up there—they'll be wanting someone's blood for it. Can't keep it from being yours if you stand out there."

Sirna followed the older woman inside. She wasn't afraid of death itself. After today she never would be again. Ptosphes had shown her that death could sometimes be your best friend.

He'd also shown her that there were good and bad ways to die. No, not good and bad. That implied a simple moral distinction. If there was anything simple about death, Sirna hadn't seen it.

Wise and foolish ways? Better, but still an oversimplification.

Useful and useless? Yes. That wasn't a universally sound way of distinguishing kinds of death, but there probably wasn't any such thing. It certainly made sense here.

Staying outside to be shot or raped by soldiers mad with rage or wine would be a *useless* death. She wouldn't risk it. What she would do another time, she would decide when that time came.

A phrase from one of Scholar Danthor Dras's seminar lectures came back to her:

The only universal rule of outtime work is that there are no universal rules.

II

Soton cursed the Hostigi and their stubbornness that was costing the Grand Host so many lives. Half the storming party was inside Tarr-Hostigos, swarming over it like bees. Both courtyards were littered with bodies, most of them Styphoni. Clouds of smoke wreathed the keep, but before they rose Soton had seen even from his distant post the savage struggle to enter it.

Why in the name of all the gods hadn't Phidestros kept back, instead of closing the breach? Then there would have been someone to go down and put matters in order.

Instead Phidestros was wounded—badly, the tales ran. Small loss, with the last defenders of Hostigos dying even now and Kalvan fleeing toward the Trygath. If Phidestros was going to make a habit of such follies, perhaps it would be best if he stormed Hadron's Caverns the next time. If he didn't, Soton would make him wish he had!

The smoke around the keep eddied. Soton turned, to summon a messenger.

He never completed the turn. Instead something as invisible as the air but as hard as stone flung him to his knees. Thunder swelled until it seemed that someone was beating on his helmet with his own warhammer. Three Knights flew off the ledge, along with a shower of rocks. Soton knew he cried out at that sight, but couldn't hear his own voice.

He lay, gripping the ground as closely as he ever gripped a woman, until it stopped shaking. Then he rose to his knees, and when they did not betray him, to his feet.

The air was filled with acrid smoke and fine ash. Looking toward

Tarr-Hostigos, he saw only a vast swirling cloud of smoke. Somewhere in that smoke was the entire storming party—one man in three of the Grand Host's strength.

One of the Knights was shrieking. "It's the Demon Kalvan! He's come to save his people! Great Styphon, save us!"

Soton smashed his gauntleted fist into the Knight's face. The man fell as if poleaxed. Soton didn't know what he was really smiting, the Knight or his own fear.

Slowly the air around what had been Tarr-Hostigos cleared. The slopes around it were alive with men, thousands of them all streaming away from the castle. Soton let out a deep breath he hadn't even known he was holding.

Another quarter-candle showed him what was left of Tarr-Hostigos. The keep was only a pile of smoking rubble, the towers had mostly lost their tops, and the walls looked to have been chewed by monsters. How many of the Grand Host lay there under the fallen stone or in fragments strewn across the hillside? The Grand Host would be far less grand by the time they were all counted, Soton was sure.

Yet—this should not have been a surprise. Desperate men will take desperate measures. Who had more experience fighting the desperate than Soton, Grand Master of the Zarthani Knights?

Soton smashed his fist against his armored thigh, insensible to the pain.

"Kalvan!" he shrieked. "Kalvan, you will pay for this! By Styphon's Wheel, I swear it!"

III

Verkan Vall finished lighting his pipe with a Kalvan's Time-Line silver and ivory inlaid tinderbox, then turned back to the data screen and its display of information on one Khalid ib'n Hussein. The second cousin of a minor Palestinian prince assassinated five years earlier—on his subsector branch—Khalid was putting together a Mideastern superstate that included just about every Moslem nation except Turkey and Libya.

As this new Islamic Caliphate emerged, on most of its time-lines its pro-Western leanings seemed to be toppling the balance between Communism, that strange atheistic religion, and the so-called Free

World. Another case of the inherent instability of the entire Europo-American, Hispano-Columbian Subsector!

Verkan made a note to send out some investigator to see if the Mideast had acquired some transtemporal hitchhiker like his friend Kalvan. One of the problems with transtemporal history was that it was always easier to spot the important historical turning points after the damage was done! There was that Paracop chief two thousand years ago, who hadn't paid any attention to an anonymous carpenter's son until the religion his death launched was already shaking whole subsectors to the foundations—

The red light on Verkan's desk lit up, announcing an important visitor. Verkan looked up to see Kostran Garth enter. The man's face was red from exertion, his breath came short as if he'd been running, and he was holding out a data-storage wafer in one hand.

"What is it?"

"This just arrived from the surveillance satellite on Kalvan's time-line. I scanned it briefly—Dalla had it red-flagged—and I knew you'd want to see it right away."

From the look on Kostran's face, Verkan knew the wafer wasn't good news; only bad news ever traveled that fast. Verkan slipped the wafer into his viewer and watched the screen light up.

The views began with a satellite's-eye scan of Hostigos and the surrounding Princedoms, from an altitude that made them all look deceptively peaceful. The next shots were close-ups of Tarr-Hostigos. Verkan sighed with relief; at least he wasn't going to see Kalvan and his remaining soldiers caught like fish in a net.

The camera panned in closer, suggesting manned control of the cameras (*remember to commend Dalla for that precaution*). A human wave was approaching the beleaguered castle; almost the whole Styphoni host seemed to be on the move. Closer still, and Verkan saw whole units going down under Hostigi shells and musketry.

Verkan sped up the fast-forward. Whatever was coming, he wanted to get it over with.

The attackers poured into the castle like ants over leftover dog food. Muzzle flashes showed that the keep still had some live defenders. Were Ptosphes and Harmakros among them—Ptosphes, who'd refused to leave his home, and Captain-General Harmakros, still worth any three men with two legs?

Suddenly everything vanished in a cloud of smoke. Verkan held his breath until the smoke began to clear. Slowly Tarr-Hostigos reappeared—or what had been Tarr-Hostigos.

Half the walls still stood, battered and leaning. Otherwise Ptosphes's seat was a pile of smoking rubble. Verkan saw where one aircar-sized chunk of stone had crushed an entire company of Styphoni. The slopes around the castle were covered with more Styphoni—lying still, crawling, stumbling, a few lucky enough to be able to run.

Verkan's fist slammed down on his desk. "By Dralm, Ptosphes did it!"

"What?"

"He did what even Kalvan couldn't do. He stopped the Grand Host in its tracks! Look at that mess! The bastards must have taken five, ten thousand casualties. That, my friend, is no longer a Grand Host. It's hardly even an army! By the time Soton and Phidestros sort things out, Kalvan will be safe in Greftscharr."

Verkan rummaged a flask of Ermut's Best and two cups out of a drawer. "A toast, Kostran. A toast to the memory of a valiant Prince and his last and greatest victory!"

Kostran gagged at the taste of the brandy, but he was smiling as he said, "To Prince Ptosphes!"

IV

Considering the Hostigi resistance, the two thousand casualties taken in entering Tarr-Hostigos surprised no one. From the stories brought in during the day with the wounded, Sirna concluded that another eight thousand at least must have been casualties of the great explosion. That made ten thousand casualties. Almost half were dead, and half the wounded wouldn't fight again this year if at all. Sirna would have liked more accurate figures, but she was relieved to know that she could go on doing a University outtime observer's work even in the middle of a battle.

It would be embarrassing if she ever returned home and had to confess that she hadn't taken advantage of her "unique" opportunity to observe historically significant Fourth Level events. It would probably cost her that doctorate!

Sirna told herself this over and over again, to keep some grip on her sanity, as the wounded poured into the Gull's Nest. It was the first time she'd allowed herself to think of First Level since the day she woke up in Menandra's back bedroom. Somewhat to her surprise it helped.

Having some extra hands helped even more. More of the lightly wounded men turned to changing bandages or helping comrades to the privies. Menandra rolled up her sleeves and went to work setting bones, a skill she'd acquired in her younger days from cleaning up after tavern brawls in Agrys City. She also turned out all of her girls who could be trusted to know a clean bandage from a dirty one, which was more than Sirna had expected.

Another of Scholar Dras's bits of wisdom kept running through Sirna's mind:

"The danger of paratemporal contamination doesn't come from the stupidity of lower-level people. It comes from the fact that they're inherently just about as smart as we are. Once they've been shown that something is possible, you would be surprised how fast they can pick it up and even start filling in gaps on their own."

Sirna knew that would never surprise her again.

By the time the western sky turned an appropriately bloody color, the flow of fresh wounded had stopped. Sirna trudged through the house on feet that felt shod in lead boots, checking splints and dressings she hadn't put on herself.

In the twilight outside she heard shouts and screams. Men, drunk or avenging dead comrades or simply celebrating being alive when they'd expected to be dead, were sacking Hostigos Town. The hard-eyed mercenary guards from the Iron Band kept the noise and the noisemakers safely outside.

At least she didn't hear the sinister crackling of flames, as she had during Rylla's campaign in Phaxos. The Styphoni weren't going to burn the town as long as they needed its roofs over their heads.

Sirna felt like a deer who'd somehow managed to be adopted by a pack of wolves. The Captain-General's men would protect her against all the other packs as long as she did what they expected. But that didn't make her a wolf. Somehow it was no longer hard to take for granted a situation she would have found unbelievably degrading two years ago. Not hard at all, when she listened to the screams outside.

She was changing the bandages on the stump of a man's arm when someone banged on the door to the street, loud enough to be heard over the din outside and the cries of the wounded inside. One of the house women looked through the peephole. Then she unbarred the door and jumped aside, with a look on her face that brought every fit man in the room to his feet.

Two of Styphon's Guardsmen strode in, their red cloaks flapping dramatically. Two more followed their white-robed charge inside, then stood flanking the door. Sirna saw hostile glances flicking over the Red Hands' clean clothing and silvered armor.

At least Holy Investigator Roxthar looked as if he'd worked today, and worked hard. His long hollow-cheeked face was coated with dust and soot and his robes were bloodstained and frayed. He reminded Sirna of a Fourth Level Judeo-Christian representation of the Devil.

For a moment she wondered if Kalvan was the only cross-time hitchhiker around. Then she remembered the file on the control time-line equivalents to the major Archpriests. On one other time-line Roxthar was purging Styphon's House almost as spectacularly as he was here. On several others he'd died mysteriously, doubtless courtesy of one of Archpriest Anaxthenes's handy little vials.

Phidestros struggled to a sitting position and raised a hand in greeting. "Welcome, Your Sanctity. Today Hadron's Hall is filled to the bursting, but the first and vilest of the demons' nests has at last been burned out."

Roxthar nodded, as though acknowledging a remark about the weather, then looked around the room. His nostrils flared.

"So this den of flesh-selling has served as the Captain-General's nest. I wondered why we had so often lacked your esteemed company at the Palace."

From the Captain-General's face, Sirna knew his patience was strained nearly to the breaking point.

"I must admit, Your Sanctity, that I much prefer the cries of honest passion in this house to the constant uproar at the Palace. No offense meant, of course. Let Styphon's Will Be Done!"

Roxthar's face paled. "Do not presume, Captain-General, or

you may yet find yourself enjoying the hospitality of my Investigators.''

''They might find a soldier too much work, after so many women and children.''

Roxthar's gray eyes turned into steel ball bearings. "Enough of this babble. We have the God of Gods to serve today. The Daemon Kalvan has fled, with the remnants of his host. The land he left behind is tainted with the evil he wrought, and the servants of his demons lurk everywhere. Let the Investigation of Styphon finish its work, *then* we can attend to lesser duties.''

It was just as well Roxthar didn't smile. If he had, Sirna knew she would have laughed out loud, hoping to wake up on the other side of the abyss between her and the sane reality of Home Time-Line, where people didn't blow up castles in wars over non-existent gods. Instead she bit her lip and unwound the last strip of bandage, then stood up to take the sterilized fresh dressing from the soldier holding the basin.

The movement drew Roxthar's eyes. Sirna felt their hard, unclean gaze on her all the time she was binding on the dressing, emptying the water into the slop bucket, and putting the old bandages into the empty basin to be returned to the cauldrons boiling in the kitchen. She was proud that her hands didn't tremble once.

At last there was nothing more to do except stand up and face the Investigator. He was now smiling, an expression to which his gaunt features hardly lent themselves. Sirna decided that she much preferred him expressionless.

''Those bandages have been boiled to drive out the fester-demons, have they not?''

''That is so, Your Sanctity.'' Sirna was relieved that she'd kept all traces of a tremor out of her voice.

''That is knowledge given by the servant of demons, Kalvan, you know.''

You're not afraid of death anymore, Sirna reminded herself. *Besides, Roxthar won't spare a heretic even if she goes down on the floor and kisses his feet. Do as you please and at least you can hope to go out with dignity, like Ptosphes.*

''That is so, Your Sanctity. Yet the new compounding of fireseed was also brought by Kalvan. With the blessing of Styphon's holy priests, the new fireseed has been used in the guns of Styphon's Grand Host, to smite Styphon's enemies. Is it not possible that the knowledge of smiting the fester-demons may also be used to aid Styphon's cause?''

Roxthar's vices did not include being at a loss for words. ''This may be so. Yet I see no priests of Styphon's House here, to bless your work so that it may drive out demons instead of letting them in. Also, it is too soon to tell what may come of this day's work. Not all demons leap forth at the wave of their servants' hands. Some bide their time.''

If it weren't that her life was at stake, Sirna would have believed this conversation about demons and their servants totally absurd. ''In your own words, Your Sanctity—that may be so. Yet I have been healing the men of the Iron Band since the siege began. In all of them, the wounds are cleaner than they would have been without my work. Ask the Captain-General or the men themselves!

''As for there being no priest here—today there were many wounded and few hands to heal them. Should I have let men who shed their blood for Styphon die, their wounds stinking and festering, because there is no priest to bless work that I *know* is wholesome and good? If I did that, then you *would* have good cause to bring me before the Investigation. I think what I have done is good service to the God of Gods, and I will pray for his blessing, and also for his mercy on you if you falsely accuse me.''

She knew that the last sentences must have been audible on the streets outside, from the way the door guards were looking behind them. Roxthar's smile froze, then he shrugged.

''As Styphon wills it. I only know what I must do in his service, and also pray for his mercy if I misjudge what that is. You must come with us before the Investigation, and hope that witnesses may be found in your behalf.''

Sirna knew that her last moment was close at hand, and also that she was going to spend it as a woman of this time-line rather than as a scholar of First Level. Her right hand was at waist level, closing around the hilt of a non-existent dagger, and she'd shifted her footing to open the distance between her and Roxthar. One of the Red Hands stepped forward—

—and stopped a yard from Sirna, as a dozen mercenaries drew entirely real swords and daggers. Two more armed with half-pikes appeared on the stairway and a third in the door to the hall, with a pistol.

"Archpriest Roxthar," Phidestros said, in a tone that reminded Sirna of a baron she'd once heard sentencing a poacher. "There is nothing but the truth in what this woman says. This I swear, by Styphon God of Gods and Galzar Wolfshead, by Yirtta Allmother and by Tranth who blesses the hands of the craftsman. My men will swear the same."

"How many of them?"

"As many as needed to make it unlawful for this woman to go before the Investigation, and ten more besides. The Iron Band knows good healing when it sees it."

One of the Red Hands started to draw his pistol at Phidestros's tone. An imperative and slightly frantic gesture from Roxthar stopped him. The Archpriest's good sense clearly extended to recognizing when he saw it a situation where one false move would leave him and his guards dead on the floor and the Investigation of Styphon's enemies in chaos.

"We value your judgment and honor you for your good work in the Holy Investigation," Phidestros went on, as big a lie as Sirna had ever heard anyone deliver with a straight face. "Therefore we will also swear to watch this woman day and night, and bring word to the Investigation of any evil effects from her healing."

Phidestros paused, then fired his final shot. "And is not one of Styphon's own signs of his presence among us his gift of healing?"

Roxthar's head jerked, but to Sirna's relief he stopped short of smiling. "As you wish, Captain-General. Clearly Styphon's favor is with you today, but this may not always be so. I shall return tomorrow, to see those wounded who have been healed in days past and to take the oaths you have promised."

The Investigator whirled and strode out so fast that the Guardsmen had to scurry to catch up with him. A chorus of harsh laughter and obscene remarks about why the Guardsmen had unbattered armor after a battle like this hurried their departure. Sirna also heard a few bawdy remarks, about who would have the job of watching her by night.

Sirna was told afterward that she didn't faint. She certainly remembered nothing until she found herself in a chair, her head pushed down between her knees and Menandra and Banner-

363

Captain Geblon chafing her wrists so vigorously that they felt ready to catch fire. She kept her head down and let the chafing go on until the giddiness and the urge to vomit on an empty stomach passed.

"Sirna—"

"Get back down on that pallet, Captain-General!"

"I need to talk—"

"When you're down on the pallet. Not a word until then!"

Sitting cross-legged by Phidestros's pallet, Sirna could hear him without anyone else being able to eavesdrop. Geblon made sure of that, with help from Menandra.

"I'm sorry if I put you in danger," she began. "But I couldn't—"

"And you didn't, and there's no need to apologize," Phidestros interrupted, with a grin. "We are the Iron Band, and we can do nicely without temple-rats chittering in our ears in our own quarters. You, on the other hand . . ."

Phidestros reached over and put a hand on her knee. "You've got a petty-captain's share of pay for this past campaign coming, and more if Styphon's House pays any of the victory gift they've promised. That's enough to be a good dowry for you, or buy you a horse and cart with traveling rations and servants to take you home—if you have any home left."

"Or you could stay here and buy into a partnership with me," Menandra put in. "I'm not as young as I once was. Somebody I could leave the place to would be a comfort to me now."

Phidestros gave Sirna a smile that showed what he thought of the Gull's Nest's prospects after the Grand Host departed.

"A partnership—" Sirna began, then pressed her palms into her eyes until the pain and the swimming red fire killed the desire to laugh. She owed Menandra too much to ridicule the idea of staying in Hostigos Town and becoming assistant madam of a bordello!

"I don't advise any of those," Phidestros went on. "Roxthar can't try anything with us—or at least anything the rest of the Inner Circle or Grand Master Soton won't stop, as long as I'm Captain-General of the Grand Host of Styphon. Soton and Anaxthenes know good mercenaries are valuable, as long as Kalvan's still on the loose.

"You, on the other hand, he'll snap up like a weasel grabbing a new-hatched chick the moment you're out of our protection. You've humiliated him before men he distrusts. He'll forgive that the day Queen Rylla begs on her knees for a pardon from Styphon's House."

Phidestros was making sense—too much sense—but not telling her what to do. Or perhaps he assumed she already knew, and was waiting for her to offer it freely.

"I . . . I suppose I could ride with the Iron Band, that is, if you've a place for a healer. I'd like to train some of your men to help me, if that could be arranged, because I really can't do it all myself—"

Phidestros was kissing her eyelids and cheeks as well as her lips. Sirna wasn't quite ready to kiss him back, but she didn't stop him, either. She managed to be deaf to the new chorus of cheers and bawdy remarks around her.

"Some of my girls may want to come with you," Menandra added. "Hostigos Town may not be the most comfortable place for a while. I've three or four who've earned out their time and may want to travel on. If you could train them too—"

It's insane! Here she was, planning to live as the healer to a band of Fourth Level mercenaries and madam to their field brothel. Not to mention, probably, mistress to their Captain-General—an idea that now left her feeling curious rather than degraded. *Although please, let the contraceptive implants not run out before I find a way home!*

It was insane—and it would keep her alive. If Roxthar's Investigators had to fight the Iron Band to reach her, they probably would give her up as not worth the trouble. If she had to sleep with Phidestros to keep his favor, she would at least be sleeping with an interesting man—and not interesting in a purely academic sense, either . . .

She would go with Phidestros and his men. She would do what they wanted her to do, and they would keep her alive until Great King Kalvan returned and took vengeance for this day and all the other crimes of Styphon's House.

Sirna was sure that day would come. It would be worth enduring much to be there to see it, and maybe, Dralm willing, help bring it about.

Tortha Karf, former Paratime Police Chief and now a Paratime Commissioner, ploughed his way through the guards and secretaries into Chief Verkan's office. He found his successor sitting behind his horseshoe desk, face buried in his hands. Verkan's face reminded Tortha of his fieldhands' wives, back on Fifth Level Sicily. When the master announced he was forsaking his retirement, the women acted as if half the tribe's men had just died in battle!

"What's the matter, Vall? Has Dalla decided on another divorce?"

Verkan looked up, startled as if he hadn't known he had a visitor. "Oh, Tortha. It's just wool-gathering. My friend Kalvan's lost damned near everything. I just finished reviewing the tape on the fall of Tarr-Hostigos.

"Instead of leaving anything for the Styphoni, Ptosphes blew up the castle, the whole Styphoni storming party, and himself. Roxthar has turned his Investigators loose, and they're busy murdering, torturing, or harassing any Hostigi who didn't flee with Kalvan."

"Sounds as if Ptosphes made the best of a bad job. Nothing sad about taking that big an escort with you. As for the other Hostigi—they're just getting now what they've already had on all the other Styphon's House time-lines where they didn't have a Lord Kalvan to save them."

The Commissioner leaned over the desk and quietly continued. "Vall, you're a realist and a historian as well as a Paracop. You know all this. What's really bothering you?"

Verkan winced as if he'd been slapped, then laughed. "You really know how to go to the heart of things. Maybe I will too, if I sit at this desk another century or so."

Not much chance of that if he keeps taking every friend's bad luck so personally, thought Tortha. A shame, really, because apart from his Kalvan problem Verkan showed every sign of being an above-average Chief for the Paracops.

"Now, once again. What's eating you this way?"

"I let a good friend down, a friend who was counting on me. Here I've got all this power and I can't do a Dralm-damned thing to help without upsetting some bureaucrat or breaking some Paratime regulation."

"You're not making sense. You're falling into outtime guilt and loyalty patterns. If you weren't Chief I'd suggest you make a short visit to our Bureau of PsychHygiene clinic."

"I'd rather be in the hands of Roxthar's Investigation!"

"That's where you might be right now, if you'd been at Ardros Field. There, or just one more corpse in a mass grave. What good would either have done Kalvan? He's alive and so are you, and I think you can do him a lot more good that way. Where is he now, by the way?"

"They've crossed the border of the Trygath—Hos-Rathon, it's called now."

"That's the Seventh Kingdom Kalvan sponsored, isn't it?"

"Yes. None of the other Great Kingdoms have recognized it."

"Then Great King—"

"Nestros."

"Great King Nestros should be a good friend to Kalvan. He must know he's next on Styphon's House's list."

"He probably is, but it's going to be a while." Verkan seemed more at ease now; his analysis of the situation began to flow with his usual fluency. "Ptosphes inflicted heavy casualties on the Grand Host and gave their morale a nasty jar. They're probably not fit for a long pursuit into hostile country now.

"Besides, the victors will be dividing the spoils. Probably falling out over them, sooner or later. This much land hasn't changed hands since the Zarthani Knights broke the Great River Confederation. Then there was only one real claimant, too. Now there are about six arguing over the pie."

"Then Kalvan should have a while to figure out what to do next," Tortha added. "In his place, I'd build a power base so that I could be a valuable ally to anyone who felt he didn't get his share of the pie."

"He could do that, selling his services in the Middle Kingdoms as a mercenary leader. Everybody's going to need soldiers, until the barbarians are beaten back. The only thing holding the Middle Kingdoms to Styphon's House was the fireseed secret, and that's blown away. King Theovacar might even find Kalvan useful against his own barons, if there aren't enough barbarians to fight."

"Vall, I think you've just described your own next opportunity. Theovacar knows Verkan the Trader. He also knows that you're a Baron of Hos-Hostigos. Who knows, you might lead him to make you one of his negotiators with his new royal guest, King Kalvan."

"Of course! It's going to take some planning and all the supplies I can beg, borrow, or steal on a few next-door time-lines, but—" Verkan frowned, then laughed out loud, a sound that made Tortha Karf want to do the same. He held his tongue, as Verkan tried to glare at him, then laughed again.

"You sly old dog! You planned this all along. Well, the penalty is going to be taking me and Dalla out to dinner at the Constellation House. We can finish roughing out the plans there."

Verkan started to swivel his chair, then stopped. "Just as a suggestion, why don't we sit on the fact that I've recovered. The rumors that I'm sitting staring at the wall have already brought out into the open a few mice who think the cat's out to lunch. If we keep the rumors going a few more days, we may find a few more mice."

"You're not thinking of hiding it from Dalla, I hope?"

"If I did that, I *would* belong in the clinic!" Verkan said with a laugh. He swiveled his chair, and the rest of the world might have vanished in mist as Verkan started punching requests for data into his computer keyboard. Tortha Karf found a comfortable chair and leaned back with a contented sigh. The Verkan Vall he'd known for fifty years was back—and on the hunt again.

THERE WILL BE WAR

Created by J. E. Pournelle
John F. Carr, Associate Editor

THE SAGA CONTINUES...

THE TOR DOUBLES

Two complete short science fiction novels in one volume!

THE BEST IN SCIENCE FICTION

GREG BEAR

☐	53172-8	BEYOND HEAVEN'S RIVER	$2.95
☐	53173-6		Canada $3.95
☐	53174-4	EON	$3.95
☐	53175-2		Canada $4.95
☐	53167-1	THE FORGE OF GOD	$4.50
☐	53168-X		Canada $5.50
☐	55971-1	HARDFOUGHT (Tor Double with Cascade Point by Timothy Zahn	$2.95
☐	55951-7		Canada $3.95
☐	53163-9	HEGIRA	$3.95
☐	53164-7		Canada $4.95
☐	53165-5	PSYCHLONE	$3.95
☐	53166-3		Canada $4.95

FRED SABERHAGEN

BESTSELLING BOOKS FROM TOR